THE HOPE WE SEEK

Rich Shapero

THE HOPE WE SEEK

a novel

Outside
Reading

SAN MATEO, CALIFORNIA

Outside Reading
P.O. Box 1565
San Mateo, CA 94401

Library of Congress Cataloging-in-Publication Data is available.

ISBN-13: 978-0-9718801-5-3

Cover painting by Donald Pass from his THWS Series, completed 2005
(for more information, visit www.thehopeweseek.com/visual_art)
Artwork copyright © 2005, 2009 Rich Shapero
Additional graphics: Sky Shapero
Cover design: Adde Russell
Lettering: Darren Booth

Printed in the United States of America

17 16 15 14   2 3 4 5

Also by Rich Shapero

Too Far

Wild Animus

The Private

On an island at the edge of the world, a few years shy of the twentieth century, the Private and his partner landed their boat.

Emerging from a thick fog, they struck the coast in a place of sheer cliffs. The current was deadly, but they made it into a small cove without capsizing. Though they were in their mid-twenties, they acted like boys, tense and laughing by turns, moving quickly, hauling their craft into the rocks out of reach of the surf, retrieving provisions and firearms. The Private's wet hair hung in black hooks around his thin face. He wore a coat of maroon felt. Its cuffs were frayed and an arm was tatted where the chevron had been removed; but the cloth still had its color, and as he loaded his packboard the sun flashed on its golden piping.

The two tramped the shoreline and mountains, heading north. It was March and the peaks were still covered with snow. The Private led the way. It wasn't a map or notes he consulted. He was guided by voices. There were ghosts in the wind, whispers from the snow or the invisible meltwater flowing beneath. It was the same presence that spoke through his dreams. He believed in the voices, and through some harmony of their natures, his partner believed in him.

On the morning of the third day, the two men crossed an icy ridge and came upon a narrow valley. The slopes of the valley were white and the small river that wound through it was frozen. In places rock was visible—a black metamorphic. Where the river met the coast, it had broken through the cliffs, forming a natural harbor. The Private scanned the harbor.

As he descended into the valley, a breeze reached him. He could taste salt from the sea, and in the wind's murmur he heard the echo of a promise. The spruce on either side were wind-sheared, with crowns like dark clouds, and the snow beneath his boots was littered with needles, as if some testament had been recorded there in a language unknown to man. He mumbled about what the text meant, and his partner mumbled back. Their heavy packs rattled and creaked as they moved.

The head of the valley came into view. Between the sloping confines of the river, a trapezoidal wall appeared, black and thinly forested, grooved vertically, as if it had been clawed by an angry hand.

The Private straddled a fallen tree, pushing aside the upstart saplings rooted on its trunk. His partner followed. They approached the river's bank. In places the ice had melted, and through the soggy mulch, yellow spikes of swamp cabbage rose, each at the center of a straw-colored star. The Private paused beside the frozen flow and raised his arm, holding his rifle barrel-up. As he stepped forward, he brought the rifle down, cracking its stock onto the river ice. The surface was solid and held his weight. But as the rifle descended, the tip of a branch cocked the hammer, and when the butt struck, a shot rang out.

The men jumped. A jay flew out of a pool and went rasping through the birch. The Private listened to the echoes, his eyes on the willow branch, watching its crystal feathers tremble. The two men crossed the river.

They were mounting the far bank when they caught sight of a bear on the trapezoidal wall, shifting against the snow that covered its crest. The shot had awakened him. He was stumbling out of his den.

The bear's back was icy. It flashed in the sun like the carapace of a beetle—an amulet worked in gold for a pharaoh's tomb. When the Private saw the bear, he knew.

The bear crossed the ridge where it was steepest, cutting through the winter pack.

A groan filled the valley.

As the two men watched, the slopes below the bear's trackline came away in a thick mass—snow, soil and trees, all churning together—and the mountain's top was dragged along. The roar mounted and the valley rumbled as the slide descended. The bear and the ridge vanished in a cloud of rock and ice dust.

They shrugged off their packs, eyes fixed on the sight.

The cloud shredded around the crest. Amid the drifting veils, a giant seam of quartz appeared—a thick white cord, stretching diagonally. Rays played over it, searching as the veils shifted. The Private saw the quartz come alive. It was turning and twisting, and the bright beams piercing its crystal found winking stars and golden flames. A translucent cord, connecting the poor to something of worth; something un-born to something timeless; someone condemned to someone divine.

The Private's partner saw the glittering cord. The Private saw the presence that had summoned him. As he watched, she froze back into the rock.

The Private looked at his partner. Then without a word, they were racing toward the bank, recrossing the river, beating through the straw and the whipping scrub, making toward the mountain and its naked quartz. The Private was in front. A prospector's pick bobbed on his thigh, its haft through his belt. His strides jarred the earth, turning seep gurgles to bird-song and gravel to grasshoppers. Thrushes called, heralding his arrival. The whistling of wrens filtered down from the trees.

It was late that night and the two men were camped by the river. Smoke coiled up from a dying fire. They were in their tent, and a lone candle lit the canvas from within. At the head of the valley, the giant white cord glimmered beneath a full moon, while on the slopes far below, the burden it had shed continued to settle. A web of splintered trunks heaved and a boulder rolled aside. From beneath the debris, the bear's arms appeared, shoving and clawing, prying the last wooden bars of his prison apart.

He crawled out of the hole and lay licking his wounds. Then he drew a few breaths and tried his legs. He wobbled and growled, then he crossed the rubble, shaking his head and chomping his jaws. His confinement had ended, but his distemper remained. He lumbered toward the river, icy crusts stuck to his back, swiping alders aside, snorting steam into the air, as if to rid his nostrils of a noxious odor.

The bear didn't see the tent. His attention was on the bluff at the mouth of the valley. Then the prospectors' light flickered. The bear shook with surprise, stopping in his tracks. A cool breeze carried the smoke and the man scent into his nostrils. He fixed on the tent. Then he was loping toward it, crashing through birch and willow, ripping up armfuls as he went.

I

A crescent moon had arced through blue sky, burying its tip in the cliffs guarding the coast. There was snow on the ridge tops, and where sun heated the slopes, steam was rising from them. The broad channel and its islands were fair, except for its southern end, where gray clouds lay like twisted blankets. A small steamer emerged from the clouds, towing a black barge behind. A knotted thread coiled from its stack.

The steamer rode the swells uncertainly, tipping and groaning. Its weathered prow read *Bocadillos*. Beneath a canvas awning extending aft of the galley, a tall man stood with an empty bowl in his hands. A shorter man stood before him, and the two were surrounded by other passengers who were spooning dinner into their mouths.

"It's a pleasure," the tall man said, shifting from one face to another. "I apologize for taking my meals below. I'm eager

7

to meet each of you." His tongue wet large lips framed by long mustaches and a pointed goatee. He was six-four, with a buckskin coat and shoulder-length hair.

"Birch oil?" The short man sniffed. He had a perfunctory smile and a widow's peak. In his left hand he held a note tablet at chest level, and in his right a pencil was poised.

Zachary Knox shook his head. "Bay rum. You are—"

"Inky Peterson. I have a few questions."

"A journalist," Knox said.

"The report on Breakaway was mine," Inky nodded.

"Thanks for that," Knox said. "What was the gentleman's—"

"Percy Schorr," Inky replied.

"With a wedge of gold 'like a melon slice,'" Knox smiled.

"A happy simile," Inky said. "It was cool to the touch and damp. His grubbing days are over. Why are you—"

Zack raised his fist toward Inky's chin. "I can see my slice here." He opened his fingers and stared at his palm. "No one will poof that, will they boys?"

"No sir," a man answered.

A bearded fellow drew his lips back. "I'm gonna plate my teeth with it."

"Your words fired me," Knox put his hand on the reporter's shoulder. "I bought my ticket and packed my trunks that afternoon." He scanned the gathering. "'Board the *Bocadillos*, raise the dead, full speed for the—'"

Just then, the ship wallowed. The men reached for something to hold on to. A black billow retched from the stack,

8

circling over them while a clucking and bleating sounded below deck. Knox clung to a crate until the steamer crossed the
trough.

"What about the *Bull's-Eye West?*" Inky straightened
himself.

Knox set his bowl on the crate. Horses stamped and nick-
ered beneath them.

"The show continues," Knox said.

"Without its headliner?"

"Mister Knox—" A teenager with long blond hair shouldered forward. "We'd like to see—"

Zack raised his hands in protest.

"Why did you leave?" Inky pressed him.

"Personal reasons."

"Was the show losing its draw?"

"What's for dinner?" Zack turned to a man at his elbow.

"Rice and beans," the man replied.

"Were you doing private sittings?" Inky asked.

Amid the onlookers, Knox noticed a young woman
dressed in black. She had sharp features and dark hair bound
against her nape. He bowed to her.

"Does your skill allow you to—" Inky persisted.

Knox shook his head, his eyes on the young woman.

"—summon the departed?"

The showman was still shaking his head. "Call me Zack."
He extended his hand to the young woman. His eyes pleaded
for help.

"There were problems with the law," Inky guessed.

The young woman took Zack's hand.

"Excuse me," Zack tipped his head to the reporter. And then to the crowd, "She's beautiful, isn't she?" He stepped through the gathering, drawing the young woman beside him, as if to permit a less public dialogue.

As they passed, a man with gray hair and a walking stick grumbled, "Farewell to culture."

His companion replied, "If you had his pedigree, you wouldn't be here."

Zack halted beside a hill of grain sacks. "Thank you," he said.

"You're a spectacle," the woman observed.

"It's my own doing. I'm sorry, miss—"

"Sephy."

She wasn't self-conscious. She eyed him with curiosity, like an onlooker at a carnival sideshow.

"An austere woman," Zack nodded, "but a kind one. I'm surprised to find you here. You're drawn by gold?"

"In a way."

Zack glanced back. Inky was weaving through the passengers and provisions, headed toward them.

"Are you cared for?" Zack asked. "You're not sleeping on deck?"

She stared at him.

"If you don't have a stateroom," Zack grasped her elbow and urged her through the galley, "you must take one of mine."

"I appreciate your concern, but—"

"I'm alone down there. It's like a prison sentence."

Sephy laughed. "You're bold."

"Please," he said, directing her attention to Inky. "The trap is closing."

"If you answer his questions—"

"There's no end to them," Zack said. He led her alongside a pile of crates. The *Bocadillos* was entering a strait, hugging the shore. A wall of spruce spires loomed a thousand feet skyward. Through a gash in the growth, a cataract hurtled from a black ledge and crashed into the sea.

Sephy caught sight of the companionway to the lower deck. "No," she said. As she halted, the chop from the cataract reached the steamer. The deck canted and she stumbled. Zack grabbed her, holding her close while he rode the heave.

"Let go," she said as the *Bocadillos* settled.

But he didn't let go. He held her and stared into her eyes with the gravity and acuity that had earned him his billing.

"The Bull's-Eye Telepath," Sephy said. "Can you hear my thoughts?"

"Test me below." He nodded at the companion ladder.

"Shall I be an actor in your spectacle?" She glanced over his shoulder. A dozen passengers were staring at them.

"You're mistrustful by nature."

"That's not true."

"I know it's not. Please." He gestured at the ladder.

She stared at him for a long moment, then she set her hand on the rail and started down.

Zack turned and bowed to the observers. Inky stood amidships, gazing one way and another. Off the port gunwale, the cliff was sliding past like wet clay beneath a deft hand.

As they descended the ladder, the sea grew calm. There was nothing but the sound of their steps in the narrow space. When they reached the lower deck, Sephy faced him.

"You're used to being favored by women."

He laughed. "I like—"

"Lots of them," Sephy said. Her expression was without bitterness or malice. "I know what a man is."

A sober silence stretched between them.

"You're in trouble," Zack said.

His words disarmed her. He didn't wait for her to respond.

"Your grief reaches me," he said. "I feel your desperation."

"This is your talent?" She tried to smile, but her lower lip quivered.

"Tell me," Zack said.

"It's no concern of yours."

"Tell me."

She weighed him—skepticism on one side, and the wish to believe on the other. He read her state and let her waver. Then his gaze turned prescient. "Our meeting is no accident," he said, and that tipped the scales.

"I've lost someone," she told him.

Zack nodded at her black garb. "Husband?"

"My brother." Sephy regarded him.

Measuring his amity, Zack thought. And his capacity for manipulation.

Her fingers unfastened two buttons below her neck. She turned aside and drew out a small photograph. "Raymond," Sephy said, handing it to him.

The yellowing image was of a young man with dark hair and features like hers. He had the same mournful lips and high brow, her sharp nose and tapered chin.

"An unusual resemblance." Zack lowered the photo. "Except for the eyes."

"Mine are different?"

Zack nodded. "I've never seen—"

"What?"

"Such sadness."

She brushed a loose curl behind her ear.

"An old photo." He handed it back to her.

"It happened two years ago, at Breakaway," she explained. "I heard the story from his partner. He escaped with his life."

"How—"

Sephy shook her head. "It was horrible." She turned her shoulder and slipped the photo back inside her dress.

"Two years is a long time to mourn."

She seemed not to have heard him. "You have some understanding of these things?" she said, half to herself.

Her words puzzled him, but he nodded.

"Raymond isn't dead. I feel his mood, his energy—in a thoughtless moment or when I'm half asleep. He's like a vapor drifting beside me. There's no comfort in it," she said. "He leaves me chilled and trembling—"

Her allure opened before Zack like a dark chasm. There

were a thousand ways to ape the spiritual, but this wasn't a fake.

He touched her chin with his fingertip and raised her head. "My 'powers,'" he said, "were just an act."

The ship lurched, pitching them against each other. This time it was she who embraced him. "Your instinct was right, Mister Knox. I'm frightened."

"Of what?" He peered into the dark eyes.

"Of reaching Breakaway. Of what I might find. He's there, with the gold and the ice."

Her dread, with all its passion and expectancy, drew him like a magnet. He felt acted upon, like a spectator in one of his shows ushered down onto the sands of the arena.

"What is Breakaway to you, Mister Knox?" She put her fingertips on his chest.

"In the world I was born into," Zack said, "every word was a cheat. Every thought and feeling was false. I played the game. Everything I touched, I cheapened."

He expected his words would surprise her, but they did not.

"And gold?" she said.

"Gold is a new life—a real one, a purer one."

"For Raymond," she said, "gold was madness."

She spoke the word "madness" in a measured tone, without prejudice.

"He gave up everything, embraced the worst perils to pursue it—the gold he knew he would find. It became his faith, his reason for living," she said. "I had to choose . . . to fight his madness or join him in it."

14

"And—"

"I fought," Sephy said with remorse. "It was meant that I should share his madness and his fate."

"His fate?"

Sephy nodded. "I wear black for both of us." Her nose wrinkled. "It smells—"

"Before Breakaway, fish slept down here," Zack said.

He motioned and they started along the corridor.

"How did this promise of a new life reach you?" Sephy asked.

"Through a bellhop. We'd played Ambrose Park the night before. He brought me breakfast and a paper. He was shivering with excitement." Zack stopped before a small door. "I left the show that day."

He opened the door. "We'll keep it ajar." Zack tapped the latch.

But she had already crossed the threshold.

Sephy stepped to the center of the room and looked around. Half a Moroccan rug covered the floor, and the remainder was rolled behind a lowboy. A large mirror in a gilt frame angled out from the ceiling. To the right, a headboard tiled with Moorish stars rose over the bed, while an Arabian coverlet lay bunched where the sleeper had kicked it. To the left, three battered trunks rested among bulging sacks, and tools leaned against the wall. Picks, shovels, axes. The lid of one of the trunks was open. A holster with a silver revolver lay atop another.

"The room next door is packed to the ceiling," Zack said.

Sephy stared at the weapon. "You don't shoot in earnest?"

"Not often. Elk, moose—"

"Never a man."

"I'm not brainsick," Zack said.

She faced him. "An unusual way to entertain people. How did you—"

"Accident and opportunity." He drew the revolver from its holster. "I learned marksmanship when I was young. I won a shoot at a fair in Wyoming. The local paper wrote me up, and I got an offer to join the exhibition circuit." He wet his thumb and touched the bead. "My second year, I toured with Doc Feldman—'Shakti the Knowing.' I started wearing a blindfold and reading minds to hit my targets." He faced the mirror. "We filled the stands." Zack raised his arm and sighted along the barrel, aiming at the reflection of his right pupil.

"Please—"

Zack lowered the gun and set it on the trunk. "It was something—" He gestured, directing her attention around the stadium. "Hearing a thousand people chanting 'Knox,' seeing the name big as a three-story hotel."

"I would expect more modesty, as well-provided as you are."

"The providing is over," he said.

Sephy assumed he was joking. "The Knox tree is large and fruitful."

"I'm the wayward limb. I cut myself off before boarding this tub."

She frowned. "I can't tell when you're acting."

"I've worn the mask so long, it has a life of its own." Zack spoke with contrition. "All I have is right here. I sent the telegram on the way to the dock."

"Why?"

"I took a hard fall in Ambrose Park."

"An accident?"

Zack shook his head. "A family matter. I invited my father to the show. It led to a—"

Sephy watched him struggle for words.

"Scandal," he said with mock hauteur.

That puzzled her.

Zack was about to give a more blunt answer when the cabin bucked, dashing them both to the floor.

He gripped a leg of the bed. The room tilted and the door slammed. He got one knee beneath him, but before he could rise, the floor plunged, rolling him onto his back. Sephy was beside him, trying to right herself, confusion giving way to fear. The ship was groaning from its depths. The cabin walls thrummed.

Zack hooked his arm around the lowboy and heaved himself up, springing for the door. He wrenched it open and peered around the jam. The corridor was twisting like an eel's gut viewed from inside. The ship swooned and he was hurled back into the cabin. His arm caught the lantern chain, and as the room leaned onto its side, Zack swung half around, seeing Sephy huddled against the hull wall, white and staring.

The doorframe cracked. The bed grunted across the planks, the bulkhead beside it gabling inward. There was a throaty noise and Zack looked down to see a gush of green water pouring over his boots. He grabbed Sephy and pulled her up. The joists above jumped and sagged. The large mirror fell, shattering on a packing trunk.

"It's over," Sephy said, watching the rift in the hull widen. The freezing sea invaded the small space, slapping and frothing over Zack's belongings.

He stepped out of his boots, gaze shifting, lighting on lowboy and trunk, coursing over the sacks with the concentration of a magician preparing for a dangerous trick. He tore off his coat and shirt, opened one of the sacks and pulled out a coiled rope.

"Glad you're down here?" he said.

Sephy watched him knot the rope.

The rift expanded, the flood nearly toppling them.

"Zack—"

He stripped his pants off, grabbed his holster belt, fastened it around his waist and hitched the rope to it. Nearly naked now, he placed his hands on the throat of her dress and ripped it from neckline to waist. The photo of Raymond fluttered free. "You know what a man is—" Zack smiled and tore open her chemise, then he lifted her out of the rags and circled her drawers with the rope's loose end, making a harness around her waist and thighs.

Sephy clung to him, shivering, watching his humor fade as the waters raged in upon them. A thick curl kicked her legs out from under her. Zack held her with one arm. She had wanted to see behind the mask, and now she saw: what remained of his panache was the rictus of a condemned man—teeth bared, powerless, scowling at a verdict from which there was no appeal.

Zack faced the gaping hole. "Take a breath."

On the main deck, the door to the fo'c'sle flew open. One of the mates bolted along the gangway and as the frightened passengers turned, he herded them aft.

"We're on a reef. To the stern—now!"

In the pilothouse, the bosun fought the wheel while the Captain glassed the seas. He cursed, collapsed his brass scope and slid it into his pocket as he faced the windscreen. A citadel of dark pinnacles rose through the fog. The ship was heeling toward it, carried by the fierce current that had caught them. "Full steam," he bellowed into the speaking tube. The wheel moved ten degrees, gears gnashing, rudder lines crying out.

A deckhand appeared. "Torn amidships," he reported.

The *Bocadillos* stumbled, listing to port. Above the bang and clatter of shifting cargo, they heard planks cracking. "Get the engine gang on top," the Captain ordered. The port gunwale was underwater and the hull was starting to buckle. Screams rose from below—timbers and horses. The Captain glanced over his shoulder. Waves were breaking across the 15-foot beam that connected the steamer to its tow load. "All travelers on the barge," he shouted.

Two of the mates started pushing passengers toward the foot-wide beam. The first of them ventured out, hugging and shinnying across. A gaunt man in a gray overcoat helped them over the gunwale at the far end, and a woman with short hair threw blankets around them.

"Save yourselves," the Captain screamed into the speaking tube. The mouthpiece came away in his hand. He cursed and stepped out of the pilothouse. Suddenly the tow beam tore loose of the *Bocadillos* and the ship rolled onto its side, pitching the Captain over the guard rail, leaving him hanging above the flood by one arm. The emerald water circled below him, cut with sharp waves, raveling with froth. He shook his boots off. "Abandon ship," he mumbled and let himself drop.

When the word "breath" left Zack's lips, the torrent roared in his face. The hull opened like double doors, and he had barely a moment to fill his lungs with air before the flood struck him. He was torn from Sephy's side, splayed against the far wall and hurled to the ceiling. Where there had been air, there was only water. He turned in a vortex, peering through green murk, the drowned cabin like a drugged remembrance of his prospecting ambitions. Pots and utensils, shovels and axes, a melee of boots and oilskins dancing with the chamois and flannels sucked from his trunk. His revolver was in the churn along with fragments of mirror and the bedding he'd slept in. His feet were already numb. The vortex slowed, he sank for a moment, feeling the water loosen around him. Then it hooked him, carrying him toward the gaping hole and through it.

He was free of the steamer now, but without any sense of the sea's expanse. It was like standing in a railyard as trains sped past, dozens of them, all headed in different directions. The sea wasn't whole. It was a wattle of disparate wills, each with the power of a god, enormous and supremely violent.

The freezing currents swerved around him, looping, crossing and interweaving. They weren't hostile to him—they didn't perceive him. He was nothing to them. Zack found his nerve, his senses reached out, along with his arms. He pulled and the currents gave around his head. They were brutal, insensible, but he wasn't powerless. He was forcing his way through them.

Where was he going? He couldn't tell which way was up. His legs were numb below the knees. He caught sight of them, battered and flexing strangely, lit by a glimmer in the distance. He could see the rope knotted at his waist, kinking and shifting with something unseen attached. He turned away from the rope, faced the glimmer and reached with both arms. The light was faint, the currents unremitting, but he found a seam in the wattle and forced himself through. Again he reached, again and again. The pool of light seemed to expand.

Then it winked out.

Zack's breath shrank, his chest shuddered with cold. *I'm sinking*, he thought. Or he'd been fighting his way into the depths, even as he imagined he was nearing the surface.

Darkness and confusion swallowed him, and as if in response, the currents accelerated. His arms were weak, his breath nearly exhausted—there was no time left. He felt for the rope at his waist and when he pulled, it gave freely.

I'm lost, he thought. But he held on. Through some fault in his reason, some abandon of heart, hope found an access.

As the currents careened around him, one especially large and powerful lifted among them, tearing the weave. Zack sensed the change dimly. Was his struggle an annoyance? Would he be dragged forthwith to the bottom of the sea? The current would be fearsome, like the others. But it slid beneath Zack and bent its back, and the waters parted around him. The current rose like a leviathan, lifting him on its freezing hump. The glimmer reappeared, and then a vivid disk of light.

The green was shot with bubbles, grew clear, glassy—

Zack's head broke the surface. He drew a stuttering breath, and the sounds of wind and waves reached his ears. His pulse was quaking, his limbs were numb.

"There," a voice exclaimed.

Zack was within a few yards of the barge. Inky's face was peering over the gunwale at him.

"Hold my legs," Inky directed someone behind him. He pushed himself toward Zack and reached out his arm.

Zack smiled and sank. The rope gathered easily. Was she alive, still conscious? Or just dead weight lifted by the flow? Sephy's naked body came into view. She looked like she was lounging on a divan, head back, hair streaming. He drew her close, grasped her around the waist and heaved her up.

They surfaced together. Inky lunged and grasped Sephy's wrist. The gaunt man in the gray overcoat got his hands on her shoulder. Then a half-dozen others helped raise her from the water and pull her onto the barge. Zack heard someone say, "Untie it, she can't breathe." He felt the rope tugging at his middle. They were hauling him in.

Inky caught hold of his holster belt. Others lifted him, dragging him across the gunwale. He lay facedown, wheezing and shaking while they covered him with blankets. All at once, his desperation burst. He closed his eyes, feeling a profound calm flowing through him. "You've been spared," a woman said. Then he heard Sephy's voice. "I'd given up," she gasped.

Zack rolled onto his hip. Inky was squatting beside him. He put his hand on Inky's knee and tried to raise himself. Inky closed the blankets around him, embracing him.

"Front page," the reporter said with emotion.

Zack coughed from deep in his lungs. Sephy was a few feet away, beneath a gray coat, hugging the short-haired woman breast to breast. The Captain was vomiting over the gunwale. There were fewer than two dozen others spread out on a tarp covering the lumpy contents of the barge. They were bundled and crouching, backs and shoulders to the wind.

"This all?" Zack asked.

Inky drew his gaze out over the chop. There was no trace of anything alive or afloat. The reef that claimed the steamer had vanished in the fog, and the barge was drifting. Zack shuddered.

"Get down," Inky said. He rose, dragged Zack against the lee of the gunwale and spread more wool over him. Across the barge, Zack saw the Captain turn and mop his face with a dripping sleeve. Three sheep were curled nearby.

The Captain straightened himself and turned to the survivors. Then he cleared his throat to address them. The gaunt man swung around, put a gloved hand on the Captain's chest and pushed him back down.

"You done enough," the gaunt man said. He glanced from face to face, wind cracking his wet overcoat.

"Who are you?" Inky asked.

"Snell," the gaunt man said. "Need to open these crates." He had long narrow teeth. Below his nervous eyes, his nose made a switchback halfway to the air holes. "See what we can use."

Snell pulled a knife from a sheath on his hip and crossed the lumpy surface. He pried at the lid of a wooden box and the lid squealed back. "Can't eat these." He reached a gloved hand inside and removed a pair of chisel-end drill bits.

A dozen men watched.

"Ya gonna help me?" Snell said critically. "You—" He pointed at a pair nearby—a brown-skinned man with spectacles and the teenager with blond hair.

The two stood.

"Take these." Snell set the drills down on a crate.

The teenager grabbed one of them and dropped it with a curse. The brown-skinned man used a corner of his blanket to grasp the other, approached one of the sealed crates, wedged the end of the bit under the lid and started to pry.

Zack rose onto one knee.

"Not you," Snell said.

Inky stepped forward.

"Come on, the rest of you," Snell motioned. "Food and matches, that's what we're needing. Not those. See the letters *BMC*? That's machinery, mine supplies. Try this one here. And them over there."

Zack watched the men set to work on the crates as the barge drifted into a thick mist. The cliffs disappeared, and most of the sea. Where were they headed? Could the barge be landed? The men called out their findings over the gulping of the waves.

"Tins of something," one said.

"Open 'em up," Snell directed him. "Use one of them nails."

"Smokes for the gents." A popeyed man held a cigar to his chattering teeth. He rummaged through the contents of his box. "Don't see any matches."

Nails shrieked as Inky lifted the lid off an oblong container. "Ladies' stuff."

The teenager shook a small box. "Sounds like carrots."

The gray-haired man, Lucky, was on his knees, prying open the door of a large crate. "What's this?" he wondered. Through the opened door, Zack could see giant gears nested inside a steel cowling.

"A crusher," Snell said with irritation, gesturing at the *BMC* stenciled on the crate's side. He swung around. "What else?"

The teenager shook a fist full of candles. "And matches," he said, raising a small box in his other hand.

Snell stepped over to him. "We won't freeze," he nodded. "What's your name?"

"Winiarski, sir." The teenager beamed.

"We had ten tons of food onboard," the Captain said, letting the lid fall back on his crate.

Just then one of the sheep bleated. Zack watched it roll onto its chest in the center of the tarp, eyes hooded against the drizzle. Its jaw shifted idly as attention turned toward it.

"I don't fancy her raw," the popeyed man said.

Snell pulled back a corner of the tarp, revealing the contents of the barge: coal.

"Who wants the honors?" Snell asked. When no one responded, he grabbed the top of the sheep's head with his left hand and put the edge of his blade to its throat.

Zack closed his eyes.

The wind spoke through his dream, like someone whispering in a foreign tongue. Or was he murmuring to himself? He stood before a framed mirror, arguing his choice of costume. Except for the broad-brimmed white hat, he had made himself red—a scarlet bolero, a blood string tie and pants of burgundy buckskin. Violent. Fearless. His right hand skimmed his holster and he twirled the revolver out, once forward, twice backward, up in the air, then skittering beside his thigh, butt slapping into his palm as he drew it toward his chest, silver barrel raised. The mirror was webbed with cracks, anticipating the lines along which it would shatter on the *Bocadillos*.

Then magically he was in the prep tent, hurrying through the horse flop and straw, trying to calm himself for the entrance. Two women followed, both elegantly dressed with complex coiffures. One was silent, the other fawned as she jabbered. Zack came to a halt, kissed her hand and urged her to leave. She pulled a feather from her fan, stuck it in his hatband and embraced him. Then she fell into tears. Zack spoke in low tones, comforting her, continuing forward. The silent woman caught up with him as he strode toward his mount. "Row five," Zack directed her. "Two o'clock from the center."

"Two o'clock," she nodded. "Everyone's in their usual positions." She hurried off. The tearful woman was still standing where he'd left her. When Zack glared, she gathered her skirts and departed.

Ambrose Park was packed. The crowd was buzzing beneath the big top. Zack could see a section of seating through the entry arch. One of his assistants stood before it, tightening his mount's cinch. Her cheeks were rouged and her hair was in braids. Above her buckskin skirt, she wore a skintight vest.

A man in a dark suit was standing beside her. As Zack approached, the man hailed him.

"Zachary? Firstborn of Charles Knox?"

Zack nodded.

"May I? It's a privilege." The man extended his hand.

Zack shook it.

"Your timing's perfect," the man said. "We caucus next week. I'm Brad Chillinghood, secretary to Congressman Tippet."

"Down from the capital for the show?" Zack said.

"Precisely."

"Are they here?" Zack asked his assistant.

"Orchestra seats," the man intruded. "It's some revenge, I must say." He gave Zack a conspiratorial look. "They're calling you the 'Thorn of Rose Hill.'"

"Over here," Zack shouted, motioning to a boy with a rake.

"No offense meant," the man said.

"Escort this ass to his stall," Zack ordered the boy.

The boy led the man away.

Zack grasped the silver pommel, sent his boot toward the stirrup and missed.

"Clear your head," his assistant said.

Zack drew a breath and nodded.

She gestured for him to raise his leg, and when he did, she guided his foot into the silver cradle. Zack swung up onto his mount.

The girl's hand lingered on his thigh. "After the show, we'll unwind."

"Marksmanship," Zack said, taking the reins. "He'll respect that." His hand was shaking. His mount stamped the straw and started forward. Zack's heart drummed in his chest. When they reached the archway, he paused, raised his arm and whistled.

The horse charged into the crowd's midst. Zack sat straight in the saddle, revolver spinning in his right hand as he circled the ring. The bandleader pricked his baton, the horns blared and the horse halted, rearing and whinnying. Zack gave her the bit, fired at the heavens painted on the big top and lifted his hat with his left hand, waving it at the crowd while he scanned the box seats.

His father wasn't there. The horse continued to rear, and as Zack surveyed the stands, he realized there were no males present. The spectators were women, every one of them. Could they sense his agitation? Did it puzzle them or mute their enthusiasm? No, the clamoring mounted. Zack's mare seemed to have lost her senses. She was groaning and snorting, twisting like a mustang as the sound from the bleachers grew increasingly shrill.

The women were cheering, crying out to him, tossing hats and combs, shaking their tresses loose, removing gowns and skirts. They were all new faces—word had reached them and they wanted a taste. But they appeared not as women do before they've been seduced, but rather as the conqueror would see them in the lantern light after he withdrew. They were sweaty, their makeup was running, their armpits had tufts. They were on their feet now, waving their arms, hurling their garments at him, shrieking, stirring harsh winds. Clothing covered the sands. Suddenly the big top lifted like an umbrella in a storm, the shrieks grew deafening and the canvas blew away. The arena was tipping, garments churning like a restive sea.

Zack reined back his mount, too late. An undertow gripped them, the downpour of clothing redoubled, the chop rose to Zack's thighs. The waves were seething, capped by bodices and knickers, spraying salt spit and sea stench while a thousand defiled women screamed from the stands—"Knox, Knox, Knox." All at once the laundry opened beneath him, and Zack and his mount plunged into a dank abyss.

2

A voice was humming.

Zack turned toward the sound and droplets of water tapped his face. He flinched, peering through slit lids, unsure where he was.

Gray sky. The ragged edge of a mountain eaten by clouds.

He shifted, feeling the weight of blankets and a human form. Beneath the wool, Sephy lay beside him. She was like a hearth, radiating warmth and safety. Her hand had settled on his chest in an attitude of protectiveness, and her temple rested on his shoulder.

"Is your chill gone?" she asked.

Her head lifted. Her face had a freshness he'd not seen on the steamer. Damp had sickled her dark hair over her brow and cheeks. He nodded, raising himself on an elbow. Over her shoulder, Winiarski, the teenager, was pulling a piece of roasted meat from a skewer. Again Zack heard the voice.

When he glanced around, he saw Snell standing at the rear of the barge with his hands on the rudder wheel, humming to himself as he scanned the fog. Through it, segments of coastline were visible: sheer gray cliffs, their tops toothed with conifers.

There were changes in the barge. Crates had been broken down. Forward, two posts had been erected and reinforced with bar stock, and the tarp had been stretched between them, raising a square sail to the wind. Leftover panels were wedged inside the gunwale to form a windbreak. Nearby a fire burned atop a steel plate, serving the dual purpose of roasting the slaughtered sheep and warming the survivors. They were all smudged with soot, huddled beneath blankets on the bare coal.

"You saved me." Sephy's voice was hushed, masked by the gusts.

Her eyes had a new depth for him. Where was her trouble now? Had the sea flushed it out of her? He felt joyful, lucky to be there beside her. He recalled his first glimpse of her face—its strict lines, its pallor, the fleeting gaze. Now it seemed like the most beautiful face in the world.

"We were so close to—" Sephy stopped herself.

Zack thought of those the sea had claimed.

"They will be cared for," she said.

"There's company, I suppose, even if you're headed for damnation."

Sephy didn't respond.

"I should be thankful," he said.

"It's no accident you were spared."

He smiled at the echo of his show spiel.

A chill gust struck them. Sephy shivered against him. "This is your new world," she said. "Your new life."

"It's a gift that must be opened," he agreed. And then, "I want to ask you something."

"Go ahead."

"It's hard for me," he tried to explain. "On the circuit, I didn't speak my mind to anyone. I was afraid I'd be exposed."

Sephy waited.

"What do you dream of—with a man?" he asked.

Silence. Sephy turned away.

I've broken the spell, he thought.

"When I'm blissful, so is he." She spoke softly, but with assurance. "When he's in trouble, I know the way. His head is full of wild thoughts, wondrous ideas—like Raymond. No one understands him as I do. The heart pounding in his chest is mine. Our spirits draw breath from the same soul."

Her words hollowed him with desire. His arm circled her and he sought her lips. She seemed to find no fault with his advance, but the mention of her brother had given outlet to her grief. A sob rose in her throat, and she turned and put her cheek to his.

Zack breathed her sweetness, feeling her loss—a moment of intense pleasure mingled with pain—feeling her longing for a man wandering the wilderness, searching for the substance of inestimable worth. It was not just Sephy in his arms—it was the passion of Raymond burning within her, mysterious and alive.

A tall man with a trolleyman's cap approached them. He had a blanket draped around his shoulders. "Hungry?" He held out a skewer of roasted lamb.

Sephy raised herself and reached for a piece.

"Thanks," Zack said.

"I'm Streetcar," the man nodded self-consciously. "You're in my underwear."

Zack glanced at his sleeves. He was wearing a red union suit.

Streetcar lifted his cap and returned to his spot beside Inky.

At the border of the blankets that covered them, Zack could see Sephy's bare foot and a rolled-up cuff. She had trousers on and was wearing a man's shirt. Her small breasts moved freely within it, and as he slid closer, their rosy points jumped.

Zack's heart raced. He put his lips to Sephy's, and this time she didn't turn aside. Her breath mingled with his own, and then her mouth opened to receive him. Were people watching? He didn't care. A world was opening inside him, a place of freedom. The breath he was drawing—from Sephy and the wind and the water—was a breath of hope, a breath that started things over.

She recoiled, gasping.

Zack held on to her.

Sephy's arm was raised. The charred lamb was dripping fat down it. "I'll be a—"

"What?"

"Quick meal for you."

"I know nothing about love," Zack said.

She tried to laugh. "You're chaste then?"

He stared at her. "Marry me."

His words shocked them both. The proposal echoed in his head, plunging him into doubt and lifting him up again, challenging his impulse. It was true, Zack thought. Thorn of Rose Hill, satyr of the exhibition circuit— Everything that came before was nothing. His life led straight to this moment.

Sephy raised her hand to hide her face.

"Answer me," he whispered.

She shook her head. "There is a lot to explain. I owe you—"

"No," Zack said. "And you've heard enough about Zachary Knox. We had fears when we met, and now we have more: we may die on this barge." He turned her face toward him. Her eyes were closed and there was a tear on her cheek. "Sephy—"

Her lips were trembling.

"Answer me," he said.

"I will," she sobbed, rocking her head on his chest. "I will, I will."

Zack held her close and kissed her brow.

"I had a hundred pounds of bacon." Winiarski, the teenager, glanced around the barge at the men seated or curled on the coal, speaking to no one in particular. "Lean cut, packed in salt."

35

No one responded.

"I'm a clothier," Winiarski said.

A few men looked up.

"A clerk," he confessed.

"Tough luck," someone said finally.

The fire snapped.

"I didn't buy a thing," Streetcar said. "Braked my trolley, told the fares, 'It's the end of the line,' and headed for the docks. Nothing but the cash in my wallet—" He stopped, came to his knees and stuffed his hands in his pockets. "Left it in my bedroll."

"Pencils," Inky said, pulling a handful from his coat.

Now the others were checking.

"Still have my ticket home," one announced, waving it.

"You boys—" The popeyed man laughed. "Arnie's got our grubstake in his boot." He glanced at the fellow seated beside him.

"I put it in the valise this morning," Arnie replied. His face drooped like a basset hound's.

"What are you saying?"

"It's in the valise, Wag."

"But you took it back out, didn't you? Shit for jam." The popeyed man, Wagner, kicked his companion. "You should've gone down with your steamer," he fumed at the Captain.

"We must count our blessings," the short-haired woman said to the group.

"For what?" Wagner scowled, gesturing at the barge. "No better than dying in the street."

No one challenged him.

"My cousin went that way," the man beside Streetcar said.

"What way?"

"Starved on a park bench."

The world they'd left hovered before them.

"A great nation gone bust," a man said.

There were nods.

"Granddad would be sick."

"Tycoons and politicians."

"It's the damn machines. They don't need men. We're obsolete."

"The school where I was teaching shut its doors," the brown-skinned man with spectacles said. "My name is Dinesh," he introduced himself, using his fingers to comb his hair. "I was taking quarter pay at the forge. After what I set by for supplies, there was nothing for transportation. I had to beg the conductor to let me sleep under the seats with the dogs."

"No work at all where I'm from."

Arnie, the man who'd left the valise behind, shook his head. "I was on the dole for a year. They took our house away. Wife's living with her folks. I got here on borrowed money, from anyone who'd give it to me."

"Borrowed's your name alright," Wagner griped.

"I hoped to make enough to start my own school," Dinesh told them.

Streetcar smiled. "Farm's what I want. Lettuce, far as you can see."

The men traded glances.

37

"My brother could be a doctor if we had the dough."

"Life of ease for me," one laughed. "Not another day of honest labor."

"I wanna be known," Winiarski said. "Someone the world respects."

"Ink's plugging for his own paper," Streetcar volunteered.

"*The Morning Sun*," Inky smiled. "'Intelligence, Fresh and Sound.'"

"Least we ain't dodging bullets like the boys overseas."

"Or freezing to death," a fellow in overalls said. "Where I come from, coal's dearer than corn. You go down by the tracks and pick up the pieces that fell off the hoppers." He gestured at the black ore. "Here we are, sitting on forty wagons of it."

Laughter circled the group and died.

"I'm not going back," Streetcar said.

"Not empty-handed," Dinesh agreed.

"We're all in the same spot."

Wagner glanced at Zack. "Not all of us."

Zack saw the faces turn toward him. He didn't respond.

"A man can rest easy," Wagner shrugged, "when he's got a fortune beneath his pillow."

Zack kept his silence.

Wagner snorted.

"He hasn't any more than the rest of you," Sephy said.

Winiarski squinted at her. The men waited for more.

"He's given back his inheritance."

Lucky, the gray-haired man, cleared his throat. "There's a question if he's mentioned in the will."

Zack regarded him. "It was a blind trust," he said.

"What's the secret?" Inky glanced from Zack to Lucky.

"The cowboy created quite a stir before he left," Lucky said. "He was the talk of the capital. He's only half a Knox, and that's fifty percent more than suits his father."

Zack felt Sephy shift. She was facing the group, allying herself with him. He wanted to vindicate himself for her sake, but when his lips parted, cynicism got the better of him. "I'm an embarrassment," he nodded.

Sephy gripped his arm.

"The ghost of a teenage trespass." Zack spoke to everyone on the barge. "My mother died bringing me into the world. Charles Knox got himself properly married a dozen years later." He peered into Sephy's eyes. "He gave his name to his second son, as if he was first. As for me—" He turned and looked out over the water. "I was Zack McDermott. Origin unknown."

The breeze died, leaving his words hanging in the silence.

"Raised as an orphan," he said. "I didn't know who my father was until I was sixteen." The rudder ropes groaned, and when Zack looked to stern, he saw Snell had turned his attention from the shoreline and was eyeing him with curiosity.

"When I found out," Zack said, "I changed my name to Knox."

"Most people think you're his lawful son," Dinesh observed.

"How about that." Zack looked at Sephy. Some of her sadness had returned.

"You gave the money back?" Streetcar was perplexed. "Don't you want to be worth something?"

"That's why I'm here," Zack answered.

"Particular where it comes from," Wagner pointed out.

"I can understand that," Dinesh said.

"I can too. It was just hush money to his pap."

"I'd keep the cash."

Streetcar shook his head. "You care what your dad thinks. They planted mine six years ago, and the old scratch is still frowning over my shoulder."

"A man spends his whole life trying to prove himself to his father," Inky said.

They thought about that.

"Pa had a dim view of Breakaway," one said. "Called me a fool."

Zack watched the grim gazes wander over the gunwales, imagining a wasting end, adrift on the cold sea or stranded on some black beach.

"We're done for," Wagner said to the Captain.

Snell turned to him. "Now what do *you* know?"

Zack felt Sephy shiver. He coaxed her head back onto his shoulder and drew the blankets around them.

A sound like thunder invaded Zack's sleep. Something sharp dug at his shoulder. He shifted, aching in a dozen places, then opened his eyes. Sephy lay motionless beside him. Her face was smudged and sooty. He slid from beneath the blankets and looked around, seeing others lifting themselves from the coal.

How long had they slept? The sun was halfway down the sky. Snell was piloting, still staring at the coastline. It was much closer now and the mists had dissolved. Burnished black walls rose from a stripe of sea crust. Higher up, the peaks were tiered with trees, rows set back one behind the other. Where the sun found aisles, the forest glowed bottle green.

Inky came to his feet silently, pointing. Zack spied the object of his excitement. Through a break in the cliffs, an arm of white water emerged. On either side, the earth was speckled with stumps where men had felled trees. Winiarski was up, grinning through a mask of coal dust. He turned to wake Dinesh.

They were entering a natural harbor. A river had forced its way to the sea, leaving a crescent-shaped beach of black rock. Above the beach, a clutch of crooked tents clung to a knoll. The thundering mounted. Sephy opened her eyes. Zack got his legs beneath him and stood, the red union suit climbing to his ankles. His feet were bare. He helped Sephy up. She followed the gazes, then straightened her trousers and tucked her shirt.

The rudder ropes moaned in the stern. Snell was turning the wheel, scanning the tidewater with a careworn smile. More tents were visible on a low hillside. The men on the barge were speechless. All stood now, blotched with soot, rumpled and damp, except for the woman with short hair who knelt in prayer.

"Sephy," Zack said.

She gave him a look of relief, but her hands were knotted on her chest.

A valley opened before them, bounded by dark forests and black palisades, its lower slopes stripped of timber. Down its middle, the river rushed, angling between the steep walls and tumbling through a mouth crammed with boulders. Above the mouth, the low hills were crowded with tents and a few small buildings.

"Breakaway," Snell said, so all could hear.

"What's that noise?" Winiarski wondered.

"Stamp mill." Snell pointed at three giant sheds, one above the other, halfway up the valley.

42

Wagner hooted and the others joined in, stumbling across the coal to congratulate each other.

"No more fares." Streetcar raised his cap and gave Zack a hug.

Zack laughed. "Look at that." The tent camp seemed a brave thing, planted in the eye of the wilderness. Canvas lean-tos, square tents, pup tents, bell tents, weathered and patched, a few blown to rags. They perched on inclines and in depressions, canted at odd angles, smoking from log fires and stovepipes—bedded at the river's end, with the ledges of gold somewhere near. He scanned the walls of the valley. Sephy took hold of his hand.

She was smiling. Her distress seemed to have vanished. Raymond, Zack thought. The camp had nothing threatening about it. Some of its inhabitants had caught sight of the craft and were running to greet them, hurrying down muddy paths, hollering and waving.

"Here's the news," Inky shouted and spread his arms.

Arnie cupped his hands around his mouth. "Make room!"

"Lead us to it," Winiarski joined in.

Lucky was troubled. "They're filthy."

"Give yourself a gander," Streetcar laughed.

"No place to spend it," Inky pointed out.

"Look." Sephy was gazing over the gunwale.

The water was boiling around the barge. A great swarm of fish circled beneath them, flashing silver and pink, quivering and clenching as their backs broke the surface.

"Here they come," Winiarski cried.

A dory had set out from a spindly wharf. Zack saw a man in a dark three-piece suit standing in the bow. He shouted, "Snell," and raised a coil of rope in one hand.

"Get that," Snell said.

The man in the suit threw the line toward them. Its end looped over the top of some crates and landed beside Zack. He grabbed it, crossed the coal barefooted and knotted it to a cleat. Then the dory pivoted and began towing the barge in.

Sephy drew beside him. The men of the camp had a strange uniformity, Zack realized. Their clothing was of similar design, spattered alike with mud and grease. They wore heavy boots with the pants cut off at the shins.

The barge settled against the piers, and two men on the wharf secured it with chains. Others extended a gangplank. The man in the suit crossed onto the barge. He was in his mid-thirties, medium height and clean shaven. His carriage was crisp. A bemused disbelief shone in his eyes. Snell made a fist over his chest and brought it forward, and the man in the suit smiled at the gesture. He stepped over the coal, shaking his head, and when he reached Snell, he circled him with both arms.

"The mayor," Dinesh observed to Zack.

"Mister Lloyd," Snell greeted the man warmly. He stood with his arms hanging, accepting the embrace with a self-conscious grin.

"What happened?" Lloyd took in the survivors on the barge.

"Steamer hit a rock," the Captain said. "Crew went down with her."

Lloyd raised his chin, as if perceiving some hidden significance in the tragedy. "Terrible." He read duty in the Captain's face. "Your boat?"

"You know whose boat it was," the Captain said bitterly.

Lloyd seemed baffled.

"To the store." Snell stepped between them. His arm thumped the Captain's back to urge him onto the gangplank.

Zack saw Snell give Lloyd a look that promised more in private.

"How many lost?" Lloyd asked.

"Twenty-nine," Snell replied. "Horses and mules too."

Lloyd blanched. "Anyone need doctoring?" He glanced around the barge. Two men stepped forward, one cradling his arm against his middle.

"I could use a banker," Lucky said. "Some of us might like to arrange a loan."

"Until we get our gold," Winiarski added.

Lloyd raised his brows, caught a wary look from Snell and answered with a thoughtful nod. "Any Cousin Jacks?"

Snell shook his head. "They're raw as your ma. The drilling goods made it." He indicated the crates. "Steel, powder, fuse. Pair of new everhards—they cost me dear." He took a breath. "What about Hope?"

Lloyd's eyes dulled.

"You want her, don't you," a voice spoke from the wharf.

Zack watched Snell face the miners and beam at them. "Sure do," he replied. "It's hell back there." His head ticked over his shoulder, marking where he'd come from.

45

Lloyd signaled to one of the miners.

"Who's Hope?" Inky asked Snell.

"Welcome to you all," Lloyd said to the newcomers, and then to the miner approaching, "Take them to the dry room." He waved the other men on the wharf forward. "Let's unload this barge."

Lloyd was treating them like cargo. Zack stared at the coal beneath his feet, trying to calm himself. His breath was constricting. Sephy linked his arm with her own.

"Can we bother you for an introduction?" Zack said. His voice quavered, but he spoke loudly enough to halt the proceedings.

Lloyd regarded him with surprise. "Pardon me. I'm Lloyd." He tipped his head. "Chemist, sawbones and bookkeeper. My time's not my own."

"My name's Knox," Zack returned the nod. "I'm free and clear."

"It must be grand," Lloyd smiled. "You're far from home."

Zack saw the irony in his eyes. "A man's freedom travels with him."

Lloyd faced the others. "It's no triumph of civilization," he gestured at the camp, "but we can dry you out and put food in you. It happens you're in time for dinner. What'll you say to that?"

"Grace," Winiarski responded.

"All choosing to be dry and fed—" Lloyd swept his hand toward the gangplank.

Lucky tugged his lapels and stepped forward. Zack met Lloyd's questioning gaze, then nodded to Sephy, and they joined those filing off the barge. He was a sight, with his showman locks, bare feet and red underwear.

The path into camp was thick with miners. Up close the dirt looked permanent, ground into their clothing. Their faces were gritty as well, but humanity shone through. They were shaking hands and talking to the new arrivals. Still, there was something covert in the welcome. Zack could sense it in their pauses and the looks they traded with each other.

On the path ahead, Winiarski had stopped to question one of them.

"Where's the gold?"

"She's there." The miner pointed up the valley.

"Hot peppers—" Winiarski followed his gesture.

Between the thighs of denuded slope, a trapezoidal wall rose. It was black with vertical grooves, giant gutters with edges that were ragged and spalled. Zack noticed a winding trail on the wall, and a dozen men strung out along it, descending. "Lots of new faces?" he asked the miner.

The man shook his head. "You're the first since February."

Zack was puzzled.

"Steamers don't stop here," the man explained. "Too dangerous."

"What about ours?" Winiarski said.

The man glanced at the barge. "What about it?"

"The new strikes have you in fine humor," Zack observed.

"Strikes?" The miner squinted and twitched his mustache.

"The ledges," Zack said. "The new lodes."

The miner returned a blank stare. Another man had stepped beside them—a big man, nearly Zack's height.

"There's only one vein in Breakaway," the mustached man said. "We hold her dear."

"She's our Hope," the big man told them, tipping his head to Sephy. "I'm Bluford," he introduced himself. "They call me True."

His jaw was square and so were his shoulders. His eyes were kindly.

"We're believers," the mustached man said.

True nodded. "It's not like it is where you come from," he assured Zack. "Here a man has something to live for." He clapped Zack on the shoulder. "You passed your first test." He gazed at the barge and the sea. "Hope's in your future."

"Is the war over?" the mustached man asked.

"They're fighting on three continents," Zack said.

The miner was surprised. True clinched his cheek, as if he expected no better.

Zack looked at Sephy. She was as puzzled as he. "Glad to meet you," he nodded to the men, and they continued up the path.

An odor reached them—fish reek—and it grew stronger with every step. There was a nimbus of smoke hanging over the camp, and as they entered it, a suspicion took shape in Zack's mind. "BMC," he muttered, eyeing the tents through the smoke.

The gravel path turned into a corduroy road that wound among the bluffs, arriving at a broad shelf beside the river where a two-story building stood amid piles of raw planking. There the road divided, one branch continuing up the valley, the other leading to large double doors in the building's side. A loud whistle blew, and as the rumble of the stamp mill faded, the man escorting the new arrivals reached the double doors and slid one open. They filed through, collecting in a dim warehouse, trading information.

There was bewilderment and dismay on every face.

"Of course," Inky protested to a half-dozen men. "I heard about the reefs when I was scouting the docks. 'I know those waters,'" he mimicked a blustering voice and glared at the Captain. "That's what he told me."

"We'd best be drying ourselves," a broad-chested bald man spoke loudly, embracing the group with thick arms. He had a genial look and it landed on Zack. "At the back of the supply store. 'Tis nice and warm." He pointed.

"Who are you?" Zack asked.

"Owen," the man said. He made a fist over his chest and carried it forward.

Zack took in the gesture and the simple smile, then he shrugged at Sephy and they did as the man suggested.

"Chatter your little hearts away," Owen said as the survivors filed past.

The corridor led between stacked drums and grain sacks. At the rear of the building, they entered a small room where a large steam heater gasped and creaked. They lined up alongside it.

49

"Percival Schorr," Inky looked at Zack. "The only man to return to the States."

"Incredible," Lucky scowled.

"The whole thing was bogus," Streetcar said.

"Who the hell was that?" Inky turned again to the Captain. The Captain didn't reply.

"There were a couple of steerers," Inky told them. "Kids in short britches. Walked right up to my desk. 'This fellow's found gold!' Took me to the Bostwick, up the stairs to Schorr's room. He was packing. 'Sure, have a look.' Big smile, black chops and chin, like Abe Lincoln." He glanced at the Captain. "Well? Say something."

The Captain stood eyeing the creaking heater. "Snell engineered it. Hired Abe to play Schorr. And the kids got sarsaparilla." He faced his passengers. "Then he bought a dry-docked tramp and found an old drunk to pilot her. Your fares paid for the ship."

Zack gazed at Sephy, stunned.

"Why?" Lucky wondered.

"They're short on men," the Captain replied.

"The Breakaway Mining Company," Zack said.

"I believed the story because it was in the paper," Dinesh said.

"Me too," Winiarski nodded.

Wagner threw himself at the Captain. "You worthless—"

The Captain held him off. "It made me sick," he said, "watching you puff on your pipe dreams."

Sweat beaded Zack's face. He turned away from the furnace.

"Zack—"

He saw the alarm in Sephy's eyes, and then he was moving, headed back through the storage area. Pipe dreams, he thought. Secrets and lies.

"Zack—"

He reached a door. Sephy's footsteps sounded at his rear. He opened the door and stepped out.

A yard spread before him. Dozens of miners stood talking. Behind them, timber tables and benches were arranged to form an open-air mess hall. The fish reek was overpowering. Zack approached, scanning the gathering for a face with the look of authority.

Someone whistled, and the sound was like ice in Zack's veins—a wordless summons, laden with contempt.

When he turned, he saw a man a few yards away, leaning against the supply store wall with one leg flexed. His hairline was low, his cheek lumpy as nut brittle. He unpuckered his lips and resumed jawing a wad of gum. "Hats off to Snail," the man said. "I'm getting hopeful just looking at 'er."

He spoke loudly enough for everyone in the yard to hear.

Zack felt Sephy beside him. Out of the corner of his eye, he saw the new arrivals filing into the yard. He fixed on the man. "Who's in charge here?"

The man kicked himself free of the wall. "DuVal," he greeted Zack. "What's the price?"

He has too much bluff, Zack thought. The man was a flunky.

"Give you seven hundred," DuVal said, nodding at Sephy.

"Swine," Dinesh spoke out.

"No disrespect meant." DuVal addressed Sephy.

She drew away from Zack, face averted, trembling. Inky stepped beside her.

"You're her cadet, aren't you?" DuVal asked Zack. "Make it a thousand. One thousand bones. That's good money, Knox."

Zack started toward him.

"Give him a pasting," Winiarski yelled. The miners were silent.

DuVal acted confused. "I'd just like to be first." He rocked onto the balls of his feet. "There's a tip—for you." DuVal's tongue slid out. He pinched the lob of gum from it. "A sweet," he said, extending the lob.

Zack sprang at him.

DuVal recoiled and waltzed aside. He stuck the gum to his nose.

"Yokel," Zack said, following.

DuVal turned to face the miners. "That's us, boys." Then he whirled around.

Maybe it was the chill of the northern sea that slowed his reflexes. Zack saw the blow coming, moved to cross it and missed. DuVal's fist plunged into his middle. He doubled over, guts twisting, and DuVal kicked him sideways into the mud.

"There's your 'tall drink,'" DuVal jibed.

Zack lay sucking the air. DuVal's comment was directed at Snell, who was watching from a spot near the cookstoves at the supply store's rear. Zack could feel the eyes of the world on him—miners, spectators in the stands, eager as magpies at a dogfight. He got his knees beneath him and heaved himself up. DuVal saw him and wheeled, but not in time. Zack's right fist hammered his temple.

DuVal stumbled back, pocked cheeks bloating. As Zack lunged, DuVal drove his boot up. The toe struck Zack in the chest. He went down, rolled, stood in time to avoid a second kick, regained his balance and spun around, pounding DuVal's ribs. His adversary heeled back and Zack aimed at his brow. The *crack* filled the yard.

"Bull's-eye," Streetcar shouted.

A babble of encouragement rose from both the miners and the new arrivals. DuVal was shuffling backward toward the cooking area. Zack closed the distance and sprang, bashing DuVal's chin, sending him clattering against tables loaded with pots and pans. DuVal snarled, kicked the loose graniteware and swung around, blinking and wagging his head. "You're making me mad."

Zack threw himself toward him. This time DuVal dodged. Before Zack could turn, he was snagged and jerked around. DuVal plowed a fist into his belly. Zack buckled without going down, gasping for air, reaching blindly. DuVal was up against him, battering his kidneys. Then something like cannon fire went off in Zack's head. He felt his legs fold beneath him and he landed hard on the gravel.

DuVal was kicking his shoulders and chest, trying to get at his face. "I'll chop your legs off—"

"Stop," Sephy cried.

"Cut off your arms," DuVal huffed. "Run you to the mill in an ore bucket—"

"Alright," a miner growled.

"That's enough," another yelled.

Through a fog, Zack could see DuVal shifting over him.

"Please," Sephy implored the miners. Inky was holding her.

"Unbutton my fly," DuVal ordered Zack.

The crowd cursed him as one.

DuVal swung toward a cook table and turned back with a grilling fork in his hand. Zack saw Dinesh fling his arms around DuVal's waist. DuVal battered Dinesh loose and continued forward. "You're the bum here, Knox."

Zack lifted himself.

Sephy was sobbing. "Someone—"

DuVal struck Zack down and dropped onto his chest, brandishing the grilling fork. "Beggin' time." The tines quivered over Zack's eye. "Beg me to take her."

Zack gripped his wrist, trying to shift the fork. Sephy was screaming.

The tines touched Zack's eyelid.

"Beg, you bastard," DuVal said.

Zack convulsed, jerking the fork aside. His back arched and his fist powered into DuVal's groin. DuVal groaned and shuddered. Then a shovel blade sliced through the air, cracking

54

against DuVal's head. His features went slack and he slumped from view.

Zack was gasping for breath. He rolled onto his hip. "He don't belong here," he heard someone say. Sephy's voice sounded nearby. "Are you hurt?" DuVal lay unconscious on the gravel beside him, eyes staring, blood leaking from his brow. The lob of gum on his nose was dashed with dirt.

A boot bumped DuVal's head. "Harder than it looks."

Zack peered up, seeing a grizzled man with sloping shoulders and a kettle belly. The shovel's haft was split in two, and he held a length in each fist. His right cheek was crosshatched with scars, and the top of his right ear was folded over. The man sighed, gaze shifting from DuVal to Lloyd and Owen, who were hunching over him. "Had it coming."

Lloyd ignored the comment. He was checking DuVal's pulse.

"He's a pit dog," Owen said, "like some paddies hereabout." He glanced at the man who'd split DuVal's head.

Zack drew a leg in. Sephy was on the ground beside him. He rose to a squat.

"Nice swing," one of the miners said.

"Run these to the shop, will you?" The man with the folded ear handed the broken shovel over.

Lloyd shouted something in a foreign language and three Asian cooks hurried from behind the stoves. He looked at Zack. "You alright?"

The man with the folded ear knelt. "This boy's beyond pain."

The cooks helped Owen lift DuVal and carry him toward the store.

"None of this should have happened," Lloyd said, glancing at Sephy. Then to the man who'd leveled DuVal, "Could have used your fist."

"Could have," the man agreed.

Lloyd hastened after his patient. The miners had turned away. Inky and Winiarski were helping Dinesh toward a table.

"Crazy," Zack said.

His rescuer laughed. "There's your madman."

Zack followed his gaze to the corner window of the supply store's second floor. He got a glimpse of a large head with thick brows swimming in the dimness on the far side of the glass. The face had a fierce intensity. As Zack met the dark eyes, the earth seemed to dissolve beneath him. Then a finger unhooked itself and the gap in the curtains closed.

Sephy gripped his arm. Zack got his feet beneath him and stood, and his rescuer stood with him. "Who are you?"

"Miner," the grizzled man replied. "Dog-Eared Bob."

"And the fellow you conked?"

"Odd jobs. He does his best to please the boss, but— He only has half a brain." Bob considered Sephy. "Got a quarrel with him?"

Zack nodded. "And with the rest of this BMC. They shanghaied us."

"We did?" Bob looked surprised.

"You're one of them?"

Bob nodded. "We all are."

One of the Asians was rattling his spoon in an iron triangle. Miners were forming a line behind the stoves.

Bob motioned them toward the line. "You call yourself Knox?"

"Zack."

Heads turned to follow them.

"Where'd you get that shave?" Bob asked. "Like a goat my uncle had."

"He was a performer," Sephy explained, "in a shooting show."

Bob eyed her as if she was a puzzle that needed solving.

"My name is Sephy," she said.

"Welcome to Breakaway, miss."

"When did this become a company town?" Zack asked.

"Six months after Hope appeared," Bob said. "Prowler came out of his hole in March, two years ago. Trevillian arrived in August and bought up the claims."

"The man upstairs?"

Bob nodded.

"Did anyone hit it? Before he got here?"

"Some of the early boys—those who were in the neighborhood when Hope first showed. Jimmy Soboleff staked a hot shoot and headed south two months later with eighty pounds of gold."

"What about you?"

Bob laughed. "They were on either side of me, jumping up and down whenever they found jewelry. I was sure it would be my turn next." He motioned upriver, at the black trapezoid.

"We were up there—where the gallows is now—two hundred feet in the air."

"In the air?"

Bob nodded. "Before the mountain got chiseled down. Hope wasn't lying flat. Once the gold on top was dug out, you had to angle in after her." Bob pointed his fingers and sent his hand sliding. "Can't do that with a pick and shovel. The boss came in. Bought up the claims, brought in miners and equipment, built the mill. Some of the boys left. A lot of us stayed on."

"To work for the BMC," Zack said.

Bob regarded him. "To be with Hope. No one understands her like Trevillian."

They were beside the cook tables now and Sephy was passed a plate. A young Asian ladled beans and greens onto it. His black hair was braided and hung down his back. Another added a plank of grilled salmon and a biscuit.

"Good chow," Bob said. "The Bangshu can cook."

A miner stood post at the head of the food line. "Lemme guess." He grinned. "Knox, Zachary." He wrote the name in a black pocket ledger.

"Give yourself a hug," Bob said.

"What's to celebrate?" Zack watched as the food was put on his plate.

"You're in Lloyd's book."

Bob got his dinner and led them among the tables.

Heads lifted and turned to follow them. Winiarski and Dinesh were seated. Worry showed in their faces as Zack passed. When Bob reached the edge of the yard, he pointed. "We'll park here."

"Expecting trouble?" Zack asked.

"You stay out of Trevillian's way till this fuss with DuVal blows over."

"There aren't any women," Sephy said, scanning the yard.

Bob looked as if the puzzle she posed had grown in difficulty. "Separate camp." He gestured up the valley, then he set his plate on the table and gave it a spin. "Let's eat."

Zack took the bench opposite and Sephy sat beside him. Bob licked the loose flour off his biscuit and bit into it.

"March, two years ago," Sephy said.

Bob nodded. "Waking Prowler. That's how it started."

"Who's Prowler?" she asked.

"Hope's bear," Bob replied. "We find her and lose her, and when she comes back, sometimes Prowler comes with her. She tests us, and that bear is one of the tests. When Hope first surfaced, she brought Prowler along. It was the Private who was tested."

"The Private?"

"He was our prophet." Bob gazed up the valley. "Prowler was sleeping beside Hope, in a den on that peak. The Private and his pal were crossing the river, where the mill is now. Hope put her finger on the Private's rifle—" Bob paused to chew his beans. "Food's getting cold, miss."

Sephy sat motionless, staring at him. Zack reached his hand out and she took it.

"The rifle went off and the shot woke Prowler," Bob

59

continued. "Crawls out of his den." He made a groggy face. "Doesn't know what he's doing. Instead of going down into the valley, he heads across the cliff through the snow pack. The top of the mountain came clean away." Bob's brows lifted. "The Private and his pal—they rubbed their eyes. They raced up to get a look. It was her alright."

"Hope," Zack said.

Bob nodded. "I can see you're believing me." He pointed with his spoon. "They pitched a tent in the wash—up there, beyond Blondetown. Prowler went down with the avalanche. You'd think, 'Well, that's the end of him.' But it wasn't." Bob wiped his mouth. "He was wicked mad when he dug himself out of the cement. As Hope intended."

Zack felt Sephy's hand pull away. She crossed her arms over her front.

"It's not a happy ending," Bob apologized.

"Go on," Sephy said.

"Middle of the night, Prowler tears open their tent. Pulls off the pal's arm. Then Prowler grabs the Private. The pal lay there bleeding, watching while Prowler dragged the Private up the side of the wash. The Private had his prospector's pick, and when Prowler raised him up, there they were silhouetted against the moon, with the Private swinging and Prowler roaring and shaking him like a rag doll. Then Prowler carried him off."

Sephy gazed into the forest.

"The Private's pal managed to bind himself up. He made it back to their boat and set it loose. A steamer happened on him a week later. When they reached Gastineau City, he told

60

the local boys everything. Plenty of danger, but they came quick. By rights, the Private and his pal should have been first to stake claims. But no one ever saw the Private again, and his pal didn't come back. Soon as we got here, Hope sent Prowler to test us. Big gash over his left eye—" Bob touched his brow with his spoon. "Everyone figured the Private did that."

"You knew him?" Zack asked.

Bob shook his head. "No one here ever met the Private."

"Why do they call him that?" Sephy wondered.

"His coat," Bob said. "He poached it from a soldier."

Just then, the triangle rang again. The miners grew quiet. A half-dozen men were filing out of the supply store. They moved as a group through the eating area and circled a vacant table in the yard's center. Owen took a position at one end.

"Here he comes," Bob said.

Through the crowd, the mine boss appeared. Zack recognized the face in the window—the piercing eyes and black brows. His expression was benign. He was average height and looked to be in his early forties, but he carried himself with the stiffness of someone much older. His gaze aimed beyond the gathering, as if there was something only he could see. He stepped onto a bench and from there to the tabletop, turned to check his lieutenants, then tipped his head back and regarded the crowd beneath the eave of his brow.

"Left the Reminder upstairs," Bob said.

"A good evening to the day shift," Trevillian boomed, "and a good morning to the night." He spread his smile through the yard. "You want her, don't you."

61

Men responded with shouts, making fists over their chests and carrying them forward. Bob was holding his fist out like the rest, brimming with emotion. Sephy gave Zack a fearful look. Twenty feet away, Inky caught his eye.

"Our band is greater today by nearly a score," Trevillian said. "Welcome them with compassion, for the trial they endured; with respect, that they survived her test; and gladly, for the spirit they will add to our own. We are all castaways, fallen from our vessel, left bobbing in the gulf."

Zack watched the miners. Most seemed to receive Trevillian's message as it had been delivered, soberly and with humility.

"This little valley, this ripple at the earth's edge, is home to a rare creature." The mine boss turned his gaze to the switchback trail. "A creature with crystalline flesh, lit with gold. She's our dream, our purpose, our sustenance." He scanned the men, picking out the new faces. "When we work and when we mate and when we pray—we are thinking of her. Hope is her name." He opened his arms. "Hope."

"Hope," a hundred voices spoke, and the echoes filled the valley.

Zack saw a range of feelings in the men around him— inspiration in one, defeat in another. Passion and dread. Pride, brazen or self-possessed. Dog-Eared Bob had intoned Hope's name with the rest, but weakly. There was resignation in his eyes, as if Hope was a woman whose favor he expected to lose.

"Remember the moment," Trevillian said. "It will be precious to you— The moment you decided to leave. Like all of us who found our way here, she reached you. The unwavering, irresistible voice—of Hope.

"What pledge does a man get from life? What promise?" He spoke softly now. "He has the certainty of the grave. Nothing more. Our prayers for worth, for purity of purpose, for the will to persist— Who can answer them? Those who give their hearts to Hope turn their backs on a doomed world."

His expression grew pensive. "We have so much to talk about, you and I."

Trevillian tightened his lips, then laughed. "Half the mountains on the continent have been mined. The earth is crawling with drillers. They have a contest every spring in the middle states. Last year, the man who won—the fastest drill in the country—walked away from his prize. He's here, in this yard." Trevillian turned his palms up. "What does my champion say? Noel?" He looked around the mess.

"I'll never go back," a voice answered from a table at the rear.

"My brother," Trevillian smiled. "And yours. We're kin here. All of us who seek her. All of us with the glow of Hope in our eyes.

"I know—it's a lot to swallow. Don't worry. I'm not going to force my beliefs on you. Hope reveals herself in a personal moment and men embrace her. That's how it happens. There's no other way. We have doubters among us." He nodded. "They want to believe, but their hearts aren't yet hers. They test our faith. Bunting. Carew—" He pointed to a man at a nearby table. "Someday you'll be with us."

Across the mess, voices rose, encouraging Carew.

Trevillian's arm fell and he stared at his boots. Silence followed. No one ate or spoke. When he raised his head, his look was distant, detached.

"Two shifts a day," the mine boss said. "Ten hours each. In the waste time, we eat and repair ourselves. Then we're back in the mountain, seeking her out. It's hard work and it's dangerous. We hear the war consumes many lives." He shook his head. "No boy on the battlefield is braver than a soldier of Hope."

"She's worth the fight," a miner shouted.

"She'll be back," another said.

"Sometimes she's mindful about the injuries we endure. Often she's not." Trevillian's expression hardened. "She's fickle. She lures us, then withdraws, slipping deeper, leaving us only a scarf to snuffle. Right now— We're chasing trifles she's thrown behind her. Hope's gone behind a cloud. We're brutes and she wants nothing to do with us. It seems like we'll never see her again. Then, when we least expect it, she'll be at our elbow, keen and reassuring, whispering in our ear."

The mood in the yard had changed. Zack could sense the unrest. There was anxiety in many of the faces.

"When I speak, Hope listens. You can see that." Trevillian's gesture took in the new arrivals and the barge moored to the wharf. "She's replaced those she's taken. Our mining supplies are restored." He was addressing his faithful.

"What about our feed?" a man asked.

Trevillian shook his head. "The groceries went down with

64

the ship. Our flour's nearly gone, and the beans and rice won't last to the New Year. We have salmon and greens, and the Bang Boys' root mash. We won't starve, but our lives will be harder. Canvas, soap, boot soles— What Snell purchased would have filled the store's shelves," he sighed.

"I'll do," one miner affirmed.

"Same here."

"As long as Hope comes back," a man said grimly.

A brown-skinned miner rose to his feet. "What's the news from Ardent?"

"Just threads," a voice answered.

"How about Slick Liver?" the miner looked around.

"Not a thing," a man replied.

"Is she saying anything to you?" the brown man asked the boss.

Trevillian raised his arms. "Faith," he said firmly.

There were curses and sour looks.

"We'll find her," the mine boss said.

"When?" A haggard man stood. "I can't stand this," he confessed.

"'Tis an urgent need," Owen said. "No one is more pained by Hope's absence than our boss."

Zack glanced at Bob.

The haggard man swore. Hope's name crossed the yard, woven through with expressions of doubt and frustration. Trevillian let them vent.

"You new fellows can see," he said when the upset lulled, "how precious Hope is to us." He smiled. "And you will share in the triumph when she returns. You're our brothers and our bunkies. We'll make room in our tents."

He looked from table to table. "Our fish sits well in your belly," he nodded. "The flesh is renewed. The meal was an advance against work in the mine." Trevillian glanced at Lloyd. "You're registered with our payroll master."

Zack put his fingers on his chest, where DuVal's kicks had landed. His blood was boiling.

"Half of the new boys will go down tonight," the mine boss said. "The others will report to the Glory Hole in the morning, 8:10 sharp. Rolls are posted by the cook shack."

"What did the meal cost us?" Wagner shouted.

"Twenty bones," Trevillian answered. "You'll make a hundred a shift, like every man here."

Winiarski held up his hand. "Do we have a choice?"

Trevillian shrugged. "If you want to take care of yourself," he motioned toward the wilds north of the valley, "dinner's on me."

"If there's more treasure, do we get some of it?" Streetcar wondered.

"I'll trade my Hope for gold," Lucky chimed in.

"I'm not going to lift a finger for you," Wagner barked.

Zack drew his shoulders back and put his hands on the table. As he stood, he saw Bob's confusion and Sephy's alarm.

"I don't care much for your generosity." Zack spoke as evenly as he could.

The yard was instantly quiet. "What are you doing," Bob growled.

"A host who claps irons on you while you're eating," Zack said, "is a freak of nature, not a man."

Trevillian turned. Zack met his stare.

"This is Hope's doing, my friend," the mine boss replied.

"Treachery put me here, not Hope."

"Step up, step up," Trevillian said. "Let me face my accuser directly."

The mine boss was motioning him to rise. Zack swallowed his fear and put his foot on the bench. He boosted himself onto the tabletop, hearing the whispers, eyeing the boss over the heads of the men.

"Our passion seems strange to you," Trevillian said.

"That's not my beef," Zack replied. There was a storm inside him.

"Well?"

"I'm not your slave," Zack said.

"No, I am yours. I serve your soul." Trevillian raised his chin, inviting a response. He could see Zack's rage. Zack was choked with it.

"My soul—" Zack's rapid breath fouled his speech.

"We're not tromping the boards here," Trevillian said. "This is serious business. Men must be led."

"Men choose who will lead them." Zack turned to the miners. "You don't applaud this. I know you don't."

The boss said nothing.

"A man has a birthright," Zack told the camp. "He's not beholden. He asks for no other man's mercy. No other man decides if he's discarded or used."

"He plays the hero nicely," Trevillian said.

"Will one of you speak up for us?" Zack asked the miners. The silence was deathly.

"Words without faith don't count for much," the boss told him. "Not here." He cocked his head, considering. "You might earn a few bones in the Wheel. '*Long John Settles the Score*,'" he smiled, sweeping his hand across an imaginary marquee. "Try your tongue on the madam."

Laughter convulsed the mess.

Zack wiped the sweat from his cheek. "Is this what Hope's done for you?" His legs were quivering. The dam was about to burst. "Have you sunk this low?"

The yard swelled with grumbles and insults.

"You're slaves—every one of you," Zack said. "You deserve your poverty, this lunatic, your worthless Hope—"

"Show us your teeth," Trevillian's voice rose over the booing miners. He nodded appreciatively and began to clap. A few followed his example, and then the camp caught his spirit and the bristling turned to applause.

Zack withered, but he didn't stop. "A man's a fool— No escape— A trap, a prison, people like you—" He was shuffling broken thoughts, trembling with abasement.

"This moves me," the boss told the camp. "Bravo, bravo!" He lifted his hands.

The men rose at their tables, raucous and whistling, giving the showman a standing ovation.

Zack looked down. Sephy was hiding her eyes. He faced

Trevillian, saw him shoot Owen a silent command. Then the boss gestured to the men. "Meal's over," he shouted.

Zack watched him descend from his table. The miners began to disperse.

He felt a hand on his foot. Sephy was peering up at him.

"You gonna stand there all night?" Bob said.

Zack set his jaw and climbed down.

"We were keeping you out of trouble." Bob spoke to Zack, but his eyes were on Trevillian. "C'mon." He grabbed Zack's arm and nodded toward a footpath. They had not gone three paces when a voice called from behind.

"Knox."

Zack stopped and turned.

Owen smiled affably. "The boss wants you."

Bob sighed and let go of his arm.

Zack was still bleary. "Watch out for her," he said.

"Watch out for yourself," Bob replied.

Zack followed Owen toward the store.

Trevillian stood waiting a few yards from the outside stair. His hand rested on the prospector's pick hanging from his belt.

"Not the way to introduce yourself," the mine boss said.

Zack didn't trust himself to speak.

"The news story, the steamer—that was Snell's work, not mine." Trevillian spoke calmly. "He lacks the power of persuasion, so he found another way."

Zack stared at the ground.

"Surprising, isn't it?" the boss said. "You'd expect a man in his circumstance to desert. Instead, he risked his life and sacrificed his scruples to return with labor and provisions. What do you call that?"

"Servility."

Trevillian laughed. "Look at me, Knox."

Zack did as he asked.

"You can help us," the boss said.

"I came here to help myself."

"Want to put your hands on some gold, don't you?"

The boss's expression was passive, but as Zack watched, the piercing eyes reached for him. Zack stiffened.

Trevillian turned to Owen. "He thinks it should belong to him."

"'Tis a common foolishness," Owen nodded.

"In the earth or out," Trevillian said, "gold isn't something a mortal can possess."

"You have a high opinion of yourself."

"Not as high as you think. I draw a wage like everyone else. We're all unfortunates here," the mine boss said, "searching out Hope together."

"Your man tried to kill me."

Trevillian swallowed his frustration. "I told him to take you down a peg."

"'Twas well meant," Owen assured Zack.

"You dig with the spades you have," the boss said. "I've put you on the day shift, to make up." He fretted. "It's a bad beginning. Snell's deception. DuVal. Falling in with—" He shook his head.

Owen brushed some straw off Zack's shoulder.

"I swear to you," Trevillian said, "there's more to Breakaway than woe. As for me, don't jump to conclusions." He tapped his chest with his forefinger. "I know what it is to feel powerless. When I wear the judge's robe, I give a man a fair shake."

Zack watched the finger move between them.

"You do the same," Trevillian said. "Steady the balance and weigh me from here forward." His expression softened. "We have something in common."

Zack didn't take the bait.

"I'll carry the blame for now," the mine boss nodded. "Sooner or later, you'll understand—it was Hope who brought you here."

Zack had recovered enough self-possession to answer him. "I don't want any part of Hope or your mine."

Command slid back over Trevillian's face like a mask. Through it, his eyes peered, invidious as a snake. "You've reached my limit. Do as I say, if you value your life. I'm not an asking man."

He turned and started up the stair.

"You'll be knowing him better," Owen smiled. "Run along."

Zack returned down the path.

"Still in one piece," Bob marveled. He motioned. "There's something you need to see."

He headed toward the supply store. Zack and Sephy followed.

"What did he say?" she asked.

71

"He threatened me," Zack replied.

"A few months ago," Bob said, "a man could chirp the way you did and get away with it. With Hope in his arms and Lloyd coaching him, he was almost civilized."

"But Hope's disappeared," Sephy said.

"That's right." Bob was leading them along the store's wall. "You were lucky tonight," he told Zack. He stopped and faced the wall. "You make trouble for the boss—" He touched the siding. "You'll play a show *here*."

The wood planking was raw in places, chafed around a vague silhouette—more a phantom than a man. The head was elliptical, the neck was absent, the left leg vanished below the knee.

"He wasn't wearing the Reminder tonight—his whip." Bob patted his hip.

Sephy put her hand to her mouth.

"The boss was schooled by teamsters. Spaniards," Bob nodded at the wall. "That's how they talk to their mules. One makes trouble—you pull it out of its traces and carve it to pieces. Makes an impression on the rest."

Zack imagined a man writhing there in full view of the yard. The heads of two bolts protruded at chest level on either side.

"He's heartless," Sephy said.

Bob laughed. "So they say. You hear a lot of babble in the camp. Truth is, the boss's Hope was more than any of us had coming—" He stopped. "*Is* more," Bob corrected himself.

Sephy stared at him. Zack said nothing.

"As cruel as it looks," Bob nodded at the wall, "it keeps us together." He motioned toward the cook shack. "We'll check the lists."

"Zack's with us," Inky reported, stepping toward them with Winiarski by his side. "On the morning shift." Inky glanced at Zack. "He put you on the spot."

"I was eating," Winiarski told Sephy, as if he'd missed the confrontation.

"You're leaking." Bob touched Zack's chest. A carnation of blood had bloomed on the union suit. He unbuttoned Zack's collar. "It needs dressing."

Dinesh approached with Streetcar and the Captain.

"I'll be back in a minute," Bob told Zack. "You stay here with your pals," he warned. Then he squinted at Sephy and grabbed her arm. "Come with me, miss." They headed toward the warehouse doors.

"I'm on tonight," Streetcar told Zack. "They put Dinesh in the forge."

Dinesh had his arm in a sling. Behind his spectacles, his deep-set eyes had a haunted look. The orbits looked like they'd been daubed with boot-blacking.

"Thanks for trying," Zack said.

"Thanks for standing up for us," Dinesh replied.

"It's like the Farnsworth Family," Inky told them. "Up in the mountains, with the god they invented. They kidnapped people and made them believers."

"And had orgies," Winiarski recalled.

"We're not staying here," Zack said.

"We have to leave," Dinesh agreed.

Winiarski eyed the valley wall. "Think there's any place we could get to on foot?"

"The shift's starting." Streetcar looked miserable. He glanced at Winiarski and patted Dinesh's shoulder. "Bye, Ink. Bye, Mister Knox." He lifted his cap and started toward the switchback trail.

Zack turned back to his bargemates. "Might be indians nearby. Or prospectors."

"From a high point, we could spot them." The Captain pulled his hand from his pant pocket and raised his spyglass into view.

Zack stared at it, then scanned the surrounding ridges.

Inky pointed at a peak on the north side of the river. It was forested nearly to its top, where a brown capstone caught the sun. "You'd see a lot of the coast from up there."

"Who's going with me?" Zack said.

"Me," Winiarski replied. The Captain nodded, as did Dinesh.

"When?" Inky asked.

"Right now," Zack said. "We have enough light to get there. By the time we're on top, it'll be bright enough to see any neighbors."

"You're barefoot," Winiarski pointed out.

Inky motioned the group to silence. Bob and Sephy were returning.

Sephy carried clothing. Bob had a pair of gumboots in one hand and bandages in the other. "Store credit," Bob said.

"Size twelve," Winiarski guessed.

"Right you are." Bob passed the boots to Zack.

"What's that?" Zack eyed a loop of cord on the clothes pile.

"Fuse," Bob said. "It keeps your pants up. Handy for other things too. Get some sleep," he told the group. He motioned to Zack and headed along the path away from the store.

Zack nodded to Sephy, and they followed. She seemed distracted.

"The Captain badgered a tent for us," Inky called after him.

"On the sea side of the yard," the Captain added.

Bob led the way to the corduroy road.

"Where are we going?" Zack asked.

"Hotel Bob," the older man answered over his shoulder. "I guess I'm your friend." He laughed to himself.

Twenty yards down the slope, they turned onto a track that twisted through the encampment. Sephy moved in front of Zack. It had grown colder and she was shivering. His feet sank to the ankles in mud. On either side, the miners' homes flapped in the wind.

"If the coast is so hazardous," Zack said, "why did you come here?"

"Back then, no one knew about the reefs," Bob answered. "Or the tests Hope would put to anyone trying to make harbor. One of the boats from Gastineau went down. I had chums on that wreck."

Sephy was looking out to sea. A red dusk glowed on the southern horizon.

75

Bob pointed. "Every so often you see them between those islands. But here in the channel, the currents are deadly. Most skippers know better. The boat that landed in February—the one Snell shipped out on—that was a fluke."

"Why didn't you go with him?" Zack asked.

"And kiss Hope goodbye? This is my pup." He gestured at a small tent pitched on the moderate incline to their left. It was patched and soiled, with a sagging ridgeline and a black stovepipe sticking out of its side. In front was split wood, a pile of small crates and some tools crusted with mud.

Up the hill, the shift whistle blew. Bob stooped, threw back the flap and drew out a small quilt. "I'll be over there, unless it rains."

"Thanks," Zack said.

Bob motioned Sephy inside. "Your love nest—tonight." He stared at her.

Sephy stared back, and in the stare, Zack saw a new side of her. She seemed defiant.

Bob took the clothing. Sephy crawled into the tent.

"Pull your suit down," Bob said, bending to retrieve a sponge from a bucket.

Zack unbuttoned his top. "You saved my hide."

The wind wuffed harder, tents flapping like a hundred flags.

"What's been saved can be spent." Bob's tone was grim. "I'm hoping you make it through the week." He put the sponge to Zack's wound.

The earth trembled and a rumbling mounted between the valley walls. Sharp cries rose from the sawmill, and as the stamps reached full volume, the cries swooped through the thunder like tethered spirits. The night shift had begun.

"I'm going to have a look around," Zack said.

Bob raised his brows. Then he laughed and shook his head.

By the time Zack had put on the clothing, Bob was settled beneath his quilt. Zack ducked inside the tent.

Sephy was drawing a rabbit blanket over her. Her eyes met his.

"It's not what I imagined," she said.

Zack thought she meant the camp, but there were other ways in which the cup had been dashed from her lips. She had watched him come apart in the yard.

Rather than speaking, he leaned forward and kissed her.

She responded warmly. But when he drew back, she acted as if she saw a different person in his place.

"What happened at Ambrose Park?" Sephy asked.

"I invited my father to the show."

"And?"

"He sat in the box I'd reserved for them. He and his wife, Rose."

"What was the scandal?"

"He was running for office," Zack replied.

Her lips parted, but she didn't speak. Zack couldn't tell what she was thinking.

"You wanted to hurt him," she said.

He ran his hand over the rabbit blanket. "I suppose so."

Sephy sighed. "You're more like him—"

Zack heard the disquiet in her voice.

"—than I would ever have guessed."

"Your brother," Zack said.

"Gold was the future," Sephy nodded. "The past was all fear and anger."

Zack didn't reply. The unlit pup tent seemed airless. The prospect of a new life had vanished completely.

"Did you speak to him," Sephy asked. "After the show?"

"He didn't stay."

"They left?"

"He did."

"By himself?" she asked.

"Rose tried to keep him there, but he shook her loose. It was after the entry. I lowered my mare onto one knee and tipped my hat to them. He looked me in the eye—taking his punishment. Then he stood and headed for the exit."

"He wasn't there to see you," Sephy said.

"No. He was proving he couldn't be cowed."

The rumble from the stamp mills filled the silence between them.

"You'll be alone tonight," Zack said.

"Where will you be?"

"Looking for some way out of this."

78

4

The scouting party crossed the river one at a time—
Zack, Winiarski, Inky, Dinesh and the Captain. The
departure was unobserved as far as they could tell,
but they were in clear view as they mounted the valley's northern slope.

They crossed a saddle and began to descend. A gentler valley lay between them and the peak they meant to climb. The
understory was thick and the bumps and pockets were hidden.
As they stumbled forward, Inky shared what he'd surfaced
after leaving the yard. In addition to food and equipment,
Trevillian had brought miners. Only a few of them knew
what they were getting into. The reefs and currents took a
heavy toll. Lives were lost, along with loads of gear and provisions. But the losses didn't deter him. When it was over he had
eighty men in the valley, mining machinery, supplies, raw steel
and enough food to keep his operation going for a long while.

The scrub was thick and their progress was slow. Dinesh had borrowed Lucky's timepiece. It was past midnight when they reached the foot of the peak. The sky was pale and the drone from the Breakaway mill was still audible. "We've got to pick up our pace," Zack told them. The Captain tripped and cursed. "You alright?" Dinesh and Winiarski helped him up.

The gurgle of a stream reached them. They descended its bank, parting drapes of sword fern while a kingfisher on a willow bough watched. As they entered the shallows, the sky's reflection made a silver-blue kaleidoscope, and where the water cupped, dark pebbles showed through.

"We've got company," Winiarski said.

Salmon striped the flow. Bullet-headed, they held their position, staring upstream, tattered but resolute. As the men waded across, the fish shuddered forward, clenching and thrashing, driving themselves through the sapphire current. Their hooked jaws gaped, cheeks flaring, waking to the challenge ahead. Upstream the watercourse veered, broken with boulders, mounting steeply. A high shelf received a white cascade, and out of the splash, a lone struggler leaped with its nose in the air.

The peak seemed to rise as they climbed. Finally the incline relaxed. It was four a.m. when they trudged onto the rocky summit. The Captain pulled the spyglass full-length and began to scan the coastline. "Ugly," he muttered at the cliffs to the south. When he turned, he saw nothing better. Breakaway was the only harbor visible. In either direction the cliffs were sheer.

"Houses," Winiarski cried. The Captain took his eye from the ocular, found the squarish objects and refocused his scope.

"Well?"

"Might be," the Captain said, stepping closer to the drop-off. "No, no—they're blocks fallen out of that wall."

They scrambled among the boulders and lichen beds, circling the heights, scouring the slopes and valleys below, looking for boats, a settlement, some sign of man. Dinesh thought he saw a jetty and the Captain passed him the scope. Then the clouds shifted and the landing turned into a rocky strand. The peak's crest was icy and the winds chilled them badly. After an hour, they were back where they started. Winiarski had the spyglass and was reexamining the blocks.

"Nothing," Inky said.

"That's a door," Winiarski mumbled.

"No tools, no weapons—" Zack eyed his companions. "And no provisions."

"Lots of fish," Dinesh observed.

"In sixty days, the salmon will be gone," the Captain said. "In ninety, it'll be winter."

They looked around them, imagining the land covered with snow. As if to drive home the point, rain began to fall. Zack imagined what it might be like in a storm. He put his hand on Winiarski's shoulder, and when the boy turned, he took the spyglass and collapsed it against the heel of his palm.

"We're stuck," Inky said.

"Until we get a grubstake," Zack nodded.

"You're sure it's an island," Winiarski asked the Captain.

"The charts say there are narrows to the south, six miles from here." The Captain pointed down the coast. "Gastineau City's seventy miles farther, over water."

They scanned the white thread of surf to where it disappeared in the haze.

"We're in his clutches," Dinesh said.

Zack wiped the rain from his brow. "We'll see about that."

On the return, they crossed the salmon stream at a different spot, higher up. The banks were gentler, the current thinned and slowed, winding through nests of dwarf violets. The sands were littered with the carnage of days. Dead salmon floated in pools or lay stranded on the gravels, mangled and twisted, cast about like rags. "What happened to them?" Winiarski wondered.

Zack turned and motioned for silence. He faced forward and continued along the bank, putting his boots down slowly. From the shallows nearby, a dozen gulls lifted. Their wings crossed, and then they coasted together, calling as they reached an embayment a hundred feet upstream. They circled the calm water and settled, lining the shore.

A circle of cedars hemmed the embayment. At its far end was a lopsided spruce, limbs lumpy with moss—like hams and thighs with gobbets torn loose. As Zack watched, a bear lumbered from the shade.

Zack waved an alarm to the others. They knelt in the willows and peered through the leaves. The bear waded into the pool. He lunged, raking the water with giant claws. His dark paw clutched and lifted a salmon, but the fish shook loose. The bear's head swung around, snout strafing the surface.

Zack motioned to the Captain. "Scope," he mouthed.

The Captain drew the spyglass from his pocket.

Zack extended the tube and peered through the eyepiece as the bear reared on its hinds. He was ten feet tall. He squinted at the sun then hunched over, studying the dorsal fins ridging the surface. The bear stiffened, plunged his head to the mane and rose with a large salmon flexing between his jaws, snapping in protest. The giant canines clamped deeper. The bear shook the salmon fiercely, drawing fish scent into his nostrils while a dewlap of water slapped from his chin.

"Is it Prowler?" Winiarski asked.

Dinesh hushed him.

Through the spyglass, Zack saw the bear lay the fish on his foreleg. He nipped the salmon's back and yanked, and the skin came loose. The bear continued to pull, stripping the fish while it writhed.

Zack turned and waved his companions away. Inky parted the willows and led them alongside the stream bed. When Zack peered through the spyglass, the bear was caressing the naked fish with his paw. He used a claw to tip its head up, as if to commune with it. The salmon gaped and the bear bit its nose off. The salmon's jaws continued to move, but the bear paid no attention. He took its head between his teeth and tore away its brain. Then he closed his eyes and chewed.

Zack lowered the spyglass. He was backing through the willows when his boot slipped. A rock *clacked* down the bed. Zack froze.

The bear raised his head. His ears perked, his snout sampled the wind. He swatted the water, then he turned and faced Zack, massive jaws chomping.

Zack raised the spyglass and the bear's head appeared in the eyepiece, giant leaves waving around it like the fans of invisible courtiers. It pushed forward, filling the lens, brown mane spiked with damp, fangs long and yellow. The emerald eyes blazed, and above the one on his right, Zack saw a lavender scar: an S on its side, like a giant worm. The scar looked soft and fatty, and it gleamed as if it had crawled out of his fur just moments before.

Prowler glanced down. Salmon were thrashing around his legs. Three gulls circled over him, whistling, insistent. Prowler chomped at Zack and then gave him his backside, returning to the fish with an obliging grunt.

Zack hurried to catch up with his bargemates.

They returned to Breakaway during the morning mess. There was some kind of stir in the yard, and when they crossed the bridge over the river, Zack could see Snell and Lloyd on either side of Arnie. Miners were gathered around them. Arnie looked like a ghost. His eyes were glazed and his face was gray. His clothes were damp and bloodstained, and his shoulders were shaking.

The scouting party split up, joining the crowd. Zack drew beside True, the big man with the square jaw.

"What happened?"

"His partner died," True said.

"Wagner?"

"Swept off the rocks. They thought they could walk out of here." True was perplexed. "Headed south, edging along the cliffs. This one barely made it back."

"Can he be found?"

"To run a dory through there—" True shook his head. "The Private did it, but none of us could."

Zack descended the corduroy road and followed the footpath through the tent camp. It was windless, and on either side the miners' homes sagged. They looked dingy and squalid.

As he approached Bob's pup, he heard Sephy's voice. She was standing, gesturing sharply. Bob was stooped over the fire pit, about to reply. When he saw Zack, he sealed his lips and rose. Sephy smiled with relief, but she didn't step forward to greet him. She wore the same baggy pants and shirt, but she had a pair of boots on now.

"Wagner's dead," Zack told her.

"We know," Sephy said.

"Get your rest?" he asked Bob.

"I've slept better," Bob said. "We had a visitor in the wee hours—" He tied his bandanna around his neck. "The Private's sis and I."

Sephy knelt by the tent opening with her back to them.

"It's our shift," Bob said. "Let's get moving."

"A hundred bones," Zack recalled.

"That's right."

"What can bones buy?"

"Whatever you like."

"It's alright if we stay here," Zack asked, "for a while?"

"You maybe." Bob scratched his cheek. "She'll be better off with the women. I can't sleep out every night."

Zack looked at Sephy.

Her back was still to them.

"My belly's growling," Bob grumbled.

"I need to speak to Zack," Sephy said without turning.

"That's the girl." Bob seemed cheered. "I'll break bread with the chain gang while you work things out."

As Bob disappeared down the trail, Sephy rose.

"I want to say 'yes' again," she said, facing him. "I want to be your wife." She took a breath. "The way these people are treating us—"

"It's a nightmare."

"It's not what you think," Sephy said.

Zack noticed a small box on the woodpile. Colored fabrics were folded inside. "Who was here last night?"

86

"They're women's things," she said. "Too gay for me. Zack— You know why I came here."

"Raymond."

Sephy closed her eyes.

Zack moved toward her. "It was a terrible—"

"He chose to be here," Sephy said. "We all make choices. It may be hard to understand—"

"Knox, I have it—" Lucky stepped through the mud. He tipped his head to Sephy, halted before them and opened his arms. "A strategy. Shame about Wagner. And it's too bad your reconnaissance didn't turn up a means of escape. But there's another way."

"Go on."

"The shelves are bare in the BMC store," Lucky said. "If there's no sea trade, Trevillian won't have any choice. He'll have to build a boat to transport whatever's needed to keep his cult going. We persuade him to let *us* do that, while he and his drudges are digging—in exchange for passage back, once the ship's completed."

"You know how to put a steamer together?"

"Our Captain worked as a shipwright in his youth." Lucky smiled. "I'm a businessman, and there's a deal to be made here. We won't have the benefit of counsel, but—" He waved his hand. "I can draft a contract to protect us.

"The Captain will work out the construction details. We'll package it up, present it and be out of this deathtrap lickety-split." He grimaced and reached for his pocket watch.

"They've threatened some ugliness if we're late.

"It's a compelling proposition," Lucky checked the time. "Let's put our heads together when we're not so rushed." And then, with fatherly care, "You make a nice couple. This is no place to raise kids."

Zack stared at him.

Lucky winked, patted Sephy on the shoulder and hurried away.

"You need to eat," Sephy said.

"You're coming with me."

They filled their plates, found Bob sitting alone and ate their fish together in silence. Sephy was the only woman in the mess. When the time arrived to ascend the switchback trail, Bob spoke.

"Everything straight now?"

"Not yet," Sephy answered.

"I'm feeling left out," Zack told Bob.

The older man made a dunce face.

"I'd like to go with you," Sephy said.

Bob shrugged and tightened his fuse belt, and they left the yard together.

As the store fell behind them, Bob glanced at Zack.

"Enjoy your night out?"

"Prowler introduced himself," Zack replied.

Sephy looked stunned.

"That's nothing to josh about," Bob said.

"We crossed a stream. He was testing the salmon."

"He saw you?" Bob asked.

Zack nodded.

"But he didn't come after you," Bob said.

"He thought about it."

"Just you. He singled you out?"

"You could say that," Zack replied. "What does it mean?"

"The boss would know," Bob said. "Maybe she's coming back, or thinking she might. You're in it somehow."

"Hope can cut me out of her plans." Zack turned to Sephy. "It's dangerous country. We need shelter, supplies. Weapons to protect ourselves." Then to Bob, "I'll put my hours in for your boss, but he'll get the minimum. You can count on that."

Bob was silent.

"We won't be here long," Zack said.

The odor of coal fire reached them. As they rounded the first switchback, a small building came into view thirty feet from the trail. Its flue added smoke and ash to the haze above it. Dinesh was visible inside the door of the forge, talking to a shorter man with a lantern jaw.

"Pollard," Bob shouted. And when the man beside Dinesh turned, "Cute babe you've got. I drew the big one and he's sucking me dry."

Pollard rolled his eyes.

Beyond the forge, staggered up the slope, were the three giant sheds of the stamp mill. They were quiet, but as soon as the shift whistle blew, rock would be fed to them for crushing.

Smoke and steam coiled from roof vents. A door in the side of the middle shed opened, and as a man stepped out, the stamp batteries were visible, lined up one beside the other, each with a large pulley wheel.

The next switchback brought them to a bridge that crossed the Breakaway River. The flow thrummed beneath the planks, charged with fish that had escaped the nets. Some fought the current, some were resting in the shallows, harboring their strength for the next hurdle.

As they started up the wall of the trapezoid, steeples of open gridwork appeared on the slope to the right—six of them, in a line.

Sephy pointed at the dark objects suspended on cables between the steeples.

"Tram buckets," Bob said.

Wheels atop the steeples were turning, moving the buckets down the mountain to the mill and back up to the invisible crest.

A miner approached, covered with grime, taking long strides. "Tough down there, cannonball," he grinned at Zack. "Think you can take it?"

Zack ignored him. When the man had passed, Sephy turned to Bob.

"What is it like?"

"Hard to see and hard to breathe," Bob said.

The pitch grew steeper with each switchback. Another bend brought them around a bluff and onto a high shelf. Three more took them just below the crest. Zack could hear the ringing of bells and muted voices. As they reached the top, a tower rose into view—a tall right triangle silhouetted against the sky, point up. The terrain flattened, littered with rock rubble. Twenty yards from them, a group had gathered.

"That's the gallows," Bob nodded at the tower.

A low hum came from the structure. There were two pairs of track on the triangle's long side, and at its top, two large wheels. A strand of taut cable ran in the grooved rim of each.

As Zack stepped forward, the top of the mountain opened before him. They were on the brink of a funnel-shaped canyon two hundred feet across. The funnel's sides had been hacked into crude shelves. The hole at the bottom was round and black as a pupil. There was a hum of life within, and as he watched, a small open-sided car poked out of the hole. The huge pit magnified its arrival, echoes groaning and shrieking as the car squealed up the tracks of the tower. The crowd turned to watch.

Zack thought of Trevillian, and what it must have taken to bend the wills of so many men to the task of disemboweling a mountain. The cable wheel stopped turning, the hum ceased and the car jerked to a halt, frozen on the inclined track beside a loading platform. As the echoes faded, two miners rose and stepped out.

Owen greeted them, and as the men passed, he turned and shouted to a half-dozen others on the landing. The Captain and Lucky were among them. They boarded the car and seated themselves. Owen shouted again and the signal bells sounded from a little house behind the tower. A loud ratcheting followed the signal bells, and the car plunged down the track, disappearing into the hole with its human freight.

"This way," Bob motioned.

Zack and Sephy followed him through the gathering. Lloyd and Snell were standing between piles of clothing. Lloyd held his black pocket ledger and made entries, while Snell sized the garments to the new men.

Bob led Zack to Lloyd and stepped out of the way.

"He's got everything but a hat," Lloyd nodded. He scratched in his ledger while Snell picked one from the pile.

"That's Alf's shirt," a soprano voice said.

Zack turned to see a small woman with quick eyes, a pointed nose and a swarm of auburn curls clinched with combs. Below her turquoise shirtwaist, she wore trousers shortened at the ankles and muddy boots, like the men.

"Alf had his moments with her," the woman said. Her eyes went misty. "I remember one of them." She touched the shirt's mended front, as if to feel its magic. "Hope blessed him to the last." She smiled at Zack. "Weasel's my name." She turned to Sephy, gave a polite nod and whirled away.

Zack glanced at Bob.

"Our Blondes," Bob said.

There were half a dozen of them weaving among the new arrivals, introducing themselves. Their flashy attire and exotic hairdos brought a jarring festivity to the grim business. Except for the pants and gumboots, the girls might have stepped out of a parlor in the bad quarter.

"Can you beat it?" One of the men from the barge faced Zack. "Ten hours a day, for vittles and kittens."

"They're fools," Zack said.

A commanding female voice surfaced above the crowd. Zack saw a woman in her thirties gesturing a few yards away. She was a platinum blonde and her long tresses rippled back from her forehead. A scarlet beret clung to one side like an obstinate crab. Her eyebrows were penciled black lines, arched high. Beside her stood the short-haired woman from the barge. Both wore gowns.

"You'll come see us, won't you," the loud woman said to Inky. "Once you've got a few bones." She placed her hand on the bulge of her breasts, letting the pinkie slide beneath her apricot bodice.

"What do we have to lose?" another man replied.

Winiarski's eyes sawed into the woman's cleavage.

"We know what *you* have to lose." She chucked his chin with a closed fan.

"She goes by 'Salt Lick,'" Bob said.

Zack laughed. "I've seen my share. Steers are crazy about them."

Just then the woman caught sight of him. She cocked her head and started toward him, and those around her followed. Zack felt Sephy grasp his arm.

"Watch what you say to her," Bob warned.

"Close to him?"

"Like one of his ribs," Bob said.

The woman with short hair smiled as the entourage drew near. "Mister Knox," she said, introducing him.

Salt Lick halted in front of Zack. "Obviously," she said, looking him up and down. Her eyes were lime green. "He belongs behind a mule." She gave the group a suspecting smirk. "Nothing frail will serve him."

Two women laughed. The new arrivals were embarrassed on Sephy's behalf. Either Salt Lick didn't notice or she didn't care.

"What a shame—that dust-up with DuVal." The madam sent her gaze to the clouds. "What can be done with the fellow?"

"I've got a few ideas," Zack said.

"Well—" She smiled. "You learn to make allowances in a place like this. *We're* delighted you're with us. Aren't we?" She looked at the women and they curtsied in unison. "We await your visit, Mister Knox. Your spirit depends on it."

"My spirit?"

"Hope speaks through us," Salt Lick said, moving closer.

"Of what does she speak?"

Salt Lick put her fingertips on his left pectoral. "A new gospel," she said softly. "A truer one. God didn't create woman to corrupt man, but to save him."

"She's the serious type," Zack said.

"Indeed," Salt Lick nodded. "She speaks of the end as if it's nearly upon us." She looked at Sephy. "Are you ready, dear?"

Zack felt Sephy's nails dig into his arm.

Salt Lick tapped Sephy's hip with her fan.

94

"We've made other arrangements," Zack said.

Salt Lick raised her brows. "There *are* no other arrangements. Sephy will be in Blondetown with the rest of us."

Zack frowned. "I don't sleep with your kind. Why should she?"

Salt Lick's jaw dropped. "*Our kind?*"

"Go back down," he directed Sephy, staring all the while at the madam. "You'll stay in Bob's tent."

Salt Lick's eyes squeezed to slits. She raised her hand to her head, drew a long pin out, shifted the crab and pushed the pin back in. Then she laughed, gathered her skirts and turned away. Sephy swayed as if faint, her brow grazing Zack's shoulder.

"Here's the manskip," Bob said with a sigh.

Zack heard the drone of an arriving car. He could see it now, coughed up from the murky throat, climbing the narrow track. Trevillian was in the first seat.

"C'mon," Bob motioned.

Zack gripped Sephy's shoulders. "Tonight," he said.

She nodded without looking at him. He kissed her forehead and followed Bob.

With a half-dozen others, they descended the steep trail to the loading platform. Inky was a few yards in front of them. Trevillian had stepped out of the car, and as they collected on the platform, he faced them. Zack saw the Reminder coiled on his hip. Its plaited rings were held by a loop buttoned to his waistband, and the popper quivered in the breeze. The blackened handle hung down his thigh.

"Who's been inside a mine?" The boss scanned the new-comers.

None of them spoke.

Trevillian straightened a man's collar. "You don't forget the first day." He regarded Zack with a welcoming smile, then he lifted his gaze to the rim of the funnel. "You're leaving a wide place for a narrow one. Amusements—sounds and colors, the buzz and blooming that's a spring to the senses—" He looked back at the group and shook his head. "You will see only what your candle lights—the black and the white. The rock and Hope's quartz streaming through it. You'll hear only our grunts and blasts as we inch toward her . . . and her moans and sighs when we're drawing near.

"Who's thinking about the danger?" The boss raised his right hand. "Or the ten hours of toil?" His hand remained aloft. "Who's afraid he won't measure up?" He laughed. "I guess I'm the only one here who doubts himself." He nodded, as if he understood.

"We live with fear. That's who we are. It's in our blood. Sometimes it's familiar, like an old acquaintance. Sometimes it's a stranger—the sort you never want to meet. I can't tell you to ignore fear, or the shame that comes with it. That's not possible. But a man can withstand fear if he sees Hope before him." He searched their faces. "Talk to your brothers. And know that in your boss's most desperate hours, it is Hope who torments him—not fear." His eyes blazed. "If I can't prove my courage to her, what use would she have for me?

"So—" Trevillian laughed. "You've lost your loved ones, your dream of wealth and the freedom it was going to buy. You'll do backbreaking work underground, risk your lives, and humor the ravings of a lunatic priest."

He lifted his chin. "What have I to say?" Trevillian looked from man to man. "You'll find her. In some crooked hole, between death and your fevered imaginings, you'll meet Hope and you'll give your heart to her, as I have. We'll cry like children and say foolish things, and you'll pray for Hope to take us all. And you'll remember this morning . . . when you imagined it had so much value—" He raised his hands and gazed at them. "This flesh of ours and the sorry world it came from." He was silent for a long moment. Then he turned and crossed the platform.

Owen was waiting for him.

"Take them down," Trevillian said.

"Sermon on the mount," Zack muttered.

"That's a shorty." Bob eyed the funnel wall. "When Hope moves him, the whole camp sits in the Glory Hole and he preaches from the skip."

Bob stooped over a box of white candles. He took them in each hand, stuffed some into his boot and passed the others to Zack. He retrieved two blocks of wooden matches from a small crate and put one in Zack's pocket. Then he approached the car.

The first men were climbing in. As Zack reached the platform's edge, he looked down. The shaft was a bull's-eye to hell—a succession of timbered arches, nestled and descending. Five lanterns were visible, each dimmer than the one before. The fall seemed nearly vertical.

The skip, as Bob called it, was a flatcar with wooden slats for seats—like a ladder with angled rungs. Bob boarded, stepping onto a slat, third from the rear. Zack followed, balancing on the seat behind him. There was nothing to hold on to. As he pivoted, the dark shaft gaped like a ribbed esophagus. He bent his knees slowly, sitting on the slat.

"You want her, don't you," Bob joked.

Men continued to board. The skip squealed and inched down the track as the added weight stretched the cable. Owen was on the last slat now, motioning.

The mine's odor billowed from the shaft, rank with must and mold. Zack choked and turned away.

"Inside air," Bob said.

High above, at the top of the tower, the steel cable creaked over the wheel. A rumble sounded from the building behind and giant gears chattered. Without warning, the skip rocked as if something had grabbed it and was tugging from below. Zack clung to his seat.

"She bucks," Bob said. "Don't lose your saddle." He put his hands on the man in front of him.

Zack grasped Bob's shoulders. When he glanced back, he saw Owen on the slat behind him, lifting his hand to yank the bell wire—four times, then twice more. A croaking noise came from the hoist house. The skip shivered, then plunged.

The timbered arches loomed closer, one inside the other,

and the lanterns ticked past. The air was tart and damp. *The gallows*, Zack thought. He was falling: the cable was the rope, the hole was the trap door, and this suffocating descent—a passage from the living to the dead. He felt a bony rhythm in his boots—the clicking of the skip wheels on track welds—and as he listened, a melody rose over them. Owen was singing.

The skip and its cable began to squeal and moan. The car slowed, grunting past a wooden loading dock, continuing to descend until the cable had stretched to its limit. Then the skip shuddered and shrank back up the track. The sign on the station's crossbeam read *400*. Three men stood waiting, covered with candle grease and mud.

Zack rose with the others and stepped onto the landing.

"Give yourselves some light," Owen said. He picked a tin lantern from a pile. Bob did likewise, pulling a candle from his boot and fixing it in the lantern. Zack and the others followed suit. Bob drew the block of wooden matches from his pocket, struck one, lit his wick and turned to light Zack's. Owen helped the rest, and when there was a flame in every lantern, the foreman led the group across the platform and into a narrow corridor.

The darkness was thick. Zack could barely see the rock by his shoulder. At some distance, a candle burned, and the shadow of the iron holder was large and ominous. It might have been the weapon of some ancient tribe, with a hooplike finger grip and a tapered spike stretching ten feet along the wall. He was crossing into an alien domain—a primitive one, where the sun of reason had never risen. The fire a man carried marked off his mind—he could have only simple perceptions, one at a time. A stretch of ragged wall, the cheek and eye of the fellow beside him, light glimmering on a pair of tracks— He was moving between steel rails.

Owen turned into a passage that branched to the left. Bob held Zack back. "They're headed for White Mint. We've got a place of our own."

Bob continued along the level, passing a shadowed opening and another. He entered the third, a smaller tunnel. After a hundred paces, it bent half around. Then the end came into view: a ragged wall. Metal rods were lined out on the floor, and there were hammers and shovels propped to one side.

Bob pulled the candle from his lantern, removed his hat, and fit the candle into the metal clip on the brim. "You too," he said.

Zack followed his example.

"Where are we?"

"Meat Hook," Bob said. "Those are drill steels and you're going to learn how to single jack." He knelt and selected the shortest drill, ten inches in length. "Brains, muscle, and a lot of patience." He picked up a small hammer.

"First, you point your holes." Bob raised the steel to the wall, chest height. "Use your brains." He angled the drill and sighted along it. "Try to imagine how the holes will come together inside the rock. There are more kinds of cuts than you can count. We're going to drill a horizontal wedge. That's two holes—one from me and one from you. We meet in the center, about three feet in. You listening?"

Zack nodded.

"There are vertical wedges and double Vs, and what they call the Vise—two Vs with a baby cut between. There's the Draw cut and the Burn cut, and the Shatter and the Pyramid. When we find Hope, we'll be drilling Pyramids. Four deep holes, pointed together."

Bob turned the drill until its chisel was perpendicular. "You put your starter where you want it—" He raised his hammer. "And hit the head like this." He swung from the side, striking the mushroomed end. "Relax, shake the steel." As he drew the hammer back, his left hand gave the drill a quarter turn, then he snapped forward and struck it again.

"The hole gets its direction from the first few bangs, so they better be right. You swing and shake, fifty times a minute." Bob started in, the steel ringing with the precision of a clock's second hand. "When the drill won't bite or the hole's too deep," he said without pausing, "get a change." He tossed the steel aside, stooped, picked up another, set it and struck it.

"Ever heard of 'going by'?" Bob drew his hammer back.

"Going by the saloon."

Bob smiled. "Going in, you mean." He swung the hammer and missed the drill head. "That's going by. Good way to break your arm."

He drew back. "In a little drift like Meat Hook, you single jack. Where you've got elbow room, one man shakes and the other strikes. That's double jacking. Or you use a machine drill if you're tired of life. Everhards, we call them. Well," he passed Zack the hammer and starter. "There's your training."

Bob retrieved a second hammer and steel and sighted into the rock from the other direction. "What're you waiting for?"

Zack placed the chisel to the spot Bob had started, found the mushroom in the flicker from his hat brim, drew the hammer back and struck the steel's head. The impact shuddered along his arm and down his back.

"That's it," Bob said. "Couple thousand more and you'll have a hole."

"How slow can I go," Zack stared at his hammer, "and still collect the bones."

"Maybe I should have let DuVal finish you," Bob said. "You want to be my partner—" He nodded at the wall. "You pull your load."

Without a watch or daylight, it was the wasting of candles that marked the hours. Time went by quickly at first. Then it crawled. A drill advanced six inches before it was dull. A fresh drill—a little longer—replaced it. When the first wedge was completed, they began another. The four holes required most of the steels, so they had to hike to the level station for fresh ones. Then they drilled edgers around the wall's border. They were nearly done when Owen appeared. He left a sack and a small tin with them.

"Alright," Bob said, after checking the final edger. "Time to blast."

Zack had his hands in his pockets.

"How are they doing?" Bob asked.

Zack drew his hands out. The fingers of his right were clenched like a bird claw. His left palm was one large blister.

Bob smiled. "Time for the payoff. If there was any sign of Hope, Owen would do the loading. But this is our affair." He knelt and retrieved the sack and tin, holding one in each hand. "You want to blow up something, it takes two ingredients. You keep them apart. Powder—" He raised the sack. "And caps."

Bob passed Zack the circular tin. Zack heard the caps clink.

"Sit here," Bob said.

Zack sat on the gravel.

"What do you know about powder?" Bob opened the canvas sack and pulled out a stick of dynamite and a coil of fuse.

"I used twenty grains with shot in my revolver," Zack said.

"Twenty grains won't rattle a beaver dam."

"It's perfect for glass balls. Folks enjoyed that."

Bob opened his knife and began measuring and cutting lengths of fuse. "Give me a cap."

Zack glanced at the tin's lid as he removed it. The dulled silver was embossed with a cartoon of a dwarf with an oversized head. And the words *Little Giant*. The dwarf's jaw gaped as if he was shouting. Zack slid a cap into his palm. It was like a bullet shell made of copper—an inch and a half long and open at one end.

"Sticks don't misbehave," Bob said. "It's the caps that cause trouble—sneeze and they go off." He found a punch among the tools, held the dynamite stick in one hand and drove the punch into its side. A sour smell filled the drift. He took the cap from Zack, inserted the end of one of the fuses into it, placed the shell beneath his incisor and bit down. Then he fed the crimped cap and fuse into the hole in the dynamite stick and tied the fuse around it. "There's your primer," Bob said.

He used a long-handled spoon to scrape the last of the drill cuttings out of one of the cut holes. Then he slid the stick in, along with another he'd slit lengthwise with his knife. He pushed them with a wooden rod, and when the rod had gone as deep as it would go, he tamped it with three light blows, leaving the tail of the fuse hanging down the wall.

Bob drew another dynamite stick out of the sack, slit it with his knife and handed it to Zack. "Load this one on top of those. Don't let anything separate the charges or knuckle the fuse," he warned. "A hangfire's the surest way to the graveyard."

Zack took the explosive. It was lighter than he would have guessed. The wrapper was waxy. "What if I blow myself up?"

"Folks might enjoy that," Bob said.

Forty minutes later, the last charge was loaded. They moved the tools back down the level and set a steel sheet on the ground beneath the blast face. Bob put notches in a short length of fuse—the spitter—and struck a match. "Zack's first blast," Bob said, lighting the spitter's end and saluting the wall with it. "We might bust into her. Wouldn't that be something?"

Zack watched him touch off the fuses. At each notch, the spitter produced a flare which Bob used to ignite the next charge. When the last fuse smoked to life, the hissing was like heavy rain in the narrow drift.

"They'll fire in two minutes," Bob said.

Zack turned, ready to beat a fast retreat. Bob caught him by the arm.

"No hurry," Bob said.

So they ambled away from the dwindling fuses, blithe as sparrows in a lane. They reached the entrance to Meat Hook and started back along the level. As they approached the second feeder passage, Bob pulled Zack into it.

The next moment, there was a deafening *boom-boom*, and a stutter of white light flashed in Zack's face. The slew of crushed rock rose through the thunder, while smoke billowed into their refuge. An acrid odor filled Zack's nostrils.

We've found her, he thought, amused by the idea. A picture of Hope came to him—a withered crone in a rocker on the other side of the blast face. She had been listening with her ear trumpet as they drilled.

"You've seen her," Zack said, raising his arm to protect his nose and mouth.

"Vouchsafe is next door," a voice answered through the dimness. "I saw her there."

Bob might have been a ghost in the swirling smoke.

"What happened?"

"I disappeared into the quartz with her," Bob said.

"Disappeared?"

"I was shaking for Noel—kneeling, twisting the steel. And then I was gone. I was like she was—fog and stars—drifting around in the cold and the dark."

"That's what she does?" Zack said.

"Hope wears a different face for every man."

"A surprise for Noel," Zack said. "When you disappeared."

"I didn't miss a shake. The blood-and-bones Bob was there with him, twisting the steel the whole time."

"Maybe you imagined her."

"I know," Bob said, "it's hard to believe."

"Let's have a look." Zack stepped out of the passage.

Bob grabbed him. "That's for our chums on the next shift. Powder fumes will kill you. The smoke has to settle."

The shift whistle reached them.

"Our work's finished. You did alright," Bob told him. "Calls for a nip." He exited the feeder and started back down the level.

"There's a place?"

"The Big Wheel," Bob nodded. "Don't forget our steels."

They recovered the used drills and hauled them to the 400 landing, where they added them to a pile. A skip was loading and they took the last seats. The car rose till it reached the 310. The miners jumped out, and Bob and Zack followed.

The group crossed the platform and entered the level corridor. Twenty feet along it, they turned into a drift. The walls were slick. Shreds of vapor crawled along the ceiling. As they rounded a bend, Zack heard an eerie tremolo—a woman's voice wandering the diggings, clothed in echoes.

The drift led into a small room lit by candles. A life-sized angel hung from the ceiling. She was naked and white, wings flexed, held by wires with one arm extended. She pointed at a portal sealed by blankets. The first man drew the blankets aside and the others filed through.

A much larger excavation appeared, twenty yards wide and forty deep. Its rugged ceiling was sloped, supported by thick wooden piers. The floor sloped too. As the men stepped forward, they descended. A crowd of miners and Bangshu were milling before a bar, where a sentry stood guard with a rifle.

"You're in Strongbox Stope," Bob said.

They shouldered through the men, already in their cups and noisy. The bar was kidney purple, purfled and scrolled, with a high polish. With the cavern arched over it and the muddy men gathered around, it was the last gasp of elegance—something subtle and finely wrought, visited on a tribe of Neanderthals. Zack watched the women dressed in bright gowns plying liquor to their customers.

"The wheel's over there," Bob said.

Zack followed him toward a barricade that spanned the stope. It was made of crates stacked to the ceiling and mortared with sand. From the narrow entrance, music emerged. Inside the barricade, a woman was singing.

As they entered the dim space, a strange tableau opened before Zack. Two dozen men were seated on furniture made of rock and timber. To the right of the seating area was a dais on which the singer stood. A man flailed a guitar, while a harmonica player rocked on a stool. Beside the performers was a cushioned chair with large arms and a high back. Salt Lick sat there. Her eyes were fixed on a miner standing on the gravel a dozen feet from her. He was watching a thick circular table turn round. The axle was iron and the table looked like a pulley wheel from one of the stamp mills. A ticking sound rose through the music, and at first it seemed part of it. But as the music trailed off, the ticking remained, slowing as the wheel did.

"What is this?" Zack said.

Behind the wheel, the wall of the stope seemed fashioned for some kind of ritual. A crude semicircle had been hewn, with alcoves drilled at regular intervals. Each had a blanket hanging within, screening its contents from view. Beside each alcove, a candle was pinned, along with a numbered signboard.

The miners were transfixed, tin cups frozen as they watched the disk slow. There was a lantern on it, near the rim. As it came around, something flashed. Zack could see now: the rim of the wheel was cracked, and a double-bladed axe had been buried there, handle up. The exposed blade caught the lantern light, and it was this that the miners tracked as the wheel slowed.

"Three," a man cried out.

"Five, five—"

A clamor rose, men standing, shouting and pointing, guessing which alcove the blade would point to when the wheel stopped. The silver edge crept past five and six, ticked its last, and came to a halt.

"Number seven."

Below Salt Lick's throne, a woman with pince-nez stood behind a lectern, gesturing at the alcove. She had a stone gavel in her hand. A placard was mounted on the lectern—*Pure and Chaste.*

The men were all standing now, eyes on number seven.

The blanket shifted in the archway, and a woman pushed her head out. Zack recognized the auburn curls.

"Weasel—" The miners yammered and nodded, as if the customer had done well. The harmonica chugged a few bars of a cakewalk. "You want her, don't you," someone shouted.

The man before the wheel smiled over his shoulder, squared himself and stepped toward alcove seven. Weasel's naked arm reached to pinch out the candle by the entrance. Then it drew the blanket back and the miner disappeared inside.

The gavel sounded and the men seated themselves. Salt Lick rose from her chair and faced the crowd. As if at a signal, arms shot up, waving to get her attention. A chorus of shouts broke out on the right. One of the miners was holding Winiarski's hand up, while others nearby slapped and goaded him. He shook his head, grinning and struggling half-heartedly to free himself.

"Winski," one man cried. And the crowd took it up as a chant. "Winski, Winski—"

Salt Lick listened, measuring the sentiment. Then she nodded.

The miners hollered and cheered the teenager on.

Winiarski stood, faced the madam, reached both hands into his pant pockets and pulled them inside out.

Salt Lick gave him a kindly look. "On credit," she said.

The woman behind the lectern, the cashier, pulled a pencil from her bun, lifted a card and recorded the debit on it amidst another round of jubilation from the men.

Winiarski glanced nervously at Inky, who was seated nearby. Then he waved, as if setting off on a trip, and stepped toward the wheel.

"You're a man tonight," one of the miners shouted.

"A lover of Hope," the madam said with feeling.

Winiarski stopped before the disk, took a breath and gripped the axe handle with both hands. The table creaked on its shaft. Salt Lick made a fist over her sternum, and the men did likewise. Then they spoke in unison.

"For. You. My. Heart."

On "heart," Winiarski threw himself against the handle, driving it to the left, and all the fists came forward. The axle squealed, the blade flashed and the wheel started around. The rhythmic clicking resumed, and the musicians launched a new melody. Salt Lick sat back on her chair, and the woman beside her began to sing. The men clapped and croaked along. Winiarski stood beside the wheel, watching the blade swing past. It made four circuits and then it was slowing, and the miners were yelling and beating on the furniture with their cups.

"Helaina's oiling up," a man shouted.

"Number three," another guessed.

"Strange way to sell fish," a voice grumbled in Zack's ear.

Zack turned to see the Captain standing beside him, stroking his beard.

The rumpus faded abruptly, along with the music. A final *click* and the disk stopped, its blade pointed at the second alcove.

"Number two," the cashier announced.

A hand emerged, grasped the blanket and drew it aside, and a pale figure passed beneath the arch. The crowd was silent. It was the short-haired woman from the barge. She wore a white nightdress, sleek and clinging, nearly transparent.

"Genuine Jo," the cashier said.

Zack realized the miners were seeing her here for the first time.

"Good lord," the Captain murmured. "She's beautiful."

Winiarski stared at Genuine Jo. A strange moment for them both, Zack thought. She didn't seem ill at ease. There was so much tenderness in her eyes, it might have been just the two of them alone. Above, an ornate chandelier hung—a hoop of glass tube flowers, each sheltering a flame. The young pair came together on the far side of the wheel, faces lit by the glow. As they stepped toward the alcove, the dimness shaded their bodies into each other.

"*There's* something to spin for," a man said.

"Put some fuse on your charge," a miner shouted to Winiarski. "Don't go off in a flash."

"Who's got a watch with a second hand?" another asked.

There was laughter.

Fingers reached for the candle by alcove two and pinched out the flame.

"I've seen enough," Zack said.

Bob regarded him, then nodded.

They headed for the exit while the cashier pounded her gavel, announcing the next spin.

"They do this every night?" Zack asked.

"And every morning," Bob said.

"Do the men know who they're spinning for?"

Bob shook his head. "The Blondes enter through a door over there, behind that pile of crates. There's a drift connecting the cribs."

As they passed through the barricade, the miners were clamoring, vying for Salt Lick's attention.

"You think we're chumps, so it won't mean anything to you," Bob said. "But Breakaway exists because of those women."

Zack followed him across the saloon. As they entered the anteroom, the face of the hanging herald appeared above him, smiling with wooden cheer.

They returned along the level in silence. The 310 platform was empty. Bob rang for the skip.

"Some public mare do you dirt?" he asked.

"A houseful of them."

"A man feels small," Bob allowed, "when he's getting his nickels pinched. These here are different." He eyed Zack critically. "They're angels of Hope."

"Hope speaks to them too?"

"She reaches them through Salt Lick. The bawd knew Hope before Breakaway—in the Bastion Mine, down south.

Salt Lick handpicked the Blondes. She sings Hope into them and waters their wings."

"She tells them what to do."

"They help us believe," Bob said.

A groan echoed in the shaft, and the skip rose unmanned from the depths.

They boarded and rattled up the tracks, the stifling air gradually mixing with gusts from above, the rock relaxing its hold, delivering them to the Glory Hole and the northern night. As they left the platform and headed up the pathway toward the rim, Zack thought he could feel the damp breath of the mine at his rear, like an animal following him.

He thought about Sephy. He was aching to see her.

They reached the rim and started down the switchback trail. The sky was clear, except in the west, where a lens of cloud hooded the sun like a lowered eyelid. In milder latitudes, Zack thought, there were as many dreams as men. In Breakaway, there was only one—Trevillian's. To the north, beyond the black palisades, the ridges were smoothed with snow, rising one behind the other. He imagined himself at the center of some disturbance that had loosed them, like circles in a pool.

"There are other veins out there," Zack said.

Bob followed his gaze.

"And the one you're chasing—" Zack turned to him. "Doesn't Hope poke her head up anywhere else?"

"She does," Bob replied. "Hope came to the surface a

couple of miles from here. See that knob?" He pointed at a peak to the south. Its top seemed to sag like whipped cream on a sundae. "The boss found some threads there and blasted the bejesus out of them. They all wriggled back to this dig."

The first switchback lay ahead.

"Now you," Bob said. "Tell me about the Bull's-Eye Telepath."

"No thanks."

"I want to know."

"'Your mind is the mark,'" Zack said. "Check the program."

"How about you read it to me."

Zack eyed him wearily.

"Trevillian got his price," Bob said. "That's mine. For lodging."

Zack took a breath. "It starts with my entry."

"You walk out?"

"I ride out, on a horse. Greet them."

Bob looked unimpressed. "Why don't you come out punching?"

"What?"

"Do some stunts right away."

"People want to know who you are. They want to see your confidence, your control. Once they've signaled their acceptance, you've got to show some humility, that you respect them. A nod, a bow. The crowd has to be with you."

"Okay," Bob seemed persuaded. "Now what?"

"*The Ten Commandments,*" Zack said. "One of my assistants picks a volunteer from the audience. She blindfolds him and hands him a target—a plate, a ceramic bird, a glass ball. I aim my rifle and using pure concentration, I order the volunteer to hurl the target where I've aimed." He spoke flatly. "'I am the master of his mind, ladies and gentlemen. He hears my thoughts and imagines they are his own.'"

Bob was staring at him.

"Then we do *Branding the Moon*."

"The moon?"

"They raise a white drumhead using ropes and pulleys. A woman from the audience is selected. She thinks of a number, writes it down and folds the paper. I read her mind and shoot the number on the drumhead with a pair of lever-action rifles," Zack scissored his arms. "She unfolds the paper and shows the number to the crowd."

Bob was enjoying himself. "What next?"

"*Shoot-Out with a Ghost*. Then the doc—my partner—is on for two acts. I come back and do *Fishing for Zack*, before the break."

"Tell me about that one," Bob said.

"My assistant selects a dozen women from the crowd—all young and attractive. They stand in a line before me, and I pick one to have lunch with the next day. I exit the arena and the women return to their seats. Except for one who's wearing a dress with a high neckline. She's upset. She rails at my assistant and refuses to leave. 'Why wasn't I chosen?' The assistant breaks down. 'If you must know, Mister Knox can see through your clothes.'"

"People laugh?"

"Sometimes," Zack replied.

"Alright," Bob nodded. "I peed and I'm back in my seat. Now what?"

"*Bull's-Eye Birds* and two more sets from Doc. Then it's *Secret Chamber*, my signature act."

"Go on."

"I hand my revolver to my assistant and walk across the ring. A volunteer from the audience is chosen. A drape is held up so I can't see what they're doing, then the assistant asks the volunteer to put a bullet—just one—in the cylinder. The drape is removed. I blindfold myself while I speak to the crowd. 'Dear friends, I don't know which chamber holds the bullet. But there is a higher power that was watching as it was loaded. A mind greater than yours and mine. Up there, out there— That mind knows. I'm going to send a stream of pure thought into the illimitable darkness. I need perfect silence— please.' I concentrate. I put the barrel to my head and pull the trigger—click, click—until I reach the chamber. Then I point the barrel at the big top and fire the shell."

The shadows had thickened. The walls of the valley rose steeply around them.

"How do you do it?" Bob asked. "What's the trick?"

"Who says there's a trick?"

Bob smiled. "People want to believe."

"It's more than that," Zack said. "Thoughts matter. The mind has powers we don't understand."

"What am I thinking?" Bob invited him. "Right now."

"That I'm a phony."

Bob nodded. "Not bad."

"Doc has a theory," Zack said, "that the cells of the brain release an invisible fluid. Thoughts are carried like twigs on a stream."

"Doc's a believer," Bob said. "Is the show over?" He looked disappointed.

The forge and the sheds of the stamp mill appeared. The western sky was gorged with purples, swirling like oil on a silver lake.

"Yes, it's over," Zack said.

"What about Doc?"

"He retired."

They stepped onto the bridge. The Breakaway River rushed beneath them.

"We packed them in," Zack sighed. "Foolish, isn't it."

"Foolish as a flea circus," Bob said. "But you're a young man."

A figure stepped out of the willows, where the bridge touched down.

"Zack—"

Sephy stood silhouetted against the sky.

He moved forward to embrace her. She looked stiff and cold, but when he opened his arms, he felt her warm body against him. Bob strode past. "See you in the yard," Bob said.

"You're alright," Sephy murmured.

"It wasn't that bad." He found her lips and she responded.

Her chest heaved against him and a whimper escaped her.

"We drilled some holes," Zack told her, "loaded a charge, and set it off. Bob watched out for me."

"He's your friend," she said.

"How long have you been waiting?" And then before she could answer, "We stopped by the saloon. I got a good look at what the Blondes do."

Sephy shivered and drew away. She was wearing pants that fit her, Zack noticed. And a pleated shirtwaist.

"Let's eat," he said. "I can pay for it now."

"The women don't sit with the men. They eat later, by themselves."

"You don't want—"

Sephy took a step back.

"Hey—" Zack said.

"Please." She raised her hands.

"What's wrong?"

"I'm not going back with you," Sephy said.

He shook his head, confused. With the sky behind her, it was hard to see Sephy's face.

"To Bob's tent," she said.

"The weather's holding. He won't mind—"

"I'll be in Blondetown," Sephy said. "With the women."

Zack was stunned. "Are you worried that—"

"No," she said.

"We'll have our own spot in a day or two. I can get credit—"

"No," Sephy said again.

"Is a roof that important?"

"The Blondes are in tents, like everyone else."

She took another step back. In the dimness, Zack lost the glint of her eyes.

"Think who you'll be with," he mumbled. A stupid thing to say. Of course she knew. Before he could close the distance, she had turned her back to him. She was taking a narrow track that branched away from the trail.

Zack hurried after her. He grabbed Sephy's shoulder and swung her around.

"What's going on?"

"Please," she spoke earnestly. "Leave me alone."

His grip tightened. "You said you'd marry me."

Sephy jerked loose. "That was a mistake."

The spite in her voice froze him.

"Leave me alone," she repeated, more calmly. Again, she turned her back to him.

The path she followed was barely visible. He watched her silhouette ascend a bank, follow its top and disappear.

5

That night, Zack couldn't sleep. He imagined Sephy was beside him. They were like they had been on the barge—there was nothing to live or die for but another hour with each other.

Before the whistle, while Bob was still snoring, he crawled from beneath the rabbit blanket. He made his way to the yard and behind the store, finding a path that followed the river. Two minutes along it, a half-dozen tents appeared on a rise. As Zack approached, he heard coughs and snuffling. A man was mumbling. The chief and his stooges, Zack thought.

"Mornin'," Snell said.

The gaunt man was on the path behind him with a water pail in his hand.

"The boss's fireside?" Zack eyed the tents.

Snell smiled. "That one, there. You can hear him."

"He talks in his sleep?"

"Not near enough," Snell said. "When Hope isn't talking to him, the diggings go dry. We been prayin' for this." He listened with reverence to the indecipherable sounds.

Zack listened too.

"Wonder what's going on between them?" Zack asked.

"Sure."

"You're aware," Zack gave him a sapient look, "I read minds."

Snell's lips parted with surprise.

Zack laughed and stepped forward.

"Where ya headed?"

"Blondetown," Zack said.

"Miners aren't allowed."

Zack bristled.

"It's not like that," Snell assured him. "Just a courtesy to the ladies. After ten hours working, they want time for themselves." He tipped his head. "If you're callin' on Sephy—" He motioned Zack forward.

Zack continued along the path. It rounded a bluff and another group of tents appeared. As he approached, a flap lifted and Weasel's curls emerged. She looked up, regarded him for a moment and ducked back in.

Zack halted. Then Sephy crawled out of the tent.

She moved toward him deliberately.

"We'll have our own canvas," he said, as she drew up before him. "This evening."

She looked glum.

"Not with the stiffs. In the trees. Or on the beach."

Sephy shook her head.

"I promise," he laughed, "I'll rein myself in."

"Poor man," she said bitterly.

"You can't stay here."

"Because?"

"These women mean business," Zack said.

"I can take care of myself."

"That's a question."

Sephy glared. "You've said enough."

"I'll make hell for this crowd," he threatened, "with or without you."

A sob rose in Sephy's throat. She wheeled and hurried back to the tent.

As she vanished beneath the flap, Weasel reemerged. Except for her gumboots, she was naked. She squinted into the sun and stretched, then she turned to face him, smiled and gave him a flutter-fingered adieu.

At the morning meal, everyone seemed to know where Sephy had spent the night. When the day shift started up the trail to the Glory Hole, the Captain pulled Zack aside to express his sympathy. It was fine, Zack told him. He asked the Captain what he'd learned as a shipwright's apprentice, and they talked in low voices about building a boat. On the loading platform, Zack was assigned shovel work at a dump on the 310. The men were new to him and he kept to himself.

That night during the meal, Lloyd gave a brief service for Wagner and those who'd gone down with the *Bocadillos*. Zack wasn't in the yard. As soon as the shift ended, he made his way down the trail, headed for Blondetown. He found Weasel alone in her tent. She refused to share anything about Sephy's whereabouts, and when he threatened to wait for her, Weasel went for help. So he tramped back to the pup. Bob had just returned from the yard and was splitting wood.

"She won't talk to me." Zack booted a rock into the fire pit.

"Got other things on her mind, from what I hear."

"Like what?"

"She's been asking the early boys about the Private—" Bob tossed the splits onto the pile and set his hand axe aside. "What happened that night. Noel thinks she'd like to find his pieces."

"Why wouldn't she ask me to help?" Zack said. "Is there anything to find?"

Bob shook his head. "A few saw what was left of the tent. Boots, packs, the samples of Hope that the Private chopped out. Far as I know, the stuff's disappeared."

The wind had picked up. All the tents were leaning the same way.

"Then Trevillian arrived and you knuckled under," Zack said. "Didn't anyone think of building a boat?"

"A few doubters, the first year," Bob answered. "They called it the *Reason*. It was a ticket to the graveyard. Worst jobs in the wettest holes, clearing jammed chutes— The boss knocked 'em dead."

Zack fought with himself. He was impatient, fearful for Sephy and upset with her. A day passed, then another. The sky turned leaden and the forest blurred with mist—a disorienting world to rise into after ten hours in a midnight drift. He returned to Meat Hook with Bob, and they continued punching holes. The outcome of a pair of blasts was nil—the fresh surfaces were no different than those they shot away. The only signs of quartz were on the 490, and there it was just ribbons and threads.

At the end of the fourth day, Zack couldn't wait any longer.

When a Bang Boy rang the triangle to clear the yard, he ducked behind the cook shack. Ten minutes later the Blondes appeared. Sephy and Genuine Jo brought up the rear.

When he stepped out of hiding, Sephy brightened at the sight of him and made a beeline toward him.

He embraced her. To his relief, she didn't resist.

"I've missed you," Sephy said. But when he tried to kiss her, she forced him away. "I want you to help me with something. Right now."

He held his tongue, nervous he would frighten her off. She took his hand and led him upriver, past Blondetown, to the wash. They climbed its steep north side together. At the top, Sephy showed Zack a spot she'd chosen. She wanted him to help her build a cairn for the Private.

Zack did his best to honor her request, wondering that this concern had swept away all others. She selected rocks from the riverbed, and as they carried them Sephy talked about her brother, their childhood with an uncle in the wheat belt, and how she and Raymond had only each other. He waited for her to speak about her decision to leave the pup, and what had happened between them.

They piled the rocks knee high as a memorial where the Private had last been seen.

"I've accepted it—that he's vanished," Sephy said when they were done. "I've thought about where Prowler took him. How Raymond spent his last hours. I wanted to be with him." She clasped Zack's hand.

"You're closer to him now," Zack said.

"I am." She smiled without looking at him. "My telepath understands."

She took a breath. "You must think me very strange. I'm sorry, Zack. It was your misfortune that you met me."

Her words baffled him, angered him. He managed to hold himself in check. She was sharing things with him that were intimate. And as on the barge, the connection with her brother lit her beauty and her soul.

"He didn't lie," Sephy said, "but there was a lot Raymond's partner didn't tell me. To spare my feelings, I suppose." She stared at the cairn. "When they were close enough to see golden leaves in the quartz, his partner went down to get a packboard. When he returned, Raymond was standing beside the vein with his pick in his hand and pieces of Hope scattered around him. In a trance. His partner couldn't get Raymond to hear or see him. When he tried to take Raymond's pick, the hand wouldn't let go."

126

Zack stared at his boots. Tendrils of twisted stalk flashed through the grass like slivers of lightning.

"He put some quartz in the pack and led Raymond down. Dragged him inside the tent, covered him with blankets and dropped off to sleep. He woke to find Prowler tugging at his arm."

Sephy spoke softly, but it wasn't sorrow Zack heard in her voice.

"When Prowler grabbed Raymond," she said, "Raymond went wild. The shock didn't restore him—he was still in his trance. Furious, attacking with no fear of the consequences. 'Like a saint,' his partner told the prospectors in Gastineau City. He painted a strange picture. But the treasure was found, and the story of the Private became sacred to them. And it's sacred to me. The man swinging the pick was the Raymond I knew."

Sephy was silent.

Zack's mind was full of things he wanted to say. She must have sensed that, because she turned her shoulder. He tried to press her—to stay, to listen—but she refused, begging his forgiveness and hurrying away.

Zack was asleep in the pup. Bob's exclamation woke him.

"Son of a bitch—"

Zack raised his head, hearing a familiar noise—the shift whistle.

Bob threw off the blanket and knelt by the tent opening. It was dim outside—the middle of the night.

The whistle was still sounding: three long blasts, then three more, and another three.

"C'mon," Bob said, pulling on his pants.

"What is it?" Zack reached for his shirt.

"Something bad."

When they hit the footpath, the camp was in a frenzy. Men were scrambling between the tents and smoldering fires, racing up the slopes, shouting, half-dressed. Lanterns were swarming around the supply store. What was the emergency? No one seemed to know. Zack followed Bob up the corduroy road. The whistle continued screaming in threes.

A big man shouldered into him, heaving and choking, his face smeared with grime. True Bluford. Zack put his arm around him, searching his face.

"Cave-in," True gasped.

"Where?"

"Tears of Joy." True eyed Zack with anguish. "Hold her dear."

"Here they come," a miner cried.

Zack could see the procession now, eeling down the switchback trail. It spoke to itself, grumbling and urgent, seeing its way with yellow eyes. Two stretchers were descending with lanterns on either side.

"McGee," True said, getting his wind back. "Russ McGee. And the new man—what's his name?" His eyes darted.

"Carew's still under it." He spotted Owen, pushed Zack aside and staggered toward the foreman. Bob and Zack hurried toward the store.

The procession divided there. Half of the eel rose up the steps with one of the stretchers, coiling before the opened door. The man was still alive. Zack could see his body shifting beneath the blanket. The other half of the eel continued down the footpath, bearing the second stretcher toward the sawmill and the morgue.

Men had gathered around Owen. Snell was at his elbow, arms jerking, talking quickly. "Every miner in camp—sixteen at a time, in three-hour sprints. That's what he wants—"

"Ya hear?" Owen shouted. "'Tis sixteen now and sixteen in three hours. And sixteen after that. Be ready—"

"'I want my Carew back,'" Snell shared the boss's words with the crowd.

Owen swung his thick arms, laying hands on men. "You and you—" He grabbed Zack's coat sleeve. "Knox, and the Irish too."

Through the doorway of the store, Zack could see men clustered around a countertop. The injured miner was on it, with Lloyd bent over him, staring and manipulating an instrument. A man beside him held a washbasin splashed with blood. Another stood by the victim's head, raising a scrolled poster. Only the title was visible—*Topographic Chart of Vessels and Organs*. Inky stood by the victim's boots, reading aloud from a book.

"Cincture the artery."

"Cincture the artery," Lloyd repeated. He put the instrument between his teeth and used both hands to pull.

The victim groaned.

"Alright," Owen shouted, facing his sixteen. "Let's rush us to the gallows."

As Zack started forward, the victim spoke. "No more fares," he gasped.

In the main shaft the whistle bursts were deafening. The skip stopped at the 400 level. A group of men stood on the landing, their grim faces staring as one.

"How many mucking?" Owen asked, jumping out of the car.

"Six," a miner replied.

Owen was already across the platform and starting along the level. Bob, Zack and the others hurried after him. Forty feet in, they turned down a narrow corridor. It jogged and veered, and then there were voices echoing ahead. Zack heard the bray of a mule, the rumble and grind of rock in motion.

The corridor ended in a large room. It had been shaped by a dream or some frightful delirium—the walls tilted different ways, the ceiling rose from four feet to ten, and the floor dipped twenty degrees at the rear. As they started across it, Zack saw a crowd of miners stooping beside the room's far wall, each with a candle on his hat-front. Lanterns were strung around them. "Where are we?" he asked.

"White Mint Stope," Bob said. "That's Tears of Joy."

Zack followed his nod to a ragged hole in the wall. A mule emerged from it, pulling a boulder by a chain. Another appeared, carrying ore pails like saddlebags. Men were visible inside the tunnel, shoveling and swinging hammers. Those outside ferried buckets, unloaded mules or led fresh ones into the drift.

Owen made his way toward the tunnel. "Hold up," he shouted when he reached the mouth. The men paused in their labors, expressions tense. "You're done, for now," Owen told them. "You four lads," he fingered Zack and three others. "Into the hole with Bob."

As they entered the drift, Zack heard Owen behind him.

"Put your shoulders to the onions," the foreman directed. "Wait on the big stuff—there's more jennies coming." Then with feeling, "Do you care for Carew, lads?"

In the tunnel were six men and a mule. The men wielded shovels, filling the mule's saddle pails, huffing and clanging in the cramped space. The two nearest the mouth straightened to admit the relief team, and three others halted and faced them. The farthest seemed not to notice. He was hunched over, running his round-point into a bulwark of broken rock. Zack could see the collapse piled steeply above the man. It looked like the smallest movement would send the pile crashing down on him.

"Boss," Dog-Eared Bob said.

Zack was startled by the figure that rose before them. It twisted around, black lips twitching, a mask of dark grit pierced by vicious eyes.

"Tears of Joy belongs to the bats," Trevillian cursed the drift. "But not till it gives Carew back."

He savaged the mute faces, then straightened, assuming a more human shape, his features composing, as if he was re-membering what it was to command. "Have we heard him?" he asked, sweeping the tired muckers for the benefit of the fresh ones.

A man nodded.

"Soon it was," another said. "After the roof came down."

"Wheezing," the first added.

"Just a bit of it," a third said. "Not a sound since."

"Carew's a doubter," Trevillian reminded the new men. "Hope won't help him." He removed his hat and mopped his forehead. "He's ours to save."

Zack saw the boss's determination mirrored in the faces of the men beside him.

"Your heart, boys." Trevillian made a fist over his sternum and brought it forward. The men joined the pledge, except for Zack.

"You, up front," Trevillian barked, facing the ordeal. "Mind the skinners and keep the buckets coming. You two, start over there. Bob and Knox," he gestured, "dig by me."

Bob grabbed a pair of shovels from departing miners and passed one to Zack. He faced the bulwark three feet from

Trevillian, motioned Zack into the space between, and ran his shovel into loose rock.

Zack stooped, buried the blade in a wedge of slide debris and heaved it up. Bob's sloped shoulders turned smoothly, arm moving like a boom, fist twisting the shank to dump his load into one of the buckets strapped to the mule behind them. "Fill the heel," Bob said, bending for another load. "Toe takes care of itself."

Zack swung his shovel toward the bucket, emptied it and turned back to the collapse.

"Tear into it, man," Trevillian said angrily. "This isn't a show."

Zack drove the shovel in with a vengeance. After a few carries, the six men found a rhythm. It didn't take long for the buckets to fill.

The boss paused and shouted at the drift mouth. The muleskinner entered to lead the animal away. "Get me a jack," Trevillian told him. "Knox, help me with this."

The mine boss grabbed a chain and dropped to his knees. Zack knelt beside him. The boss started the chain around a large boulder. Zack reached from the other side, found the boss's arm and fumbled along it, getting hold of the chain's end. "That's it," the boss said. A large mule was backing into the drift. Trevillian brought his end of the chain forward, and Zack followed his example. As the boss clipped the chain to the harness, Zack saw the pleasure in his eyes.

"He's all yours," Trevillian told the muleskinner. He stood

and slapped the beast's haunch, and the boulder groaned out of the drift.

They retrieved their shovels and turned back to the collapse. Their blades entered together, and as they did, a dull knocking sounded from within. Suddenly the ceiling was crackling, like a hot skillet when something cold's dropped in, and then the entire bulwark was shifting. The slide was letting go—everything in the drift would be crushed. Zack eyed Trevillian, ready to flee. The mine boss smiled. A mule with empty buckets was backing toward them.

Trevillian pivoted with another shovel load. Zack glanced at the others. Their expressions were fearful, but they were following the boss's lead.

Trevillian leaned closer to Zack. "You're with me," he said reassuringly.

Zack was too shaken to laugh. Did the boss imagine he'd earned Hope's protection? Maybe he thought his company would make an agonizing death agreeable. Zack swallowed his dread and forced his round-point back into the collapse.

The precarious slope held, and with each mule haul, there was less broken rock and more room in the drift. But there was no trace of Carew. As the three-hour relay advanced, Zack's perception of the mine boss changed.

Trevillian was a brute, but he was brave. There was no denying that. When an unwieldy span appeared, he put himself beneath it, in the place of greatest danger, levering it loose while men and mule pulled. He did everything he could to save the buried man, and it wasn't because it was his office. What did he know of Carew? Where did his passion come from, and his endurance? The challenge was to keep up with him, and Zack gave his best.

When the three hours had ended and relief arrived, the boss thanked the five shovelers as if nothing on earth mattered more to him.

Bob sighed and leaned his round-point against the wall.

Zack had his eyes on Trevillian. The boss was going to shovel with the next relay.

"I'll stay," Zack said.

Trevillian faced him, only half surprised. "You've seen Prowler, I hear," he said, as if he'd sniffed out some evil. His blackened cheek twitched. "You're just what she wants."

Zack was speechless.

"Stay," the boss recanted, swallowing his venom. "We'll give her our hearts."

He grappled Zack's shoulder and shook him like a friend. Then he turned and motioned the fresh team into the drift, and the work resumed.

At the end of that sprint, they found Carew. Trevillian caught sight of his pant leg through the puzzle of loose rock. He halted the shoveling, went down on both knees and began issuing orders. They worked quickly, removing the surrounding material with care, trying to avoid further harm. When they were finally able to lift Carew onto the floor of the drift, he was limp and motionless. His lips were swollen and a leg was fractured. Curled there, covered with blood, he looked like a stillborn infant.

Trevillian wept, unashamed, and the men joined him.

"He was a doubter," one of the miners lamented.

"At the last," Trevillian shook his head, "he held her dear." He made a fist over his heart and brought it forward, commending Carew to his reward.

The next relief group arrived in time to bear Carew to the store. The miners who'd uncovered him returned through White Mint Stope and up the main shaft. Zack's intent was to follow them. But as he was crossing White Mint, he collapsed from exhaustion.

The morning shift whistle woke him. His head ached and he was stiff in every joint. He was in White Mint, where he'd fallen. Someone had lain a coat over him. When Zack raised himself and looked around, he saw Trevillian seated on a powder box, staring at him.

"Coming back?" the boss asked.

Zack rubbed his face. "Long shift."

"You're off today," the boss said. He grabbed his coat and

put it on. Then he rose and helped Zack to his feet. "I don't want to use you up."

Zack glanced at the ragged entrance to Tears of Joy. "Dead ground?"

"That's what I said."

"Is there quartz in there?"

Trevillian nodded. "Up top."

"Show me."

The mine boss studied him. "Alright." He pulled a candle from the wall, turned, and led the way back into the drift. As they reached the end, he waved the candle over his head.

A thin white line angled across the ceiling and vanished into the collapse.

"Gold?"

"Not much. Hope's back in there." Trevillian gazed at the slide, as if he could see through it.

Zack imagined a white river running past them, sinuous and frothing, with this thread of spume trailing back.

"She's in your thoughts," Trevillian said.

"Not like she's in yours," Zack replied.

The steely eyes narrowed.

"She's talking to you," Zack said without blinking.

"And you're listening in," Trevillian said.

"With your permission."

"Well then," the boss nodded, "you must know how disappointed she is."

"Because—"

"You don't believe," the boss said. "She wants me to help you with that."

"How about helping me with Sephy."

Trevillian seemed confused.

"She's garrisoned in Blondetown," Zack said.

The boss shifted his jaw, taking stock of the problem. "You know what you need?" He put his hand on Zack's shoulder. "A bath."

Zack thought he was joking.

"This way," Trevillian motioned.

He exited Tears of Joy and Zack followed.

They arrived at the platform, boarded the manskip and ascended to the 310 level. As they pulled up to the landing, Inky emerged from the shadows. He didn't acknowledge the boss.

"I let the boys know," he told Zack as he climbed into the skip.

"Streetcar?" Zack said.

Inky nodded. "He's making stops in the golden city now."

Trevillian led the way across the landing and along the level. He took the cut-off to Strongbox Stope. The clamor from the Big Wheel reached them.

"Trying to shake off the gloom," the boss said sadly. He continued through the anteroom and into the stope.

The miners were carousing, but their abandon was forced. There were haunted faces everywhere Zack looked. Trevillian strode up to the bar, grabbed a bottle from behind it and turned, leading the way back to the anteroom. They circled the small space and slid into a narrow passage. A few steps brought them to a pink drape.

As Trevillian pushed the drape aside, a miner appeared. His clothing was caked with mud, but his face was clean-shaven and his wet hair was combed back.

They entered a roughhewn chamber—a cave, but for a half-dozen logs wedged between floor and ceiling. A woman sat on a stool beside a tub full of water, rasping her nails with a drill file. As they approached, she pulled back a cape of red hair and lifted her face. It was powdered chalk-white.

Her painted lips parted and she gave the boss a toothy smile.

"Helaina," the boss introduced her.

She eyed Zack. "Dirty?"

"Blind?" Zack said.

Helaina stooped for a sponge. "Cost you forty."

"It's on me," Trevillian said.

Zack took his coat off.

"He needs a trim," Helaina said.

"Put it on the bill," the boss told her.

"Bubbles?" Helaina nodded at the bath.

Zack laughed as he stripped his shirt off.

"On me," Helaina said. She leaned forward and spat in the tub.

Zack unbuttoned his pants and slid them down, watching her breast tops quiver in the candlelight. Tarnished shears glided into view, blades clashing menacingly.

"What about Sephy?" Zack asked.

"I'm going to fix that," the boss said. He handed Zack the bottle. "You'll want this."

Zack raised the bottle to his lips. The liquor was tart and caustic. It bit his tongue and clawed his throat. "What is it?"

"Hooch," Trevillian said. "Our own brew. Well—" A burden seemed to descend on him. "I've got things to attend to." He seemed reluctant to leave. "He's caught Hope's eye," he remarked to Helaina. "Don't make him a clown." Then he turned and strode out of the Grooming Parlor.

Ten minutes later Zack was settled in the tub, arms trailing, eyes closed. Helaina was scrubbing his chest. Drops fell on his face as she hefted a pail and poured water over him. He raised the hooch and downed the last of it. His hand opened and the bottle landed with a tap on the surface of the bath. Helaina clashed her shears by his ear. Zack felt a tugging at his temple, the shears dipped toward his neck and climbed the back of his head. And then they stopped.

He heard a *swish* at the Parlor's entrance, and when he opened his eyes, he saw Salt Lick twisting forward, the train of her gown flashing over the rocky floor. The gown was covered with tiny blue beads. She held a lantern in one hand, and as she approached the tub, she raised it to light her face. The other knuckled into her waist. Her lime eyes peered down at him.

"I'll stuff my mattress with that." She glanced at a wooden box beside the tub, where Helaina had dropped his hair.

The madam wore a straw hat decked with fruit. Beneath, her face was divided. The high brow and broad cheeks were

140

moonlike, sage and beneficent, while the aquiline nose and sharp eyes scouted their prey.

"What do you think of my establishment?"

"It needs dusting."

"Still strutting like a banty," Salt Lick said. "You don't understand— There's no Hope without us."

"The gold I understand. The Wheel is whoring. Don't whitewash it."

Salt Lick pondered him, as if debating whether he was worth the effort. "The vein comes and goes. When Hope's distant, the boys still feel her care. The Wheel nourishes their affection. Their love keeps it turning."

"Lust keeps it turning," Zack said. "Goat spunk."

The madam's reaction surprised him. Her temple creased with pain. She pursed her lips, as if accepting his condemnation. Then the lime eyes pierced him, questioning his past. The pointless liaisons, strange partners in strange beds—

"What do you suppose goat spunk is for?" she said quietly. "It serves begetting, but there is something more."

Zack saw the passion in her eyes. Real feeling and theater were so mixed in her, they were inseparable.

"Hope is his, when a man needs her," she said. "Thank the Blondes for that."

Zack laughed, admiring the performance. "There's more than one?"

"We're all blonde beneath the skin. Aren't we, dear?" Salt Lick spoke over her shoulder.

The pink drape shifted and a woman stepped forward.

"The lady who warmed your bones on the barge—" Salt Lick passed her lantern to Sephy. "She'll warm many more down here."

Sephy approached him. She carried the lantern by her waist. She came to an abrupt halt, like a bird striking a window, one wing flexed, one hanging limp. Her head was turned to the side, and it seemed to take an act of will for her to face him. When she did, he saw the admission in her eyes.

Salt Lick motioned, and Helaina followed her out of the Grooming Parlor.

"What have they done to you?" Zack rose dripping, feeling the hooch, the rocky chamber pivoting around him. She wore black, as she had on the steamer. A stark black dress with a white collar.

"Nothing," Sephy said. "I'm resuming my old life. The one I had before I met you."

Zack shivered, shrinking from the cold.

"I'm sorry," she said. "It was a fantasy. I thought there might be—" Her gaze wandered, features tense. "I worked in the High Quarter. I heard about Snell from a girl on the Square. He was recruiting for Breakaway. Raymond—was calling me. I sought Snell out."

Sephy grew older as she spoke.

"I don't expect you to understand," she said.

Zack remembered the moment he'd first sought her lips.

"You had such majesty," she said. "I thought I'd been given a new life." She shook her head. "I've put myself in Salt Lick's care. I agreed to that when Snell hired me. He paid my debts

142

before we left. He bought me things too. It all went down with the steamer, but the money was spent." Her eyes hardened. "That business with DuVal—"

She struggled to express her remorse.

Zack's mind brimmed with images. The sickles of hair, her protecting hand on his chest, her tear-bathed smile saying *yes*.

"It changes everything, doesn't it," Sephy muttered. There was a hesitation in her voice.

Zack felt his heart hitching, rage welling up, drowning his pain and bewilderment.

She lowered her gaze. "It was my weakness. I misled you. But you are . . . easily misled." She seemed to recover her composure. "Perhaps you will accept some of the blame."

Her show of dignity stunned him. He stepped toward her, not knowing if he was going to clasp her or strike her down.

"Raymond knew what I had become." Sephy stood her ground. "He never lost his faith in me."

"Faith?" He lunged, grabbing her with one hand. As she tugged loose, the cave twisted around him. Zack grunted and wagged his head. His gaze fell on his gumboots, and he stepped into them. Then he was striding toward the exit, sweeping the drape aside. He stumbled along the narrow manway, and when he reached the anteroom the wooden angel greeted him, swooping out of the darkness, pointing toward Strongbox Stope. Zack parted the blankets and lurched toward the bar. The men made way, sensing his ire, amused by his nudity. Zack scanned the faces, looking for a BMC stooge or the boss himself. He spotted the sentry.

The man saw him coming and twisted between two miners. He grabbed a tin-can lantern as Zack reached him, and when he swung around, the flame scorched Zack's chest. Zack clutched the man's shoulder and sent a fist crashing into his jaw. He caught the man's belt with his free hand and lifted him over his head like a bale of hay. The rifle fell to the floor.

The crowd recoiled as Zack heaved the sentry over the bar. The oblong mirror burst, there were cries, splintering wood, the sentry falling amid a torrent of curses.

Zack picked up the rifle, levered the handgrip and checked the chamber. Then he strode through the gathering, headed for the Big Wheel.

The crash had interrupted a spin, and as Zack passed through the barricade, he saw the spectators on their feet, regarding him with surprise, the disk still clicking around on its axle. The cashier had left the lectern and was crossing the sitting area. Salt Lick stood before her chair with a murderous expression. From a couple of alcoves, faces peered out.

"Stripped for Hope," a miner shouted.

The assembly erupted around Zack, baiting him with catcalls. He rested the rifle on his shoulder and stepped toward the dais. A half-dozen men circled him, but Salt Lick raised her hand.

"Back from your honeymoon," she hailed him.

"Empty-handed," Zack said. "And bare-headed."

"I smell goat spunk." Salt Lick pinched the air beneath her chin.

"Sugar for Blondes," Zack said.

The miners hooted and banged their seats with their cups, and then a chorus of whistles rose, goading the madam to action.

"The mirror will cost him dear," the cashier shouted. She stood in the barricade archway, surveying the damage.

Jeers filled the Wheel.

Salt Lick waved for silence. "He'll owe us for the bar," she said, "and spin on the house." A flurry of approval followed, and the madam spoke over it. "Who can live without Hope?" She faced Zack. "Hand over the rifle and grab the axe."

Zack ignored her, closing the distance to the wheel and vaulting onto it. He rose atop the wooden disk, finding his balance, rifle held high.

"Spin me," Zack shouted, aligning himself with the blade.

Men in the front came forward. Zack saw hands grasp the axe handle and braced himself. Salt Lick stared at the miners, then nodded.

"For. You. My. Heart."

The men lunged and the wheel turned beneath Zack, tipping him, starting around. A skirt stay had been nailed to the table's center, and Zack could see it clicking against the axle bolts as the disk rotated. At the sound of the measured beat, the musicians cracked open another tune.

Zack flexed his knees, centering himself. The blade passed the dais—where Salt Lick stood, hands on her hips—then tracked the curving wall, alcove entrances sweeping past. Four of the seven candles were lit. Zack slapped the rifle barrel, sending the trigger guard cartwheeling around his finger.

The miners shouted and he could see their faces rushing by as the rifle turned end over end. Salt Lick was stamping the dais, joining her voice to the singer's. "Give, give, give her your heart," she sang, as if the refrain urging men toward Hope had been written for him.

Zack jerked the rifle from his finger and sent it twirling into the air before him, recapturing it as the seating area swung back into view. The men shrieked and yowled, the axe blade winked light as the alcoves passed. He pictured the women inside, on mattresses of human hair, gowns fringed with roots and beaded with balls of dirt. The picture aroused him.

Salt Lick's voice froze in her throat as he swung past the dais. Now the men could see, and they wailed as he turned before them. Zack jutted his jaw and pumped his knees, gumboots heeling in time, dancing for his brothers in hell.

The wheel was slowing. Alcove number one and two. Three and four. Five, six, seven— Then the singer and musicians, and the staring madam. Past the seating area, still slowing. Zack felt with his boots, shuffling backward until he bumped the axle cowling. Number one, two, three. He put his heel on the cowling, feeling the axle turning beneath it. Number four, five— He eased his weight onto his leg, braking the disk. Number six, number seven—

The last click sounded and the wheel halted, pointed directly at Salt Lick.

Zack cocked the hammer and lifted the rifle, drawing a bead on her chin, pulling the gunsight up the bridge of her nose. Shouts from either side, and then he squeezed the trigger

146

and the bullet snatched her hat and went ricocheting off the rock.

The bullet's scream echoed in the silence. Salt Lick stood rigid, her face as pale as her hair.

"Crack shot," a miner said. There were cries of outrage, laughter, and snickers from those who thought the madam fair game. Salt Lick tried to collect herself. She took a breath, touched her hair and faced Zack.

"The boss's minx," Zack said, as if surprised at his good fortune. He spoke in a stage whisper.

"Hold her dear." True Bluford stood and saluted him, clenching his fist over his sternum and bringing it forward. The others followed suit.

"Hooch—" A man waved to a Bangshu, and with that cups flashed, and the babble mounted in anticipation of the next spin.

The cavern was still circling Zack. There was no feeling in his fingers. He squatted on the disk and lowered himself over the rim. He started toward the dais, knees wobbling. Salt Lick was talking to the cashier, watching him approach. Her agitation was palpable. As he drew up, he could see her breasts throbbing in the beaded bodice.

"The grand prize," he mumbled, handing the rifle to the cashier.

Salt Lick smiled, her charm thin as greasepaint. "My boudoir—" She gestured toward the shadows behind the dais. She retrieved a lantern with one hand and extended the other, expecting he would help her down.

Zack circled her back and thighs and lifted her from the stage.

"What're you doing?" the cashier demanded. She had retrieved the madam's hat.

Salt Lick searched Zack's face. "It's alright."

The cashier put the hat on Zack's head. "You could have killed her."

"There's still that chance," Zack said to the madam.

Salt Lick looked away.

He carried her toward the place she'd indicated. It looked like a softness in the rock. Velvet was hanging there, and when he shouldered through, he found himself in a room twelve-foot square, walls planked and papered with scarlet cabbage roses on a pink ground. The odor of fish filled the space. Zack let Salt Lick down. She set her lantern on a dresser. Then she turned to a washstand and lit a lamp. An earnest Cupid fluttered across its porcelain ball.

"Well," she sighed, "what's the man's pleasure?"

Zack snatched the fruit hat from his head and skimmed it toward the pillow. His pulse was racing, his skin slick with sweat.

"Facedown? On all fours?" Salt Lick pulled the combs from her hair, and ivory waves spilled over her shoulders. "Or does the cowboy prefer a rider?"

She couldn't have been colder.

Outside, the men were chanting, "For. You. My. Heart."

"The truth is—" Salt Lick put her hand on the rail of the

bed. "A man's best experience with me is in the position of prayer."

He stepped out of the gumboots.

"Sit here." She touched the bed.

Zack sat.

She grasped the hem of her gown and gathered it up, skirts and all. Her pale thighs came into view above stockinged calves. She put her fingers to her tongue and slid her hand into her drawers.

"Look at that," she admired his weapon with a practiced soft-soap. Then with her skirts still hitched up, she rose and put one foot on the bedstead.

Salt Lick's thighs opened around him. She parted the slit in her drawers, and through the gap Zack saw a mons white as quartz. "There's your gold," she whispered. "You can catch the gleam," she glanced at the floor, "on your knees."

Zack shook his head. "Here," he pulled the coverlet away. "With your back on the griddle. Take everything off."

Salt Lick made a hurt sound. It came from a playbook—a melodrama in which a maid's honor was forced. "Hope asks for better," she said.

"Leave Hope out of this."

"Don't say that." But she was unfastening her gown.

He watched her step out of it and slide her petticoats off. When she released her bust bodice, large pointed breasts swung toward him, feeding his hunger and his loathing. The nipples hardened in the cold, as if they had a will of their own.

She unclipped her garters and stepped out of her dresses and drawers. "Enough?"

All that remained was a garter belt and her stockings and shoes. Zack nodded.

Salt Lick opened her nightstand, drew a bottle out and poured liquid into her hand. The reek of fish oil was overpowering. She reached between her thighs and slicked herself. Zack's repugnance peaked, and then his desire joined with the stench. He stood to embrace her. She caught his wrist.

"You look like a madman," Salt Lick said, turning him toward a mirror.

His hair had been cropped in places and hung long in others.

"Don't be rough with me." She kept hold of him and climbed onto the bed. "Like this?" She lay on her back.

"That's fine." He parted her thighs.

She turned her face. "Gently," she whispered. "Gently."

Salt Lick's warmth made him shiver. The damp manway was dark and close. The likeness struck him—he was no stranger to dismal corridors. He ventured farther, feeling the familiar wariness. His senses grew sharper. Without warning, hot breath reached his ear. Fingers crossed his haunch, wriggling like grubs. He drew back.

"I'm going to test your purity," Zack told her.

"Whatever you find," Salt Lick said, "is hers. I have none of my own."

Her voice was dark and soft, like the mud that sucks a miner's boots.

Zack drove into her—slowly, but all the way. Did she gasp? It might have been a heave from his chest. He could hear his breath in his ears. He drew back and loomed forward again, and again. His wind was entrained, his pulse and his hips— Damn measured steps and sly delays. All the way, all the way—

In a flash, Zack saw Salt Lick on the dais, pinching the air beneath her chin. He was watching himself in the mirror, trimming his goatee, a prinked-up fiend. Zack, Mister Z. The omega of man—the beast, not the meek.

It reared, starved and angry, like a tapeworm emerging from the jaws of a corpse. Inside that corpse, another corpse curled, and another and another—a cradle of gnawed women, nested in his depths like Russian dolls. Starved and angry, out it came—a panther lunging, a hooking bull, a spastic ape.

His pride was gone, and his foolish dream. The marriage of minds? Elk snort, rat seed. She's slick and warm, made to gore. Ripe or withered, soft or firm— Love? Love? Twitching limbs. Churning jellies and putrid guts. The beast is hunching over his feast. A looter's eyes, a displaced grin; the wine from your bowels is dripping from his lips and chin. He'll eat your marrow, the bull's-eye beast—

You know your mate, you worthless pelt. It's Zack, the bastard—boon to maggots, nothing else. Slimy entrails— carnival treats! Gall-green syrup on speckled meats. One dark penny, nothing else. Hurry, people! Take your seats! Hear him grunt, watch him shoot. Balls of glass and peanut shells— A hot dog dinner, nothing else.

The body beneath Zack was shuddering. He raised himself, drenched in heat, smelling the carnage, seeing the blood flowers opening around him in the half-light. A whimper— Something was dying. He lunged at it, thrusting back into the wound. The whimper turned quizzical, retreating—dazed and weak, focused on itself. Breathing its last, he thought.

Then the voice swelled with fresh life. It seemed to have detached itself from the woman beneath him. As he listened, the sound grew throaty, deeper. A stream of words was resolving out of it. A song, he thought, reaching him from the dais of the Big Wheel. But it came from a greater distance than that. Somewhere deep in the mountain.

All other sounds faded: the squeal of the bedframe, the *whish* of sheets, his own labored breath— Muffled, distant. The madam's cave and the world of the mine was a dissolving mist—nothing remained but the voice. It spoke of advancing and retreating, of appearing and vanishing. Of making its way toward him through winding drifts, the dark unknown—

Hope, Zack thought.

The voice didn't hear him. It was foolishness, he knew. Whoever he was listening to, it wasn't Hope. But there was magic in the voice—

It took hold of his senses, and as he listened, it grew. He was no longer conscious of the movement of his hips. His body seemed to have lost its thrust. But he still felt desire. The charms of that voice worked on some other instinct, apart from flesh.

There, on the Wondrous wall— She wasn't aware of him.

Or if she was, it was only dimly. She was singing to herself, or to some vague recollection of men, whoever and wherever they might be. *In Ardent's roof, a treasure you'll never own.*

The thought of Hope and everything promised to the miners welled inside him. He pictured the Private alone on the peak, staring at her with his pick in his hand. He hated Trevillian's use of her, and the poverty of spirit that kept men enslaved. But he burned to imagine her.

There was a drift called Sublime. He had never been to the place, but he saw it before him now.

He was alone in the drift, peering through a crack in the headwall.

He could see a bath—much larger than the one the stiffs used—with a cloud of steam eddying and pearling around it. The bath brimmed with a dazzling fluid, thick and white, like boiling cream. Beneath the surface he could see body parts shifting—a knee sliding through scallops, a mosaic thigh, a translucent shoulder, threaded with fire—

The nimbus closed over the bather. Then, on the rim of the bath, a crystal forearm appeared. It was lathered with froth and feathered with glass. The arm tensed as he watched. The bather was rising. Her body was hidden, but above the steam he saw the arc of spread wings, the tips of white pinions and the crystal webbing between.

Hope wasn't surprised. She knew he was there.

He could see her eyes. Amid all that strangeness and swirling, there were two points of light—distant but knowing, focused with feeling.

He pushed his arm into the fracture, reaching. His hand emerged on the far side of the wall, and when he spread his fingers, they burst into flames. Hope's glow dimmed abruptly. She sank back in the cloud, and the boiling bath froze. The rocky bed that held Hope was visible now, above and below, like the folds of a robe. It was closing around her, entombing her.

His hand was no longer burning. Its flames had quenched, leaving a dark claw. Then Hope's voice faded and Sublime winked out.

Zack was on his back. The bedframe was squealing beneath him. The boudoir came and went, light pulsing as the Cupid lamp sputtered. The cabbage roses seemed about to explode. Salt Lick was straddling him, hunched like a gargoyle. Her eyes were closed and she nursed his windup, rocking shamelessly.

In her panting exertions, Zack heard a low note—a remnant perhaps of Hope's introspection. The tips of the bawd's breasts dragged on his chest, catching and dipping. As the moment arrived, he arched between her thighs, imagining it was Hope who received him, and that the passion brimming out of him was borne away with her, frothing and white.

The lamp rattled over the edge, struck the floor and burst, splashing the scarlet petals with gold. Zack rose to the surface and went under again, in a warm river with waves passing through him. Salt Lick clung to him. He rolled there beneath her for a time, pulsing and wasting. Then a stray current pushed them both aside.

Zack lay motionless, gasping, delivered back to the Breakaway mountain—the dark place where men drilled the earth.

His limbs were numb. His jaw seemed locked.

Salt Lick shifted over him, dismounting.

He shivered.

"The real Zack," the madam murmured.

His mind swung back, seeing Hope through the steam. Wishing she was still with him.

"She reached you," the madam said. "Didn't she."

Zack turned toward her. Salt Lick's face was wan. What had happened was unexpected—for her as well. She retrieved her straw hat and covered her breasts. "I did my best."

What did she know of the Hope he'd imagined? Nothing, Zack thought. But it would be cruel to unmask her.

"Blondes have feelings," she said.

He accepted the chastening.

"I care for you. For all the boys."

"The Wheel won't replace Sephy," he said.

"She was never yours."

"I was going to marry her," Zack muttered. "And now—"

"Allow us some virtue," Salt Lick said.

The lantern still burned on the dresser. Her features had hardened.

"It's our part—playing Hope. That's what you need." Salt Lick's voice echoed up from an ancient well, tinged with bitterness. "I know my business. I've spent half my life with men like you."

She set her straw hat on the bed between them. "You're a peach, with an ugly crease." She touched the fruit on the brim. "Something cut it when it was young. The older it gets, the deeper the scar."

"*Hor*ticulture," Zack said.

Salt Lick nodded. "We're rooted in the same manure you are. We dream of being a wounded man's angel. We imagine we're his highest reward."

Zack regarded her. "Cripples and martyrs."

"And we're all for sale," the madam said.

There was something like helplessness in her eyes.

"A young woman fell in love—" Zack stopped himself.

Salt Lick was perfectly still.

"With a young man named Knox," he went on. "When she got pregnant, he found a place for her. With women like you. At the last hour, they cut the baby out—one of them fancied herself a surgeon. My mother bled to death. Whores will do anything for a dollar, so it was all kept below public view."

Shouts reached them—a scuffle in the Big Wheel.

"I'm sorry," Salt Lick said.

Zack looked away.

"We're doubles, substitutes—every girl here. We've been abused and disgraced, seduced and defiled. To find the one who can't be corrupted, you must look through us."

"It's Hope I want," Zack finished her thought.

"He's coming along," a deep voice observed.

Zack started. The silhouette of the mine boss loomed over the bed. How long had he been standing there?

"Tough customer—" Trevillian tinkled the lamp shards with his boot.

Salt Lick rose. "He's soft as nanny cud now." She reached for her bust bodice.

Trevillian put his hand on Salt Lick's wrist and drew her close. He ravaged her mouth and she didn't resist. Zack saw them as in a globe of frosted glass.

"Shall we play Punish Hope?" Salt Lick teased.

"Tell me how Zack was," Trevillian said.

"Try him yourself—"

"I couldn't receive him," the boss said.

Salt Lick laughed. "He's an effort, even for an old hand."

"He jiggered the wheel?"

"Hope put him up to it." She eyed Zack. "She had something planned."

"Did she?"

"Zack's important—you were right about that. It's late. I'm missed." She shooed Trevillian toward the velvet.

The boss departed.

Zack eased himself off the mattress and stood.

"Always in a hurry," the madam said. She drew a flushing syringe from the bedstand. "Helaina will fetch your clothes and finish your trim." She smiled. "Pass me the basin. I need to wash myself out."

The singer's voice reached them from the Wheel.

"Where did that music come from?"

"Where do you think?" Salt Lick pulled the plunger, filling the syringe with water. "When Hope's fled the diggings, your boss finds her here. Afterward, I write things down."

6

The rescue relays were still searching for victims at Tears of Joy. Chains had been run around a boulder, and as a mule pulled the boulder clear, a man's body appeared amid the debris. It was Zack, his back crushed, face and hands blackened. He was conscious, but he seemed unaware that men were trying to save him. He saw only the bright points of Hope's eyes through his narrowed slits. A rapturous moan passed through his lips. His mind echoed a line—"I'll be your bride"—while the song it came from died in his ears. Far beneath the collapse, the thread of Hope's voice was winding away, receding into the depths of the mountain.

Zack jerked up and thrust the rabbit blanket aside, shaking his head to rid it of the nightmare. He measured the light coming through the canvas.

The tent flap lifted and Bob's head appeared. "Yap at this." He tossed a hunk of dried salmon to Zack.

Zack held the salmon between his teeth and buttoned his shirt.

"They put a price on the damage," Bob said.

"Steep?"

"Thirty thousand bones," Bob replied.

"That's a year in the mine."

"Pretty close."

"I dreamt I was buried alive," Zack said.

Bob ducked through the opening and knelt beside him. "I dreamt I was back in the ring."

Zack pulled his boots on.

"That's what I get for bunking with a pug." Bob jerked his right up to protect his face and sent his left at Zack's jaw, stopping short of impact.

Zack regarded him over the frozen fist.

"His arm's covered with blood," Bob said. "My blood. But I'm not going down."

"Long fight?"

Bob sniffed, nudging his nose with his knuckle. "Fifty-eight rounds."

"When was this?"

"Couple of lives ago. Ever hear of Paddy Ryan? He was a giant."

Concentration molded Bob's face.

"For a while I was reading his moves. Then he started to surprise me. Those days, it was no gloves, fight to the finish. Round fifty-one, it begins to pour. The crowd runs for a barn, but we keep on. Soaked, sliding in the mud, teeth chattering.

That red arm coming at me." Bob laughed. "I took everything he gave. He made me the mutt I am."

"Barely roughed your bark."

"The shots went deep," Bob said. "I lost my nerve. That was the end of battling for the purse. After that I sold muscle by the pound."

"By the pound?"

"Collecting for shylocks," Bob said. "Twisting arms on election day. I had a wife. Sweetest apple on the tree. I was useless to her. When she left, I came west."

"To get rich."

"It wasn't like that," Bob said. "I was just jumping into a well, thinking it would be over. And then—Breakaway. And Hope."

"She's important to you."

"She's been my reason for living," Bob said. "We're pals now, so I'll tell you—"

Zack saw the strain in his eyes.

"I'm missing her more than most," Bob said. "These couple of months— We've lost Hope before, but the boss knew how to get her back. Maybe she's tired of him. Or us," he sighed.

"Losing your faith?"

"It's always been weak," Bob admitted. "I never expected Hope to hang around with an old, beat-up guy like me."

"You've been with her—how many times?"

"Ten. Seven of them in the Wheel."

"You've spun more than seven times."

"Oh sure. No one likes to say it, but the Blondes are spotty. Sometimes you can tell they're pretending. Sometimes it's her, but just barely. When she comes out of the quartz, in the diggings—that's the Hope that winds your clock."

"When was the last time you saw her?"

"'Bout a month ago. In the Wheel. Just a little of her."

"A little?"

"Sometimes Hope's inside the Blonde's body. It looks and feels like a woman, but you know it's not. Sometimes the Blonde turns to quartz—all glass and crystal, with spars and wings—like the angel that Salt Lick paints in her songs. There's the truer Hope, strung with real gold—the Hope in the diggings we all pray to see. And there's the Hope reserved for prophets and priests."

"The Private," Zack said.

"And Trevillian," Bob nodded.

"What do the Blondes say, about how it's done?"

"That's their secret," Bob replied. "Kate was the best. She passed of pneumonia. I was with her once when Hope took her over. All she would say was, 'I remove myself and Hope comes through.'"

"It takes a generous spirit," Bob observed.

"Sephy will play the part well," Zack said.

Bob was silent.

"You knew, didn't you," Zack said.

Bob turned and crawled out of the tent.

"She was in on Snell's stunt," Zack nodded as he rose beside him.

"Don't be a fool."

The slope was busy, miners emerging from their dwarfish abodes. "Time to bury the dead," Bob said. He led the way up the trail.

In the east, the sun was hidden by clouds. It began to drizzle. Down by the water, a horse-drawn wagon departed with the last of the barge's coal, bound for the bunkers beside the mill.

When they reached the corduroy road, two miners fell in beside them. One limped.

"Top of the morning," Bob greeted them.

"On the mend?" Zack said.

The man shook his head. "This leg's for keeps." There was pride in his voice.

"Prowler's work," the other said. "Len passed the test."

"Never lost Hope," Len told Zack. His smile revealed a broken incisor.

"She was pleased?"

"Mightily," Len smiled. "I was in the infirmary when they blasted the holes I drilled at Dazzle One. Hope was bigger than life. She stayed with us for a month."

"Someone should turn Prowler into a rug," Zack said.

The others laughed.

"You'd get my vote for that," Len nodded.

"He's thick with warts," Bob said, "from all the bullets he's taken."

"He'll drop sooner or later," Len waved his hand.

"When he does," his partner explained to Zack, "she'll just send us another. Hope told the boss that."

"We should have gone after him," Bob said, "that time with Len."

"Should have," Len's partner agreed.

"What happened?" Zack asked.

"Snow had just fallen," Len told him. "He would have been easy to track. We thought, ''Fore long, Prowler'll be in a hole 'neath some tree.' So we laid poison fish around the camp and killed some birds. Morning, Noel."

A man with turquoise eyes joined them. "For you, my heart," he saluted with his fist. His clipped orange hair stood straight up, as if he'd been shocked by electricity.

"Noel-the-Mole," Bob introduced him.

Zack shook his hand. "The champion," he said, remembering.

Noel smiled. "Just another tormented soul."

Zack heard the passion in his voice. Noel was a young man, but something had driven him quickly through life. "You want her, don't you."

"She's everything," Noel replied.

"You've been close to her. In the mine."

"As close as I am to you," Noel said.

"Where?"

"The first time was at Ardent. Half the headwall was quartz. I was spitting the rattails and—" Noel's hands sprang apart. "She busted out of the rock."

"Someone was with you."

Noel shook his head. "My shaker had left the drift."

"What did she look like?"

"She had wings that time," Noel said. "They were sparkling like the combs my mother used to wear. She folded them around me."

"Did she say anything?"

"I had to scramble," Noel said. "The charge was about to go off."

"What about Sublime? Who's seen her there?" Zack asked.

"I have," Len's partner spoke up. "Right after a blast. The boss helped me."

"Helped you?"

Len's partner smiled. "She wasn't an angel. She was a long spiral shell, like you'd find on the beach. I got sucked inside."

Zack regarded him. "I'll give you boys credit for a lot of imagination."

"You'll see what happens when Hope speaks to the boss," Noel promised.

"What happens?"

"Hope tells the boss where she'll be. We drill, and she's there." Noel looked at the others.

"That's the way it was," Len's partner nodded.

Len was silent.

"She'll be back," Noel insisted.

"Seen Webster lately?" Len asked him. "He won't leave his bedroll."

Bob glanced at Zack and raised his brows.

"He has to get through to her," Len said. "There's no time left."

"Faith and sacrifice," Noel said. "When the boss gave Hope his heart, he set us all an example."

"That he did," Len agreed.

"Cut it out himself," Bob winked at Zack. "With a straight razor."

"He does pretty well without it," Zack said.

"It's the truth," Noel said. "The cut was made." He drew his forefinger down his left pectoral.

"I've seen it," Len's partner nodded.

"It was at the Bastion," Noel said. "Hope had disappeared. He did it to bring her back."

"Good thing he didn't kill himself," Zack said. "He'd be with Hope now, and Streetcar and Carew would be stuck here with us."

Bob gave him a wary look.

"Don't mock him," Noel said. "Our boss is the only light in the tunnel. Of all the creatures on this miserable earth, we're the closest to paradise."

"You got a taste last night," Len grinned at Zack, "from what I hear."

They took the path that led to the supply store, but when they reached the fork, instead of heading to the right, up the hill, they continued on the level. To the left were the sawmill and carpenter's shop. Straight ahead was the gutting area, and beyond that the smokehouses.

The stench mounted. The air was busy with gulls, hovering and diving, fighting over the scraps. As they entered the gutting area, the earth turned sodden, puddled with viscera.

Three silvery hills rose before Zack, a hundred eyes staring from each. Men were backing away from wooden slabs, wiping the slime off their arms, setting aside knives and cleavers and removing their aprons. Kegs brimmed with glistening roe, ember-red. On the trail beyond, wheelbarrows piled with salmon were lined up, ready for the smoke.

Again the path forked. They headed down the hill. Beside the sawmill was an open structure with a plank roof that served as carpenter's shop. It was crowded with men, and as they approached, three coffins were raised. A loose procession formed, heading around the sawmill toward a bridge that crossed the river. Zack and his companions followed the cortege into the graveyard.

It was a protected spot hedged by thickets, tranquil and apart. On the slope above, red alders bent over the dead. Three pits had been dug, and the coffins were set down on sawhorses before them. The men of the camp collected among the grave markers. Dinesh and Pollard stood by one of the pits. Dinesh was staring into it, his arms folded across his chest, as if he expected to be interred himself.

Noel wanted to be in front, and Len and his partner went with him.

Zack and Bob hung back. The boss's lieutenants were behind the sawhorses.

"Over there." Bob pointed at a low rise.

The rise was riddled with holes—open graves. Trevillian stood among them, his back to the camp, lost in some reverie.

"The first that died last winter got buried," Bob said. "The rest we stacked behind the hoist house. With the ground frozen, it would've been four men working a month to put them under. In the spring, we dug homes for them." He nodded at the open graves, "Along with thirty spares."

"Thirty?" Zack said. "What about the rest of us?"

"Behind the hoist house?" Lucky turned to Bob. "Don't you people have noses?"

Lucky had donned his suit coat for the burial. It was tracked with mud.

"It takes a while here," Bob squinted at him, "for dead things to go bad."

Inky and Winiarski were approaching, and the Captain was right behind them.

"We heard—" Winiarski smiled at Lucky. "Zack was dancing on the wheel, naked as a worm."

"Tell Knox what you raked up," the Captain prompted Inky.

"Breakaway belongs to Florenzo Fugazi. Robber baron. They call him *The Fog*."

Zack glanced at Bob. The old fighter was amused.

"Fugazi owns the Bastion Mine. Trevillian was boss there," Inky continued. "When the miners ousted him, Fugazi sent him here."

"There's a blockhouse beside the store," the Captain looked upriver.

"The gold they mill from quartz is locked up there," Inky nodded.

"The Fog's made a killing," Lucky said smugly.

Bob burst out laughing. Lucky seemed not to notice.

"I've been mucking," Winiarski told Zack.

"They gave Streetcar a choice," Inky said. "Run trolleys or swing a sledge. He'd still be alive."

Zack thought of the good-natured man with the cap.

"Lloyd made a mess of him," the Captain said.

"It was terrible," Inky swallowed. "Until the end. Streetcar died with a smile. He thought she was with him." He looked from face to face.

There was a stir in the graveyard.

The Blondes had arrived. They were in black, with Salt Lick in front, wearing a cloak and a porkpie hat. The others were veiled, so it was hard to identify them. One paused to scan the crowd, fixed on Zack and continued forward. The women crossed the graveyard and took a position to the right of the three pits.

"Quiet," Lloyd shouted from behind the coffins.

Zack noticed DuVal beside the doctor. His head was bandaged.

Conversation had ceased, and Trevillian was making his way down the slope. He was geared for work, pick in his belt, the Reminder looped on his hip. He'd come from the diggings and looked ready to return as soon as the bodies were lowered. A brief ceremony, Zack thought. The camp, however, seemed to expect something more.

Inky led Winiarski toward one of the coffins and the Captain followed. Lucky wandered among the overgrown plots and collapsed with his back against a marker, facing the wrong way. The drizzle had ceased, but the leaden sky was descending as if it meant harm to the mourners.

Trevillian stopped behind the center pit. There was a thick roll of canvas on the ground beside him.

"Maybe it's the hour," the boss began. "Or these clouds." He looked at the sea. "I'm remembering a day, eleven years ago. At the Paymaster, in the Chocolate Mountains." He nodded to a man in front. "You know the place." He studied the coffins. "I stood in the boneyard, watching five men disappear into the earth for the last time. One of the handsorters had been a priest. He was starting the last rites when a miner beside me turned and whispered in my ear."

Trevillian inclined his head, as if listening. "'No man sees beyond the headwall.'" He rapped his knuckles on the center coffin. "For him, there was nothing more than this."

Zack glanced around. The men watched the boss closely.

"It was ice down my collar," the mine boss said. "I had no Hope yet, and his error wasn't clear to me. The eyes can't see beyond—but a wall may have glass for a deeper faculty to peer into. Stars and threads, reflecting light from a hidden source." He shook his head. "I was blind. Like our poor brothers," he gestured toward the river, "I was another fool fish, beating myself to nothing."

He scanned the assembly. "We're going to die. Today or tomorrow. We're already pierced, bleeding. In a few hours—just a few—we'll be limp and motionless. We're men, wanting to be more. Pitiful flesh, barely risen from the earth and churned right back into it."

One of the Blondes fell to her knees. Another lifted her hands, and the women on either side of her clasped them. Some of the miners bowed their heads.

"Condemned," Trevillian thundered. He turned, taking in everyone with his steely gaze. "Time is eating you alive. Who among you is willing to shoulder the blame?" He faced the coffins. "Their retreating dreams, the misery they endured—" His head shifted oddly, tics punctuating his words. "The earth loaded on their backs was a mountain of shame. It would have broken them . . . without Hope."

Hope. Hope. Her name rumbled through the graveyard.

Trevillian turned to the coffin on the left. "Russ McGee." His voice was heavy with homage.

Men clenched their fists before their chests. The woman on her knees began to sob.

"Russ had his moments with her."

The sobbing woman clawed her hair.

"And in those moments," Trevillian said, "he felt her perfection. He was included in that fearless embrace. He saw the light which does not fade.

"Life's dearest triumph," Trevillian spoke to the dead man. "You forced your unworthy flesh, your blood and bones, toward something of consummate power and grace." The boss paused, ducking his head as if trying to compose himself. Then he turned to the coffin on the right. "And the man we called Streetcar? Did he find Hope in his final hour? He spoke her name with his last breath. I believe he knew: that's what's out there, beyond the fire zone." The mine boss spread his arms, taking in the two men. "They died gasping for Hope, feeling their desire welling out of their chests—departing as their senses dimmed. Those furious hearts." His voice trembled with emotion. "Their bodies are in these boxes— The passion that knew Hope has another home."

One of the Blondes had begun to sing. Not something designed for the memorial, but a spontaneous outburst, a wordless yearning.

"And what of my Carew?" Trevillian shouted. "Sniveling drifter to the end?" He glared with outrage at the center coffin as he drew the pick from his belt. "Still the doubter?" he stormed at the dead man, swinging his pick back. "Speak to us! Speak!" He buried the pick in the coffin's corner and wrenched mightily. "What are you now but guts and mud?" As the lid shrieked back, Trevillian caught the coffin's head with his hand and heaved it upright.

Zack was choked with horror. Purplish organs and raveled entrails slid to the foot of the box, mixed with rags and clods of dirt—Carew's remains, jumbled and disarticulated, already rotting. The rest of the camp shrank as well, filled with mindless dread as the box tipped on its side and crashed to the ground, spilling its contents into the grave pit.

"My brothers," Trevillian regaled them, "she's brought him back!"

Owen and Snell had unrolled the canvas. It was Carew, rising to his feet between them, one leg splinted, chest bandaged, alive and smiling. He turned to the mine boss, and at the sight of his face Trevillian shook from head to toe. His eyes brimmed, he embraced Carew and began to weep.

Zack shivered, feeling a reflexive elation. "Quite a trick," he muttered without looking at Bob. The graveyard was full of laughter and sighs. The restoration had been staged, but Trevillian's emotion seemed real. Everyone knew how desperately he'd worked to save Carew. And Carew was alive.

"Excuse the clumsy theatrics," Trevillian turned to the camp, laughing through his tears. "Now that Zack is here, I'll get some schooling."

Faces turned. Zack smiled, sharing the joke.

Trevillian regarded Carew lovingly. "You who were with me saw him, broken and unconscious. We carried him down the hill, never suspecting." He glanced at Lloyd.

"His ticker had stopped," Lloyd explained.

The mine boss nodded at Carew. "Tell them."

Carew drank from his eyes, then grabbed the boss's arm to steady himself. "She came to me," he said in an uneven rasp. "When I was buried." He scanned them like people he'd known in a former life. The wild knowledge in his face held the camp rapt.

"My chest is a leaky boiler," Carew remembered, "hissing and shaking. The last steam escapes. Everything's black. I pull a breath, but— I can't pull another." He turned his ear. "Then—" He closed his eyes. "I heard her," Carew said softly.

The Blondes were silent, and so were the men.

"Hope," Carew whispered, reliving his state. "She's near. She can hear my heart. She's right over me, listening to it." His jaw trembled. "It's all I have left."

173

Zack saw the joy in Trevillian's face twisting strangely.

"I gave Hope my heart—" Carew's voice broke, recalling that devastating moment. "She still has it," he said. He looked at Trevillian.

The boss nodded and glanced at Owen.

"Hold her dear!" Owen shouted. And a hundred voices answered, "Hold her dear!"

The cry filled the narrow valley.

"There's more," Trevillian said solemnly. "More good news to share. Hope is speaking to me. She's been in my dreams all the past week."

A wave of relief swept through the crowd. Men patted and hugged each other.

"Your devotion has softened her," Trevillian told them, "and the brave pledge of Carew has warmed her ice. As always," he raised his arms, "there are things she wants. Things she says she must have."

Zack saw the sober looks.

"But—" The boss smiled with confidence. "She's coming back to us. All who are bound to Hope—" Trevillian held his hand level before his gaze, then lowered it.

The camp fell to its knees.

Zack saw Bob hesitate, then descend beside him. The doubters stood staring at each other—a couple of dozen men, including many of Zack's bargemates. Lloyd and the smith, Pollard, remained standing, and so did Dinesh and the Captain. But Arnie was on his knees, along with Winiarski. When Zack turned back to Trevillian, the boss was staring at him. Zack could feel the man's power pulling him down. But he chose to defy him.

The boss sank, kneeling with the faithful.

"We are far from home," Trevillian said. "The world is nothing and the flesh is less. Give Hope your heart."

"Give Hope your heart," the camp chorused.

"You shall not preserve your pride," the boss said.

"Give Hope your heart," the camp repeated.

"You shall not preserve your property."

"Give Hope your heart."

"Only she survives. All but Hope, I abhor."

"Give Hope your heart," the believers shouted.

Trevillian's head shook. "Speak to me!"

The Blondes began to hum, and Salt Lick's voice rose over them, reciting. "The journey's over. You stand on the threshold." She stepped forward. "The lamp is lit. Your beloved lies within." She removed her hat. "Through the wheeze of your fading wind, you hear me sighing. What deep and twisted workings these have been.

"Your back is hunched. You're cut and bleeding. There's little left but longing. That's the cost. So many dark and dead-end tunnels. But—" She caught her breath. There were tears streaming down her cheeks. "You found your way to the one you thought you'd lost."

"Take it," Trevillian implored.

As Salt Lick stepped back among the Blondes, the mine boss clenched his fist over his sternum. "It's yours," he sobbed, bringing his fist forward. A few words followed, choked and indecipherable. Then a freakish sound came from his throat. It was like a young boy laughing.

Zack shuddered. The assembly was perfectly quiet.

Trevillian rose slowly and turned with an abstracted look, as if waking from a dream. The believers stood. The mine boss motioned to Owen and DuVal. They bent on either side of the coffin on the left and grabbed the ropes beneath it.

"Wish us well," Trevillian said to the corpse in the box. "She'll weigh herself out as she judges—till our flesh falls like tailings, and our love, like yours, is proven pure and welcomed into that blessed place."

The two men lifted the ropes, bearing the coffin off the sawhorse and over the rim of the pit. Snell and another were doing the same thing with the coffin on the right.

"Cradle them down," Trevillian said.

In front of Streetcar's grave, Inky stood between Winiarski and Dinesh, scribbling on a piece of paper. Men welcomed Carew back, turning from the burial site to face the camp. The Blondes moved through the damp grasses, returning the way they had come. Zack saw Salt Lick leave her retinue and make her way toward Trevillian.

"That's why he's boss," Bob said.

Zack nodded. In the maze they'd drilled, a man was as easily crushed as a mayfly. Who could persist without Hope or something like her?

Dinesh scowled as he passed. "He's leading us to slaughter. *That's* the shame."

The mine boss turned to confer with the madam. Zack spotted Sephy. She was wearing the same black dress he had seen in the Grooming Parlor. Stern, priestly—appropriate in a graveyard. He couldn't imagine her attired like the others. In an alcove, waiting for the wheel to stop.

"It's a miracle—" Salt Lick swept beside Zack and looped her arm through his. Her black gown circled his boots like a pool of tar. "Don't you agree?" Beneath the porkpie, her lime eyes glittered.

"Trill wants you," she said.

"Trill?"

She put a black-gloved hand over her mouth to mute her indiscretion. "Come along now." She urged him toward the grave pits and Trevillian.

Zack glanced at Bob, then nodded, letting her lead him to the boss. Despite the gravity of the occasion, she was wearing a revealing dress. The bodice was trimmed with ermine and her breasts swelled within, like overripe fruit ringed with mold.

"The flesh is cruel," Salt Lick said, still in the grip of Trevillian's sermon. "We must care for each other." She pulled his elbow against her corseted waist. "Splint the breaks, cleanse our wounds, bind the wreckage together."

She was speaking to him out of the intimacy they'd shared in her chamber.

"My nurse," he said. "You put me right."

"When she's back in the diggings," Salt Lick sighed, "it will lighten our load in the Wheel." Her brow furrowed.

"'Things she wants.' What could that be?" She smiled. "I'll bet it has something to do with you." She squeezed his arm. "You're her peach."

Men were shoveling dirt into the pits on either side. Owen was down in the vacant one, raising Carew's coffin into DuVal's arms. The boss was talking to Lloyd.

"Here's our man," Salt Lick announced.

DuVal picked a blister of sap from the coffin lid and placed it on his tongue. "Shoulda took my money when you had the chance," he sneered at Zack.

Lloyd swung around. "I was two hours sewing your skull."

Zack stared at DuVal. "You left his brains on the table."

DuVal erupted, but before he could round the pit, the shovelers grabbed him. "Two-bit high horse," he seethed.

Trevillian pulled the whip from his belt loop.

"I'll be looking in on you," DuVal told Zack.

Trevillian whirled, bludgeoning DuVal's brow with the whip handle. The goon doubled over, holding his head in his hands. The boss turned to Zack, lowering the Reminder, forefinger hooking its coils. Zack felt Salt Lick let go of his arm.

"You've got a new assignment," the boss said.

"This morning?"

Trevillian nodded. "I'll take you there myself."

"Hope wants me," Zack guessed.

"That's what she says," Trevillian smiled. "I'm going to serve you to her and see what she swallows."

Zack laughed. "With any luck, she'll settle for an organ. You can show me how it's done."

The words registered on Trevillian. His eyes blazed and his arm swung around. The coil struck Zack in the face, and his legs gave beneath him.

"Make light of that again," Trevillian raged, "and I'll cut out your tongue."

A siren mounted in Zack's head. He put his hand to his right ear. He could feel a thick bug crawling out of it. People were helping him up—a shoveler on one side, Salt Lick on the other. She eyed Trevillian with distress.

"Was that necessary?" Lloyd glared at the boss.

Zack looked at his hand. It was covered with blood. He noticed Bob a few yards away. Most of the camp had stopped to watch.

"A test," Trevillian said quietly.

Salt Lick faced Lloyd. "You need to tend to this." She glanced at Zack's ear.

"I'll get my tinctures," Lloyd nodded. "Have Bob wash it and try to stop the bleeding," he told Zack. "I'll see you in your tent." Then to Trevillian, "Hope can wait."

Zack turned and retraced his steps toward Bob. The old pug lifted his fist and nudged his nose with his knuckle. His look was ugly. He might have been staring at Paddy Ryan's red arm.

7

It was an hour past dawn and the night shift had ended. Zack was splitting wood before the pup, jacket buttoned against the cold. His ear was bandaged.

Five days had passed since the resurrection of Carew. After Lloyd treated his wound, Zack was given the shift off. Following that, he'd worked as a driller at Vouchsafe. He saw Trevillian in the yard or the workings, but the boss didn't speak to him. There were no signs of Hope's reappearance in the diggings. Zack tried not to think about Sephy, and he kept away from the Big Wheel. The men knew better than to talk about her in his presence.

He heard bootsteps on the path, and when he looked up he saw Bob returning from the night shift.

"Hope?"

Bob sat on the woodpile and shook his head. "You?"

"Not a thing."

"Trevillian's out of tricks," a voice razzed.

A man with a handlebar mustache and a broom of peppered hair stepped toward them. Zack didn't know him.

"Marcus Bunting," Bob introduced the man. "The knee that never bends."

Bunting's coat was in rags, his pants patched with sacking and pieces of fur. He cocked his head at Zack. "Standing with the doubters in the graveyard. Stood on the wheel and shot the witch's hat off. Tried to stand up to the boss the day you landed, but that didn't go so well." His eyes narrowed. "How's the ear?"

"Still mucking Slick Liver?" Bob said.

Bunting nodded. "Till there's something worse."

"What you got there?" Bob asked.

Bunting raised his arm. Hanging from a short piece of twine was a thirty-inch salmon. It had a stick through its gills and was motionless. Its jaws were open and the long canines gleamed like penny nails.

"Breakfast," Marcus swung the fish toward Zack. "You won't have to pay Trevillian. I caught him myself."

"Thanks," Zack said. The black eye of the fish glared at him.

"He's a scuffler," Marcus admired his catch.

"Look at that build," Bob agreed. He touched the fish's tail.

The salmon convulsed, jerking wildly, fangs reaching for Zack. He seemed unaware he was tearing out his own gills.

"It would take a fellow like this to bring Trevillian down," Marcus nodded at the fish. He drew a knife from the sheath on his rump and sliced into the salmon's back. A strip of red flesh curled up. When he raised it toward Zack, it twitched between his thumb and forefinger like a hungry leech.

Marcus looked at Bob. "They're fools, but if the right man stood up to him, they'd come along. Isn't that right."

"Could be," Bob answered. "If Zack will oblige me, I'll help myself to this troublemaker. Too pooped to drag myself to the yard."

"You don't believe," Zack said.

Marcus feigned shock. "Hope? I'm flying her banner." He smirked at Bob. "There's no gold left, Knox. No cause for anyone to believe. I know. When a stiff reaches his limit, he comes gabbing to me. These men that are dying— He's going to answer for it." Bunting's iron mustache lifted over a yellowed fang. "The big finger's going to point at *him*."

The salmon was gripped by fresh spasms.

"Relax," Bob told the fish. "You're bunking with me," he patted his belly, "and I'm a good man." He took the salmon from Marcus.

"Why didn't you leave here when you had the chance?" Zack asked.

"There's a score to settle." Bunting drew his weathered face closer. "I'm going to skin Trevillian. I'm going to grill him and eat him. And when I'm done, I'm going to grind up his bones and brush my teeth with him."

"Alright," Bob said. "That'll do."

Bunting stepped back, his eyes on Zack. "You boys have a good day." He turned and retreated along the trail.

Bob laid the salmon on the woodpile. He grabbed his hand axe to put it out of its misery, then realized the fish was finished and set the axe aside. Through a rift in the mist, the sun struck its limp body.

"He's ready for a scrap," Zack said.

"You want trouble, Marcus can get it for you." Bob turned to the tent. "I invited him to drop by." He stepped out of his boots, threw back the flap and crawled inside.

Zack entered behind him. "What was that about—'flying her banner'?"

Bob rubbed his neck. "Marcus was the last fellow to get a slap on the back. 'Changing his colors'—that's what the boss called it. Gave him more stripes than Old Glory."

"The whipping wall," Zack said.

Bob glanced at him, grasped the pallet Zack slept on, folded it over and lifted the hemlock boughs.

There were umber stains on the tent floor.

"That's his blood," Bob said. "I dragged him here when it was over. Took him three days to recognize me."

Zack imagined Bunting lying there.

"He was hanging from the chains, naked, shouting over his shoulder. Never stopped cussing the boss." Bob's eyes clouded. "It was freezing and the cuts were steaming. Trevillian would have killed him if Lloyd hadn't checked his wounds. Gave the boss time to calm down."

"What were the men doing?"

"Watching."

"How could you let—"

"Marcus didn't belong in the ring with the boss," Bob shook his head. "And I was part of the struggle."

"For Hope—"

Bob nodded. "It was her we were dying for. She seemed worth it. When I was close to Hope, I was more than a used-up pug." He peered at Zack. "Marcus is right. Last night, one of the early boys went to pieces. Ten hours mucking without a sign of her, and the poor fellow just curled up. Crying like an infant. We had to carry him to the skip."

"Your fists are hardening," Zack said.

"They are," Bob replied. "When Hope was with him, it was different. Now, I hate what he's doing to us."

"We can topple him," Zack said. "Bunting. Some of your tribe. Some of my pals from the barge."

"He'll put up a fight."

"We'd need weapons," Zack said.

"Every stiff has one," Bob shrugged. "To chop wood."

A hand axe could rip a man's body open. Its blunt end could crush a man's skull.

"Are you ready for that?" Bob asked.

Zack didn't reply.

"You've got style," Bob observed. "The energy of youth. And you know what everyone's thinking," he smiled.

Zack returned the smile. "My volunteers were plants. My assistants signaled me."

"What about the *Secret Chamber*?"

"The chamber was marked," Zack said. "We scraped the nap off so I could see through my blindfold."

"They wanted to believe it was real," Bob said. "This crowd isn't any different."

"We'd need firepower," Zack said.

Bob slid his arm beneath the bedding, drew out a tarnished revolver and handed it over. "It's a mongrel, like you."

Zack weighed the gun and sighted along the barrel.

"No lack of guns in the camp," Bob told him.

"Where do you get bullets?"

"You don't. I fired my last round at Prowler when he busted Len up."

"The BMC has arms—"

Bob nodded. "Heavy artillery."

The mongrel was single-action, overly large with a molasses butt. Zack clasped the thick handgrip and inserted his forefinger in the trigger guard, taking the gun's balance.

"Flip her over a few times," Bob said. He pushed Zack toward the tent opening, and the two men rose outside the pup.

"Go ahead—" Bob motioned. "Flip her over."

Zack jerked his hand up, twirled the revolver backward twice and twice forward, lifting it from his hip to his chin and sending it cartwheeling into the air. As it descended, his finger caught the trigger guard. Another pair of twirls, then the crook of Zack's thumb cocked the hammer and the butt slapped against his palm.

He shifted the barrel to an invisible adversary and squeezed the trigger. The *click* sounded in the quiet.

"Don't think I won't," Zack said.

"Won't what?"

Trevillian's voice startled them. When Zack turned, he saw the boss twenty feet away, at the bend in the footpath, watching.

"I've been known to react suspiciously in situations like this." Trevillian looked from Bob to the mongrel as he approached.

Zack passed the gun back to Bob. His hand was trembling.

The boss stopped before them, regarding Zack soberly.

"I'm going to cook my friend." Bob faced the salmon.

"I'm going to see if Zack can change our luck," the boss said.

Trevillian led the way through the tent camp, up the corduroy road and into the yard. The men were lining up for breakfast. Zack felt their eyes on him. He followed the boss up the outside stair of the supply store.

"You're angry, I know," Trevillian said over his shoulder. "I shouldn't have struck you." He reached the landing. "I'm sorry I did that."

He opened the door and motioned Zack inside.

The mining office was ringed with desks and drafting boards. Ore samples, instruments and sheaves of paper covered the table tops. There was a large sectional map on the wall opposite. Noises came from behind a shoulder-high bookcase to the left—the clink of metal tools and the purr of a furnace.

"Sit here," the boss said.

Zack sat.

One of the Bangshu stepped through the outside door. He set a plate loaded with breakfast on the table before Zack. Lloyd, wearing an apron and padded gloves, emerged from behind the bookcase. He spoke to the cook in an Asian tongue, replaced his goggles and returned to his work.

"You know how the vein was found," Trevillian said. "Go ahead—dig in. The Private was just a nipper, but Hope opened her robe."

Zack bit into a salmon cake.

Trevillian stepped over to a bank of shelves beside a rack of rifles and shotguns and came away with a wooden tray. "The Private had his moment. Then she put Prowler on him." The tray was heavy enough that he had to hold both arms beneath it. "Did he pass the test? Only Hope knows."

The boss set the tray on the desk. It was loaded with rock fragments of various shapes and sizes, a number of them quartz.

"He was our prophet," Trevillian said. "But he didn't have long with her, and he just kissed her toes." Trevillian lifted an oblong sample. "I've gone deep beside her, felt her body with a hundred hands. That's a piece of her." He passed the rock to Zack.

It was like a prehistoric club, banded and heavy. As Zack raised it, light from the window shone through. The bands were translucent, webbed with facets and massed with tiny gold leaves—hives of lanterns, each with a petrified flame.

"Stand up," the boss said.

188

Zack stood. Trevillian grasped his shoulder and turned him, and the flashes from the crystals lit the underside of Zack's wrist. The bright pattern seemed to have a life of its own. As he turned, the pattern moved along his arm, onto his chest.

"From Moonblood," Trevillian said. "She was there for three weeks. All as precious as this and shoulder-high."

The boss took the club from him, twisting it slowly, six inches from Zack's face.

The golden leaves rayed needles. They stung his eyes and pricked his cheeks; they danced around the room, starring wood and glass, leaping from edges and pointing corners. For a moment, he was the Private standing beside the vein.

"So that you know," Trevillian whispered in his ear.

The familiarity startled Zack. He could feel the boss's breath on his cheek.

"Picture the quartz body this came from." The boss drew away, pointing and stepping toward the map on the wall. "She ran through those stopes."

The mine cutaway looked like the work of an ant colony. Above, the tunnels intersected big rooms where the vein had been removed. Zack could see how the rooms angled into the mountain as it was mined, and where they vanished below the level labeled *490*. Drifts frayed and fanned into manways around the empty stopes.

"She's in the mountain somewhere," Zack said.

Trevillian nodded. "Maybe here," his hand swept into the unexplored region east of the digging. "Or down here," his hand slid toward the bottom of the map.

"You're showing me this for a reason," Zack said.

"What I do," the boss answered without turning, "I do because of her." He glanced at Zack's breakfast. "Finish your grub. Lloyd will take another look at you. After that, meet me on the 490 landing."

Trevillian grabbed his coat and exited the office.

A moment later, Lloyd appeared around the divider, carrying something that looked like a muffin tray. In each cup was a pale cube, the size of a child's alphabet block. He set the tray down and removed his padded gloves and apron.

"Still painful?"

"Not bad," Zack said.

Lloyd retrieved a bottle of tincture from his medicine cabinet. "Face the light." He removed Zack's bandage and inspected the wound. "It's coming along."

Lloyd bound a pencil end with a scrap of cloth and sprinkled fluid onto it. "Just luck," he muttered as he dabbed the wound. "He could have deafened you." His anger was unconcealed.

"You speak your mind," Zack said.

"Our relationship precedes Hope. I was at the Bastion."

"With Salt Lick."

"Francine," Lloyd corrected him. "He should have married her. I wouldn't be treating injuries like this." He paused, inspected his work and put the stopper back in the bottle. "There's another faith here, if you're interested. Talk to the cooks."

"You don't believe."

"No, I don't. When things are going well, I enjoy the pursuit. But now—" He gestured at the ore samples and the map as if they were relics from a barbaric past. "It's obvious that all this *wanting* is a disease. That's what keeps the stamp wheels turning. That's the engine of our misery. Wanting something outside ourselves, beyond our reach."

He met Zack's gaze. "There's a cure for our ailment." Lloyd looked down at the muffin tray. "He knows it's coming. You see this?"

He lifted one of the white blocks from the tray. There was a depression in its top, and in the depression was a dark residue. "Nothing but dust." Lloyd nodded at the others. "The gold's gone."

"I'm surprised you're telling me this."

"Trevillian has no gripe with me voicing my opinions. It doesn't take an assay to see that Hope's disappeared."

When Zack stepped from the skip onto the 490 landing, the boss was waiting. A dozen miners saw Trevillian greet him and motion him toward the level tunnel. Their surprise was palpable.

"I've never taken a stiff on my morning inspection," Trevillian said.

Zack heard the edge in his voice.

"There's a risk in doing that," the boss said.

Zack was silent. The risk he could imagine, but the reason he could not.

Trevillian led the way along the 490 until they reached Outside Chance, a drift that angled to the left at the level's end. Owen met them at the entrance and the three proceeded to the headwall, where the blast from the previous shift had deposited a load of rock onto a mucking sheet. As they approached, the muckers raised their shovels and stood aside. Trevillian stepped forward, talking to himself as he surveyed the broken rock. Then he swung his lantern up to the freshly cut wall. Zack saw the dark eyes searching.

There weren't any traces of Hope on the wall, but as Trevillian's lantern rose, Zack saw a strand of quartz in the ceiling. It was thin as a fuse, and it pinched to nothing two feet from the drift head.

Trevillian had backed away from the face and was eyeing the strand. "What are you doing?" he muttered. He turned to Owen. "She's somewhere beyond Ardent. We'll find her with Breastwork. Between there and Milky Way—she's got no place to hide." He thought for a moment. "We shouldn't have pulled out of Dazzle One. She flattened to nothing and we passed right through her." He smirked, admiring Hope's cunning. "Take the team from Snuff o' Kate and get back in there. Twenty paces behind the head—start running crosscuts."

"And here?" Owen asked.

"Keep on. North and ten degrees east—" Trevillian gestured at the face as if he had a grudge against it.

"She's shunning us," one man said.

Trevillian faced him. Zack braced himself.

"That's her way," the boss replied. He scanned the faces, giving them a look at his desolation, making the fist over his heart. He brought the fist forward, but instead of offering it, he clenched his jaw and shook it with a vicious look. "When you find her, we'll make her remember what it was to be pleased by us."

The grimy faces nodded. One smiled.

"Lift those loving arms," Trevillian said to a big man with a sledge, motioning the group back onto the mucking sheet as he stepped aside.

"Four rounds on that bearing," Trevillian told Owen.

"North, bending east," Owen said.

The men with D-scoops resumed their shoveling. The big man secured his stance by one of the boulders, grabbed his sledge at each end and raised it over his head. His trunk buckled and the sledge arced through the candlelight, striking the boulder, cracking it like a clay pot.

The boss put his hand on the man's loins. "Break your back for her."

He motioned to Zack and they headed for the drift mouth with Owen behind.

They returned along the 490 till they reached the entrance to Sublime. The tunnel rose into the rock. Zack followed the boss, climbing a wooden footway beside the tram rails. Caves and cloisters opened on either side. Sounds echoed from the shadowy recesses—the hum of a blower, a trickle of water, the throb of hammer blows like a hidden pulse. It was nothing like the Sublime he'd imagined in Salt Lick's boudoir.

They crossed a small chamber and entered a horizontal drift at its rear. When they reached the drift head, the boss greeted the miners. "What have you seen?"

"A bit of her hair," a short man said.

"Charley—" The boss opened his arms. The short man grinned as Trevillian embraced him. "There she is." The mine boss knelt before the headwall. Owen drew beside him, ready for orders, while the others watched. Trevillian studied the rock in the light of his lantern and gestured to Zack.

Zack approached, dropping to his knees beside the boss. He saw a translucent thread. It ran for twenty inches and dove back into the rock. Trevillian pulled the pick from his belt, slid his wrist through the thong and swung it, grabbing the handle just before it struck. A fragment cracked loose. He caught it with his free hand and lifted it to his mouth, running his tongue over it as he drew a magnifying glass from his shirt pocket.

Trevillian examined the fragment, then passed the magnifier to Zack. Under the lens, the thread was beaded and glittering, like spider silk dotted with dew.

The boss gave drilling instructions, then they strode back down the corridor.

"What does the hair tell you?" Zack asked.

Trevillian shook his head. "Signs, my friend. Some false, some true. Hope is a puzzle with many pieces. You're seeing a few."

The next stop was Dazzle Two. Muck was being loaded into a car while a pair of miners double-jacked the wall. The shaker knelt, holding the steel with both fists. The man standing swung a long-handled sledge, nostrils sucking, senses keyed on the drill's end. *Clang, clang, clang.*

"Hold up," a mucker shouted as Trevillian began picking through the blast fragments.

"Nothing," the boss grumbled. Then he snarled, "What's this?" He pointed at a wing of rock jutting from the side wall, sweeping the group as he straightened, eyes gleaming with contempt. "You'd think we could manage a clean cut." He faced the mucker at his elbow. "Something to say?" Trevillian's right arm hovered over the Reminder.

"No sir."

Zack watched the others. Some were with the boss, taking the blame on themselves. And some weren't.

"Straighten them out," Trevillian fumed at Owen. He turned on his heel and stomped back down the drift.

Zack fell in beside him.

"A hint—" Trevillian shook his head angrily. "That's all I need. It's not indifference—she enjoys my distress."

His voice echoed down the corridor.

"I want her all the same," the boss said. "All the more."

Their boots crunched the gravel.

"That was stupid," the boss muttered.

He was talking about his outburst.

"It's my nature to bristle at failure." Trevillian spit. "She's left us hanging before. But that doesn't help." His eyes met

Zack's. "You're never prepared when a streak ends. Everything seems desperate." He tried to smile. "It's a heavy load, being Hope's anointed."

This wasn't the same man, Zack thought, who'd shown him a piece of Hope's glory in the mining office an hour before.

"Doubt is contagious," Trevillian said.

"Lloyd surprised me—"

"He's the worst."

The boss read his confusion.

"There's no faith without temptation," Trevillian said. "Lloyd's a subtle tempter—a kindly one—but he serves the purpose." The power bled from his features. He seemed suddenly younger, vulnerable. "To escape from desire is to withdraw from life. Their doubt doesn't touch me, Zack. But—" He faced forward. "Sometimes a man wants a mirror to talk into."

They visited Ardent, Slick Liver, Wondrous and Moonblood. Each had empty rooms where Hope had been mined, and each had an exploratory drift. But there wasn't a thread of quartz in any of them. What was Trevillian's purpose in showing him the diggings? The question remained on Zack's tongue, but the boss was in a hurry, and there seemed no occasion until they exited Moonblood.

They stepped along the level in silence. On the left, a

pair of iron air pipes ran waist high, quivering in the halos of candlelight.

Zack drew a breath. "Why—"

"You should have had it out with him," Trevillian said. Zack gave him a blank look.

"Charles Knox," the boss said.

Zack's hesitation put some distance between them. "I missed my chance."

"Chance?"

"We were only face to face once."

Trevillian waited.

Zack stared at his boots. "I wasn't supposed to know. Once I was in college it was plain. Private tutors, equestrianism— The Home didn't have that kind of money. Finally they told me the truth and I went to see him."

"And?"

"He said he'd done what he could to make amends." Zack saw Charles Knox standing behind an oversized desk in his smoking jacket. Watching his teenage son trembling, struggling for words. Trophy heads lined the walls of the study. "'I have a brother and sister,' I said. 'In this house.' 'I'm sorry, but you don't,' he said.

"A week later I came again, but they refused to admit me. His wife handed me my mother's death certificate in a sealed envelope."

The sounds of Trevillian's boots reached him, splashing through a puddle. It was easy to imagine being led into a dream world down here—seeing things in the shadows, listening to the echoes of your breath.

"I tracked down the man who signed it," Zack said. "I learned about what had happened from him."

"He killed her," Trevillian said.

"In a way, he did."

"To hide the affair."

"I was—" Zack stopped himself.

"Afraid to confront him," Trevillian said.

Zack held his tongue. The boss was nosing through him like a worm in an apple.

"And after that?" the boss asked.

"I left school and headed west."

"A man who hates his father—really hates him—doesn't have any rails to run on." Trevillian spoke slowly. "He has to set them down himself."

Bells jingled—an eerie sound, mounting as they rounded a bend. Zack saw a mule and a man alongside holding a lantern. The tracks gleamed before them. The mule pulled a pair of ore cars.

"They never see daylight," Zack said.

"Not unless there's a good reason," Trevillian replied.

They passed the trammer and continued to the shaft station. The loading platform was empty. Trevillian stepped across it, grabbed the signal wire and tugged.

Moments passed. Then from the bowels of the mountain a low moan rose. The sound of the skip was like something from beyond the grave.

An empty car emerged from the darkness, creeping up the track toward them. It slowed with ghostly cognition and squealed to a halt beside the platform. They boarded it and seated themselves, and Trevillian yanked the wire. Four bells for the level, a pause, and one to rise. There was no sense of a human agent—the skip yelped and growled and began to climb. The lanterns ticked past. Ore was being emptied somewhere above, and its rasping echoed in the dark throat.

"What draws your attention to Francine?" the boss said.

"She's a handsome woman," Zack ventured. "My charms haven't worked. She wants a year's wages for that mirror."

"What nonsense. Who needs to look at himself when he's drinking?"

"You don't mind that I—"

"No," Trevillian answered. "We have a friendship, but she's for the men, like all the Blondes. If you have the bones."

Zack laughed. "You don't expect me to go a year without—"

"No, of course not. But—" The boss seemed to consider his words. "Appreciate their purpose—Francine and Sephy, and the rest of them." He spoke in a tone of renunciation. "I was a hound for frails when I was younger. I finally realized that it was *her* I was looking for." He paused. "That's what makes Casanova fickle. He dreams of finding Hope's perfection in a human form."

The 400 station came into view. The car prattled to a crawl and stopped.

Trevillian stood, stepped onto the platform and crossed it. Zack came up beside him, and they walked shoulder to shoulder along the level. The drift leading to White Mint Stope appeared on the left. After ten yards, another corridor opened to the right, and then two more farther along. The passages were black and quiet.

"My first meeting with Hope," Trevillian said, "was in the Bastion. I'd been a boss for three years. A difficult time of life." He spoke as if to himself. "I was confused. And I was dead on my feet with the influenza."

The air of intimacy put Zack on edge.

"Things were going well. At the bottom of the diggings, we found a quartz body two feet thick. There were golden branches winding through it, with fat buds. For a week, I worked and woke in a fever, steaming with pride at every blast. Then Fugazi showed up. The man I most—and least—wanted to see. My report was outrageous—boastful, jealous. I wanted his praise, but I wanted the triumph for myself."

The mine boss paused to look at Zack.

"Halfway through it, he raised his gloves. 'Hear, hear!' He was laughing at me. 'Give it your best.' And he left."

Trevillian stared down the level. "I stumbled away, shame-faced, cursing him. Down I went, seeking comfort from the only thing I knew—my diggings. My diggings! And then the truth struck me. The diggings weren't mine, and neither were my dreams of wealth. It was all a dark labyrinth with Fugazi at the center.

"I rode to the bottom and staggered along the drift, groaning over my pathetic delusions. It wasn't till I saw the eyes of the rattails that I realized I'd walked past the firing team. They were screaming at me when the blast went off."

Trevillian smiled. "My despair drew her. I'd recognized my poverty—" His fingertips tapped his left pectoral. "In an instant, she was all around me. All I could see was this shattering curl, a breaking wave with a million facets all slick and sliding—and inside each crystal, a golden taper that quivered and flashed as if it knew me.

"I was guiltless. The time of judgment and execution was over. Hope had been waiting. I was the man she meant to save."

"The blast changed you," Zack said.

"Utterly." There was rapture in Trevillian's eyes. "She took me into her perfection. The wave broke and her body coiled around me. Many strands, many limbs— Or perhaps just one, thick and close. I could hear her whisper in both my ears, and then it came from inside me. And where my ribs were—" His hand touched his front. "I could see crystals drawing apart like teeth. There was a space for her, like a druse. And inside this space, Hope made a home, her light growing whiter and whiter, pulsing like my poor heart never had—"

Trevillian halted, watching Zack for his reaction.

"It's a mystic's vision, from the Middle Ages."

"Perhaps it was her they saw," the boss nodded. "Perhaps it was Hope who transfigured Christ."

He scanned the walls, remembering. "Through her milky pulse, I could see the drift. It had changed. Everything was fresh and new—the rock was alive with color, the fumes braced you to breathe them. And then I could see *through* the walls—countless crystals, like drifting motes. The rock—the world I had known, that had seemed so substantial—was nothing but mist in a mineral night.

"A strange thought came to me. I imagined I was a Pharaoh's son. I had died when I was young and been entombed as a mummy. I was returning— My windings were gone and I could see. It was paradise I had awoken to."

A drumroll of boots sounded behind them, and a miner passed carrying a bundle of drill steels.

"And in this paradise," the boss said, "I was twelve again, shaking and gasping."

Zack saw a secret surfacing in Trevillian's eyes.

"When they dragged me to safety—" The boss raised his brows. "My pants were a mess. There was too much gold. Too much light."

"Why are you telling me this?" Zack asked.

"Hope wants you to know," Trevillian said. "You're special to her. Special!"

Zack saw the venom in his eyes.

A lantern appeared ahead. Around it, shadows shifted. They were approaching an active drift.

"Reading minds," the boss said half to himself. "You may have reached out to her without even knowing it."

Men's voices surfaced through the dimness.

"Humility Shaft," Trevillian said.

On the left, Zack could see a large inclined tunnel with

rails running up it. The tunnel descended through the floor of the 400. As he watched, a loaded gravity tram roared down.

"This way."

Trevillian led him to the mouth of the tunnel and then up a crude stair hacked in the rock. At the top, the boss hailed two men on either side of a second tram. They were filling it from an ore cart, while the mule that had brought it relieved himself.

"Give Hope your heart," one of the men said. He raised his blackened fist to his chest and held it toward Trevillian.

"You're her favorite, Lew." The boss put the fist to his cheek.

Another drumroll of boots, and the man who'd hurried past reappeared without the steels. He saluted the boss and descended the stair.

At the top of Humility, the rails vanished. Trevillian led the way forward. There was hardpan beneath Zack's boots and the passage was dark, lit only by the flames of their lanterns.

"Use your hand," Trevillian said.

Zack felt for the wall. Nubs and crusts came to him, clefts, shatter scallops. For an instant he entertained Trevillian's madness—that here beneath the earth, some beneficent presence awaited him.

"Where are we?"

"The Relentless Extension," the boss said.

The trammers let their car loose, and Zack heard it roar down Humility. Then they rounded a bend and the Extension grew quiet.

Something was wrong with the air here. Zack's breaths felt woolly. They lodged at the top of his chest. Claustrophobia was winding like a muffler around his head. He tried to surmount it, focusing on the ragged space his lantern opened before him. But the acrid air poisoned his thoughts. He imagined the passage was tapering, then realized he wasn't imagining.

The walls were converging. The ceiling descended as they moved.

"My father was a wheezer," Trevillian said. "Every year he had less wind. They say, 'The steps to the pulpit are the surest way out of the mine.' Well, that was his way. He begged the pastor to make him a lay preacher and pounded the camps for miles around, worried for his lungs more than his soul."

The boss laughed. "That's how I got started. I'd stand on a pail and sermonize my pals. He pulled a congregation together. Built a church called Holy Heart. Two months later, the church went up in flames and the flock scattered. Their preacher was sent back to the mines."

The ceiling was a few inches above Zack's head. He touched it, dragging his fingertips over the rock, trying to anchor himself in sensation. But his mind rebelled, lifting a picture before him: he was trapped here alone, without light or air, and the walls were closing in. The boss was silent. Was he going to speak? The sound would calm him. Then Zack's lantern sputtered out.

The dark clenched around him, and he felt a mindless fear—his throat was stopped, his lungs were seizing, the chain of his thoughts transformed into an endless scream.

"This is what we call a doghole," the boss said.

They had reached the end of the Extension. There was a wall straight ahead and an oval opening on the left. Trevillian stopped before the opening, hung his lantern on a spike and turned to face him.

"When you strip away a man's pride and pretense, there isn't much left. Some stiffs never face that. For others, life's a cruel teacher."

Trevillian was unbuttoning his shirt. Zack felt a moment of powerless dread. Why had the boss brought him here? What did he intend?

"Are you one of those, Zack? Do you know the truth—" The boss unfastened the top of his union suit and held it open with both hands. "How little a man is, how close to nothing." He tucked his chin, directing Zack's gaze down.

There was a deep groove in the boss's left pectoral—a red seam that ran from sternum to nipple.

"You've heard the story," he said. "I cut out my heart."

Zack searched his face. "A miner?"

Trevillian's lantern flickered. "My father." He spoke simply, with bewilderment in his eyes as if to summon the moment. "He took Mother's life, then Freddie's. After he'd finished with me, I watched him stab himself."

"He was crazy," Zack said.

"Crazy with loathing," Trevillian nodded. "Crazy with despair." He glanced at the rock. "He couldn't bear to be down here. I can see him standing over me, that wild look, his bald head shaking. He used a boning knife."

Zack stared into the dark eyes.

"I was captain of the West Side waifs for a year," Trevillian said. "When the law rounded us up, I was sent to a home. But the home didn't lead to college. I came west in a boxcar."

Something in the boss's look beckoned Zack.

"You can touch it, if you like."

Zack didn't move. The boss grasped his hand and brought it forward.

The wound's edges were like the wings of an ill-fitting vest straining against its buttons. Zack followed it with his fingertips. The torn muscle was hard as rock. Below the scar, Zack could see the dark taproot of hair on the boss's belly.

"Violent acts surface things we fear most," Trevillian said. He let go of Zack's hand. "And things we most desire. Sometimes both in one stroke." He buttoned his union suit and shirt. Then he motioned at the oval opening in the wall to the left. "This is Threadbare."

The boss stooped to retrieve the bundle of steels and a hammer that had been left by the entrance. He grabbed his lantern and gestured Zack into the passage.

Zack started forward and the boss followed.

The space was just tall enough to stand up in. It allowed only a few inches on either side. Twenty feet in, the boss called a halt to light a candle that was spiked to the wall. "Put your wax on your forehead," he said. Zack removed the candle from his lantern, relit it and fixed it to the brim of his hat. "Alright," the boss said.

Zack bridled his fear and continued forward. Points of rock caught his hips and shoulders. The light thrown ahead made the passage look like a series of cutouts. Zack imagined one blast after another driving the outline of a man deeper and deeper into the mountain.

His boots made sucking sounds and the air turned rank. The end of the passage appeared.

"This is your spot," Trevillian said.

Using his lantern, the boss lit a pair of candles in the side wall. The starved flames squiggled in the darkness.

"My spot?"

"This is where she wants you," Trevillian said.

"Why?"

"To stage her return, perhaps. We'll find out." The boss handed over the hammer and steels. "I'll be back at the end of the shift." His gaze narrowed on the rock by Zack's shoulder.

A white braid kinked to within a foot of the headwall and then frayed, like a lock being combed. Zack examined the quartz in the light from his brow.

"You know, the real Hope isn't in the quartz we crush," the boss said.

When Zack glanced at him, he returned a cagey smile.

"The treasures we gloat over— They're dead skins the snake has cast. The real Hope is thin as fog, a stream of vapor without beginning or end.

"It's a story every geologist knows." He held his hands up and made claws of them. "When it was young, the flesh of the earth was torn." His fingers pried as if opening a fruit. "From the depths, gases rose, charged with metals—some of them precious. Hope entered our world through those fissures and laid her gold down there." The boss touched his fingers to the scar beneath his shirt and set them on Zack's left pectoral, over his heart.

"She has a talent for finding faults," the boss said. "Certain men draw her."

"Ten hours is a long time to spend here alone."

Trevillian nodded, eyeing the drift head. "Speak to her, Zack. Perhaps she'll come."

8

The first day at Threadbare was a long one, and so was the second. Zack fought his fear moment by moment, his wits in the balance till the shift whistle blew. On the third day, resistance failed him, and when the walls closed around him, he gave himself over and let the darkness crush him. During the ensuing hours he saw unaccountable things, heard babbling and the moans of a creature chained on the other side of the wall. But he worked. Through the remainder of that shift and the days that followed, he kept drilling.

There were blasts at intervals, but no signs of a quartz body. At times he reached out to Hope, but without conviction. Trevillian's face reappeared, expectant, increasingly sullen. It was the axis around which Zack's delirium turned. The eyes, black as midnight, with a flame raging in each. The voice that remained with him, chanting, when the face had vanished. "Where is she, Zack? You need Hope to live."

He'd been drilling Threadbare for eight days when the sound of the shift whistle rose through his hammer taps.

Zack set his tools down, dizzy, weak on his feet. He tried to draw a breath and mustered a spasm of coughing. Then he was stumbling and groping his way along the passage. When he reached the Relentless Extension, someone was standing beneath the candle.

"Sephy?"

Her presence washed over him. He leaned toward her, seeing the glimmer of care in her eyes.

She embraced him. He was unable to speak.

"You'll be alright," she whispered.

A dry sob rose in his throat, a tremor shook his chest. Her face turned up, but it was obscured by shadow. He felt a hand caress his cheek. He was consumed by gratitude, and then he remembered what had divided them.

"He'll pay for this," Sephy swore.

Zack drew back, getting her in focus. Her cheek was smeared with grease from his candle. He removed it from his brow, let it fall from his hand.

"You're a Blonde," he said.

She looked away.

"One of Salt Lick's whores."

"If we're going to speak, you'll have to master your contempt."

"Why are you here?" Zack asked her.

"To give you—whatever strength I can." The candle on

the wall flickered. Sephy wavered in the light. She was wearing the black dress.

"Strength?"

"You don't understand," Sephy said.

"Understand what?"

"Trevillian didn't invent Hope."

He was lost in her words. What was she saying?

Sephy's head tilted. "That night with Francine—"

"Hope is a delusion."

"No," she said softly, "Hope is a true faith. It's the priest who's corrupt.

"I want you to forgive me. For being a stranger to myself." She put her hand on his sleeve. "My life as— It isn't what you think. Our hostess was a brave woman. We took pains with our callers." She met his gaze. "They needed me, Zack. I allowed them to speak to something purer."

"Purer?"

Sephy nodded.

Her hair was swept to the side, held by a comb. Zack saw a wild intensity in her eyes.

"I had never seen gold in quartz. I had never heard Hope's name. But I knew her—" Sephy touched her collar. "She was Raymond's faith, and my own. Even then."

She drew a breath. "When we met, I didn't know how much I had to give you. Now we're here in this dream—" She gazed at the entrance to Threadbare. "In this nightmare— together. And I have more, so much more— Raymond is alive, in this mountain. These are Raymond's trials, this is Raymond's search. It was Hope he sought—"

"Madness," Zack mumbled, remembering her words below deck. The murk and flickering— They'd gone down with the steamer. His last breath was leaving him at the bottom of the sea.

"My flesh isn't precious," Sephy whispered. "I'm willing to spend it."

What did that mean? What was she thinking?

Feeling welled in her eyes. "I wanted to be your wife. I'm not too proud to be your Blonde."

She pressed herself against him.

"I didn't take your mother from you," Sephy said. "I love you like she did, and so does Hope." She wiped the grime from his face and gave him a lingering kiss.

Was he going to resist? The walls pivoted around him.

Zack was going to faint. He clung to her, stooping, lowering himself onto one knee. She descended with him.

"Say you forgive me," she whispered.

She was loosening her collar, unbuttoning her dress. A drop of wax starred on her shoulder. Her skin flashed ivory beneath the flame. A breast appeared, spare and pointed, flawless.

"It's important," she said.

"Why?" Zack closed his eyes. "I'm nothing but a slave."

"I know better."

Sephy opened his shirt. He felt her hands on his chest.

"I'm afraid of him," he confessed.

"Hope doesn't serve Trevillian," she said.

Zack's eyes were still closed. She was untying his belt.

"What is it like?" he asked. "In the alcoves."

"Darkness conceals them," she said. "Their differences disappear. You are no longer prey to discomfort or a girl's misgivings. You are a bird on the wing. A dream men desire."

A scent reached him— Was it quince or gardenia? He felt Sephy caress his thigh, and then her caress seemed to divide.

"I still—" The words choked him. "I forgive you," he sobbed. "You're all I've ever wanted."

Someone who loved him was beside him. He felt a pressure on his chest, pushing him down. The chill air made him shiver. The fingers on his leg grew longer, stretching. He imagined his lips found Sephy's. Their tongues met—

Harbor for his soul, Zack thought. A refuge—

Forget her, a deeper voice said.

His eyes were still closed. The image before him was painted on his lids. He was staring at the wall of the Extension. A thick lens of quartz had appeared in the rock. He reached for Sephy and his fingers touched crystal. The jewels were cold, lit dimly by the candle. He could see the lines of a bas-relief, barely incised—an angel with her head bowed toward him, knees flexed, one wing folded behind. The other was extended, its pinions on his thigh.

He was delirious, dreaming—

Hope, Zack thought. His need was so powerful, it sculpted the rock. As he watched, the relief deepened.

The wall rumbled above and below, and a white leg pushed

out, sleeked and glassy and marbled within. Its calf tapered to a toeless ribbon. The angel was emerging, but not from sleep. She was newly arrived, pinions quivering, still trembling with speed, the fires of heaven sighing from her pores.

He crawled or craned forward, drawing closer with his eyes.

Her arm split free, sharp-edged, crystalline, fingers still threaded into the clinging bed.

Show me your face, Zack thought.

The angel's head tipped up and it was Sephy's features he saw. But the eyes peering out were from some other world. Hope's crystal was steaming. Hope's icy breath fogged the air. Through the irising mist, it was Hope who watched him. Her shoulder emerged, then her breast—a cone of white agate with a crystal stud.

Zack reached and lifted a lock of her hair. The filaments were cool as rain. The flames in her neck rippled as she shifted, and the strands slid through his fingers.

She was free of the seam, her wings opening over him, webbed with glass, fanning, lifting—

He reached out.

The edge of Hope's wing seared his palm. Her icy breath etched his cheek. He clung, circling her trunk as she rose, pressing against her. The jewels pricked his chest. Beneath Hope's crystal skin, a million gold fishhooks were twitching their barbs. Her wings stirred winds, rising and dipping like the boughs of a tree. The mine and the mountain turned onto its side. The elastic legs and fine white fingers stretched like the strings of a puppet. Then they snapped and Hope bore him away.

The strange lover he held, or who was holding him, knew nothing of bondage. The labyrinth of drifts, the rock the miners pierced inch by inch—had all dissolved. It was nothing but mist, stars winking in a midnight void. He was lost in the speed and smoke, the blasts of wind and the shrieking of puzzlework wings. Her myriad facets hissed as she flexed, and out of the hissing came words and a voice.

Is it Hope you want?

She spoke with inhuman strength and assuredness.

Bring him down.

How? Zack thought.

I've made him desperate, Hope said. *He will go deeper. I will test him to prove his faith. And I will test you.*

Tell me how, Zack thought.

Get close to him, Hope said. *Be who he wants you to be.*

I'm afraid of him, Zack thought.

It's the only way, she said. *Hope makes promises. Here's one for you: if I don't save you, you'll die in the diggings. They'll bury your mangled body before the first snows.*

Zack came to himself midway down the switchback trail.

The sensations, the images—it was all still with him. The angel emerging, the wild flight, the words she'd spoken before she cast him loose.

It was Sephy he'd held, Sephy he'd heard. She was stirring him to revolt, or drawing him toward the center of Trevillian's web. He could hear Hope's voice echoing in his head, and for a moment he imagined that the tear in his eardrum was a door that Trevillian had purposely opened. An entrance for Hope that could never be closed.

In the south, the sun warred against a platinum sky, hurling smoke and birds at it. On his right a thick fog curtained the valley wall. He rounded a bend and peered down at the river. Where its banks pinched together, a giant white bloom was opening. The petals were endless, unfolding each moment as the torrent fed it. The river's breath lifted toward him, and as Zack inhaled it, a deep calm infused him. A hint of the freedom and confidence he'd felt in Hope's arms.

At the next bend, the stench reached him. There were salmon rotting in the shallows by the river's edge. At the mouth of the inlet, a dory was visible. The men on board lifted the net. The dory tipped till its gunwale took water, then the sea boiled and the salmon rose, bodies braided in a thick mass, writhing and rolling over as they poured into the boat. The men descended on them with clubs.

Bob was waiting for him by the bridge.

Zack could see the concern in Bob's face as he approached. "What took you?" Bob asked.

"You mean 'who.'" He laughed.

Bob frowned. He'd seen Zack's condition deteriorate day by day.

"Sephy," Zack nodded. "It was Sephy."

"Can you read my mind?"

"You think I've lost my grip," Zack said.

"We've got to get you out of there."

Bob motioned and turned, and Zack followed him.

It was late in the break, but the miners were still in the mess, eating and talking. Lloyd was standing on the BMC table, reading balances from his pocket ledger.

"Tollefsen, 940, bad. Voorsanger, 154 bones, bad. Noel, 357 to the good. How does he do it?"

Bob led the way to the cooking area, they got their dinner and found a table with a vacant bench. Inky and Winiarski were seated at the table adjacent.

"She refused to undress," a man beside Inky recounted.

"The old Helaina," another nodded.

"She gave me her buttonhook," the first went on. "Left shoe, then the right. Then she had me unclip her garter. Made me use my teeth."

"Nice touch," Arnie said.

"Worked like a charm," the miner told the group. "By the time I reached her drawers, I was twitching like a cave cricket and Hope was floating over me."

"When was this?" Inky asked.

"January," the miner replied. "Now she's strictly business."

"She's takin' it hard," said a brown man with a beard.

"Weasel's still got the spirit," Winiarski said. "Right?" He grinned at Inky.

Arnie laughed and slapped Inky on the back.

"She was in number five last night," Winiarski told the

others. "Genuine Jo and Sephy were lights out, and so was Wong. I'm thinking, 'It's Helaina.' But no—" He slinked his shoulders. "Out comes Weasel, wearing nothing but a corset. It was six spins before she relit her candle."

Heads turned to Inky.

"She inspired me," the reporter said. "Hope is a writer's dream come true."

"He's a believer now." Winiarski smiled at his friend.

"She's really something," Inky nodded.

Their eyes glazed each other with a reciprocal hypnotism.

"You new boys," the brown man growled. "You think the wheel's gonna keep turning? If Hope don't come back?"

As Lloyd finished his payroll, the yard grew quiet. Trevillian was making his way through the mess, and Owen was behind him. The boss had a brooding look and his jaw was set. He climbed onto the table.

"What's the news?" Trevillian scanned the men and then glanced at Owen.

Owen seemed reluctant.

"Let them hear," Trevillian said.

"Outside Chance is dead."

"Sublime?" the boss asked.

"Not a thing."

"Ardent?"

"The same."

Trevillian looked around. "Word-to-the-Wise?"

"Not a what-for," Owen said.

"She's gone below," the boss told the camp. "And she

doesn't think we'll follow." He pointed at the mountain. "We're going after her, boys."

"Farther down," Noel-the-Mole shouted.

A rumble of assent followed.

"Sink the main shaft," Owen nodded.

"That would be the safe way," Trevillian said.

"We'll find danger, sure," Owen laughed.

"Safe," Trevillian shouted at him.

"Aye," Owen said, puzzled.

"I'll not risk losing her." Trevillian faced the men. "We're going straight down."

The miners exchanged glances. Owen was stunned. Lloyd pursed his lips.

"A bucket winze," Trevillian announced, "from the toes of the 490 landing. A well, with an iron bucket to deliver us to her. 'Telegraph,' we'll call it. Hope will hear our charges like a key on the wire."

"That's suicide," Marcus Bunting shouted.

"What do you say?" Trevillian asked the camp.

"Straight down." True Bluford rose to his feet.

A dozen men echoed "straight down" and stood along with him.

"We'll shutter the mill and save our coal," the boss said. "Danger and privation— A hundred dogholes if that's what it takes." He clenched his fist. "When Hope has fled, when it seems you may never see her again— Hold her dear, imagine she's close—"

"Must it be a winze?" a man asked.

"Last time I rode in a bucket," another laughed, "I was in knickers."

"Is this Hope's idea?"

"Lower your heart to her," Trevillian said threateningly.

"Lower your own," Marcus Bunting barked.

The crowd froze. Trevillian was unbuttoning the Reminder from his hip.

Zack stood. "No hearts go to Hope," he said loudly, "before mine."

Trevillian stared at him.

"I'm tired as hell, hearing about her," Zack told the camp. He tapped his left pectoral. "I'll hand it over myself." He took a breath, gathering his courage.

"This winze," Zack faced the boss. "It's a shaft plumb with the station?"

The boss nodded, reading Zack with a suspicious eye.

"Point my chisel," Zack invited him.

"We'll cut by machine."

"I'll go first behind the everhard," Zack said.

"There's a stiff," a miner cried. Affirmations circled the mess.

Trevillian was still staring at him.

"How far down?" Zack asked.

"You'll know when I say 'stop,'" Trevillian replied. "Pick your oiler. Who's lead for the second team?" He narrowed on Noel-the-Mole.

Noel nodded. "If the boss wants his bottom drilled, I'm the man."

The miners laughed, and with that Trevillian stepped down from the table. The shift whistle blew and the men began to disperse.

Bob rose. "Nice performance."

"Hope cooked it up," Zack said.

"Any idea what you volunteered for?"

Zack watched the boss climb the stair to the office.

"When the drilling's straight down," Bob said, "the muck comes straight up. Can't have rocks falling on you, so they seal you in." He held his hand flat, an inch over his head. "Only time they lift the lid is when you fire the round. You're climbing out with fuse hissing in your ears. You slip, the ladder gives—that's it. Are you listening?"

"I'll ruin him," Zack said.

"You'll be sorry you're in that well."

"I can't take another shift at Threadbare," Zack told him.

Bob raised his brows. He understood.

"It's a chance to get inside his defenses," Zack said. "Besides, you'll be down there with me."

On the 490 landing, the shift whistle was blowing. It echoed in the cavernous space like the cry of some netherworld spirit calling men into the depths. Twenty feet from the platform, a well had been blasted. It was ten feet across and forty deep, and there were ladders staggered from ledge to ledge.

Zack stood on the rim beside Trevillian. As the whistle faded, the boss spoke.

"Don't get cocky. Keep your eye on the walls."

Zack ran his bandanna around his neck and knotted it.

"Hope's watching over you," Trevillian said.

Zack turned and held his candle over the boss's lantern. When the wick flared, he attached it to his hat brim. Something was wrong.

"The piers may be twisting," the boss said. "The ceiling cracking— But the man with Hope passes through. Stopes crumble around him, drifts spew fumes and fire—"

He sounded miserable. "What is it?" Zack asked.

"With Hope," Trevillian said, "everything's a test—of courage, of duty, of will." His gaze clouded. "Sephy's seeing you outside the Wheel."

"She still cares for me."

"Hope's done nothing to reach you?" the boss asked. "When you're drilling? When you're asleep?"

"Sephy acts the part," Zack said.

Trevillian waited for more.

"She speaks with Hope's voice," Zack said. "Sephy believes."

"What does she say?"

"Not much that I understand." Zack touched his temple and glanced into the well. "I'm sending her thoughts when the everhard's going."

"And?"

"Nothing yet."

222

"You have youth on your side," the boss said. "Keep sending."

Owen trudged past with a half-dozen men, hauling boxes of powder. "'Tis ready," he told the boss.

Trevillian's eyes were still on Zack. "Here—" He drew the prospector's pick out of his belt. "Hope wants you to have it."

The sharp point flashed in the light from Zack's brow.

"Drive it to the haft," the boss said, "and bring a piece of her back."

Zack slid the handle into his fuse belt, swung onto the first ladder and descended into the well.

Trevillian watched, hands on his hips. When Zack was near the bottom, the boss spread his arms. "Our Eden awaits us—" His deep voice thundered in the well.

Zack's foot left the last rung. Across the puddled floor, Dog-Eared Bob was lifting the machine drill onto its mount.

"Hold your breath, dog bone," DuVal called from the rim.

"Get a job," Bob grumbled.

"Got one." DuVal swung the wooden boom over them. Another man appeared to help DuVal lower a semicircular section of bulkhead into the well. The ticking of the boom crank sounded and the decking descended. Zack reached the mount as Bob took a wrench from the toolbox.

"What's that?" Bob eyed the pick.

"Gift from the boss," Zack said. "He's having bad dreams."

Bob set to work on the drill bolts.

"Hey," DuVal shouted.

Zack raised his hands, grabbed the panel and guided it onto the steel pegs, securing the wooden ceiling seven feet above the floor, then releasing the boom rope.

The ticking resumed.

"Where's my air?" Bob demanded.

There was scuffling on the rim and a black hose slithered down. Zack grabbed it, dragged it across the floor and attached it to the drill housing.

"Here she comes," DuVal yelled. The second panel descended into the well.

Zack checked his pockets and boot for candles and matches. The giant semicircle tipped toward him like a half-moon. He reached to right it, got it onto its pegs. "Dust to dust." DuVal's jibe dropped between the panels and the section slid into place.

Except for the hiss from the air hose, silence. Except for two flames on the wall, and the two on their heads—darkness. Panic rolled over and opened one eye. Zack knew what to expect. His senses would suffocate. His thoughts would hunt and feed on each other. It would be like lying in a coffin with the lid closed and the nails pounded in. It wasn't a question of hanging on to your mind. What mattered was that it came back at the end of the shift.

He stepped behind the mount and put his hands on the drill. "Alright."

Bob grunted to his knees, grabbed a fresh bit and fit it in the nose. Zack hefted the drill by its rear, aimed it at an extreme angle and cranked the screw, bringing the chisel toward the floor.

The steel grated against the rock. Zack lifted his bandanna so it covered his nose and mouth, and rode his chest up the butt of the machine, hunching over it.

Bob dipped the can in the water bucket and knelt, ready.

Zack filled his lungs and hit the bolt on the housing. The hiss of air turned abruptly to a wild clatter, and the drill jerked in his hands like a wounded animal. He mated himself to it with all his strength, fighting to control it with his arms and legs.

For a long minute, he was a man in the grip of a seizure, feeling it as something beyond him, just trying to hang on. Gradually he absorbed the machine's rhythm—the borrowed power felt more like his own. The fury grew familiar, uniting with his struggle to control it, until he could no longer tell where the fury ended and the control began.

It was like a disease of the nerves, some Dark Age plague. Or a medieval ecstasy—the Dance of the Blessed. The nimbus of dust rose around him like an aura, and he imagined himself as the deliverer Trevillian prayed for—protected, utterly possessed, quivering at the thought of his longed-for Hope.

The following week, Zack and Bob met Sephy in an abandoned raise on the 310. They extinguished the lanterns and

Sephy lit a stub candle. She knelt and placed it on a small boulder beside her, and Zack and Bob sat across from her.

"Bunting is with us," Zack told her. "He has a rifle."

"Can you trust him—"

"He won't do anything on his own," Zack assured her.

"The hard part will be keeping him quiet," Bob said.

"Who's next?" Sephy asked.

"Another doubter," Zack said, "whose spleen is deep."

"There aren't many like Marcus," Sephy said.

"Two. Maybe three," Bob agreed.

"And a few of our bargemates," Zack told her.

"Who has Hope left behind?" Sephy thought. "The Captain—"

"And Lucky," Zack added.

"Do you want Lucky—"

"Hell no," Bob said.

"There will be more who doubt." As Zack spoke, the wavering flame made the shadows shift on the wall behind Sephy. "Soon."

"That depends on Hope," Sephy said.

Bob nodded. "Hope's holding the cards."

Sephy put her hands in her lap. "There's no revolt without the faithful." She peered at Zack. "These people have given their hearts to her. The way to sway them is to speak to their belief. Hope made Trevillian their leader. Only Hope can bring him down."

The shadows behind Sephy dissolved and returned, as if

226

the spirits of the miners were with them, shifting their loyalties as they spoke. Hope was real, Zack thought, for the men who'd mined her. And for the Blondes who played her night and day in the Wheel. But for him, Hope was a phantom. The encounter at the mouth of Threadbare had jolted him and given Sephy a new sense of purpose. But neither of them had seen or heard a thing from her since.

"Zack will be our new priest." Bob was looking at Sephy.

Sephy didn't respond.

"What the boss does is mostly show," Bob said.

"Many of the boys know Hope better than Zack does." Sephy glanced at Zack. "He can't just pretend."

"A pug's a pretender until he takes the title," Bob said. "Then he's the champ."

"I have some experience," Zack reminded her, "with the popular mind."

"*The Secret Chamber*," Bob nodded, "and *The Ten Commandments*."

"That was entertainment," Sephy said. "Those people just wanted a good time."

"They believed," Bob said.

Zack nodded. "A lot of folks thought it was real."

She weighed Zack's words, lifting the stub candle and dashing the hot wax to the side. The wick had been drowning. Now the flame rose steady and strong. "Where will it come from?" she said softly, following some thread of thought she chose not to share.

After a moment, she raised her head. "You may be right."

"We'll pick carefully," Zack told her.

"For the doubters," Bob said, "we'll use doubt to turn them. For the man who believes— He'll never see Hope again, unless Zack leads."

"We've got problems," Zack pointed out, "if Hope reappears in the diggings, in the middle of all this."

"She won't," Sephy said.

Zack stared at her. When he turned to Bob, the older man raised his brows.

"What about the Blondes?" Zack asked. "Will any of them help?"

Sephy's expression turned the question back to him. "They all believe."

"How does Hope reach them?" Bob asked.

"Each girl has her own line to Hope. And we have the stories worked out by the boss and Francine."

"Drawn from his dreams," Zack said.

Sephy nodded.

Bob was surprised. "The boys don't know that."

"Certain things," Sephy told him, "you're not supposed to hear."

"It's not really her," Bob said.

"Not always," Sephy replied. "It's no different than it was in the High Quarter. You wanted it to be real, so you did your best. And sometimes it was."

"This is a hard place to keep secrets," Zack said. "And there's the question of odds—how many is enough."

"Nine men bunk on the hill with the boss," Bob said. "We've got over a hundred boys here. If it comes down to numbers, the decision will go whichever way they lean."

"We'd want a bunch of them in our pocket," Zack said, "before we made a move. And we'd want firepower—"

"Bullets for our guns," Bob nodded. "And explosives—powder and caps—so we can make a stink if we have to."

"We'll start a little war." Zack felt the chill and the damp in the derelict drift.

Sephy was silent.

Was she conferring with Hope? Zack imagined for a moment that Hope had invaded her as they sat there and was now a party to their plan to bring down the boss.

Sephy met his gaze. "Are you really going to do this?"

9

Zack and Bob focused their efforts on the three men Bob knew to be doubters and foes of the boss. Then they recruited the Captain. They hid the identity of each man from the others. All anyone knew was that Zack was in charge. No mention was made of Sephy, but word got out that she and Zack had reconciled. As for her working in the Wheel, he acted as if he was resigned to it.

They looked for chances to steal explosives. There weren't many. Even in the smallest drifts, it was hard for one man to do anything unobserved. They managed to take two dynamite sticks and a handful of caps. Bob hid the explosives in the pup, wrapped in a shirt.

Zack and Sephy were together often—an association that was technically barred. But because Zack had "made a new start," the boss let the infraction pass. Between shifts, they'd meet in a corner of the mine, in the trees by the river, or beside the cairn. The trysts provoked the camp's curiosity. They let word circulate that Hope visited their intimacies. But the stories were lies. Zack's connection to Sephy grew deeper, but Hope kept her distance.

Zack's work on the winze boosted his standing with the men, and Sephy's influence in the Wheel grew. With her stoic garb and her earnest manner, she balanced Salt Lick's extravagance. The girls were soothed by her piety, as were the miners.

It took a month to sink the Telegraph Winze to 770 feet. No new quartz was found and the assays weren't encouraging, but this was the depth Hope had revealed to the boss in his dreams. So a new level was struck and they began sending out drifts—Tempting, Wallflower, Promise and the Lovesick Raise. Zack and Bob returned to hand drilling. There was a sense of anticipation. Hope wouldn't caboodle the boss—she was about to reappear. But Trevillian was guarded. His sermons were brief and his proclamations were cautious.

The northern summer ended. The nights grew dark.

It was in the dim hours before the morning shift break. The mill had been boarded up and the valley was quiet. The tent camp slept beneath a swirling mist. Pale shreds drifted through the conifers on either side of the river. Around the forge, it was especially thick. The plank walls of the small building were drenched, and a cloud boiled behind as if a kettle had overturned.

Zack and Dog-Eared Bob followed the path from the switchback trail toward the straw-colored light puddled around the door. Zack looked like a miner now. His face and hands were the color of the earth, and his Vandyke had disappeared into a mat of beard. He glanced over his shoulder and then pushed the door open, and the two men stepped inside.

Dinesh was stooped over the brazier, pulling a pair of tongs from the coals. He signaled them to wait.

The shack's interior had an air of sorcery. It was windowless, lit only by two sulfur lanterns and the brazier's vermilion. Rods bristled from the shadows, and drill steels were piled in a half-dozen places, partitioning the chaos of tools and machine parts left for repair. A workbench stood in front of a pair of anvils with a slack tub between. Over the coals hung a giant bellows and a metal hood that fed smoke to the flue.

Dinesh straightened, turned, examined the glowing part between his tongs, and dropped it in the slack tub. As the steam rose, he peered through it, his face gray with soot.

Bob raised an armful of steels. Dinesh gestured, showing where he wanted them. Then he saw Zack's expression and realized they wished to talk.

"You like working for the BMC," Bob nodded.

Dinesh laughed. "I do?" He picked spatters off his leather apron.

"It's hard here for doubters," Zack said.

"I shouldn't have been on that steamer," Dinesh replied. "Gold was never my goal. I won't worship gold or Hope."

"Or visit the Wheel," Zack said.

Dinesh looked away.

"You're thinking, 'I'm odd man out,'" Zack said. "But you're not. You're the man we want."

Dinesh removed his spectacles. "What's this about?"

The visitors exchanged looks.

"Bullets," Zack said.

"I don't have any here," Dinesh answered simply, polishing a lens with his sleeve.

"But you can make them," Bob observed.

Dinesh stared at him.

"The jackets and heads," Zack said. "You'd need powder."

Bob acted thoughtful. "You could use dynamite for that."

"There are a lot of things you can do with dynamite," Zack nodded.

Dinesh replaced his spectacles. He looked at Bob, then back at Zack, brows pinched, lips parting.

Zack nodded, reading his question. "We're serious."

The coals had crusted over, but scarlet was glowing through the cracks. Dinesh glanced at the pair of anvils. "I don't have this place to myself, you know."

Behind the shack, the kettle cloud was drifting. A crescent shred floated aside and Hope's shaggy harbinger lifted his head above a cranberry thicket and drew scents from the breeze. Prowler cringed at the fumes. His giant paw raked the gravel. Then he shouldered through a lattice of speckled leaves, his emerald eyes focused on the lone tent behind the shack.

He circled it slowly and stopped before the opening. He sniffed and the force of his breath shifted the flap. With an indignant grunt, he raised himself and lunged with both arms, piercing the canvas with the long knives of his claws. There was a startled cry within, and movement. Prowler lifted the tent and shook it. An arm appeared through one of the tears.

Prowler sank his jaws into the arm and tugged, using his claws to rip the canvas around it. Pollard emerged, screaming for all he was worth.

The three men in the forge hurried outside. "Pollie?" Dinesh saw what remained of the tent.

"There," Bob pointed.

Prowler was dragging Pollard up the slope. He reached a boulder and hurled the man onto it. Pollard's body went *rup* and a leg hung limp, but his arms continued to flail. The bear shook his head, as if amused. The smith was croaking like a frog.

"Rifles," Bob shouted. "Rifles—"

A handful of men spotted them from the switchback trail, saw Prowler and hurried toward them. Two sprinted for the store to get weapons and reinforcements.

"Leave him alone," Zack yelled at the bear, stepping closer.

Prowler closed his jaws on Pollard's shoulder. Pollard struggled to free himself and Prowler chomped again. Then he lifted Pollard between his teeth and shook him. Zack began hurling rocks and so did Bob and Dinesh.

One struck Prowler's chest and he dropped the smith, startled. His ears pivoted, eyes focusing on the three men, nostrils steaming. He turned back to Pollard, huddling over him like a squirrel with a nut. Then he scooped the smith up and rose onto his hinds.

Zack was forty feet away, throwing rocks and shouting, narrowing the gap. Prowler watched him approach, Pollard clasped to his chest. The smith was moaning. His right arm was wrapped around the bear's neck. They might have been dancing, but Pollard's boots were four feet off the ground.

The men from the trail halted behind Zack, adding their shouts, stooping for rocks and scrap from the junk pile, heaving whatever they could find. Zack continued toward Pollard and the bear.

Prowler's green eyes locked on him, gleaming with recognition, including him in the strange intimacy with Pollard. A grumble issued from his muzzle while his giant arm crushed Pollard's chest. Pollard screamed, and then the scream turned into a warble as Prowler's arm lifted and pressed, playing him like a bagpipe.

The bear tilted his muzzle and spread his jaws, taking Pollard's head between them.

"No," Zack cried.

A *crump* sounded and the warbling ceased. Prowler's jaws parted, releasing the smith's head.

Zack was fifteen feet from the bear, with the horde of men behind him. Prowler held the smith to the side, draped over one arm, while he batted missiles with the other. For a moment it seemed he might be yielding. Then his lips snarled back, he clamped Pollard's chest with his fangs and flung him into the air. The limp form arced over a patch of wild celery and crashed into a thicket.

Gunshots. A mob of men were hurrying up the trail from the store, firing rifles into the air. Zack watched Prowler let himself down, thudding onto his fores with a belligerent grunt. The beast seemed indifferent to the danger. He swung his head from side to side, nostrils flaring while he worked his chops, as if picking his next victim from the men before him. He settled on Zack.

Zack heard boots retreating behind him.

He could see nothing but Prowler's eyes. They grew larger and larger—green, emerald green. A green abyss, an ocean of contempt that could swallow the earth and drown every star in the sky. The harshest judgment on the worth of man was visible there. The fur below one eye twitched. Above the other, the lavender scar twisted like a segmented worm.

More shots. And yells. A crowd pounding closer.

Prowler bucked his shoulders and rose. His head craned, taking in the mob and Zack, arms pedaling to either side, black claws clicking. Then the giant jaws gaped and Prowler roared—a blast of air and emotion that was like a bucket of lye in Zack's face, burning with scorn, stinking of rotting flesh and roots. Prowler's huge arm swung around. The knives struck Zack's hip, knocking him sideways.

A bullet whistled by Zack's ear.

Prowler's front quivered and the emeralds fogged. His shoulder spouted blood.

He wheeled and went charging up the slope.

Someone grabbed Zack's arm, and then the rifles let loose. The mob of cursing men scrambled up the incline after the bear, barrels smoking. A second group was hurrying through the huckleberry beside the mill. Another shot struck Prowler's flank and a cheer went up. Prowler wrenched around, snapping at his pursuers, then plowed into a thicket, leaves flying. He was in full stride, entering the forest with a crashing of boughs. For a few moments the havoc made his path visible, and then he was lost to sight.

The volleys ceased and the clamor faded.

"Did you see his look?"

"It was Zack he was after."

When Zack turned he saw a crowd of men behind him. Their eyes were on him. "Hope," one muttered, and the word "test" sounded from another. Noel nodded to him.

"That's a tap on the shoulder," Noel said.

Bob drew beside Zack, breathing hard. He motioned and Zack followed him toward the thicket where Pollard had landed. Lloyd had arrived and was giving directions, medicine bag in hand. As they drew closer, Zack could see Pollard through the web of branches. He was on his belly, facedown, arms quivering. They pried the boughs apart, and men on either side grabbed hold of him. As they lifted, Pollard's face appeared. His forehead had caved. Below his tortured eyes, the flesh had been torn like clay, leaving a hideous grin, impossibly wide.

"Is it bad?" Bob asked, eyeing Zack's hip.

Zack looked down. His shirt was in shreds.

The attack put an end to the shift. Pollard was carried to the mining office and Zack went with him. Beneath the remains of Zack's shirt, claw tracks were barely visible. Trevillian cleaned the scratches while Lloyd worked on Pollard. Owen knelt beside the groaning man, threading needles and squeezing out sponges.

Through the window, Zack could see the miners below, gathered in the yard. They were standing, not seated, and no one was in the food line.

"How good is Dinesh?" the boss asked Owen.

"He's got some to learn."

"Damn her and her wild pig," Trevillian said bitterly.

"'What does it mean?'" Owen's brow rumpled. "That's what they're asking."

"False clues, fresh tests," the boss said. "No answers, just omens. She can't be trusted—that's what it means."

Trevillian taped Zack's hip. "Does it please you? Seeing the boss in a corner?" He spoke like a parent scorching a disobedient child. "You're like the rest of them. Behind my back, you're chewing my gizzard."

Zack made a bewildered face, but Trevillian just laughed.

"You think I don't know?" The boss eyed him as if he was something he'd fought for and lost. "Things were simpler here when Prowler was boss. He didn't play father to his boys. He ate them."

"The bear had his eye on Zack," Owen observed.

239

"It must be Zack she's testing," Trevillian said with an impish look. He inspected his tape job, patted Zack's shoulder and waved him toward the door.

Zack stepped down the outside stair and found his way through the crowd. Men spoke with urgency to each other, like soldiers in a fort under siege. Faces turned in Zack's direction.

He approached Bob. "Is Hope making trouble for us?"

"She might be," Bob said.

Silence filled the yard. Trevillian was descending with Owen at his rear. He strode quickly through the mess and mounted his table. Bob elbowed Zack and glanced up the valley. A group of Blondes were filing down the switchback trail.

The mine boss scanned the gathering. "You want to know what this means," he nodded grimly. "Is Hope near?" He paused, as if waiting for someone to answer. "Yes. She's very close."

There were expressions of relief, a few gave the salute. Many had misgivings.

"She's testing our belief," the boss said. "We need to show our spine."

"No one loves her like we do," a miner cried.

"Kill that bear," another shouted.

The yard swelled with agreement.

"He's diddled us for the last time," Trevillian promised. "We're going to dig pit traps—two north, two south—and bait them with salmon. The Bang Boys will make us Prowler stew."

"Is that what she wants?" a miner asked.

"Hunt him down."

Trevillian raised his hands for quiet.

"Why Pollard?" someone wondered.

"He's a doubter," another replied.

"The attack wasn't meant as a test for Pollard," the boss shook his head. "This is the test—right here. This upset, this discord. It's a test of determination, for all of us."

"You know her best," True Bluford said loudly. "Tell us what to do."

"Stay buckled to your tasks," the boss said. "I'll take care of Prowler."

"You Hope spooners are fools," Marcus Bunting shouted. "He's a bear and we're sleeping outdoors. We want barracks."

"I concur," Dinesh said.

Zack glanced at Bob.

"Excuse me," Lucky turned. Beneath his tired eyes, his cheeks sagged like oysters. "Should we consider building a boat? Before winter sets in?"

"I'd board her," one man volunteered.

"There will be no *Reason* here until the boss orders it," Owen said.

"She was testing Knox," Noel-the-Mole observed.

"That's right. Prowler singled him out."

"Barracks," the Captain demanded. "You'll build them *now*." He stepped forward, glaring at the boss as if he'd been waiting for this chance to declare himself.

Trevillian put his hand on the Reminder. "You'll curl in the dirt."

"You boys from the night shift feel like turning in?" the Captain asked.

"Not me."

"We're chestnuts in a bag," another agreed.

Salt Lick was descending the corduroy road, drawing attention to herself with a wave to one and another. A half-dozen Blondes were behind her, including Sephy.

"It's a terrible thing—to wish for Hope and to live without her, to watch our brother Pollard torn up by Prowler." The boss shared a careworn sigh. "I try to keep my grief on a leash, but I cannot. We have our memories of her. We have our courage, the will to endure— These crutches must hold us while Hope is at a distance." He opened his arms. "I hear your thoughts, boys. They're reaching me. You love Hope as I do, but she's testing you sorely."

His naked longing brought fists to a few chests and remorse to a few faces. "Hold her dear," one man said, and the invocation spread slowly through the crowd.

"Our love for her still burns within us." The boss nodded solemnly and then showed them the steel in his eyes. "There is no pause in our dream."

"There'll be paws in mine," the Captain said. He rose onto a bench not far from the boss and stamped his boot on the boards. "You'll not get another hour of labor till my berth has walls around it."

Trevillian laughed.

"Who's got the grit?" the Captain insisted, looking around. No one spoke.

"Step down," Owen said.

"Speak out!" the Captain urged the men.

"You'd betray her," the boss said darkly. His right hand unbuttoned the Reminder.

"You don't frighten me," the Captain said.

The whip straightened beside Trevillian's leg. "We can fix that."

His arm jerked and the long thong reached low, snaking around the Captain's shins. The boss tugged and the Captain upended, his shoulder striking the tabletop, then his head. He slid over the bench and landed in the gravel, groaning and sucking his breath.

The assault stunned Zack. There was poison in the boss's eye.

Owen hurried toward the Captain, stooping as Trevillian descended from his table. "There's your lesson," Owen said, but he seemed more intent on shielding the Captain than reproaching him.

Trevillian smacked his foreman aside. He rocked back, skimmed the braid of the Reminder across the dirt and snapped it forward, slicing the Captain's pant leg.

"Aren't you grand," Trevillian seethed. His frame buckled and again the whip cracked. The Captain shook as if he'd been struck by lightning. "A minnow rules the deep— A snail's turned into the moon!" Bent to the right, sidearming, Trevillian lashed the convulsing form again and again.

"There's the real man," he proclaimed. The Reminder heeled by his knee. A scarlet stripe crossed the Captain's thigh

243

and Trevillian was glaring at it. He shuddered and his right arm spasmed. Zack saw the popper snap, leaving a frog of blood on the gravel. Then the boss drew back and the whip struck the Captain's leg again, opening the wound.

"Enough," Salt Lick shouted from the rear of the crowd.

But Trevillian couldn't be reached. Again and again, arching and hunching, lost in his strokes. Venom pulsed through his legs and spit from his lips— He was as ravished by the Reminder as his victim.

A few stiffs were repelled, a few were detached. But most, Zack saw, were transfixed, unable to turn away—as if they were enduring the strokes themselves. For the first time, Zack sensed how utterly the camp mirrored the boss's state. Trevillian's mine was now a place of humiliation and despair. And they were all in it with him.

"No more—" Salt Lick parted the gathering.

Trevillian bellowed in triumph and wrenched around, the popper dancing before him. He grabbed it and ran it through his fist. "Adam," he opened his palm for them, showing the Captain's blood around. "Adam to the quick—"

"The Bastion," Salt Lick cried.

She was ten feet from the boss, arms out, on the verge of tears, drawing Trevillian's attention to the shocked faces.

He acted as if he'd awoken from a hypnotic state. He stood swaying, blinking, recognizing Salt Lick and the others around him. He saw the Captain, leg drenched in blood, huddled on the gravel. The boss took a breath and stared up the valley, then he turned to Salt Lick with devastation in his face.

"The scourge—" Trevillian gazed at his right hand. He opened it, and the whip fell to the ground, eeling in the dirt. He eyed his shirtfront with a helpless expression. It was covered with blood.

The yard was silent.

"Pick it up." Trevillian scanned the faces. "Someone." He gazed at the coils. "I'll take the same as the Captain. No—Twice as many."

No one moved.

"A zealot of Hope—" Trevillian bowed his head. "Is a vile creature. He thinks he's ordained by glory. When he's nothing but meat for the butcher." His gaze fell on Lucky. "Remind me."

Lucky stared at him.

The boss bent, grasped the whip by its braid and rose. "Make me bleed," he said, extending the handle.

Zack saw the relief in Salt Lick's face. She had led Trevillian out of his madness and now a show was under way.

Lucky was motionless. The silence drew out. Trevillian began to coil his weapon.

"I pray," he said softly, "she will be as generous as you are."

He was speaking to them all. He meant them to forgive his atrocity. And he deemed that he deserved their forgiveness. He wasn't a cruel man. He wanted no harm to come to any of them. His heaven was submission—a submission that would make them all, finally, children of Hope.

Lloyd stepped forward with DuVal. They helped the Captain put his weight on his good leg and, supported between them, he hobbled toward the store.

"What can be done about Prowler?" Salt Lick asked.

"The bear must die," the boss said.

He was resuming command. He'd never really relinquished it.

"Some of the boys are hunters." Sephy stepped forward. "Perhaps they can track him down. There's one here who's quite a good shot." She turned to Zack.

Trevillian's gaze shifted between them.

"Why not?" Salt Lick gave the boss a piercing look. "Zack's a deadeye," she lifted her skirts and surveyed the men. "And he has a sensitive nose."

That drew laughs.

She glanced at Zack. "What do you say?"

In the aftermath of the lashing, the crowd's reaction was subdued—scattered nods, mutters of approval. Zack faced Trevillian, recognizing his authority.

"I'm not believing he can do it," Owen advised.

"I'm not either," Trevillian said. Then a smile spread across his face and he raised his arm, inviting Zack to try.

The tension in the yard dissolved. Voices rose and men began speculating on the outcome. Zack saw Salt Lick tip her head to him. Sephy was curtsying to the boss.

"Is an ear enough?" Zack asked Trevillian. "Or do you want all of him?"

"Bring me his pizzle," the boss said. "I'll wax my boots with it." He gestured toward Snell. "Take my best—he's been around bears. And three more, your pick." Then to the gaunt man, "Get the rifles."

10

Six hours later, the trackers were in mountains to the north, winding through a stand of towering spruce. The trees around Breakaway had been thinned for timber and firewood. But here, not one bore the trace of human hands. A gray ceiling hid the sun. Cool droplets fell—from the sky or from high boughs, there was no way to tell. Zack watched them tap Snell's shoulders.

"Good you're with us," Snell said.

"We need to find him first."

"In the diggings, I mean."

Zack was at the center of the file, a lever-action rifle held ready. Winiarski was behind him, then Inky. Bob led the group out of the spruce stand. As they descended, the brush closed in. Zack scanned the magenta scrub.

"You know bears?"

"Before the boss, I worked on Gray's Island," Snell said. "We had 'em there."

"Is it true you bought the steamer with our fares?"

Snell nodded. "Should've given it a closer look. Too busy seining for Francine."

"She's particular."

"You got no idea." Snell hesitated. "Sephy's a rare one."

Zack heard the respect in his voice.

"The Wheel was different 'fore she arrived," Snell said.

"Different how?"

"She's Hope's kind side. She sees the good in everyone."

A stream gurgled nearby. Bob was wandering to the left. He stopped and Zack saw him shake the end of a freshly broken branch. "Not losing any steam," Bob said.

"Mis'able temper." Snell pointed his rifle at a bush that had been torn to pieces.

"It's undignified," Winiarski said.

Bob laughed. "Bring your tape measure?"

"He'd turn heads in a collar and cravat," Winiarski smiled. He glanced at Zack. "Thanks," he said as they resumed the descent.

"What for?"

"Picking me."

Zack kept his eye on Snell.

"They don't know what I can do," Winiarski said.

Zack nodded. "You're a fine fellow."

Winiarski swept an armful of branches aside, peering

through the undergrowth like a stalking maharajah. "Folks in my town, they didn't think I'd add up to anything."

They hit the stream and followed it, walking on moss and soaked gravels. Rills slid past, bright as quicksilver. The banks were dotted with berries—orange beads, crimson thimbles, purple baubles strung on strands. Giant devil's club leaves spread over them, tiled together like a roof of green glass.

"Print," Bob reported.

He'd reached a bend in the stream. As Zack drew closer, he could see the impression of Prowler's paw. The mud was slotted where the claws had dug in.

"Size twenty," Winiarski said.

Bob was examining an ash frond and shaking his head. Blood smeared the leaves. He ran his thumb over one. "Already gummy. He could be days away by now."

The group considered this.

"Part of the test," Zack suggested.

"Let's keep on," Snell agreed, motioning with his rifle.

Bob continued through the scrub. He fought with a tangle, then pulled the machete from his belt to clear the way. Prowler's track led down into a hollow. As they descended, shadows thickened. The bushy crowns grew murky. Fingers of mist appeared on the rim above them, winding through aisles in the brush.

The trail led through webs of downed saplings with bear prints among them and places where the huge paws had dished moss away. A hole had been torn through a devil's club thicket. Prowler's blood streaked the leaves, and tufts of his fur were caught on the spines.

The fingers of mist were lanes now, rippling and curling and gliding together. The sound of cascades reached them, and through the branches a cliff appeared. Waterfalls had worn a quartet of hourglasses in the slate-colored rock. The way grew marshy and passed through thigh-high swamp cabbage. The giant leaves looked petrified, frozen in time. Near the low point of the hollow, the understory vanished. Bob led the group across an open bog. Lobes of moss lolled in the runnels, green and maroon. The dry spots were tufted with sedge.

"Flagpole," Winiarski said.

They stepped through the mire, approaching a solitary tree, barkless and twisted. Its one fingerless branch was draped with moss.

"He was here," Bob said, pointing at prints.

"Half mast." Inky looked up.

Zack scanned the surrounding thickets. "Any idea where we're headed?" He glanced at Snell.

Bob pointed at the paw holes in the muck. "Only one of us knows the way." He lifted his boots and continued across the bog.

"How far does he go before he's left home?" Winiarski muttered.

He followed Bob, and Snell fell in behind him.

"Prowler was made," Snell said, "out of things we don't know nuthin' about."

Zack went next and Inky brought up the rear. They were ascending, leaving boggy ground, tramping through crowberry and heather.

"Hope put him together with us in mind," Snell said. "That's how he tells it."

The mist was still with them, but the currents had lost their borders. The vapor was a commingled mass, churning over them.

Trees rose as they mounted the slope, and they were again in a woodland. Here the understory was leafless. Gazing between the trunks, the mesh of skeletal branches looked like gray smoke. The leaf mold was damper and deeper. It crept beneath Zack's feet—countless quiltings of it, bedded over the centuries.

"Nothing changes for that bear," Snell said. "His ways are set. Brushes this tree every time he passes. Puts his paw on that rock."

The trees turned silver. Zack felt the damp prickling his face. The mist had descended. As he moved, he imagined the cool swirling was Hope. Not Hope in a human form, not Hope the angel. But a Hope much larger and more powerful, diffuse and encompassing, like the one Trevillian spoke of, who rose into faults to deposit her gold. The forest had given her its fragrance, steeping her in resins. The tree trunks before him were the pillars of an ancient cathedral, and this bracing fog was the living body of the god, stirring within. This was her home. From here, she breathed herself into the world. Prowler was wandering some outlying cloister like a brooding monk, lost in half-conscious rituals, sniffing her smoke.

Zack recalled the jolt the bear gave him. The moment was vivid—one he wouldn't forget. If Hope was a fog that brought gold into the world, Prowler was her assayer come back to check, testing to see if anything of worth was absorbed. Zack had survived the run-in—a good sign. And Hope had done him a grisly favor, giving Dinesh a chance to make ammunition without being observed.

The ground leveled and they began to descend.

"What's the news?" Inky asked.

"There's a print," Bob replied.

The mist swirled around them. Zack peered through the forest.

If there was a Hope, he thought, what would attract her to him? He didn't have the Private's passion. He didn't have Trevillian's discipline and command.

His boot landed on a fallen branch—the *crack* was like lightning, a flash of energy passing into formlessness. If a man ended like that, Zack thought, what did it matter? A little more time and Zachary Knox would be here. His virtues and faults, his desperate dreams, his ruinous fears—weathered and spongy, mixed faceless into the seeding and burial ground of the ages. What use would Hope have for him then?

If Hope exists, Zack thought, she knows what I am.

"Wait a minute," Winiarski called a halt.

Zack turned to see him looking skyward, pointing through the mist.

"The flagpole," Winiarski said.

The tree was unmistakable, the frozen standard on its lone arm hanging ghostly over them.

Bob looked around, then faced the group, perplexed.

"We've gone in a circle," Winiarski said.

Snell pointed at Zack's feet.

The grass had been flattened, and there was a puddle of blood to one side of Zack's boot. From where he stood, over a hedge of dwarf spruce, the flagpole was in clear view.

"He looped back on us," Zack said. Prowler had stood watching them, not a dozen feet away.

Inky swung around, scanning the foliage. Then they were all looking.

The bear was nowhere in sight.

"Don't like this," Snell said.

"He's closer than I thought." Bob glanced at Zack.

Zack nodded to him, and Bob started forward.

They skirted a wet spot, rose over a low spur and descended toward a stream. The mist thinned and a drizzle fell through it. They were in swamp cabbage again and the leaves twitched like elephant ears as the raindrops struck. The stream was deeper than it looked. The water climbed to Bob's thighs, he lost his footing, then stumbled up the bank. At the top, he burst out laughing.

"What's the joke?" Inky wondered.

As Zack mounted the stream bed, he saw Bob stooping over a wallow four feet wide—a mass of berries, twigs and sludge splattered on the ground with steam rising from it.

"He's telling us something," Bob said.

Snell ignored him, circling the wallow. He was focused on a bough in the scrub. A broken branch—a loose V—had caught on the bough and was swinging like a pendulum. There wasn't a breath of wind, and the leaves around it were like chips of stone.

Zack raised his rifle and hurried forward. As he broke through the scrub, a jay swooped out of the trees a hundred feet ahead. It cawed and dove back into the woods, screeching and scolding.

"Movin' fast," Snell called out.

A steep meadow lay before Zack. He bolted toward it, scrambling up, quivering with anticipation and fear. The quick steps of his companions sounded behind him. A spot of sun flared through a chink in the cloud cover. Fifty yards higher, the meadow ran into rocks and a ridge jutted from them, narrowing, turning away from the sun. Along that ridge a dark hulk was moving. Wet flakes laced the air. Above the meadow, the rain became ice.

Zack charged after the bear, sleet flying in his face, slipping and skiing over the sodden leaf cover and new-fallen snow. On the crest, he struck a path that tacked through trees like none he'd ever seen—twisted and bent, trunks tied in knots, curving out of the earth like weathered tusks. Skeins of lichen hung from the trees, and as he passed they caught and clung.

The ridge ended in a drop-off. There was a long descent to a snow-patched plateau. Prowler had reached the bottom and was galloping across it.

"There he is," Inky gasped, halting beside Zack.

The bear was a blur, obscured by veils of mist, his distance difficult to judge. Zack spread his legs, anchoring his boots in the rock. Prowler was at the plateau's edge now, climbing a black boulder pile at the base of a wooded slope. The mist there was milky—he was like a cork bobbing on it. Zack raised his rifle and sighted along the barrel.

"Can't hit him from here," Inky murmured.

Prowler surfaced suddenly through a gap, silhouetted on his hinds, snout in the air. Zack nailed his bead on the giant head and lifted it, accounting for the long arc. "Can't I?" He stopped his breath and tensed his trigger finger.

But Prowler sank before he shot. The mist swallowed him and there was nothing more to see.

Zack heard labored breathing behind him. He lowered the rifle. "If that was the test, I don't think I passed."

"No one could've—"

"Look at that," Winiarski said with surprise.

Zack turned.

To their left, at the plateau's western edge, an outcrop rose two hundred feet into the air. It was concave, and its cliffs were washed by beams raying through the chink. It glowed ocher and amber, and its crest gleamed with rocky thorns and bosses of snow. At its rear, a blanket of cloud stretched to the horizon. An odd scallop of mountain—like a shell on the beach, stuck upright in the sand—and the tidewater behind it, sliding back to the sea.

"We'll never catch him now," Bob said.

Snell shivered. "Can't sleep up here." He gestured his rifle at the slope before them. Prowler's prints led down. Snell took the lead and Bob fell in behind him. Zack went last.

Unprotected by peak or woodland, the slope had been ravaged by the elements. On the left, between patches of beaten heather, the leaf mulch had ruptured like morbid skin. On the right, broken hellebore stalks were heaped like translucent intestines. Prowler's track arced toward the concave outcrop. His prints were as deep as cisterns. Zack watched his boots descend into them.

"Nice of him to leave these," Winiarski observed.

"They were here before Prowler," Snell said.

"He's kidding," Inky told Winiarski.

"No I ain't. His pap used 'em, and his grandpap—all the way back."

The cisterns didn't give beneath Zack's boots. The earth had hardened around them.

As they reached the plateau, the southern sky was flooded with burgundy. It was as if some great bladder had been punctured by the beams of sun. They walked beside Prowler's track on cushions of peat. The tawny surface gave beneath Zack and the peat bled, maroon pools collecting around his boots. As they drew closer, the scallop rose up, pleated by ribs, its amber and ocher rickracked horizontally. Between the ribs, silver threads descended the walls. Along the curving crest, the rocky thorns appeared.

"Hoo," Winiarski exclaimed, scanning the heights.

Invisible creatures whistled from the ledges.

"What is that?" Snell mumbled. He'd mounted a rise and

was the first to spot it—along the base of the scallop was a pink scroll woven with scarlet threads.

"It's pushing up," Snell pointed. "Can you see?"

Zack saw. The giant scallop was like something alive, emerging from the plateau. Beams played over the contact zone, lighting rock that looked like a wave curling over on itself—a pink wave with scarlet sea straps.

They continued forward. Snell was still following Prowler's track. The burgundy spill had drowned the west. Directly above them, perforations in the mist let rods of sun through. The bright pencils darted, subtle as thought, drawing lines and dots on the mounds of moss and patches of snow. They approached the scallop with the runes shifting before them. And then Prowler's prints vanished.

"That's it," Snell said, puzzled, looking around.

The soil was sandy and puddled. Spindles of trapper's tea quivered in the grass.

Inky was staring at the earth before him. Zack moved closer.

There was a depression, matted with fur. On one side, a plum-colored boulder rose like a back cushion. Its surface was studded with crusts of black lichen and yellow moss stars. On the other side, a small boneyard had collected.

"Nice place to lounge," Bob said.

The sofa was fifty yards from the base of the scallop. Zack eyed the trail of prints they had followed. It wasn't just Prowler who had dined here. Generations of bears had used the spot, retiring here for their feasts.

"He might come back," Winiarski said.

They glanced at each other and scanned the plateau.

There were trees, Zack noticed, flanking the scallop on either side. Hemlocks, straight and spear-headed, fifty feet tall. For a moment, the outcrop wasn't just a time-honored haunt in Prowler's domain. It was his Throne. And these trees standing by it were monuments to his ancestors—a line of beasts that Hope had set loose when she cast her first lifeline to man.

On the left, at the front of the grove, one of the ancients had been beheaded. All that remained was a splintered snag.

"Hope's here," Winiarski said.

"She wouldn't look kindly on the burping and farting," Snell replied. "Prowler's got plenty of spots like this."

It was growing darker and colder, and they were hungry, so they gave up the notion of finding a safer spot and bedded down a hundred yards from Prowler's sofa. While the others slept, one man kept watch.

Midnight had come and gone. Zack sat cross-legged with a rifle in his lap. He shivered, feeling the chill through his miner's clothing. He stood, warmed his hands with his breath, watching the men sleeping beneath a pair of tarps. Then he stepped quietly toward the one closest.

He knelt, put his hand on Bob's shoulder and jostled him. Bob lifted his head. "Ready?" he whispered.

Zack nodded.

"Go slow. A few jabs." Bob scratched his cheek. "Let them open up."

"They're friendly targets," Zack said.

"The kid maybe," Bob allowed. "Inky's changeable as type."

"We'll see."

Bob rose and Zack edged away.

He stood alone, breathing the night wind. The encounter they were staging would be the first with believers. An exclusive performance for the two bargemates. And for Hope, if she was watching. He listened, fixed on the spot where Inky lay and started forward, laughing beneath his breath. It wasn't Hope that spurred him, it was survival. And defiance. Revenge had a life of its own inside him—its own purpose and plan.

A noise startled him—a purring and squealing. Zack stopped, scanning the ground. As the sound lifted, he turned. A dark sheet was rising from the base of the Throne, wings rustling like leaves in the dimness. The swarm of bats crossed the moon and disappeared into the night. The crest of the Throne was visible. A cloud had caught on one of its thorns.

The little man was curled with his blankets around him. Zack scooted beneath the tarp and shook him, and when his eyes opened, he put his hand over Inky's mouth.

"Sh-sh-sh."

"Prowler?" Inky raised himself.

"I want to talk," Zack murmured. "Without Snell." He motioned Inky up.

Inky studied him. Then he unwrapped his blankets.

Zack led him away from the campsite to the Throne's left shoulder, where the grove of tall hemlocks rose into the sky. Bob and Winiarski were waiting by the snag.

"What's up?" Inky wondered.

"Just between us," Zack said.

"Sure," Winiarski nodded.

Inky pursed his lips.

"Well?" Bob pressed him.

"Reporters have a code," Inky said.

"What's it about?" Winiarski wanted to know.

"Hope," Zack said.

Winiarski glanced at Inky.

"You're thinking about Sephy," Zack told the teenager. "About the attentions I've gotten outside the Wheel."

"There's a lot of talk about you," Inky volunteered.

"I'm a different man than you fished out of the drink," Zack said.

Inky moistened his lips. "Hope visits you often."

"She cares for me," Zack said.

"Great, isn't it." Winiarski smiled.

"You don't understand," Zack said.

Winiarski waited expectantly. Bob was staring at the ground.

"She's left Sephy behind," Zack peered into the night. "Hope visits my dreams. And my waking hours." He spoke as if from a distance. "She wants something from me."

"What does she want?" asked Winiarski.

Zack seemed not to hear. "She's given me promises."

"Like the boss," Inky said.

Zack fixed on him. "Hope doesn't think enough of Trevillian to promise him anything."

Inky blinked.

Winiarski was confused. "The boss says—"

"I know what he says."

The disdain in Zack's voice darkened the silence. The cloud on the crest of the Throne was stretching, shaped by an invisible wind. "His communion is a sham," Zack said. "He's feeding us lies."

"Weasel agrees with you," Inky said. "She doesn't think we'll see Hope again." He nodded, as if he'd gotten the point. "So Breakaway's finished. Why should we kill ourselves if she's not coming back."

"You love her," Zack said.

"He loves Weasel," Winiarski laughed.

"The Hope in her," Inky avowed. "I hold that dear."

"I know you do," Zack said. "You need Hope, like all of us." He put his palm on Inky's shoulder. "She *will* come back," he said with emotion. "Once the boss is out of the way."

Winiarski eyed Zack uncertainly.

"What are you saying?" Inky was fearful.

"She's through with him," Zack said. "Prowler singled me out for a reason. It was a sign from Hope—to everyone in the camp."

Bob looked surprised. Was it Zack's audacity or the quality of the performance?

"Hope wants me to put the bit in his mouth," Zack said

heatedly. "Until then, Breakaway will be an open grave."

Bob drove his fist at Winiarski's middle, stopping just short of impact. "A shot to the slats." He glared at the cringing teen and the stunned reporter. "The camp's going to blow up in the boss's face."

"We're trickling powder out," Zack told Inky. "Stick by stick."

Winiarski swallowed. "What will he do if—"

"His command's been honored because Hope favored him," Zack said. "But the favor is gone, and the command will go with it." He looked up. The cloud had detached from the Throne and was drifting north. "I shied from the thought I was special to her. The idea that she had chosen me to lead. What can a man do but be surprised and bewildered? Until he is certain the summons is real."

He gazed at the three men. "I've not seen her in the diggings. But I know who Hope is. I've pressed her close. I've heard the hissing of her crystals, smelled the smoke from her flames—" He drew a breath. "It's still strange, speaking this aloud."

Zack closed his eyes. "She's drowned me in froth— Held me suspended, mingled with her bounty: that precious fruit, grown without sun or rain—a million blazing peaches, each perfectly shaped, swollen around a golden stone."

The words rolled off his tongue.

"I've lived through that moment— When between Hope and her closest there is no distinction. When the treasure was mine. When *I* was her gold. From nothingness, from vapor: a creature of supreme worth, with an infinite soul. My heart is Hope's. I see with her eyes. And every thought burning inside me, every word springing to mind, has Hope as its source."

Zack drew the breeze through his lips. When he parted his lids, Inky and Winiarski were staring at him. Bob was squinting— He had changed in Bob's eyes.

"You're crazy," Inky said.

Winiarski sighed. "I had dreams about her," he confided, "when I was a kid." His eyes glistened at Zack. "She was a caterpillar, soft as cotton. I rode on her back."

A chill wind struck them, and they shivered as one.

Zack grasped Inky's arm. "Hope wants you with us."

"How many are there?" Inky asked.

"More than you'd think," Bob replied.

"Trevillian's steak on the hoof," Zack said.

"And then Hope will return?" Inky frowned.

Zack nodded slowly. "Hope will return."

The statement was so bald, it left little room for question. Inky just stared at him. Bob scratched the gravel with his boot.

Zack gazed at the plateau with its sofa and boneyard. "When we've had our fill of her, we'll fell some trees. Build a boat. Head back south." It was an afterthought.

"That's why we came on this chase," Winiarski glanced at Inky. "So Zack could ask us to join him." He smiled at Bob. "The test was for us."

Zack laughed. He eyed the teenager, closed the distance and embraced him. "We've been in this together, from the start," Zack said. He stroked the boy's hair.

11

The next day they headed back. Snell was none the wiser. Inky remained noncommittal, but there was no mistaking—he saw Zack in a new light. Bob was quiet, still digesting the performance.

As they approached the pass above the Breakaway valley, it began to rain. The climb was steep and Zack was breathing hard. By the time they reached the Glory Hole, he was soaked. But the cold and the headwind only lifted his spirits. He was the rebel, dead set and valiant, battling forces allied against him.

As they came around the rim, the giant funnel appeared. The runoff was pouring from all sides, converging at the collar. In the water plunging down the shaft, Zack saw an image of Hope—not that pristine creature the camp yearned for, but something muddy and lank, scaling beneath the lanterns, track ties piercing her skin like a broken spine. For Trevillian, this was all that was left of her.

The boss must have spotted them descending the switchback trail. As they drew near the store, Zack saw him waiting on the front deck. His oilskin slicker slapped in the wind.

"Get him?" the boss asked.

Zack shook his head. "We found a place he visits."

"Might snare him there," Snell offered.

Trevillian waved the suggestion away. "Start digging those pit traps." He nodded at the firearms and Snell collected them from Inky and Bob.

"Guess I'll be takin' that now." Snell looked at Zack's rifle.

Zack was handing it over when Trevillian stopped him.

"Bring it with you," he said, motioning toward the store entrance.

The boss turned and passed through the doorway. Zack mounted the deck and started up the inside stair behind him.

Trevillian opened the door to the office and the two stepped inside. Salt Lick was standing by the window. There were shadows beneath her eyes. When she saw Zack, she stiffened.

"Did he get the bear?" she asked.

The boss shook his head. He took the rifle from Zack, tossed him a blanket and approached the gun rack, working the handgrip till the magazine was empty.

Lloyd was there too, just as Zack had last seen him—stooped over the cot with Pollard on it. The smith was still alive, his body shifting beneath the blankets. Lloyd was about to apply fresh bandages, but as he reached toward him, Pollard shrank.

"Cuck hin oken," Pollard pleaded.

Pollard turned and Zack froze. One of the smith's eyes was bulging with horror. The other was sunk like a button in an overstuffed pillow, scotched on all sides with stitches. There was a bloody bowl where Pollard's mouth had been, and the rest of his face formed a kidney around it, purplish and inflated, beaded with sweat.

Lloyd set the bandages aside and retrieved a damp rag from a basin on the floor. He reached to cool Pollard's face, but Pollard recoiled. His scarlet mouth twitched. A tongue was wriggling down in it.

"You're safe," Lloyd said.

"Cuck hin oken—" Pollard's head shook, desperate to be understood.

Lloyd gripped his shoulders and forced him back down.

"The fog's rolled in," Trevillian traced a zephyr past his head.

Hope had delivered this atrocity to the boss, and he was living with it.

"Thinks Prowler's swallowed him," Trevillian scowled. "He's inside the bear's gut, trying to get out."

A flurry of rain landed on the roof of the store and slid down its backside, clawing at the planking. Nickel gloom filtered through the windows.

"We were having a discussion," the boss said.

Salt Lick turned and stared through the glass.

"Francine's angry with me," Trevillian told him. "She wants me to slow down. Lloyd thinks we should do as the Captain suggested—build barracks."

Lloyd let his rag fall into the basin and stood up, looking from the boss to Zack.

"Explain yourself," Trevillian directed him. "I want Zack's opinion."

"Why are you drawing him into this?" Salt Lick said.

Lloyd took a breath. "There's some ill sentiment. Hope's in hiding, and men are wondering why they're here. It's going to be a long winter. Building shelters will buy us time."

"And the flogging—" Trevillian prompted him to continue.

"The Captain's in the infirmary," Lloyd nodded toward the warehouse below them. "The wound would be manageable—but he's got scurvy."

The Reminder was on the boss's hip. Zack remembered how he'd drawn the bloody popper through his fist.

"Go on," Trevillian said.

"Men are—" Lloyd hesitated. "Upset."

"My power is no longer secure—" Trevillian cocked his head. "What do you think of that?"

Zack was silent.

"Is it time to take a breath?" Trevillian asked.

The boss stepped closer. His eyes were steely, impenetrable.

"You know Hope's mind," Trevillian said.

Zack stared at his boots, heart racing.

"She's speaking to you," the boss said, "isn't she. What happened out there? I know her too well."

Zack felt Trevillian's breath on his face. His thoughts churned.

"What does Hope say," the boss hissed.

"We're failing her test," Zack muttered.

"What test?"

"The test of belief." Zack raised his eyes. "We dig, but we doubt."

The boss stood rigid, searching him. "She's left us for dead."

"No," Zack replied. "She's in the mountain."

Salt Lick turned from the window.

"Where?" the boss asked.

Zack looked helpless. "She wouldn't tell me."

"This came through Sephy?"

Zack shook his head. "Hope answered me last night. For the first time."

Rain swept across the panes and swished down the siding.

"She's using you to torment me," Trevillian said. "Doubt? I bow and scrape," he waved at the trays of fresh assays. "I shuffle on my knees for flimsies jotted with insults." He faced the sectional map. "That's faith enough—" His gaze wandered from the barren drifts into the uncharted rock below the 770.

"You've made a hell of my life," the boss said. He drew a new pick from his belt. "You're too free with your disgust," he threatened the map. "I'm going to earn it."

"She barely thinks of us," Salt Lick said.

Trevillian didn't hear her. "If I have to dig to Gehenna," he brandished his pick, "I'll find that dainty hand. Kiss it? No, I'll chew it off— I'll strip you on every side and mount my hundred stiffs together, mules too. All at once, every spike to the nuggets in you." He powered the pick at the map, and the point sank with a shriek.

"Trill—" Lloyd moved toward him.

When Trevillian turned, his desolation was naked. He was shaking from head to toe. "Look what she's doing—"

Lloyd opened his arms, and the boss found harbor in the sawbones' embrace. "Hope stinks," Lloyd said.

Trevillian rocked his face on Lloyd's shoulder.

"We'll put roaches in her knickers," Lloyd said.

Trevillian laughed. "That'll fix her."

Zack glanced at Salt Lick. She looked away.

The boss drew a breath and wiped his cheek. "Doubt, you say?" he muttered at Zack.

"I'm learning," Zack said, "how cruel Hope can be."

"First thing tomorrow," Salt Lick told the boss, "we'll start milling boards for the barracks."

"Hope means more to us than safety or shelter," Zack said.

Salt Lick ignored him. "If Hope reappears—"

"It's a Blonde's job to care, and a doctor's to heal," Zack said. "The priest must lead."

Trevillian's eyes met his.

"Your devotion will be used," Salt Lick warned the boss, "to breed revolt."

"Any Judas in the camp," he said, still focused on Zack, "will find my whip around his neck."

"I'm done here," the madam said. She turned to leave. The boss didn't stop her.

Lloyd collared Trevillian with his arm. For a moment, the two were scamps tussling in an alley. Then Lloyd returned to Pollard's cot and sank down beside it.

"Get your rest," Trevillian waved Zack away.

Zack descended the inside stair. The rain had ceased. The madam was waiting for him at the bottom.

"Shabby stagecraft," she shook her head.

"I'm doing my best for him."

"You're playing rat to the snake." Her lime eyes seethed.

"Rat?" Zack laughed. "I'm Hope's peach."

"You're not to be trusted, Mister Knox."

"You're jealous, Missus Trill, and that's foolish. You're the one I want." He wagged his finger and hooked it on her bodice.

She slapped his arm away.

"Stick with Sephy," she said.

"You're closer to Hope."

"You're so wrong," the madam said. "No one serves up Hope like Sephy. Ask any of the boys."

She saw her words had pierced him, and she hurried with more. "A spartan soul—that was her idea. No paint or undergarments—" The madam's brow creased. "Solemn and righteous— With Sephy, there's nothing held back. She makes the full sacrifice."

Zack turned away.

"You're a lucky man," Salt Lick said. "You and Trill. He can't get enough of her." She seemed to gag on her words.

When Zack looked again, her jaw was quivering. A nostril twitched, as if some foul odor had reached her. She exhaled sharply. "What do I know?"

With that, she turned and started along the path toward Blondetown.

Zack watched her go. She moved slowly, like a woman much older, bent in the middle and unsteady without a cane.

When she had disappeared from view, he started for the corduroy road, ascending the switchback trail alone.

Sephy was in the Big Wheel. He got word to her and she agreed to meet him in an abandoned bulldoze chamber on the 400 level.

It was a small cavern littered with boulders. Rich ore had been loaded into trams here, back when quartz had been bountiful. It was quiet now, except for the ringing of drops in hidden pools and the whispering of Hope's ghost in the cloisters. Zack had met Sephy here before. He found the slab and sat down.

A few minutes later, a lantern appeared at the cavern's entrance and floated toward him. Sephy clambered onto the slab and knelt beside him, the black skirt riding up her calves.

"Prowler survived you," Sephy said.

Zack nodded.

She set the lantern down. "And your two—"

"They're with us," Zack said.

"So you passed your test." Sephy removed her boots. "Poor Pollard. It's terrible, what he's going through." She peered into the darkness. "And there's grief in Blondetown. Helaina is pregnant."

Zack was silent.

"Have you seen a child come into the world?" she asked.

"The wrangler's girl let loose one night." He stared at her. "You're playing Hope to Trevillian."

She bowed her head.

"How long has this—"

"It started after the winze was cut," Sephy said.

"Our lies about Hope's visitations," Zack nodded.

"It's his privilege," she said. "He's the boss."

"Why didn't you tell me?"

"I knew how you'd react."

Zack held his tongue.

"It's not because he has any yen for me," Sephy said.

"Has Hope spoken to him? Through you?"

"Do you mistrust her?" Sephy asked.

Zack didn't reply.

She lifted her arms and unbound her hair. "She despises him as I do." Her hands went to the neck of her shirtwaist and she began to unbutton it. "She wishes you could protect me—"

Zack shook his head.

275

"But she knows you can't," Sephy said.

"What has she said to him?" Zack demanded.

Sephy stared at him.

"It has to stop," Zack said.

"I'd like to bring this mine down on all of you," she muttered.

The reaction silenced him.

Sephy seemed to retreat into some interior refuge. She opened the shirtwaist. "Hope thinks of no one but you," she said.

The black top fell from her shoulders. Her hands slid the black skirt from her hips. And the priestess of Hope was naked before him, her white body framed by the grotto, its ragged walls dark and gleaming.

He reached for her. His fingers touched ribs, sliding over the smooth corrugations.

She knows you can't—

Sephy's words ripened in his head, swollen with reproof.

The slab seemed to lose its mooring. She was easing him back. Her face descended, settling to one side, her lips by his cheek. Both lanterns were flickering, and the syncopated flashes seemed to reach through the walls. He wasn't seeing the dripping rock, he was peering through it. The bright flecks were drifting motes, distant stars in a mineral sky. The piers of the chamber rose into it, like the columns of a ruined shrine.

Illusions fed by longing? His humanity seemed to be slipping away.

Sephy lay in pieces. Her cheek was here, her knee there, her hip, her arm— Her presence circled him like fragments of a shattered mirror, memories and sensations without a center.

She knows you can't, she knows you can't—

Her whisper echoed in the distance, obscured by hissing. The body of an angel was settling over him, her chest lit like a cut-glass chandelier. On either side, wings arched like glittering spouts, trembling, loosing halos through the smoke. An icy face resolved, rigid, chiseled for eternity, razor-edged facets glinting in crystalline eyes.

Sephy was gone.

Hope's limbs streamed back, her long pinions drawing from the grotto rock. Her trunk flashed, her face fogged and pearled as he watched. Then the gleaming wings closed around him, swaddling him in a polyhedron of stretching glass. Again, Zack felt Hope's blessing. Her power, her confidence— Trevillian was an impotent puppet shaking its stuffed head.

The angel convulsed. Her webbed wings sprung back. Her jaw was spasming, and the flesh below drooped and quivered like a lizard's jowls. A cry escaped her, thin as a lamb's. Then the angel's head sank, her nape cracked like a molt, and a thick white torrent came roaring out. The liquid quartz hurtled forward like a train on tracks and eeled behind like a river racing down a mountain.

You don't know me, Hope said.

She was wingless, faceless—

You've never touched me or held me—

Her voice was throaty, changing with the flow.

I'm a dream to you, Zack. Something you imagined.

The cast skin clung to her: an ivory robe with a jeweled lining. Rubies and garnets were studded there, glistering and dripping while Hope's serpentine body slid through it. Beyond his feet, Zack could see a white tail tapering in the distance. Forward, her neck had looped, rising and vanishing into a fog. Directly before him, Hope's thick trunk sang and squealed, the sharp-sided crystals gliding and melting an inch from his palm.

Look in this glass, Hope said.

The drenched facets were annealing. Her smoky flesh cleared. The gold flames still burned behind flashing panes, but it was as if a million wicks had, all at once, been turned down. Hope's body was a mirror of burnished shards, and as it rushed past, he saw his reflection: a grinning mask with holes for eyes.

See what you are.

A false face, Zack thought.

He stared at the empty orbits as Hope hissed past.

A man with no soul—

Not even that, Hope said. *Not a man at all.*

Zack closed his eyes.

A severed child, she said. *Your fears imprison you. You will die inside them, like a bird in a cage.*

I've done my—

Your deceptions are vile, Hope said.

There is no other way—

You will never defeat him, Hope said.

Zack heard the contempt in her voice.

You don't have his nerve, his daring. And you don't believe.

Men will follow me—

Those who do will perish, Hope said. *To the rest, you will bring misery and despair. And when Trevillian cries, "Hope, where is Hope," you will hold him and kiss the tears from his cheek.*

Help me—

Don't think of me again, Hope said. *Put me out of your mind—*

Zack opened his eyes. The mirror had fogged. Hope's voice was fading.

Don't fish for me in Sephy, Hope said. *Don't speak my name.*

The ivory robe closed. The current froze and its long body shrank back. Arms and legs appeared, impossibly stretched.

No, please—

I don't exist, Hope said.

The last vestige of the river collapsed. It was Sephy's pale body before him.

Zack reached to embrace her, breathless, distraught. She turned her back to him and curled away. When he placed his hand on her shoulder, she hid her face.

Zack wanted to speak, but fear held his tongue. What might Sephy say—in what voice, with what feelings? He stared at her back, wondering, dread mounting. The game they'd played, the fantasy that nourished their love and fueled the dream of rebellion— These longed-for possessions by Hope—

They'd turned onto some dark byway, Zack thought. Crossed some line that shouldn't be crossed. As he lay there in the cold, watching Sephy's motionless body, he imagined he'd lost her.

When he woke, she was gone.

Zack returned to the pup for the evening and was in the yard the next morning for grub. He descended to the 770 and put in ten hours behind a sledge at Peephole. Was it weariness, Hope's words in the bulldoze chamber or his fears about Sephy? Everything seemed rushed, his shift mates in a frenzy, the struggle for Hope without purpose.

When the whistle finally blew, his shaker rose and departed. Cart wheels squealed down the drift, and a light winked into view. The man backing a mule toward him was Marcus Bunting.

The mule stopped and Marcus bent over the cart. Zack drew beside him, watching his fingers feel along the bottom. Marcus lifted a foot-square plate. Beneath, a small compartment lined with moss held four sticks of dynamite.

Marcus passed him the sticks.

"He'll get them back," Zack said.

Bunting smiled.

The mule snorted. Its ears cocked, pivoting full around. Someone was coming.

Marcus replaced the false bottom. Zack slid the sticks beneath his coat and headed down the drift.

Twenty minutes later, he was in the warehouse on the ground floor of the store. Beyond the hills of grain and beans, the summer's salmon catch had been stacked—a maze of walls, red and oily, eight feet in height. With a lit candle stub, Zack threaded the maze, waded through a battery of equipment and entered a clutter of cots and pallets. The sick and injured tossed and slept here in darkness thick as the mine.

He saw a pair of lanterns on the far side of the infirmary, and glints on coifs and gowns. Blondes on their shift break. They had their backs to him and they didn't turn.

There were no cots available, so Lloyd had put the Captain in a ruined dinghy. Zack caught sight of its prow. As he approached, the little boat emerged from the gloom, floating in a brace of logs and grain sacks. The Captain sat inside with his back to the stern and his elbows on the gunwale.

Zack drew up beside him. "How does she fare?"

"Heeling badly," the Captain said.

"You need ballast."

The Captain drew his blanket back.

Zack pulled the four sticks of dynamite from beneath his coat and passed them over the gunwale. The Captain slid the cartridges into a canvas sack. Zack retrieved a handful of bullets from his pocket and those went into the sack as well. He could see the mottled bandages wrapped around the Captain's thigh.

"She's testing me," the Captain said.

Zack could see the foreboding in his eyes. He had a few choice words of his own for Hope, but he swallowed them. He closed the sack and helped the Captain bury it beneath his good leg.

"Give it time." Zack drew the blanket over him. Then he found his way back through the maze.

12

fter the encounter in the bulldoze chamber, Zack saw
no more of Hope. His fears that he'd lost Sephy were
false, but things were different between them. The
subject of Trevillian's attentions was avoided. They spoke of
Hope, but there was no hint of her presence in Sephy's ca-
resses. When Zack called Hope to mind in solitary moments,
his impressions faded as quickly as he formed them. She was
like a morning fog that the heat had burned away.

For the sake of the rebellion, they maintained the fiction
that Zack was intimate with Hope. To believers, he pretended
he was her chosen. They continued to add to the small cache
of munitions and explosives, and the recruiting advanced.
With the help of Inky and Sephy, Zack drew Weasel in. He
was successful in enlisting two more men—one from the
barge and one of Bob's pals. But most of the miners were

unapproachable. Men like True Bluford remembered the days of Hope's glory, and the memories inspired a fierce loyalty to Trevillian. Those who'd arrived on the barge had no attachment to the boss, but most were too cowed to defy him. And converts like Carew had to be counted out. He would defend Trevillian with his dying breath.

The ever-present fear of discovery added to the exhaustion of long shifts and the gloom that pervaded the camp. At times it was more than Zack could bear. Sephy did what she could to support him, but when the topic was Hope, her words lacked conviction. Hope's silence didn't mean she'd left them for good. Who knew what she intended? Hope might return, Sephy said.

There was no evidence of that in the diggings. The drifts on the 770 were pushed farther and new ones were started. Threads surfaced at Lovesick, lenses at Peephole and Giblets— just broken traces that came and went. A ribbon appeared at the end of the level—Vestige they called it—but when they blasted, the ribbon unraveled. No one was surprised when Trevillian announced that the winze would be driven deeper. The everhards were employed, and when the well reached 930 feet, a new level was struck. The initial results were discouraging. The boss's preachings didn't cease, but they grew increasingly confused. He would pause and gaze into the distance, searching for words, lost in thought. When he called a halt to the drilling at Slick Liver, he had his cot put there and his inspections redoubled. Men saw him at all hours, scouring the blast faces like a pilgrim searching the stars for a sign.

Zack felt Trevillian's moods keenly. The boss would laud his labors and then use him to vent his spleen. For a time, the boss clung to the idea that Zack would give him access to Hope. But as the prospects in the drifts faded, it was consolation he sought. "That energy," Trevillian lamented. "Having Hope inside you— I can't live without that."

The boss continued with Sephy, summoning her to his tent, or entering her alcove in the Wheel through the back passageway. Word circulated, and there weren't many who cared to spare Zack's feelings. If there was a chance that, through Sephy, the boss could determine Hope's whereabouts, that was cause for cheer. But when Zack grew bold enough to ask, Sephy's descriptions of her courtesies to Trevillian were bleaker than anyone would have imagined. The boss had grown weary of failed attempts to find Hope between her thighs and would abuse her instead, pour his grief out to her, or curl on her pallet with his head in her lap.

Chatter about Hope's pique or her fickleness ceased. Even those firmest in belief now accepted the possibility that Hope might not return. Was it a judgment she had levied against them? Punishment for weakness of spirit, the conflicts surrounding Prowler's visit, the way they'd bungled one test or another? Many thought her loss was on account of them.

A succession of grim events followed, one after the other.

A week after Prowler's attack, Lloyd removed Helaina's unborn child. The Blondes wrapped the remains in white linen, ascended to the rim of the Glory Hole with the bundle and found a place for it in the forest.

The week following, Pollard died. In the graveyard, the words the boss said over the smith chilled the camp more than the cold. His elegy became a tirade against Hope. "She's idling below," Trevillian raved, "combing her hair with the Private's ribs."

The next day, while charges were being tamped at Lovesick, a blasting cap went off in the loader's pocket and destroyed his leg.

As September gave way to October, the hours of light grew shorter. The mists were thicker, swallowing distant peaks, then nearer ones. Rain fell and it wouldn't stop. There were empty seats at the tables in the yard. Men were sleeping through the shift whistle, missing meals, hiding in their tents. A lung sickness spread, leaving a dozen miners wheezing and feverish, and it was three weeks before the last of them was out of danger.

Brute winds joined the rains, and together they thrashed the slopes. The first freeze left the devil's club hanging like rags. The week following, winds flattened the fern beds and the last leaves were torn from the thickets. One afternoon seals appeared, drifting offshore with only their heads above the surface, staring at the camp like observers from another world. The next morning a shelf of ice edged the inlet. That night, one of the Blondes broke down. She emerged from her alcove stark naked and went stumbling through the Wheel, pleading with the miners. "She must be found, she must be found." The woman was confined to her tent, and when she reappeared it was as a cook. She remained constant to Hope, but she was no longer fit to play her.

The footpaths hardened and a winter storm struck the valley. The air in the diggings was colder and drier, and the stiffs on the 930 struggled for breath. Redirecting the air flow was urgent, but as the equipment was being readied on the 490 platform, two Bangshu lost their hold on a section of ventilation pipe. It fell down the winze and crushed a miner in the bucket. Before the camp could put him under, another storm hit. It tore up a dozen tents and forced men into the warehouse for shelter. The winds continued through the next day, letting up after the evening mess.

It was dark. The walls of the Breakaway valley gleamed with ice, and an ember was winding between them. Someone was descending the switchback trail.

The ember reached the bridge and floated across. It circled the store, paused at the cook shack and approached the side door. A figure in woman's dress appeared in the lantern light. She opened the door and slid through.

At the front of the warehouse, miners who'd been driven there by the storm were seated or huddled half-clothed in their bedrolls, some talking, some eating, some trying to sleep.

"Fool," a man cursed his half-eaten salmon. "Shoulda stayed in the ocean."

Inky was ten feet away, reclining against a grain sack.

"Fish don't have any sense," another observed as he chewed.

"There's a theory," Inky said, "they come back to the river they were hatched in."

The first man laughed. "Why would they do that?"

At the rear of the warehouse, Sephy emerged from the salmon maze, dimmed her lantern and entered the infirmary. The cots and pallets and the patients on them were barely visible. She made her way to a quiet corner, where the Captain's dinghy rode the darkness. She drew beside it and put her hand on his shoulder.

He surfaced from sleep.

Sephy put her fingers on his lips and raised a canteen. "How is it?"

The Captain pushed his blankets back. His thigh was swollen twice its normal size.

"Drink your spruce tea like the rest of us." She handed the canteen to him.

"Our good fortune, I suppose," the Captain said, after he'd taken a draft.

Sephy pulled three sticks of dynamite from her coat pocket and passed them over the gunwale. The Captain flexed his good leg and added the sticks to the sack beneath.

"Good fortune?"

"Where else would we stow this stuff?" the Captain said.

Sephy stroked his cheek.

The Captain kissed her hand. "I'll harbor here long enough to see them used."

At that moment, Owen and DuVal were investigating a hangfire on the 930. DuVal had touched the charges off, but when the round fired, the count had been short. He found Owen, and the two men were at the Maidbraid drift head, sorting through blast rubble.

Owen reached between twists of smoke and forced the sharp end of his pick beneath a scorched block. He levered it up and turned it over, and a flame jumped to life.

"There 'tis," he said, going down on one knee.

DuVal crouched opposite, chomping a wad of gum.

Owen raised the sparking fuse, opened his pocketknife and cut the cord ahead of the spark. DuVal worked over the broken rock, uncovering the remnants of the shattered drill hole.

"There's the primer," DuVal said, raising an unexploded dynamite cartridge with a cap buried in its side. "And the one behind it—" He raised a second stick and his chomping stopped. "Look here."

Owen examined the stick and then stooped over the remains of the drill hole.

"She's packed with mud, not powder."

"The boss will spit blood," DuVal said.

Owen stared at him. "Who loaded this?"

The tent camp was lit by log fires, and smoke was threading from the stove pipes. Snows from the recent flurries covered the ground. Men's voices sounded, muffled by canvas. Zack and Dog-Eared Bob were inside the pup.

Bob knelt in front of the oil drum stove, feeding wood to it. Shouts sounded from up the hill. He turned, concern wrinkling his sweat-slicked face.

The two listened to the voices answering nearby. The next moment, boots pounded along the path, splashing through puddles and mush ice. Bob reached for his coat. Zack threw back the tent flap.

"What's up?" he shouted as a miner hurried by.

"Someone on the whipping wall," the miner answered.

Another man passed. "Winiarski," he said, glancing at Zack.

Bob hooked the lantern bail with his fingers and scrambled out.

Zack turned back the bedding, grabbed the mongrel revolver and felt for the two bullets he carried in his shirt pocket. He tucked the mongrel into his belt, drew on his coat and rose in front of the pup.

The slope was alive, men hustling up the paths toward the store. Bob gestured with his light. They hadn't gone ten paces when they heard the *crack* of the Reminder. As they crested the rise, they heard another. Noel-the-Mole appeared on the corduroy road in front of them. Bob grabbed his arm.

"Hangfire at Maidbraid," Noel said, answering the question in their eyes. "Two sticks where there should have been five. Winiarski did the loading."

Another *crack*. Bob winced.

They hurried forward.

"No blood," a voice shouted as the yard came into view.

Zack saw the men gathered around the wall. Winiarski was naked, spread out with his back to Trevillian. The circle of lanterns and the rising smoke made it look like some barbaric ritual. As the followers watched, their priest brought his scourge back, then his arm shot forward and the whip cracked.

Winiarski spasmed and sagged, his gasp turning to steam in the chill air.

Zack's stomach turned. A pair of large welts crossed the boy's shoulders and a third spanned his thighs.

"Seven," DuVal announced. "No blood."

Zack made his way through the gathering. Bob was behind him.

"The game's up," Trevillian said.

Winiarski glanced back. He was trying to smile. He wore iron cuffs attached by short chains to the bolts in the siding, and he rattled them helplessly. "Can't I put my drawers on?"

Zack could see the terror in his eyes.

DuVal stood on Trevillian's right, holding a shotgun.

"Where did the powder go?" Trevillian demanded. The Reminder switched at his boots, then it arched its back, doubling by his shoulder. The boss drew it behind him, rose onto the balls of his feet and brought it around like a mainspring unwinding. The air was split by another *crack*.

"Eight," DuVal said. "There's blood."

A stripe appeared, running from shoulder to buttock.

Zack saw Inky staring wild-eyed at him, ten feet away.

"Talk to me," Trevillian raged. He twisted, cocked his arm over his shoulder and threw himself into the downstroke. "Talk!" Again he struck. And again.

"Stop—" Lloyd descended the outside stair and barged through the assembly, swinging his medicine bag angrily. "The infirmary's full," he shouted at Trevillian.

The boss paused, his whip raised, popper dripping.

Winiarski turned to look. His cheeks were wet.

"Let me have him," Lloyd said.

But Trevillian was bunching his arm. He rocked forward and struck again, and again the lash cut deeply.

"You'll clip him apart," Noel-the-Mole shouted.

Trevillian turned, snagged Noel with a glance and cracked the Reminder at his face. Noel threw his hands up and collapsed into his fellows' arms with blood leaking through his fingers. The crowd receded before Trevillian's gaze. Lloyd threw himself on the boss's back, but Trevillian dashed him to the ground.

Zack shuddered. His hand was trembling. He raised it and felt inside his coat for his shirt pocket. Bob was at his elbow, watching him. Zack fished in the pocket for the bullets. His fingers were rough as spruce cones, and the metal objects slipped through them.

"See what you are?" Trevillian snarled at Winiarski, raising the dripping thong and shaking it. "A few buckets of blood, standing between Hope and her believers."

"Give Hope your heart," Winiarski cried, his voice breaking.

Trevillian lifted his arm. The whip collected in the air behind him and struck again. A razor cut divided Winiarski's loins.

"I believe," he sobbed.

"You disgust her." Again the boss struck. "She loathes you." Again. "She coughs up empty carts at the sight of you."

Zack had a bullet between his thumb and forefinger, but as he drew it from his pocket, he bobbled it. The bullet landed in the gravel between his boots.

As the Reminder struck, Winiarski bucked against the planking. "I believe," he said, "I believe, I believe," as if he meant to outdo the boss's passion for Hope. Steam was rising from his back, and a scarlet fringe was dripping down it.

Zack got hold of the second bullet. With his right hand, he palmed the grip of the mongrel beneath his coat, moving forward, forcing his way through the crowd. His other hand drew the shell from his shirt pocket, holding it firmly, his thumb against the seam where the head disappeared into the casing. He opened the mongrel's chamber and slid the bullet in.

Trevillian stood now with his right arm hanging at his side, chest heaving. The Reminder's popper was coiled in the dirt. A choked sound came from his throat—a sob of his own. Just one, as brief as a sneeze. "Where's my count?" he demanded.

"Twenty," DuVal said. "Is it twenty?"

Zack's heart was racing. He was near the front of the

gathering now. He saw Dinesh follow him with his eyes. Marcus was doing the same. Zack forced himself to look at the boss, cocking the hammer of the mongrel and easing it up his midline. His hand was shaking, the barrel twitched beneath his coat. He stared at his boots to calm himself.

Crack. Crack. The office door slammed.

Zack looked up to see Owen and Snell descending the outside stair with shotguns trained on the crowd. Trevillian wiped his eyes with his wrist, and the whip came looping back beside him. There was a snow-covered buckboard by the warehouse door, a dozen steps to Zack's right. He shouldered through the miners, moving toward it.

Trevillian growled and threw himself forward, striking repeatedly with no pause between. He was cutting on every stroke now.

"Harden yourself," Owen shouted from the stair. His words seemed meant for all of them.

Zack swung behind the buckboard and peered over it in time to see Winiarski faint. The boy hung limp from the manacles, head lolling. Trevillian snapped the lash back and circled it overhead. Pinpoints of blood spattered the snow in the buckboard bed and stung Zack's face.

He raised the mongrel, hugging the rail, straightening his arm behind the seat as the Reminder hummed. His palm was sweaty, his vision blurred. He leveled the bead on Trevillian's ear hole, but his hand shook so badly, he knew he would miss. Something flashed at the corner of Zack's eye. Through the open warehouse door, a lantern glimmered, hanging on a post amid the baled hay. As the whip broke its circle, Zack swung the mongrel toward the lantern. At the *crack*, he squeezed the trigger.

The revolver spit a foot-long flame and the lantern exploded.

Zack turned his shoulder to the buckboard and tucked the mongrel beneath his coat.

"Fire!" a miner shouted.

Through the door, flames were splashing the floor and climbing the hay.

Lloyd hurried beside Trevillian. "The whistle," he pointed at Snell. "Fetch buckets," he cried to Owen. "For heaven's sake!"

Owen cursed, glanced at Trevillian and lowered his shotgun. "True—" He descended the stair, motioning. "Blankets—" Smoke was filtering through the plank wall. Owen faced DuVal. "Take the Bang lads and run the hose to the river."

Lloyd had unlatched Winiarski's manacles and was dragging him away from the warehouse. Zack watched Trevillian turn, following the sudden activity with a dazed look. He was breathing hard, tongue on his lip, the bloody whip curled around his boots.

"Get the sick out of the infirmary," Lloyd shouted.

Zack's fears shifted to the Captain and his freight. He sprang forward, joining a half-dozen others who were headed into the warehouse. Flames were mounting the inside walls. As they reached the entrance, a crazed mule bolted through the smoke, pulling an empty wagon. Men threw themselves aside, but Zack stood his ground, watching the wild eye come. He caught the harness and fell with his weight on it. Just then, the alarm whistle blew. Zack held on while the mule screamed and bucked. Carew threw his coat over the animal's head. Others surrounded it, laying hands on the hitch and collar, and together they hauled it back into the building. The alarm continued to blow.

Inside, the western wall was a sheet of flame. Fire spouted from the hay piles and dripped from the second-floor planks. Zack led the mule and the choking men down the wagon lane of the warehouse, hearing shouts through the smoke ahead. Beyond the salmon maze, he could see figures tottering among the cots, crawling on the floor. The blaze came balling along the rear wall and the Captain hove out of the shadows, craning over the gunwale, riding a scarlet wave.

Zack clipped the mule's harness to a post chain. "Captain first—" He gestured the men toward the dinghy. The Captain's eyes found his. Zack could see the prospect of the ignited explosives in them. Two men appeared on the other side of the dinghy and reached to lift the Captain out. He bellowed, waving at his leg.

"The whole boat," Zack ordered them. "Get under it—"

Carew and three others went to the stern, and with a man on either side of the prow, they lifted the dinghy off its braces. Zack slipped the mongrel over the gunwale to the Captain as the boat rose. Then he stooped and put his shoulder beneath the hull. They turned the dinghy's prow and beached it on the wagon bed, then they lifted the other patients in. Zack unclipped the mule from the post and led it back down the wagon lane, hauling the cargo.

As he passed through the doorway into the yard, a gang emerged from the store's front, loaded with blankets. Inky was among them.

"Like this—" Owen took a blanket, dragged it in the snow and threw it over a man's shoulders. "Bring me a sack of beans—" Owen motioned at the others. "Put a blanket on. Fetch our grub. Go!"

Zack stopped Inky with an urgent look. He nodded at the mule collar and Inky grabbed it, seeing the dinghy with the Captain inside. "Get them away from here," Zack motioned. Then he turned, plunging through the crowd, headed for Winiarski. A mass of flames grew from the spot where the boy had been chained. Thirty feet away, in the trampled yard, Lloyd knelt beside him. Trevillian stood over them, coiling his whip slowly, his pants soaked with blood.

As Zack approached, Trevillian turned. "The office," the boss mumbled, waking from his trance. He turned on his heel and hurried toward the front of the store.

"How is he?" Zack asked.

Beneath Lloyd's lantern, Winiarski lay motionless, face up. His eyes looked like pebbles. Lloyd sighed and shook his head.

"Better help with the hose," Lloyd said.

Zack turned, boiling with rage. Below the mill shed, DuVal's team was hauling a hose and pump through the scrub. Around them, men were racing past with buckets, carrying water from the river. Zack's legs kicked beneath him and he headed after the boss.

Trevillian had entered the store's front and was climbing the inside stair. Zack leaped after him. Flames forked through the treads. Higher up, they were weaving a nest between the balusters. He saw the boss put his head down, and he did the same, bursting through the orange swarm, heat and venom hissing in his ears. The boss rose before him—a specter, legs lost in smoke. He was unaware he was being followed. He reached the landing and shouldered through the burning door.

Zack mounted the charred platform and paused by the jamb, covering his mouth to keep from choking. Trevillian was on the far side of the office. He'd retrieved a table furnace from the assay area, and as Zack watched, he heaved it through the window. Flames were eating through the floor from beneath. The boss was at the shelves now, coughing, clearing them with both arms, gathering bottles, mortars, molds and assay tools and hurling them out the window. He lunged for the rack, pulling firearms free, tossing them through the opening. Then he rummaged in a cabinet, found a satchel and loaded it with boxes of bullets and shotgun shells. His face was pocked with Winiarski's blood and his hands were gloved with it.

Zack pulled the pick from his belt, watching through a scarf of flame. The boss sprang across the room, tore the sectional map away and stuffed it in the satchel. A fountain of fire erupted beside him. He glanced toward the door. Zack recoiled, shuffling behind a blazing curtain. Trevillian's eyes were wild. He hurried forward.

Zack raised his pick, crossing the threshold to meet him. At that same moment, the roof collapsed. The office walls buckled, the planks burst apart. A joist swung like a boom, catching Trevillian's shoulder. He crashed to the floor beneath falling timbers. Wind blasted into the space, roiling the smoke. It circled the boss in a thick mass. Zack stepped through the ruins, gasping, left hand clearing the air by his face, pick ready in his right.

Trevillian lay pinned on his side, still clutching the satchel, a giant beam across his middle. He struggled to free himself, silvered with ash, glittering with cinders, the red loops of the Reminder slapping his thigh. Zack hovered over him, breathless, pulse pounding, looking for an opening as the smoke churned.

Trevillian wrenched onto his back, cloth ripping across his front, staring straight at Zack as the pick reached its height. His left pectoral was bare, its deep crease the target, and the pick was descending—

"Boss!" Owen rushed forward, brandishing an axe.

Zack veered the pick, spiking into the beam between cuffs of fire. Through a veil of sparks, he saw Trevillian's shock dissolve.

"Grab him." Zack heaved the pick up, lifting the burning beam.

Owen pulled Trevillian from under it.

Zack let the beam drop and jerked his pick free. "Down," he shouted as Trevillian came to his feet.

Owen grabbed the satchel and bolted through the smoke. "Down—" Zack motioned to the boss.

Trevillian stumbled after Owen, but as he reached the threshold, the floorboards tittered. With a burst of glowing motes, the landing crumbled into chars and fell clean away. He reeled backward into Zack's arms. The boss was about to speak when the blaze rumbled beneath them. The floor opened and Zack sank to his thighs in a vat of flame. Trevillian sank with him, clinging to his arm. Owen's frantic voice reached them.

Zack thrashed for footing—there was nothing beneath him. His sleeve was on fire. Trevillian held on to him. The chars supporting them collapsed. They fell together, but not far. A wall on the first floor with shelves to the ceiling tipped and caught them. They hung suspended, peering into the inferno below, the shelving now a flight of steps leading down.

Zack felt Trevillian's arm circle him, saw the ashen head turn, facing the test. The boss urged him down onto the next shelf. A black scud slipped between them. The smoke bit Zack's eyes, he was gagging, choking— Beside him, he heard Trevillian's breath seize. The fire reached for them, orange and crackling. The boss gripped his front and dragged him into it, forcing him down. Another shelf and another.

The warehouse opened below them. Stacked barrels were glowing pillars with snapping gold flags. Sealed oil drums rumbled and gonged, while the contents of exploded ones pooled and spread, thronged with blue flares. Tools clattered, crates burst— Kegs cracked, tongues of orange roe emerging, a wave of fish reek rising with the smoke.

Zack set his boots, hoarding his breath, following close. Flames speared from both sides—spikes of copper, pokers white and yolk yellow. Another shelf and another— Showers of sparks, gold and vermilion. Rattling cascades, colored liver and kidney, pouring from cliffs of rice and beans.

The heat was unbearable. Zack's coat was on fire. He grabbed the cloth and tore it open. His right side was stinging, eyes flooding with tears. He felt for Trevillian— The shelving below was a mass of flame, planks fanning, about to collapse. The boss leapt into the breakage and Zack went with him. They came down together, crashing onto a bed of fire, embracing each other and turning full over, coals cracking beneath them. Zack felt the scarred pectoral against his chest.

The blinding glow pulsed as they tumbled together, writhing for breath. Then they divided and rose.

Zack saw night and staggered toward it. He passed through an archway of fire and emerged a human torch on the stoop of the store. Shouts greeted him. He was struck by freezing cold, smothered with snow. Men grabbed him, carried him off the porch and set him down in the slush of the road.

I'm alive, Zack thought. His right side felt seared.

He heard gasps close-by.

Trevillian was crouched, drenched with sweat, grimacing. Snell came up behind him and put a blanket around his shoulders. The boss closed it over his torn shirt.

A crash came from the store and the alarm ceased abruptly. The building was a shell now, gutted by fire. Flames pierced the siding in a hundred places, bright feelers weaving like ivy across the smoking planks. Above, the roof was thick with orange tendrils. The wind curled and teased them as Zack watched. He shivered. The flesh beneath his right arm felt like it was burning. He opened his blanket to look.

"Below the whipping wall—" Trevillian motioned to Lloyd. "Cooker, equipment." He rose to his knees with a groan.

Zack turned, seeing the people of Breakaway around him—a hundred men and women standing and watching the store burn. Buckets were scattered across the snow. The kinked hose lay torn on the gravel, a shaft of ice visible within. Salvaged crates were in scattered piles, sacks of beans, blanketfuls of salmon—

"Hear them?" Trevillian said. "The orphans are burning."

Zack looked from the boss to the store. It bore no resemblance to the Home he'd grown up in. Then the voices reached him—scores of gagged throats, shrill and helpless, trapped in a cage of fire.

A section of roof collapsed, and a moment later the north corner sank beneath a geyser of sparks, lighting the pall of smoke above with an amber glow.

Owen had his eye on Zack as he approached. "Half the food's saved." He directed Trevillian's gaze to the piles. The largest was covered by the tarp from the barge and secured with tram cables. "'Twill be the mill for shelter tonight."

A moan rose in the east, as if questioning the foreman.

As the boss stood, the wind struck with unexpected force. People huddled beneath their coats and stepped closer to the fire, like a family gathered around the hearth. Another section of roof slumped. It took part of the second story with it, sheets of flame winging to either side. Zack saw Bob in the crowd, staring at him, drawing his attention toward the yard. They'd bundled Winiarski's body up and were lifting it into the sick wagon. A couple of Blondes were standing nearby, Sephy among them.

"What's this?" Snell complained, the blow whipping his coat.

The wind was growing fiercer and it was carrying snow.

"We'll be snug in our barracks." Marcus Bunting scowled at the gathering. He looked twenty years younger, his thatch blackened by smoke.

Trevillian eyed the frost collecting on his blanket. Zack rose.

All at once, the blast came with such fury they had to turn their backs to it.

"It wants our vittles," Owen shouted, bolting toward the supply piles. The wind was tearing at the sacks and boxes, turning them over, scattering them. A dozen men hurried to join him.

With a shriek, the wind swooped beneath the tarp, lifting it, pulling at the cables that secured it. Cries, shouts muffled by a sudden wave of snow. Through the white blur, Zack could see a loose cable switching over Owen's head like a demented serpent. The storm plowed beneath the tarp, clawing crates free, dashing them against the slope and bearing their contents away on the flurry as the store's southern wall collapsed.

A Blonde screamed. A box tent was tumbling through the crowd. "That's mine," a man swore. The next moment, a pup glided over their heads, beating its wings like a petrel and sheering away.

Farther up the valley, sounds of something cataclysmic reached them. In the light from the store, they could see the snow whirling wildly, wind twisting the thickets and scouring the rock. And then a great torrent appeared between the valley walls, roaring toward them, raving and white.

"To the diggings," Trevillian boomed.

The bewildered faces turned.

The boss aimed his arm at the mountain. "Now!" Then the blizzard obscured him.

Zack faced the blast, stooped and shivering. In an instant he was covered with freezing fur. He pulled the blanket close and stumbled through the melee, joining the beaten army headed for the switchback trail.

In a dim corner of Strongbox Stope, Zack sat with his head hanging between burnt-away shirt shoulders. His right side was bandaged from armpit to hip. The prospector's pick was tucked in his belt, its blackened haft against his thigh. Bob sat beside him.

"He was brave," Bob said.

Zack held his breath. He shook his head and tears came again. All that eagerness and well-wishing, he thought. The hope the boy clung to—that his day would come— How could men do that? Couldn't they remember?

Bob joined him, sobbing and rocking, arms beneath his kettle belly. "The ugly pugs live and the lovelies die." His face crumpled.

Near the bar, a group had gathered. Genuine Jo stood wrapped in a black shawl, leading a prayer for Winiarski. Inky and Weasel were among the mourners. They held hands, gazing at Jo and each other.

Bootsteps approached. It was Dinesh. Zack wiped his cheeks.

"They buried him in an abandoned drift," Dinesh said. He licked his lips. "The Captain and his dinghy are safe. No one's the wiser." He looked at Zack with vexation, as if Zack's grief was a weakness.

Zack stared at him.

"The fight's not over," Bob said.

Dinesh's eyes narrowed behind his spectacles, then he turned and stepped away.

The stope was crowded. Miners were resting, tending to burns or arranging themselves a spot for the night. Blondes tried to make the sick and injured comfortable in a quiet corner where the ceiling descended. The Bangshu worked to set up a pair of stoves near the entrance.

Snell approached. "Boss wants you," he said.

Zack drew a breath and rose.

They crossed the stope in silence. Snell seemed to be trying to muster the courage to speak. "You could help him," he said finally.

Zack didn't respond.

"The boss don't think more of any man here," Snell said.

"It was terrible, what he did."

"Terrible," Snell agreed. "He's hurting bad inside. You understand."

"I do?"

Snell swallowed. "I believe you do."

The gaunt man led him through the Big Wheel barricade, toward Salt Lick's boudoir. When they reached the velvet drape, Snell stopped, made a clumsy bow and departed.

Zack drew the drape aside and entered the madam's room.

"It's murder," Salt Lick was saying. "There's no dressing it up."

Trevillian was sitting on the edge of the bed. Salt Lick stood over him. She wore a black skirt and jacket and had a handkerchief in her hand. As Zack entered, she turned her upset on him. "Isn't that right?"

Zack glanced at the boss. He looked like a chastened schoolboy. "There's a lot of sympathy for Winski," Zack replied.

The drape shifted and Lloyd entered. He was in his shirt-sleeves, and his clothing was grimy and soaked with sweat. He went to Salt Lick's washbasin, poured water from the pitcher and began scrubbing his hands. "I can't stay long."

"How are we?" the boss asked.

"Lots of burns, a broken arm," Lloyd replied. "One man's lungs may be damaged. I put a dozen stitches in Noel's face." He turned. "I need to see your legs."

Trevillian waved his concern away.

"Well?" Lloyd faced Salt Lick. "What is it?"

"The shot," she said.

"It was fired by someone who wanted to stop the flogging." Lloyd looked at the boss. "I should have turned a gun on you myself."

"You fool," Salt Lick barked.

"He's losing them, Francine. The miners, the Blondes—everyone."

She faced Zack. "What's your role in all of this?"

"Role?"

"There's powder missing, if you haven't heard."

"I've heard," Zack said.

Trevillian gazed at him.

"And the gunshot?" Salt Lick asked.

Zack tipped his head. "It wasn't fired at the boss."

"Winiarski was your pal," the madam said.

"I liked him," Zack replied. "I don't know what he was doing with the powder, but it couldn't have been anything sinister. He was too artless for that."

"Trouble's never far from Mister Knox," Salt Lick said without shifting her eyes from him.

"He saved my life," Trevillian rasped. His voice filled the small space.

"Owen says he was going to kill you," Salt Lick shot back.

"I've given Hope my heart," Zack protested.

"You phony," she snarled.

"Leave us alone," Trevillian murmured.

She turned with fury in her eyes.

"Please, Francine."

"I take it the tribunal is over," Lloyd said. He exited the chamber.

Salt Lick stood staring at the boss, then she flung her arm out, swept aside the drape and disappeared.

"She's jealous," Trevillian said. There was a hint of amusement in his eyes, then they clouded over. "Sit here, will you." He touched the mattress beside him.

Zack did as he asked.

"She's right, isn't she." The boss regarded him sadly.

Zack didn't reply.

"She'd do anything for me," Trevillian said. "No Blonde could play Hope like Francine, back in the day. Sephy's a truer Hope for me now." There was bitterness in his voice. "She loathes me." He peered into Zack's eyes. "You know that."

Again, Zack was silent.

"And *I* hate *her*," the boss said.

"Hope."

"I'm to blame for her absence," Trevillian said wryly. "I'm the cause of her discontent. The fault is mine." He gazed at the lone candle guttering on the nightstand. "The hardships I've put upon you—and the favors—were urged by her. You were going to change our luck. She assured me of that." He paused. "She has her reasons, I suppose, for deceiving me. And for driving us apart." The boss faced him. "Why did you follow me into the store?"

Zack saw more than suspicion. Trevillian knew. "Winiarski," he replied.

"How could I do that," the boss said quietly.

"He was just a boy."

"Not at the end," Trevillian muttered. "At the end, he knew more than most men. The prospect of death ages a boy quickly."

The boss was still wearing his torn shirt. Zack remembered the moment they were chest to chest, rolling through the flames.

"It was him," Trevillian said.

Zack heard the revulsion in his voice.

"It was his hand on the Reminder," the boss said.

As the candle glow steadied, a char streak on Trevillian's neck seemed to divide it. Zack saw what looked like a severed head floating before him. The boss's eyes searched his own, as if he yearned to trust him.

"To be a child," the boss said, "is to love yourself. To live in the light and find happiness in things of no consequence. To be cherished by others for who you are." He closed his eyes. "To be a man is to hate yourself. To covet things of great worth, to claim a power over fate that you know you don't have. To be a man is to live in darkness and sleep with shame."

The words seemed terrible to Zack.

"Help me—" Trevillian said. "I'm hurt."

The boss was leaning back on the bed, struggling to open

his trousers. The burnt fabric came away in his hands. His legs were covered with blisters. Some had burst. The fluid gleamed in the candlelight.

"I'll get Lloyd."

Trevillian grabbed him. "No. Please—" He calmed himself. "Just stay here with me."

Zack was motionless.

The boss tightened his grip on Zack's shoulder and drew him down onto the bed beside him. "I need—" He shivered violently.

Zack felt the boss's forehead on his shoulder. Another fierce shiver shook him.

"Hold me," Trevillian begged.

Zack's breath had frozen in his throat. His body was rigid. Was he going to kill Trevillian or care for him? He could hear Trevillian's gasps, rapid and high-pitched, like a child who'd been frightened but knew comfort was near.

"Boss?"

Zack looked up. Owen's big-chested silhouette stood inside the drape.

Trevillian's lids parted. "We're on break," he said quietly, focused on Zack. "This shift and the next."

Owen didn't respond.

"Did he hear me?" the boss asked.

"'Twill be as you say," Owen said.

"Tell Francine to bed down with her girls," Trevillian said. He closed his eyes.

Owen turned and departed.

A few moments later, the two men were asleep.

On the surface, white waves crashed over the Glory Hole. Between the valley walls a torrent raced, polar and crystalline. No lights burned in the mill sheds or forge, and the remains of the store and tent sites were buried. Around the switchbacks the miners had trod, the blasts raised ghosts, whirling and amorphous.

In the mountains to the north, the winds had died down. The clouds were turning over, swamping the air with woolly stars. They settled in thick mats, covering everything. Drifts rolled white to the edge of a glassy rivulet, where black-rodded alders grew icy leaves. A shaggy hulk appeared, following the rivulet, lumbering toward a cave beneath a tree.

Prowler's face was crusted white. His sides were roped with rime. A mantle of ice had frozen over his back, and as he barged through the cave's entrance, points of rock scribed it. Inside, he glanced at the frozen walls. Root arms emerged from the rocky soil, and a half-dozen bats hung from them, heads down.

The bear tramped the dry boughs and turned once around. His shoulders bumped the ceiling, and the load above shifted. In the dimness, an object descended from the web of roots: a boot at the end of a leg.

Prowler stiffened. He stared at the boot, his massive snout wrinkling, beaded ears laid back. From deep in his throat came a menacing grumble.

Just then, a vole scuttled over his paw.

Prowler looked down, watching the vole cross the floor. Before it reached cover, he grabbed it, and with the little creature wriggling in his fist, he put his rump to the world and sank. He worked his hip into the bedding. The dead branches squealed and cracked. When he shifted his arm to rest his cheek on it, the vole's head popped out. Prowler grunted with mirth, opened his paw and watched the vole scurry away.

His jaw chomped loudly, then not so loudly. He drew a deep breath, then one not so deep. He eased his head onto his arm. Some lingering thought stirred his digits, making the black claws click.

Then he tucked his snout into his belly and curled himself with a self-satisfied groan. Slowly he drifted into the oblivion of winter. One of the bats opened its wings, stretched and folded them back around itself. Falling snow rustled onto the hemlock spray that eaved the den's entrance. As the flakes feathered thicker, the spray began to droop, like a heavy lid edging down.

13

While the storm raged, the camp got some shuteye and the first meal was served in the stope. Men found places on the floor by the entrance, around the bar, against the walls. The Blondes slept inside the Big Wheel barricade. Every few hours, Owen sent someone to the rim to see if the weather had changed. When the two rest shifts were over, the boss called two more. There had been no stoppages of that length since his arrival. Was it his wounds? Remorse for what he'd done to Winiarski? Fear of an uprising? Or had the setbacks discouraged him? Was the boss still confident that Hope would return?

No one knew his state. No one but Zack.

Trevillian kept to the madam's boudoir. Except for the visits from Lloyd to treat his burns, or from Owen, who had updates and needed orders, Zack was his sole companion. At his request, Zack bathed his legs. Zack went for food and they ate together. And Zack listened to his rambling confessional.

"For me to confide in you—" The boss laughed. "That's the last thing she wants."

"Why would she care?"

"She knows I suffer," Trevillian said. "She means to deprive me. To make every minute of my life an ordeal. I must face doubt alone. I must believe when no one else does, because I'm her priest."

Trevillian gazed at his damaged legs.

"We went a week without even a thread of her," he recalled. "Just before you arrived. The boys were in the dumps. It was dawn and I was standing on the loading platform in the Glory Hole, sending them down. Russ McGee steps forward. His face is gray. 'I'm sorry, boss,' he says. 'Sorry and ashamed. My faith is slipping.' He was asking for help.

"'It happens to the best of us, Russ,' I say. A dozen of his brothers were watching and listening. 'And you're one of the best. Don't let that shame you. We're born with doubt in our flesh.'

"'I gave Hope my heart,' he reminded me.

"'I know you did.'

"'I've been wishing I could take it back,' Russ said.

"An hour before," Trevillian waved his hand, "I was twisting in my bedroll, calling Hope a lie." He stared at Zack. "I was doubting her even while Russ asked for my help."

"It's a lot to hold on to," Zack said.

"I believed in Hope Thursday," Trevillian whispered, "but

today I don't. That's the secret that can't be spoken—that none must hear." He glanced at the dresser where the Reminder lay coiled. "When I rage, it's fear speaking. Fear that I've lost my faith. Fear that I've lost my reason, and I'm preaching insanity to a hundred lost souls to hide from the truth."

During his trips to the cook tables, Zack avoided questions. He did what he could to put on a good face for those he'd recruited. He kept an eye out for Sephy, but only saw her once, grinding root mash with her sisters on the other side of the stope. He waited for a chance to be with her, knowing he'd have to explain how the fire started and what had happened inside the burning store. On the third night, when the Bangshu were dishing out supper, an opportunity arose.

Genuine Jo addressed the camp.

She mounted a small island of crates near the bar, and before anyone knew it, she was wringing her heart out for all to hear. The food lines dissolved and the camp gathered around her.

"I love Hope," Jo said. "She's with me when I lift my head from the pillow and open my eyes, and she's there when I set my head down for the night. I thank heaven for Hope and the blessing she's been to our barren lives. But—"

Jo's fine features and the classical lines beneath her nightdress did nothing to soften the picture. Her poise had vanished. She was drawn, and her movements were nervous.

"We can't let our love," Jo scanned the faces, "justify things that we know are wrong. She doesn't want us to lose our humanity. Our compassion. Our sense of good and evil. Hope is our angel, our ally. She's not a tyrant, raising herself up. She doesn't want to be the only thing that matters. That's not Hope. I know it's not."

While Jo was speaking, Zack saw Sephy emerge from the infirmary with a basket on her arm. He moved closer and caught her eye.

She waited in the shadows, and when he reached her, they backed into the dimness together.

She fell into his arms. He pressed her close and kissed her. A sigh escaped her, then she shivered and held him tightly. Zack had dreaded the moment he'd have to recount his actions, but the darkness of her mood lifted that fear. It was as if she knew, without his saying a word, that Hope's predictions in the bulldoze chamber had come true.

The camp was buzzing with speculation about the source of the shot, how the two men escaped from the store, what they were doing together in the madam's boudoir. Zack told her the truth.

When he'd finished, Sephy rested her cheek on his chest. "I thought I knew her better," she said.

Zack shook his head.

"I was sure she was with us," Sephy said. "That she meant you to lead. That she would take your side in a struggle with the boss and turn these people your way. And make us partners for life."

She spoke as if she'd been naive.

"She's wrong about you, Zack. You're brave. You risked your life to save me."

"She wasn't happy," he said. "With me."

"Maybe Hope wants things that men can't give her," Sephy replied. "Things that she has no right to ask for. She betrayed Raymond, after all."

Salt Lick had appeared at the doorway of the Big Wheel and was making her way through the crowd, giving an affectionate smile and an understanding nod to people on either side. When she reached the crate pile, she held out her hand to Jo.

"I know you're upset, dear," Salt Lick said sadly. "All of us are."

"I have to speak my feelings," Jo told her.

"Of course you do."

Salt Lick curled her fingers, inviting Jo to take her hand.

"May I continue?" Jo asked.

"Let's calm ourselves first," the madam smiled. "After a while." She clasped Jo's hand, coaxing her down. When Jo reached the floor, Salt Lick folded the girl's arm over her own. "After a while," she said again, stroking Jo's wrist.

The madam led her away through the crowd.

The pause in the diggings lasted six days, and still the storm raged. Trevillian remained cloistered. While relief from their grueling work was welcomed by some of the miners, the prevailing reaction was distress. There were exploratory holes on both the 770 and the 930. Lovesick had a ribbon showing, and before the last blasts at Vestige, there were threads. Wouldn't they be better off looking for Hope than sitting on their biscuits?

People did what they could to make the stope habitable. The women stitched pallets out of sackcloth. The Bangshu added a pair of tables to their cook station, along with a collection of hoods and pipes to conduct the steam and smoke into existing vents. The liquor bar was used as the foundation for a wall; barrels, grain sacks and bundles of salmon were stacked to the ceiling around and on top of it. The resulting enclosure became a replacement for the warehouse, and the salvaged provisions were stored within. It also became temporary quarters for the boss's men.

On the evening of the sixth day, a strange rumor went round. Winiarski had been a doubter secretly, in league with others who pretended to believe. The group was plotting to bring great harm to them all. No one knew how the rumors started or who the plotters might be. But as the camp was bedding down, Owen and DuVal circulated. All the miners were stripped and their belongings sifted. No dynamite or firearms were found. Fortunately for Zack and his recruits, they didn't disturb the Captain.

The following day, the storm's fury subsided. Owen and a small team descended the trail to have a look at the camp. When they returned, they made a dispiriting report: there was little left. The miners' tents had been crushed or borne off by the wind. Blondetown had suffered the same fate. Owen and his men searched the wreckage. No explosives were discovered, but there were rifles and pistols buried with the miners' possessions. They were hauled to the stope and secured in the new enclosure. The owners didn't squawk—without shells, the weapons had been useless for quite a while. Two escaped detection: a rifle owned by Marcus Bunting that he'd buried beneath a rock pile north of the graveyard, and Bob's mongrel revolver, hidden in the Captain's dinghy with the stolen powder. This did nothing to cheer Zack or his recruits. The spirit of the rebellion had all but died.

Zack watched the boss grow stronger daily. After hearing the report on the ruined camp, Trevillian released him. Zack found a spot to bed down in the stope.

Within hours, Trevillian emerged from the boudoir, bandaged and hobbling. He was back among his men, stern and purposeful, giving orders as if nothing had happened. Relief was widespread. The memory of the lashing of Winiarski was indelible, but the camp was in peril and they needed their leader.

As if acknowledging the boss's command, the storm ended abruptly. Trevillian dragged himself down the mountain to see the damage himself. They had no choice, he told the people when he returned. Other than the mill sheds, there was no shelter above ground. They would haul what remained of the camp up the trail and down into the stope.

It took two days and the hard labor of all but the infirm.

319

When the hauling was completed, the rocky cavern looked like the hold of an immigrant freighter. The boss gave orders and the people bent to their tasks. A relict drift on the west side of the 310 was turned into a sawmill. The bedding area was leveled and heated using the miners' stoves. New pipe was run to pump air into the stope and additional ventilation shafts were drilled in the ceiling. They were cheered by their own grit and inventiveness. Perhaps it was all according to Hope's plan. The boss returned the boudoir to Salt Lick, shifting his residence to what the camp now called "the BMC enclosure." That same evening, he addressed the camp.

Trevillian exited the enclosure with the Reminder looped at his hip—the first the camp had seen of it since the lashing. He strode into the cooking area, grabbed a dented pot, banged it against a barrel and boosted himself onto the barrel's top. The miners in the sleeping area rose from their makeshift bedrolls. Zack and Bob, and the others lined up beside the cook tables, turned to listen. A moment later the Blondes exited the Big Wheel.

"I've been tested before," Trevillian began, "but never like this."

His sober mood settled over the stope.

"I've looked in the mirror," the boss said, "and what I've seen has caused me great pain. I've had help these few days, as many of you know. The help has raised my spirits a little. I'm not ready to give up. But I'm going to leave that decision to you."

He pointed at the floor.

"You've lain here with your ear to the rock. Have you heard anything from Hope?" He scanned the haggard faces. "True?"

"Not a whisper," True said.

Trevillian gestured at Noel.

"I sleep pretty deep," Noel replied through his bandages.

"You've got the ear," Owen volunteered. "That's why you're boss."

"I've been listening," Trevillian nodded. "I'll be honest with you all. I haven't heard a peep."

Zack saw Sephy among the Blondes who'd joined the rear of the gathering. Salt Lick wasn't with them.

"I don't know if she's down there," the boss said. "If she is, I'm not sure we'll find her. I have no guidance. I don't know where to look." He raised his fist. "But I'll dig if you will. I'll give you everything I have. I'll devour this mountain to find her. Or—" He scanned the faces. "We can embrace our defeat, bide our time and crawl back to a world of starvation and war next spring."

The stope was still. The boss was serious.

"I'm for Hope," True said.

No one was surprised.

"We'll find her at Vestige," Carew chimed in.

"Or on the 930," another agreed.

"Let's not be hasty," Lucky protested.

"We'll make a coffin," Marcus Bunting said, "for each of you boys."

"Give Hope your heart," Arnie stepped forward.

"Give Hope your heart," another said, rising from his bedroll.

"Where do you stand?" Trevillian asked them. "I need to know."

"Give Hope your heart—" Pledges sounded on all sides, but no one gave the salute.

"'Tis for Hope," Owen said. "The votes are counted."

Trevillian nodded and drew a deep breath. "We'll sound the whistle at the end of this meal. You'll have shift assignments by then," he pointed at a spot on the wall behind him. "Our search for Hope will continue." He smiled at the Blondes. "And the Wheel will resume."

The comment met with cheers.

"Those with hooves will have it hard," the boss said. "We lost more than half our winter hay. The rest of us are provided for." He gestured at the food stored in the BMC enclosure and locked in its walls. "We'll feel no storms here and waste no time shuttling up and down the trail."

Zack felt Bob's elbow. He was staring at Lucky, who was shaking and red in the face.

"You can't be serious," Lucky sputtered.

"The time of darkness is upon us," Trevillian said. "The cold descends from the pole. If we mean to find Hope, this must be our home."

Lucky looked around, at the walls and the other men.

"I can't give you a rousing sermon," Trevillian said. "The best I can do is a quiet prayer."

He held his arm out, palm down, and then lowered it. Slowly, the believers sank to their knees. Zack and Bob went down with them.

"Hope is the fountainhead," the mine boss said softly. "The milk of creation. Hope will make just the bloody sacrifice of man."

The miners returned to the drifts. Zack's burn made wielding a sledge impossible, so he took shaker duty. The drill teams applied themselves with fresh energy, and there was excitement when strings surfaced at Wallflower. But three days later, they vanished. Elsewhere on the 770, and in the new holes on the 930, there were no signs at all. Life in the stope was harder than anyone had imagined. Men were packed so close, they were sleeping on top of each other. Wood was ferried from the valley, and from time to time a miner went up to look at the sky. But they left the diggings infrequently, and that added a new dimension to their defeat. Hope's absence became oppressive—a reality no one could escape.

Accidents and mishaps mounted. With the infirmary packed and their spirits sinking, the camp was struck by its first suicide.

There was a doghole near the end of the 930. Arnie dubbed it "Hermes," after a statue with no testicles he'd seen in a museum. The man drilling Hermes spit the charges and didn't crawl out. Three days later, Helaina disappeared. It took a while to find her. She'd left the mine, climbed a tram tower, secured a rope to one of the struts and hung herself. She was stiff as bar stock by the time they cut her down.

The lamentation among the Blondes shook what was left of the camp's morale. The men had never seen such despair, and no one was more doomful than the madam. Trevillian was morose and stone-faced. He strode through the diggings grinding his teeth. There was a ceremony for the two who had taken their own lives, and it was Lloyd who presided. When the service was over, Zack returned to the Wheel with Sephy.

Mingling with the others, she seemed the least affected. The other girls leaned on her for strength. She led Zack along the back passageway into an empty alcove.

The space was twice the width of the bed and little more than the height of a man. A candle burned in a tin can nailed to the wall.

"How could she do it?" Sephy muttered. She held out her hand.

As Zack sat on the mattress beside her, Sephy's composure gave way.

"How could she let this happen to us?" Sephy loosed her grief. "I'm not a bitter woman," she cried, "but I'm bitter about this."

"You have a right," Zack said.

"My devotion has always been to those who need Hope. To Raymond, the men in the High Quarter, the miners in the

324

Wheel. And you, Zack. You most of all. I would do anything to wish her back—for you."

She's giving up, Zack thought.

"Hope has the power to change everything," Sephy said. "I truly believe that. But we're not her chosen. Hope's not coming back."

Her hand lay limp in his. He struggled to find something to say. It had always seemed that his actions mattered, that the course of life depended on what he would do. But the time for action or words—anything that would make a difference— seemed to have passed.

Like a bird in a cage, Zack thought.

"We should have gone down with the others on that steamer," she said.

Sephy listened to the moans and sobbing on the other side of the blanket covering the archway. Then she slid her hand from his.

The hours that followed, Zack spent in a daze. He was turning a drill, then he was in the bucket. Then he was in the infirmary, beside the Captain's dinghy, retrieving the mongrel. He put a bullet in every chamber, slid the revolver inside his waistband and stepped across the stope toward the BMC enclosure.

He held a lantern in his left hand. It wasn't trembling. His breath wasn't short. Would killing the boss make any difference? No, it was just unfinished business. Sephy was in his thoughts, not Trevillian. And when he reached the enclosure's entrance, it was Sephy he saw.

The gray blanket drew back and she emerged. Her strict hair lay draggled on her shoulder. Her white collar was torn. There was a spot of blood on her lip.

She didn't see him at first, but when she did, her face twisted with anger and she waved him away.

Zack was stunned.

Without thinking, he obeyed her, stumbling toward the anteroom, crushed by her rebuff. He had caught her with Trevillian's venom still coursing through her veins.

Somehow he found his way to the bulldoze chamber.

He seated himself on the slab and doused his lantern. In the darkness, he cocked the hammer of the mongrel and rotated its cylinder, feeling the scoops in the casting. There was no *Secret Chamber*. They were all loaded now. He recalled the night he'd stood facing the crowd with his gun in his hand, thinking he would favor the bullet instead of avoiding it. Instead of an evening's entertainment, it would be an encounter with death for everyone present.

Zack put the muzzle to his cheek, as he had so many times before, feeling the cold zero over his molar. He whimpered like a child and began to sob. His hand was shaking—he was fearful now, as fearful as he would have been facing Trevillian or his father. But he could do the job. His finger tightened on the trigger.

A long time had passed, but it seemed no time at all. He had been tunneling with all his strength and concentration—swinging the sledge, aiming the everhard, casting his mind into the threatening unknown—searching for Hope. His thoughts reached out for her, he sang to her with his heart.

Hope, you knew me. You saw through me. You were right.

The darkness seemed impenetrable. And then it had depth. Pale clouds billowed in the space before him, a translucent face in a mineral sky. A portrait of Sephy. Her eyes were closed, her features immobile. But as he watched, she stirred, feeling his presence. Her lids parted and she fixed on him through the leagues of night, seeing the spirit of the Private inside him.

The face was changing. It was no longer Sephy he saw, but the moonlike face of Salt Lick. Then the madam faded into his favorite assistant, and the show girl into an earlier love and an earlier. The need that drove him, his desperate longing, was mining his past, divining and distilling—the bliss bestowed, the hearts he'd stolen. The kaleidoscope ended with an unknown mother—stray glitters in the smoke of a featureless head.

Every word of love, every whisper— They had all been translations: Hope singled out, Hope sequestered. The face in the sky was once again Sephy's. Her lips were moving, but they were Hope's thoughts. Hope was speaking—had been speaking, it seemed, for a very long time. Her words were diffident, guarded. The meaning was hard to grasp. Had he listened to and understood everything she'd said—had he been able—he would belong to a different world. The perishing earth would not be his home.

In this mineral night, this dream exploration, Hope's mask was dissolving.

Before the light, Zack thought, *there was just you and I.*

The vapor stretched and glittered across the boundless sky, compressing, winding like a ghostly river.

It is Hope I love, Zack thought.

The serpent of stars was impossibly distant. He would never touch it or hold it.

I believe, he swore to her. *I believe, I believe—*

And then . . . he was no longer a wandering mind. He had substance.

He was a man, naked and barefoot, crossing a transparent stage. It was crosshatched by cracks and freezing cold—quartz or marble or ice from the pole. Ahead was a lookout, a turret fronted with crystal panes, like a large bay window. And through it, he could see an inlet fed by a finger of the sea. Flames crowded the swells—ships with golden sails. A great armada was returning, heavy with treasure, welcome in the land where men worship Hope.

He was finally here. Through wishing and wanting, baffling tests and fitful resolve, he had found the way. As he reached the overhang, other turrets came into view, lining the inlet on either side. They shifted, they flashed—the glassy casements budged like the valves of mussels in a rocky cove.

He reached out, and as his hands touched the panes, the casements swung open.

The inlet was hissing below his window. The folds of Hope's robe frothed like surf. Her winds were biting—

And then, as if the harbor had been waiting for this moment—

The inlet froze. The golden sails remained, suspended, encased in light with the wind still in them, flickering with life—frozen flames in a channel of mirrors, perfused with embers and traversed by smoke.

He leaned forward. He could feel the strop of Hope's gusts on his chest.

He made claws of his hands, found the seam in his pectoral and pulled, reopening the scar. Then he reached his right in and dug out his heart. He raised it before him in the spectral light, a fist-sized ruby, faceted and throbbing, trailing scarlet arteries.

Below, the shore appeared as Hope's frothing tide pulled back. A garnet beach, and each grain was pulsing. Hope's ivory robe lapped and hissed over a tribute of hearts—an infinite number, cast to her at moments like this.

Hear my sigh, this wishful night.

No weakness. No wavering.

My vow, my pledge, Zack swore. *My first and last.*

He held his heart out.

It's you I want. This heart I give to the one I love best.

The ruby slipped from his hand and fell. It winked light once and was lost from sight, joining the others on the strand below.

Would his offering strip Hope's veil? For a moment, the waters of the inlet cleared. A vapor drifted above, with eyes shining through it— Eyes he had wished for all his life. Eyes that miss nothing, from which nothing is hidden. Eyes that bring pain and wash pain away. All at once the casements had sprung—every one of them. From the faithful of Hope, arms reached out and a great cry arose. Hope saw them, Hope smiled and all her golden flames had wings. A fervent wind sent them flying. They were like birds beating toward him, birds passing through him. Boundless energy without a hint of fear—

That terrible need— The love he'd wanted— It was finally his.

He'd given Hope his heart and he was one of the blessed.

The passion of the moment abated. The inlet grew opaque, the steady hiss of the waves returned. The Hope that Zack had imagined faded. Had she heard him? Had Hope been listening? It didn't matter. He didn't care.

My heart is yours, Zack thought. *It belongs to you.*

He woke in darkness some time later. He was stretched out on the slab in the bulldoze chamber with the butt of the loaded mongrel in his hand.

The following day was a strange one. A test, of sorts.

Zack was put behind the everhard at the end of the 930, in a new digging called Nightpool. His side was still bandaged. The machine drill shook his burn and rattled his bones, while doubts beat back and forth in his mind, rattling his conviction.

It was a dream, nothing more. A fantasy fed by Sephy's delusions. The blind faith of the camp. Trevillian's preaching. In a moment of weakness, he'd been overcome.

The doubts didn't touch him. Everything had changed.

At his center, where fear had hidden—in the place of despair—his pledge now abided. There was no Hope in his world—inside him, around him. But he knew she was real.

If he'd lost his wits, it was for the better. This was what he needed. Only this would see him through.

When the shift ended, Zack's first thought was to share all that had happened with Sephy. But by the time he returned to Strongbox Stope, his perspective had changed. He'd done nothing to halt what Trevillian was doing to her. That and the memory of Sephy's angry dismissal filled him with shame.

14

Zack kept to himself. He felt an urgency to help Sephy, and the camp's state was desperate. But despite that— It was a time to say little. A time to put others at a distance and be alone with his thoughts and feelings. He rose and he ate, he worked and he slept with the prospect of Hope drifting through him. He dwelt in this suspension and waited.

The waiting lasted four days. It ended an hour before the shift whistle at Nightpool.

Zack was bent over the everhard, his humpbacked shadow shaking on the headwall. His shirt was soaked, his face beaded with sweat. Inky Peterson was in water to his shins, using a pail to flush the drill hole while the chisel clattered. Behind them, lame Len mucked.

Zack turned the jackscrew to advance the drill, squinting through splatter and spray to keep his angle. Suddenly the headwall gave like a trap door. Inky shouted. A groan sounded from the hollow. Zack threw himself back, landing in the slop while the wall on his right rumbled and slumped into some unimaginable declivity.

When he turned, he saw Inky in a puddle beside him. The rest of Nightpool had drained. Len crawled forward to join them, and the three rose together. Zack grabbed a lantern and they picked their way over the breaks. The everhard lay on its side beneath the rubble. At the rim of the subsidence, Zack extended the lantern. A chaos of fractured boulders lined the chasm. Beyond that, there was a void as far as the light reached.

"Cavity," Len said.

Zack heard a ticking, glanced up and recoiled, dragging the two men with him. A giant gray blade hung over the rim, held by a puzzle of chocks.

Len put his hand on the wall. "Still shifting." He eyed Zack. "When I was at Heyday, we hit a hole like this. It connected to a cavern as big as the mill shed."

"Go through it?" Zack asked.

"Didn't dare. It collapsed a week later."

"Hope wouldn't lead us into a deadfall," Inky shook his head.

Zack stared at the opening. "Maybe it's where she lives." He stepped between his companions, lifting the lantern. At the rim, where the gray blade met the drift wall, a band of solid quartz striped the rock. It was thick as a woman's thigh.

Silence held them for a long moment.

"I'll fetch the boss," Len said. He wheeled and hurried away.

Zack moved the lantern between himself and Inky, giving his comrade a window into his mind. Then he stooped beneath the gray blade, crossed the broken rim and started down the slump. Inky followed.

After a dozen steps, the rock shifted beneath them. They shuffled until the breakings found an angle of repose, and then stood peering into the darkness.

"Is that smoke?"

"Dust," Zack said. The darkness had swirls. His lantern flickered like a beacon signaling. "Smell?"

A breeze blew from the chasm, carrying a strange odor.

"Gas," Inky said.

Zack felt the chill on his chest. "Hope," he muttered.

"What are you thinking?"

Zack faced him, uncertain what answer to make.

"You've changed," Inky said. "Since Winski died."

Zack saw the gravity in his eyes. "So have you."

Inky nodded.

"We're playing for keeps," Zack said.

"For Weasel and Sephy," Inky agreed. "And for—"

"We have to find her," Zack said. "Wait for me," he toed the breakings. "Don't leave." He pulled his bandanna up over his nose.

"I'll pray for you," Inky said, sinking to his knees.

The reaction jarred Zack. A friend, eyes closed, summoning divine guidance for him in this barren place— Zack turned, raised the lantern and crookt his left arm in front of his face, finding his way over the loose rock and boulders, through the dust and darkness.

The slope steepened. Fins of rock jutted from an invisible ceiling and a ragged wall appeared, forcing him to the right. His eyes stung. He wiped them with his sleeve and the decline slurried before him as if he was underwater. The odor of gas grew stronger. He felt a tightness in his chest. His shoulder struck something, he stumbled and reached to steady himself. In the wavering light, his hand rippled across the corrugated rock.

A sigh sounded close-by, like a voice in his ear. When he shifted the lantern, the rock popped and a blue jet speared out. The flame pointed the way: fifty feet farther, the ceiling descended and the leaning walls met in a cave.

He moved his boots through the shifting gravel. Sighs reached him now from all sides. In the glow from his lantern, he could see the cave's vault. It was ribbed like the tomb of a saint. He passed beneath it, sinking into its shadows, swaying, gasping for breath. He thought to turn back, but his legs gave beneath him.

Was he facedown? No, he was lifting his shoulders, forcing his lantern closer.

Whoosh—the sides of the cave spit sky-blue fringes—and through the raveling fire, Zack saw Hope at the rear of the cave: quartz, white and glittering, as thick as a man. She was gliding through a dark berth with the fires of heaven hissing from her pores. Blue lozenges slid over her body—glowing, growing and winking out. Hope had no head or tail, no arms or legs. She'd pierced the material world as a winding serpent, without a trace of humanity.

Can you hear me? Zack thought.

Her white length swelled as he watched, flexing and sliding out of the seam. An endlong crack split her trunk, and the molt was like an ivory robe pulling at its fastenings. She lifted from the blue pillows—the robe opened and Zack could see Hope's naked body. It glittered like a lizard's, scales irising as the flames of gold licked within.

Touch—

Had Hope spoken? No throat made that sound. It was the hiss from an eddy of oil and sand, the grinding and crushing of sentient crystals—

Touch, Zack heard.

He reached his hand to her front, feeling the facets, slick and cool. The contacts bubbled with froth. Hope's scales were shifting, every crevice was leaking, dripping icy pearls. On either side, he could see the robe's jeweled lining—a myriad rubies and garnets threaded together, glistening and alive.

Open—

Zack felt himself choking, his face was drenched.

Your chest, Hope hissed.

He found the scar with his fingers and parted his wound, feeling its silky inside. Hollow, empty—

Pitiful man, Hope said.

His heart— How had he lost it? Had he given it to Hope, or was that just a dream? Had Trevillian taken it, or Sephy? Or had he borne the loss all his life without even knowing?

337

Come to me—
Zack drew nearer.
Close.

His chest touched Hope and he twisted away, racked with pain. He could smell his flesh burning—

Close, Hope hissed.

Zack forced himself, gagging, shuddering— And then Hope found the breach. He felt her enter him, her creamy essence invading his chest. A draft of her steam rose into his nostrils. Confusion, mistrust— In what corner of his mind had this shrinking been born? Hope was inside him, her crystals were growing, her points pushing out. She was making him her own, filling the emptiness at his center.

Hope's way, she said.

She spoke as a woman now—not Sephy or any woman he'd known, but a presence from another world, whose mission was to nourish and protect. Her strength was releasing from the crystal core, traveling every vein and nerve in his body, transforming him. His flesh was like hers now, lit from within. There were mirrors inside him, shifting and flashing. His body pulsed with Hope's fire—

And then time stopped. The blur of moments halted, and there was only one, stretching out.

I've found you, Zack thought.

You've found me, Hope said.

They will honor me, follow me— I'll bring the boss down and be your priest.

That's not what Hope wants, she said.

She could hear his thoughts as he formed them. *What does Hope want?*

Trevillian must share your glory, she said.

Why? Zack asked.

He will teach you, and Hope will test you. Brotherhood, then betrayal.

I'm afraid, Zack said.

No man can hurt you, child. Hope is inside you.

Stay with me, he said.

Stay with me, Hope echoed. *Stay with me, stay with me—*

The crystal bounty began to shrink and retract. The kindliness faded, and the dazzle with it. Zack's body no longer pulsed and flashed. The Hope within him was clouded and dimming. He felt her slide through the wound and exit his chest, and despair took her place. A darkness and poverty like never before.

Zack hugged the serpent body, fearful, shaking in every part. An odor bit his nose—sulfurous, caustic—then Hope cringed and withered. What Zack clung to was oily and cold. Hope squirmed free of him, gliding on her belly.

He watched, numb and empty, as the coronation of his dreams eeled back to its furrow in the dark vault of rock.

He struggled to his feet, drew his pick from his belt and drove it into her.

Zack had no memory of his return. He was cresting the slump, holding the lantern before him, when he came to his senses. His shirt was open. His chest was heaving, but his breath seemed shallow and he was gasping for air. Every muscle in his body ached. He passed beneath the gray blade and halted, spying the buried machine drill. Inky rose from the shadows to greet him, face spattered with grease.

Zack swayed, took another step and sank into the smaller man's arms.

Inky dragged him to the air lines, yanked the everhard hose from its coupling and forced the rubber between Zack's lips.

Gradually, his strength seeped back.

"What's that?" Inky asked.

Zack had something cradled in his arm.

Lights appeared at the mouth of the drift.

They listened to the hurried bootsteps.

Trevillian's voice could be heard, then he emerged from the darkness with Owen beside him and Len behind. He came to a halt a few feet from where the everhard had fallen. Owen knelt and began moving rocks to free the machine.

"A soft spot." The boss stared at the collapse.

"Holy ground," Zack said.

"Where's the quartz?" the boss asked Len.

Len pointed at the pale stripe on the wall.

Trevillian approached it. As he was stooping beneath the blade, a chirping sounded.

"Boss—" Owen sprang to his feet.

As Trevillian drew back, the blade dropped six inches.

"We 'ave no business here," Owen said.

Trevillian eyed the floor of the drift. "It's not Nightpool anymore."

"'Guillotine,'" Owen said. "There's the name for it."

"She's tempting us." The boss faced the dark hole.

"I've been to see her," Zack said.

Trevillian laughed.

Zack raised the quartz in his hand. "She's bedding where there's room to stretch out."

Trevillian stared at him. "On your feet."

Zack rose.

"Lead the way," Trevillian said.

Owen exhaled. "Shall we give a thought—"

"Dismiss them," Zack told Trevillian.

"Use your wits, man," Owen snarled.

"Leave us," Trevillian said.

"Boss—"

"Now," Trevillian commanded.

Len grasped Owen's arm, Inky rose to join them, and the three men retreated down the drift.

"Zack—" Trevillian sprang open like a shot squirrel, embracing Zack and kissing his cheek. "Have we found her?" he said in a breaking voice. He clung for a moment and then pushed himself away, burying his emotion. "Alright—" Trevillian grabbed his lantern.

Zack stepped between him and the collapse.

The steely eyes glinted with suspicion.

"There are conditions," Zack said.

"Who do you think you're talking to?"

Zack looked down. "If you get too close to her—"

Trevillian's right hand gripped the Reminder.

"She'll abandon us." Zack met his stare. "She doesn't want you near her. Those are Hope's words, not mine."

"Hope's words?" Trevillian's fingers fumbled to free the whip from his belt loop. He was shaking with rage—

"I'm the one she's chosen," Zack said.

A chill wind struck them.

Zack saw the prick of fear in Trevillian's squint. The boss raised his hand, sensing the wind, taking its direction. He pushed Zack aside and peered into the collapse.

"What did you see down there?" Trevillian demanded. A faint echo followed, rising from the invisible depths.

"Hope's in her glory," Zack told him.

Trevillian faced him.

"She's thicker than a man," Zack said. "Translucent, like she was at Moonblood."

The boss noticed his charred shirtfront.

"There's gas," Zack told him. "Torches flamed over us."

Trevillian's lip quivered.

"I lay with her," Zack said.

342

"How was that?"

"She's no angel. But—" Zack raised the quartz chunk between them. It caught the light from Trevillian's lantern. "She's ours for a while."

Trevillian eyed the gold barbs winking through the crystal panes. He clutched the rock. "Hope," he mewled. The quartz trembled like an animal in a trap.

"You, after all." The boss searched Zack's face.

"What do you see?"

"A boy fresh from Venus," Trevillian said weakly. "You please her as I did. Gas you say. And the rock is pitted around her?"

"Like swiss cheese."

"Take me to her," Trevillian said. The quartz fell from his fingers.

"You'll view her from a distance—"

"Now," Trevillian demanded, "or I'll cut you into stew cubes."

"You'll do what Hope says—"

"I'll do as I please." The boss's eyes gleamed like ball bearings in oil.

"You're to be celibate."

Trevillian's jaw dropped, then his lips pulled back, showing his teeth.

"You're not to touch her," Zack said. "Or Sephy. Or any other Blonde, except Francine. That's Hope's condition."

"Sephy will bunk down here and take leftover strokes."

343

"You don't understand—" Zack struggled for breath, trying to imagine Hope's indomitable nature filling his center. "Hope hates you. It's over."

"Now," Trevillian roared. His arms jerked, he hooked the lantern bail with his finger, faced the collapse and swung beneath the gray blade. Zack followed him. As they clambered down the rubble slide, Zack grabbed his arm. The boss whimpered and wrenched free. They descended in silence together.

It was the end of the meal hour in Strongbox Stope. Miners were eating, others had curled with their blankets over them or were pulling on their clothes, getting ready for the next shift. Near the entrance, two men in union suits fed wood to a stove. The blankets shifted and the boss appeared with Zack behind him. The men stared. Zack was shirtless. In his arms, the boss carried something wrapped in charred cloth.

Lloyd was by the cook shed, making marks in his pocket ledger. He saw the boss signal to him and he turned, grabbed a ladle and clanged the bell. Miners put their meals down, sat up in their bedrolls. Trevillian mounted his barrel as the bell continued to clang. Zack stood close-by, facing the camp. Men were rising, gathering around. Others emerged from the Big Wheel barricade, followed by a string of Blondes in shifts and chemises.

"Brothers, sisters—" Trevillian scanned the crowd.

There was no fooling any of them, Zack saw. No possibility

for drama or suspense. They could tell by the boss's jaunty manner, by the lightness in his voice.

The crushing load was about to be lifted.

"I have hold of something," the boss said. "It's bigger than this mountain. Bigger than the frozen world above us." He laughed. "I'm happier than I've ever been."

The people drew closer.

"Hope cares for us," Trevillian said. "Why else would she have returned?"

A Blonde cried out, there were gasps from the men, shouts and sobs of relief. Some fell to their knees, clasping their hands or kissing the ground. Some looked to a partner or friend—another to share their joy with. Others stood silent, watching the boss, feeling his confidence. It seemed to fill the cavern.

He raised the object wrapped in cloth. "Bluford—" Trevillian nodded.

True stepped forward and the boss lowered the object into his hands.

"Undress her," the boss said.

Men crowded around, holding candles and lanterns to see. Bluford peeled away the remnants of Zack's shirt.

"It's Hope," he said.

Fresh hollers and sighs. Men yammered at each other and the Blondes kissed cheeks. Zack saw Sephy among them, watching him through the crowd.

"She's on the 930." Trevillian looked at the floor, as if he could see through it. "At a place she painted in my dreams. Four feet wide, with smoke and fire in her."

Zack saw Bob and Inky staring at him.

"Not the fire that turned our store to ash," Trevillian said. "These flames heal and save. The man who feels them is a different man.

"I see Hope among us." He pointed through the crowd. "There. Right there. It looks like Katz, but that's Hope under that crooked smile and those greasy clothes. And there—that's Hope, brightening Sid's gloom, bringing cheer to Billy. Hope's there and there—" He picked faces out. "And right here in front of me." Trevillian's chest shook and he began to cry. "Make her welcome. Take Hope in your arms. Go on now—"

Men turned to each other.

"Tell her how glad you are to see her," the boss pressed them through his tears. "'I love you, Hope.' That's right, that's right."

Zack saw Salt Lick threading the clamor, eyes wide, patting shoulders and stroking faces. Trevillian stood watching, shaking his head at his mawkishness while a smile paid homage to the camp's fidelity. He wiped his cheeks and drew a breath.

"Now who do you think," he looked around the cavern, "is the first stiff I summoned when I found her?" He smiled at Zack. "Finally, the lad has seen Hope for himself. Tell us," he urged him.

Zack faced the camp.

"I came here," Zack said, "to fill my pockets. From the first, the boss saw how pinched in spirit I was. 'Give Hope your heart,' he told me. I sneered and I growled, but he didn't give up. An hour ago, he came to me. 'Are you ready?' he asked me. 'Ready to meet Hope, face to face?'"

Zack saw Marcus shaking his head. Inky and Len looked stunned.

"I'd had hints from many of you." He nodded to the face at the rear of the crowd. "From my favorite Blonde—"

Sephy went pale.

"—and from two run-ins with Prowler. But nothing prepared me for. the real thing. She was bedded in a vault. I pressed myself against her," Zack said. "Hope tore through me like the jet from a steam nozzle."

The mirrors before him cast a dozen reflections. Hope's latest conquest, the boss's favorite, the cowboy charlatan, Trevillian's stooge. Through his bandages, Noel eyed him soberly; Lloyd with mistrust; Carew with emotion—hearing, believing.

"She's tested us all," Zack said. "But those tests are nothing compared to what lies ahead. The place we called Nightpool is 'Guillotine' now. She's raised a blade to mark off those who venture deeper from those who won't. Hope's in a maze of riddled rock, with hellfire and gas."

"The lamp is lit," the boss said, "and our beloved lies within." He swung his arm down, pointing at the floor of the stope. "Who will spend his life for her?"

"I will." A miner stepped forward.

"She's all I want," another said, making a fist over his heart.

"Take me," True shouted.

"Take me," Arnie echoed, falling to his knees. And then

the camp was chanting, "Take me, take me," and the floor was a throng of supplicants, tendering their hearts. Trevillian lowered himself from the barrel and gestured to Zack with an open palm.

Zack stepped forward. "I will not sit wasting in this prison of flesh."

The faithful bowed their heads.

"I will not let doubt crush my spirit and mind. I will not linger here, stranded and fearful, waiting for the gulls to peck out my eyes."

Zack saw Salt Lick moving toward him.

"I'll breathe your gas," he said. "Dare your fire. Fill myself to bursting with too much power and too much light."

"Here's to you," Salt Lick cried.

She raised a bottle in one hand and smiled at the boss, offering him a cup with the other. Trevillian moved in front of Zack to receive it. The camp watched as he drank.

"And to my partner—" Trevillian turned, toasting Zack. "The new straw boss of Guillotine."

In honor of Hope's return, Salt Lick gave the Blondes a holiday and let the hooch flow on the house. The girls put on skirts and shirtwaists and mingled freely with the boys, while the singer and guitarist sat on a crate pile and played for the camp during the evening meal.

Zack was challenged. They treated him differently. He

had a new position among Trevillian's faithful—many were deferential. Things were different with the doubters as well.

"Honestly, Knox—" Lucky reproached him.

Marcus was furious. "Wiping his dump-hole with your hankie."

"If you don't like the flag I'm flying," Zack said, "go find another."

Bob, shaken at first, found his feet quickly. "If you were a fighter, you'd understand," he told Marcus. "He's lowered his guard."

But the biggest challenge was Sephy. What had happened pulled their relationship inside out. Zack found her at the end of the mess and they retreated into the shadows of the empty Wheel to talk.

He told her of the collapse and his encounter with Hope. And the face-off with Trevillian that followed, along with the arrangement they had agreed to. Her reaction was not what he expected. She turned and sank onto a bench.

"So much deception—" Sephy spoke half to herself.

"It's what Hope wants," Zack said, sitting beside her.

"And you?" Her hands settled in her lap. "It pained you— to be an actor, to live a false life."

"This deceit is founded on belief. I'm spinning a web with Hope inside me." Zack touched her cheek. "He's going to leave you alone."

"I'm relieved," she nodded. "But you've strengthened his command."

Zack saw the doubt in her eyes.

"It means everything to these people—that Hope has come back." Her voice whittled away. "Their faith is renewed—in Hope and in him. He's still their priest."

"He won't put his hands on her in the diggings," Zack said. "The craving they have will be satisfied by me."

"You really believe."

"I've given her my heart," he said.

"I wasn't sure if—" She took a breath.

"Hope is guiding me." Zack kissed Sephy's cheek.

"Can you trust her?"

The question rang inside him. Sephy seemed to sense that. She straightened and put her hand on his arm. The pale fingers tensed, and when Zack looked up, he saw a new kind of strength in her face. Not the power of sacrifice and faith, but a power that gave her patience and endurance.

"You still love me," he said.

15

Thirty days later, Guillotine looked as perilous as the day it appeared.

Trevillian stood before the gray blade with his lantern raised, measuring its height, inspecting the chocks on either side. Then he stooped beneath it and headed down. There were piers from floor to ceiling now and candles to light the way. The slope had been stabilized with muck, and track had been laid for the trams that rose loaded with Hope.

At the bottom of the incline, the track cut to the right. Air lines were mounted waist high on the wall. The mine boss passed Mind's Eye—the name given to the cave where Hope had revealed herself to Zack. It was a drift now. There were candles by the entrance and a faint clang in its depths. Beyond that, the way descended because that's what Hope did. She had been wanton at first, swelling at their attack, the gases thicker and more potent with every blast. Then she narrowed and twisted, leading them into a hive of fractured rock. Trevillian passed Dream Song and a pair of exploratory drifts. The men were threatened there, more than they'd ever been. But the threat wasn't that Hope would vanish.

It had been a glorious month, with more precious moments than anyone could count. The pace was feverish and the camp hung on the news from each blast. Every other shift break, Trevillian led an hour of communion, an emotional sharing of personal encounters. Some of the doubters had found belief. The naysayers pointed to the gas, the danger of cave-ins, and their barbaric living conditions. "Look where Hope is taking us," the Captain lamented. But the skeptics had no converts. The people could see Hope was real. Trevillian had a recess blasted inside the BMC enclosure, and the new high-grade quartz was secured there under lock and key, along with the gold amalgam that had been stored in the blockhouse before they'd taken up residence in the stope. Except for those hauling wood and water, few left the mountain. The Breakaway valley was sunk in darkness and given over to storms.

The mine boss descended toward Sacred Breath.

Earlier that week, Hope had tested them. She dove and frayed, and as the ribbons peeled off, the drill teams tunneled after her. The trails were false—all but one, but that one fattened quickly, running glassy and pure. As Trevillian approached, he could see eight men crowded before her, drillers stripped to the waist, muscles swollen and gleaming. The charges were set—there were holes in Hope and fuses hanging down.

The men weren't spitting the fuses. They were huddled together.

"The boss," Snell said, turning.

Trevillian halted twenty feet from the gathering, raising his lantern as the men hailed him with salutes. He motioned them aside, eager to see the focus of their interest. As the huddle opened, Zack was visible with lame Len beside him.

Len was stripped to the waist and the moment was his. He stood there facing the vein, trembling violently. From the look in his eyes, he might have been alone with her. He seemed to see none of the men.

Zack took hold of Len's arm and raised it.

Len stiffened. He looked fearful, about to recoil.

Zack whispered something and Len seemed comforted, but still insensible that another was beside him.

Zack drew Len's arm closer to the vein.

Len shuffled forward, surmounting his fear.

To Trevillian and the others in the drift, Hope was wondrous—translucent and glittering, with a sinuous ess where she touched the right wall— But static.

For Len, Hope was alive.

Zack hadn't noticed the arrival of the boss. He was barely aware of the miners around him. The candles flickered. The gases were thick. He heard a rhythmic sighing, and in the strobe of light he saw a misty portrait of the man needing his help.

"She's ready," Zack told him.

Len shuffled closer. His fingers touched the milky quartz

and his eyes narrowed. In that faraway look, Zack imagined Len could see the long body of Hope through the headwall, winding into the distance.

"Give me your heart," Zack said.

With his free hand, Len made a fist and carried it forward.

"Now," Zack said. He circled Len's shoulders with his arm.

Len's features went slack. His eyes filled with dread.

Zack forced him forward, against the quartz.

Len's arms twitched.

A strangling sound issued from his throat. Len cried out.

He stood perfectly still, then his legs buckled. He lay on the floor of Sacred Breath convulsing, writhing and gasping while the miners watched.

Zack fell to his knees and raised Len's head. Len's cheeks and chin were covered with froth, as if he'd swallowed an infusion of Hope and she was bubbling out.

"Help me," Zack said to Snell.

Snell nodded to another man and stooped. "We'll get him to the sane side of Guillotine."

"No," Zack said. "He's had enough. Carry him to the stope."

As Zack rose, he noticed Trevillian. He saluted.

The boss returned the salute as Len's shivering body was lifted.

"Our charges need sparking," Zack told the men. "Noel and I will spit. The rest of you—beat it home."

"Fine shift, boys," Trevillian lauded them. "Report," he ordered Zack.

"Tapering in Dream Song," Zack replied. "Nothing left at Mind's Eye. You see how strong she is here. There's more farther down. That's where she's taking us."

"That's where we're going," the boss concurred. "Alright—" He motioned at the miners stepping toward him. "Is that muscle or rock?" he squeezed a man's arm and slapped another's back, returning along the drift with them.

The shift whistle sounded from down the level. The departing men turned a corner, and Zack was alone with Noel-the-Mole.

"He's in high spirits," Noel said, opening a pocketknife. He notched a short length of fuse.

Zack took a candle from the wall and held it beneath Noel's chin. A red furrow split the right side of Noel's face, from nostril to earlobe. "How's the cut?"

"It itches," Noel said.

His energy hadn't dimmed, Zack thought, but Noel's smile would never be the same. The scar had pulled up the right side of his mouth.

"The high spirits are a show," Zack said.

"There's always something eating the boss."

"You know what a spade bit is?" Zack asked.

Noel nodded.

"He's wearing one," Zack said. "His limit is twenty feet." He glanced at the spot where Trevillian had stood. "He can't lay his hands on Hope or put his pick in her."

Noel stared at him. In the silence, they could hear the whisper of gas leaking from the headwall.

"Why would—"

"We have an agreement," Zack said. "Those were Hope's terms. She wasn't coming back."

"Why are you telling me this?"

"Hope wants you with us," Zack said.

"Us?"

Zack nodded.

"I'm not going to forget what he did," Noel said, "but a man has principles—" He pursed his lips. "Light the spitter."

"You know how much Hope cares about principles?" Zack laughed. "Your honor? It's a mystery to her—the pride of blood sausage. What Hope wants, Hope wants. Your heart is with her or it's not."

"You're a new man, that's for sure."

Zack heard the enmity in his voice. "Doubt has left me, Noel. It's what she demands of a priest."

Noel didn't turn away. He was listening.

"You accept the worst kind of tyranny from Trevillian because you think Hope is with him. But she's not. Hope is speaking to you right now, through me."

Zack snuffed a candle on the wall, so the only light was the one in his right hand. Then he raised his left hand beside the flame and turned it slowly.

"I've seen the change, Noel. I've watched Hope flow into me, until nothing human remained. *I am the dream now: Hope's crystal, Hope's milk.* As a man, I received her. Now as Hope, I go forth. My muscles eel, my skin glitters as the scales shift. Flames burn inside me, and the light raying faith into everything around me— That light is mine."

Zack swept the blankets aside and stepped into Strongbox Stope. He halted for a moment, taking deep breaths to purge his lungs and clear his head.

"Groggy?"

Dinesh drew beside him and lifted something halfway out of his coat pocket. "For the mongrel and Bunting's rifle."

Zack nodded and Dinesh let the packet slide back.

"Give them to the Captain," Zack said.

"Not much room left."

"I know," Zack squeezed the smith's arm.

Genuine Jo and Weasel crossed the stope and entered the infirmary. DuVal was with Owen, and the two were stepping toward them, headed below. Dinesh hurried away.

The stope made a strange billet. The breath of its lodgers had accumulated on the walls, where it glistered and dripped. Because the coal supply was supplemented with timber, and because the fires never went out, the stoves ran red-hot. They pulsed and glowed through the smoky miasma.

The boss was standing by one of the stoves with his arms extended. He was giving a bouquet to the men on the last shift. Miners were sitting in their bedrolls listening. In the middle of some expostulation, Trevillian spotted him and raised his arm, motioning him toward the BMC enclosure. Zack nodded.

He strode past Owen and DuVal, ignoring the foreman's greeting. The boss entered the enclosure. The Bangshu paused in their yammering to bow to Zack, then returned to their tasks.

The door to the enclosure was fashioned from crate lids. Zack swung it open and approached the boss's corner, an area cordoned off from Lloyd's assay lab and the cots where the inner guard bunked. Zack drew the blanket aside.

The boss's quarters were dim, lit by two candles, each burning in a halved tin can. Trevillian had his back to him and was removing his shirt. He faced a washbasin and mirror, seeing Zack in the reflection.

"How many shifts since you warmed your bedroll?" the boss said without turning.

"Three."

"You need a rest." Trevillian poured water into a shaving cup. "Len's made of strong stuff—"

"You think I went too far?"

"No. It's a dance with death, getting close to her. The last of my soap." Trevillian worked his brush and lathered his face. "My point is—there's only so much help you can give." He paused to eye Zack in the mirror. "It's Hope who will save them, not you. Share their triumph, but stay out of their rapture. And," he lifted his straight razor, "keep a sharp edge on their fear. Men are like mules."

Zack watched the razor glide beneath his jaw.

"Being boss feeds you," Trevillian said. "Daily you grow."

"There are moments—"

"Mmm?"

"—when they're toiling and panting together. I'm like a man hunched over his lover, looking down, seeing my strength, the power I'm wielding."

In the glass, a smile ripened between the stubbled cheeks.

"I'm putting Noel behind the everhard," Zack said.

"A waste of talent," Trevillian replied.

"The rock is so loose, I can't get the steels pointed."

"Have the carpenters build a guide brace," the boss said. "Keep Noel with his sledge."

"I'm going to use Mind's Eye as a powder cache."

"No you're not," Trevillian said.

"We're wasting time."

"That's crazy." The boss bent over the washbasin and splashed water on his face.

"The powder must be closer. It's what Hope wants."

Trevillian dried his cheeks and turned to regard him.

"Why?"

Zack made a baffled face and shook his head.

"Alright," the boss said. "But there will be a cage with doors, and the doors will be locked. Owen will have the key."

"Thanks," Zack tipped his head. The Reminder lay tangled on the floor, looking harmless amid dirty socks and hand tools. "For keeping your word and your distance. For trusting me."

"Trusting you?" the boss grunted. "I'm impulsive, self-deceiving. But I'm not a fool. The only thing I trust about you are your designs on me."

His face was a mask, but Zack could hear the resentment in his voice.

"You're sweet cake with broken glass in it," Trevillian said. "Tell me I'm wrong. Look me in the eye and lie to me."

"Bastard—"

Trevillian raised his brows. "The magic word."

The scar on the boss's chest was purplish. Its color changed with his moods.

"I like it when you wear your feelings on your sleeve," Trevillian nodded. "It's exciting. 'This is my doing,' I think. 'Zack is more and more like me—live nitro in a runaway cart.'"

"Why don't you pay the Wheel a visit," Zack said. "Chew on Francine."

"She's the only door you've left open," Trevillian laughed. "But there's nothing inside. Francine's unable to summon her. There's no Hope for anyone here—without you."

Trevillian stepped closer. Zack looked away.

"You wonder, don't you. 'Could it happen? The monster she made of Trevillian— Could she make another one, out of me?' Oh she could, she could. I'm here, Zack. Not over there with the laundry."

Zack faced him.

"A mantle of power. And inside, nothing but fear. When Hope vanishes, that's what you'll be." The boss tossed his head. "The real test is coming. You'll hear how loudly rage roars, how hateful the sound is to the whole universe."

"Will I roar?" Zack said.

"I believe you will," Trevillian replied. "You'll never be as fine a boss as I am, but you might wear the whip some day. You've seen me tested, and you'll have my example to fall back on." His eyes glittered with amusement.

"When you were a boy," he said, "did you have a blood brother?"

Zack shook his head.

"What a great time that was," Trevillian sighed. "The excitement, the danger— Bailiffs and bigwigs, chaplains and coppers—they can all go to hell." He cackled. "Blood brothers on the streets of Gotham. Tough town, you say? Not for us. In the Seedbed of Vice, blood brothers are welcome. All the doors are open. And all the windows too."

Trevillian turned away. "We should be closer. For better or worse, we're in this together." He retrieved his shirt from his cot.

Zack realized there were two cots in the boss's quarters now, side by side.

Trevillian pulled his shirt on. "Men of purpose, bound by Hope. There's no disgrace in that." He buttoned his front. "The priest's life is a lonely one."

The boss tucked his shirt into his waistband.

"You know—" Trevillian stooped and grabbed his whip. "There are times when you remind me of my father."

Zack watched him.

"He kept me at a distance," the boss said, "and I was never sure why."

Trevillian coiled the thong in silence. Zack said nothing.

"He might be a few feet away, just as you are now. I would say something, and it was as if he didn't hear me. As if I wasn't there."

A moment later, Zack exited the boss's quarters. As he strode past the assay table, he was surprised to see Lloyd hunched over the furnace. He'd entered the BMC enclosure while Zack was with Trevillian.

"Let me see that burn," Lloyd said, straightening.

Zack stepped toward him and unbuttoned his shirt.

"You were listening," Zack said.

"Well done," Lloyd muttered, loosening the bandage.

Zack heard the irony in his voice.

"You're his new dwarf," Lloyd said.

Zack struck him across the face. Lloyd lurched against the makeshift shelving, sending beakers and cupels clattering to the floor. "Tweak my nose and you'll be mending yourself," Zack said.

As Trevillian emerged, Zack turned on him.

"Why do you put up with this?" he snarled, tearing the bandage free and chucking it at Lloyd.

The doctor regained his feet, hand on his cheek.

"He's losing his balance," Trevillian told Lloyd.

They turned together and stared at Zack.

In the silence, song reached them from the Big Wheel. *The man who feels what Hope feels is a different man,* the voice declared. It might have been Hope, observing the three of them from a distance.

"You've brought me along," Zack said. He turned on his heel and strode out of the enclosure.

16

Hope guarded Zack and nourished him in the diggings and in his dreams.

Then one night Prowler appeared, rising as if from hibernation, enormous and brown, a mountain with ice on its shoulders. His green eyes turned through the darkness, knowing Zack was there. The shaggy arms opened, black claws clicking. And then Hope's sigh blew over them. Prowler collapsed like a clown suit, and from beneath the brown mass, the white serpent emerged, gliding toward him over broken ground.

She was sleek, without head or limbs, and as her body eeled, it left translucent ribbons like cast skins. Hope's front lifted into the air. She loomed over him, her robe swinging open. He saw its lining—the fabric of hearts, pulsing and glistening.

It's time, Hope said.

Zack shivered.

The man will live and the boy will die. Her thick body flexed against him, taking him between the wings of her robe. He felt the golden flames twisting inside her. The odor of blood filled his nostrils and the rubies and garnets drummed in his ears.

I've retreated to a place where drills won't find me.

Her panes dimmed with smoke.

Hope must be cruel. And so must her priests.

Zack was shaking. His bones ground, his limbs jerked. He was shaking loose of Hope, turning and falling through unlit space.

Farther he fell and farther. And then he stopped. The shift whistle was sounding.

Zack woke in darkness. He was in his bedroll.

He felt beside him. On the rough-sawn top of an over-turned box, he found a block of matches. He snapped one off and struck it, and a pool of light spread around him.

He was on his cot in Trevillian's quarters. He propped himself on an elbow, wiping the sweat from his face as the whistle died. The boss's blankets lay twisted beside him. Zack raised himself and slid into his pants.

Heads turned when he exited the BMC enclosure. The miners were stretched on their pallets or standing by the stoves. Those assigned to his drill team stepped toward him, dressed and fed, ready to go. As he crossed the stope, they tipped their heads and fell in behind him. Two months had passed since Zack had become the boss's bunkie. A feverish time—one long shift, one reckless spree with Hope. The early boys likened it to the heyday of the 310. The conditions, of course, were different—with the riddled rock, the gas and their confinement beneath the earth.

They were a ragged lot now. As their garments wore through, they'd patched them with canvas or scraps of sacking—whatever could be found. In the first week in February, they reached the end of their grain and canned goods. The fish kept them alive, but the portions shrank. As he passed the cook station, Zack grabbed a cup of spruce tea and chugged it.

When the team reached the 310 landing, Zack waved his men into the skip, giving one a smile, squeezing a shoulder, swatting a hip. They all felt it—the anticipation of another day close to Hope. Zack stood, yanked the bell wire and sat on the tread, and they headed down.

By the first week in March, all the quartz had been mined from Dream Song and Sacred Breath. Hope took them deeper. At a place they called Rapture, she ravished them— thick flames in clear glass. But they paid a price for the gift of gold so pure. In the gassy drift, flares from candles set a man's pant leg on fire or melted his ear. A woozy driller missed his steel, crushing his shaker's fingers. Zack rotated the men at the headwall, two hours each—the gas was that bad. Some got nauseous, some giddy. Some couldn't stop chattering or sobbing and had to be restrained. In two locations, Hope kinked.

Little Twist pinched out after forty feet. Big Twist led farther. That was where they were headed. At Big Twist, Hope
was waiting for them, naked and rich.

The skip pulled up to the 490 and the drill team stepped
out. As Zack faced the winze, he was surprised to see Trevillian. The boss stood among piles of steels and crates, giving
orders.

"Where's this going?" Zack asked Arnie, pointing at the
equipment being loaded.

"Big Twist," Arnie replied.

Zack came up beside the boss and put his hand on his
back. "Thanks."

Trevillian turned. "Ah," he smiled. "Drills first," he ordered DuVal. Then he grabbed his lantern, motioned to Zack
and swung around.

The boss crossed the loading platform and Zack followed.
When they reached the darkness at the entrance to the level,
Trevillian halted and faced him.

"You're not going down this shift," the boss said.

"Who's going to boss Big Twist?"

"The teams will dig as they do elsewhere," the boss said.
"With my guidance."

"Don't be a fool."

Trevillian's jaw clenched. Zack saw venom in his eyes.

"You're breaking our pact," Zack said.

"I've already broken it," Trevillian replied.

What did that mean? Had he been below?

"You'll drive Hope away," Zack said angrily.

368

Trevillian's severity dissolved. He shook his head. "She's taken me back," he said, sharing his astonishment.

A prickling chill climbed Zack's neck.

"She spoke to me," the boss said, "as we slept. I woke and—" He glanced at the winze.

It's not true, Zack thought. *He's lying. Deluded.* He peered into the boss's face, reading his mind, feeling his power and confidence.

"Hope flows into you," Trevillian said, "and Hope flows out."

A voice in Zack's mind cried out to her. He imagined he was at the Big Twist headwall, on his knees.

"Your days as straw boss are over," Trevillian told him. "No more drilling or mucking. You'll be on the mule gang—dumping slag into the worked-out drifts."

The boss feared him, because of the position Zack had with the men. "Blood brothers," Zack said.

Trevillian raised his lantern. "Nothing's changed. We're still partners and bunkies. I'm doing what Hope wants. I'm her priest."

Zack stared at him.

"'Keep him away from me,'" Trevillian said. "Those were her orders. I'm sorry." He sighed. "I gave you my blessing when she favored you." He opened his arms. "Give me yours, now that I have her back."

Without waiting for a response, Trevillian embraced him. Zack felt the boss's chest against his. Zack's legs wobbled, he struggled for breath.

"You've got pals in the stope," the boss said. "Take the shift off."

Trevillian turned and headed back to the winze. Zack stood in the darkness, watching the men load the bucket.

He crossed the platform, avoiding the glances. He boarded the empty skip and signaled the hoist house. As the car crawled up the track, Zack closed his eyes.

In the Big Wheel, the seats were empty. A corner had been set aside as a Toilette Room and the women were gathered there, making themselves ready. As Zack entered, Genuine Jo brightened and turned. He fastened the back of a worn gown for her. The cashier saw him and directed his gaze toward Sephy, then she ushered the Blondes to the passageway connecting the alcoves.

Sephy stood quietly, regarding herself in a mirror. She'd set her puritan garb aside and was wearing an organdy dress. When she saw him, she gasped and hugged his chest. He held her, wondering at her emotion. Did she know what had happened?

"He's gone back on our agreement," he said.

Sephy looked up.

"I'm not straw boss anymore."

"Why not?"

"He says Hope's taken him back. She wants nothing to do with me."

Sephy shook her head. "Is it possible?"

He didn't reply.

"He's deceiving you," Sephy said.

"I'm not so sure."

"What reason would Hope have to leave you?"

"I had a dream last night," Zack told her. "She said, 'It's time.'"

"The old priest and the new," Sephy guessed.

"I can't bring Trevillian down without her," Zack said.

"Maybe Hope means you harm."

"Maybe she does."

"We have no power over our lives," Sephy said.

"I don't know what to do," he confessed. "I've given her my heart and so have you."

"Everything I give to her now," Sephy said, "I give for us."

He gazed into her eyes.

Sephy stifled a sob. "Pity the boss."

"The boss?"

"He gave her everything. Look what she's done to him. And poor Raymond. Maybe she's playing false with Trevillian right now. Hope is ruthless. She has no conscience." Sephy looked at him. "I don't care who she favors."

There was love in her eyes.

"It's time then, with or without her," he said.

Zack expected her to join his resolve. Instead, she turned away.

"You said you'd seen a child come into the world," Sephy muttered.

371

"After the show," Zack replied. "In the livery tent."

"What happened?"

"She managed it. I tried to help her. I thought something was wrong—it was white as soap."

Sephy faced him. "I'm pregnant," she said.

Through her agitation, Zack saw an irrepressible cheer.

"The cooks think it's a boy," she added.

"His," Zack said.

"Only the wheel knows."

"It's time," he said.

Bob and Inky were in the sack, and so was Noel. Zack roused them, and not long after, the four men and Sephy were kneeling on the gravel at the end of the Snuff o' Kate drift. They'd extinguished all but one lantern. The light flickered on their faces.

"The boss has his eight," Inky said.

Bob nodded. "And the true-blue stiffs."

"Call it two dozen," Zack said.

"We're twenty-two now," Inky said. "Plus Sephy and Weasel."

"There's another," Sephy said. "I haven't spoken to her yet, but she'll be with us."

"The rest," Noel shrugged, "will have to choose."

"They'll choose Hope," Inky glanced at Zack.

"It's our man who speaks to her," Bob agreed.

"Things have changed," Zack told them, "as of this morning. I'm not straw boss. I'm on the mule gang."

Sparks flew from Noel's eyes.

"It's how he wants it," Zack said.

Inky was nervous. "What if Hope disappears?"

"Has the boss put his hands on her?" Bob asked.

"She won't let him," Zack said, imagining Trevillian at the end of Big Twist, with Hope spread before him. "She hates him and she'll show it."

Noel and Inky were silent. Sephy looked down.

"That's why we're going to act now," Zack said.

Bob was nodding, but there was a question in his eyes.

"Are you with me?" Zack pressed.

"Of course," Inky replied.

"No question," Noel said.

Bob continued to nod.

"You're Hope's priest," Sephy said, looking up.

"We've got three firearms and four rounds for each." Zack ticked them off. "I'll have Bob's mongrel, Bunting has his rifle, and Noel will use the pistol I lifted from Owen's batch."

"Who's stuffing the vent holes?" Inky said.

"You and Bob will relay sticks from the Captain's dinghy. Noel will be up top to receive them."

"How many?" Bob said.

"Forty, maybe fifty," Zack replied. "Get them transferred by the end of this shift. I'll load the ceiling at the break. If

Trevillian's gang doesn't go along, we'll bury them beneath it." He scanned the four faces. "While I'm up there, you'll gather the boys."

"I'd like to be there," Bob chuckled. "See the look on his mug."

"Where are you gonna put him?" Noel asked.

"The powder cache at Mind's Eye."

"It's locked," Noel said.

"Dinesh is making me a key," Zack told him. "We'll have the camp to ourselves."

There was silence. The confrontation was hard to imagine.

"You'll turn them," Noel said.

Bob scratched his cheek. "Maybe we should put the boss out of his pain."

"It'll be easier," Inky agreed, "if they know he isn't coming back."

"For all his crimes," Noel conceded, "I couldn't kill him. But—" He frowned at Zack. "What's his job here afterwards? Who is he, when it's over?"

"A man who's learned something," Zack said.

Bob shook his head. "That's not Trevillian."

"I hate his butchery," Zack said. "I'm not carrying it forward."

Quiet closed over the five.

Inky looked at Bob.

Bob brushed the grit off his palms.

"Any other questions?" Zack asked.

At that moment, Trevillian was waving his arm before the headwall of Big Twist. A thick current of Hope was bedded in the rock. The spitter in the boss's hand sizzled and flashed as he touched off the last of the fuses.

"Fire in the hole," he boomed.

The men with him turned, and together they stumbled back along the drift with the gas whispering around them. Where the corridor widened into Rapture, they took cover, and a few seconds later, the blast stutter sounded. The rock roared, the digging shook and the dim tunnel was filled with dust.

In the Big Wheel, a miner stood watching while the disk turned around. Zack skirted the seating area, headed for Salt Lick's boudoir. When he reached the velvet, he spoke her name.

"Francine?"

"Come in."

Zack drew the velvet aside and entered. The madam was sitting on her mattress with her knees up, wearing only knickers and a bust bodice.

"I didn't mean to surprise you in bed."

"That would be difficult," she said.

Zack's eye fell on a small box on the dresser beside him. Inside were the shards of the Cupid lamp. He picked one and held it up.

"Someday," Salt Lick sighed, "we'll repair all these broken things around us."

"Weasel said you wanted to see me." Zack returned the shard to its box.

She studied him. "You've had quite a run with Hope, haven't you."

"I owe you," he said, "for the introduction."

"He thought you were his salvation."

"I was," Zack said, "for a while."

She laughed. "Your faith is as crooked as mine. Really, between two actors—" She rose and put on a negligee. "This Eden of ours is a cheerless place."

"Not for the boss. He has Hope."

"Yes," Salt Lick nodded, "they're together again. We're on the outside now, you and I."

She was drawing closer to her purpose.

"Maybe we should be thankful he's back in Hope's graces," the madam said. "I don't have to take his abuse. And you don't have to play priest." Her voice softened. "Sephy needs you right now."

Zack eyed her coldly. "Who else knows?"

"Lloyd and the Bangshu, and most of the girls." She reached out.

Zack felt her grip his arms, watched the painted moonface draw near.

"I read minds too," she said. "The minds of men. You want to destroy him, even more now. And when he finally sees how deep that desire is, he'll destroy you."

"A man with my thoughts," Zack said. "What can he do?"

"Banish them," the madam replied. She let go of his arms and took a breath. "Who is Hope? How did she enter our lives? For a woman, she's a poor substitute. A dream, growing inside us. Something we nourish with our love, in place of a child."

"Those aren't the words of a believer," Zack said.

"Perhaps not."

"A more punishing faith would burn you as a heretic."

"Our faith is punishing enough." She swept her blonde waves back. "There's a treasure in this mine—a woman who loves you. Take your heart back from Hope, and give it to her."

"And leave Hope to the boss," he said.

"Men are fools," the madam reproached him. "Absolute fools—" Her lips were trembling. "Do you think your mother—"

The poison in Zack's eyes stopped her.

He swung around and swept the velvet aside. Salt Lick followed him.

"She would have done anything to save you," the madam said to his back.

She stood there alone, staring at the spots of light ringing the Wheel. A moment passed, then the scrabble of footsteps startled her.

Genuine Jo emerged from the shadows.

377

Salt Lick embraced her. Then she drew the velvet aside, and the two entered her room.

Zack's boots left the gravel of the 310 level and stepped onto the platform. He stopped at the center of the station and looked around. Then he turned down the wick of his lantern and approached the scaffolding at its rear. A rope dropped out of the darkness above. Noel descended toward him, hand over hand, breathing hard.

"Ten feet in," Noel said as he reached the landing. "Behind a block."

A parked skip cried out, and the two men jumped. The skip rocked on the track and sank with a whine, summoned from below.

"Nerves of steel," Noel muttered.

Zack passed Noel his lantern, put his hands on the rope and was about to haul himself up.

"Zack—"

Noel raised the lantern. "The first time I drilled for prize money, I was up against the best stiff in the state. I had to pull my hero down."

"He's no hero of mine." Zack put his arm around Noel and shook him. "But thanks. Get word to our boys."

Noel nodded and Zack muscled his way up the rope.

A minute later he was in a dark crawlway above Strongbox Stope. Minutes after that, he was crouching, holding a cable and peering down through a ventilation shaft. Owen and Lloyd were exiting the BMC enclosure. They passed under the vent and disappeared from view.

Zack shifted his legs and took a deep breath. A candle flickered behind a rock ten feet away—all the light he could risk. He steadied himself, craned over the vent and loosened his hold on a cable that descended into it. The cable crept through his fingers. At the end was an iron plate. He maneuvered the plate past a nub of rock, then pulled the cable back up. The nub crumbled as the plate came against it, and a stream of dust slid down.

He peered through the vent. All was quiet in the stope. No one had noticed.

He let the cable go again, dropping the plate farther, past another nub. He squinted, held his breath and tugged on the cable. This time the plate caught, wedging itself in the shaft. Zack kept the cable taut while he fixed it to a bolt set for the purpose.

He wiped his eyes, turned to the bundles of dynamite piled beside him and grabbed one—a half-dozen sticks bound with twine. He placed it in the vent and lowered it by its priming fuse. It came to rest on the plate.

Zack ran through the calculation again. It was just a guess. If the loads weren't right, an explosion would bring the roof down on everyone in the stope.

A clanging sounded below. He scooted along the crawlway to the next vent hole and looked down. The men were assembling and they were noisier than usual. He heard groans and protests, the clamor that arose when things weren't right. They were all facing the same way—toward the BMC enclosure. Zack couldn't see the barrel Trevillian used when he spoke, but he imagined the boss standing on it, raising his hand for silence. The crowd settled and Zack heard the boss's voice.

"Many of you have the news from your pals—those who were with me, examining the morning blast at Big Twist. What's showing? What's the look of our headwall?" The boss would be gesturing, picking someone out.

"Black," Owen's voice sounded. "All black."

The clamor resumed.

"Hope's not with us," the boss said. "Not right now."

Zack gripped the rock with both hands.

"Things have changed on the 930," Trevillian was saying, "as many of you know. I spit the last blast. There's a reason for that."

Silence.

"Hope's got a gripe with us." A pause for emphasis. "We've done our best to please her, but we've failed."

A stir of speculation. The boss called for quiet.

"The source of Hope's disaffection," Trevillian said, "is my brother. Zack." His voice sank with humility. "She loved him. She let him mine her. But a man in his pride, who thinks he's more than a man— Hope won't abide that. She'll return to us, but she's laid down new terms and I've sworn to obey them."

"Soon?" a man asked.

"What terms?"

"When's she coming back?"

Zack saw the miners' agitation through the vent hole. They incited and harangued each other, trying to make sense of the bad news.

"She's left us in the lurch again," one lamented.

"We've lost her," another cried.

"What does Zack say?"

"Where is he?"

"As far from Hope as I can put him," the boss said. "That's what she wants."

17

An hour later, Zack was moving down Snuff o' Kate with Dog-Eared Bob. The drift was quiet. Bob's lantern lit the way.

They reached the bend and four hat candles appeared at the headwall. Zack saw eyes—many, watching him. Nineteen rebels were packed in the narrow space. He halted, regarding them silently. He lifted his hand to the brim of his hat. Then he hurled it at the wall. The gathering jumped.

"The boss is useless," Zack said. "To Hope and to us."

"What's happened to her?" a man asked.

"Will we get her back?" another wanted to know.

"Once he's out of the way," Zack said, "there will be more Hope than any of you can imagine."

"What a joker," Bob sniffed. "Trying to blame Zack."

"If he'd kept his distance at Rapture," Zack told them, "she'd still be with us. Hope hates him—you all know that."

"He put his paws on her," one said.

The man beside him raised a sheath knife. "I'll cut his throat."

"The pig, the rat—"

"We'll set everyone straight," Zack said, "as soon as I've got the stage."

"DuVal's finished," a man said.

"And Lloyd—"

"Sweep the place clean."

"Where's Len?" a voice wondered.

Faces looked around.

"Cold feet," Bob said. "He'll come across with the others. Genuine Jo—she's one of us now. Sephy gaffed her at the break."

"In this election," Zack's voice rose, "there's only one vote that counts. One kiss to victory." He scanned his soldiers. "Hope loves you, boys. She'll be with you when you shake your fist at the boss."

"I'm for finishing his daddy's work," Marcus Bunting said, "first thing."

"He'll be below," Zack said. "Till the show's over."

"Bring the Reminder back with you," Noel told Zack. "That'll ease their minds."

There were grunts of agreement.

Zack held his hand before him, palm down, and then lowered it. As one, the men sank to their knees. They needed Hope now, Zack thought. And so did he.

"Minutes are passing. Hours and days. I watch with fearful eyes. Falsehoods fill my ears, words that condemn me, cries of despair— I see, I hear, but help doesn't reach me." He clenched his fist over his chest. "There is only one cure."

Zack was trembling. "The Hope we have," he carried his fist forward, "Trevillian didn't give us. And Trevillian can't take her away."

Every man's hand was fisted, every arm straight. He gazed at the miners for a long moment, honoring their pledge. Then he motioned and they rose.

"Two a.m.," Zack said. He drew the prospector's pick from his belt and handed it to Bob.

"Two o'clock," Bob affirmed. "One hour after the next shift starts." He slid the pick through his waistband and scanned the faces. "Follow the plan, Marcus, or I'll crush your skull."

"Those below," Zack said, "leave your drifts, give yourselves enough time. Those in the stope, watch for my return after I've dumped the boss below. That's the trigger."

"First round," Bob said. "The BMC boys throw the sponge in. Or we'll flatten 'em."

The men nodded, sharing a moment of silent resolve.

Then Zack stepped forward and embraced one of them. The others followed his lead and when the clinching was done, they departed in twos and threes.

Zack entered the stope without a lantern. He found his way to the infirmary unnoticed, approaching the damp spot where the Captain's craft was moored.

"Ahoy, there," Zack said softly.

The Captain was resting with his back to the stern.

"It's in motion," Zack said.

"Come for your weapon?"

Zack nodded.

The Captain drew his blankets back, raised his good leg and passed a small canvas pouch over the side. Zack put the pouch in his coat pocket. Then the Captain handed him the mongrel. Zack slid it into his waistband.

"When does the show start?" the Captain asked.

"Two a.m." Zack eyed the stope entrance. "When I part those blankets." He shifted his gaze toward the Big Wheel, searching the darkness. "How's the leg?"

"Soft as dough," the Captain said. "I've had some strange fancies."

Zack faced him.

"About Hope," the Captain said. "I'm being carried to meet her. In this little ship of mine." He squinted. "There she is, spanning the horizon. Will she welcome you home? You'll know soon. The currents are strong. Ship your oars and ride the flood."

He set his hand on the gunwale. "A dying man's dream."

"You're not dying."

"How many times have I seen it?" the Captain said. "There's a fish on the deck. It was swimming, then it was

386

struggling on a hook. Someone dropped it there and left it. The sun goes down and the purser lights the lamps. The fish is still thinking. It imagines it's moving its fins." He peered into Zack's eyes. "What great ocean of dreams must that poor fish cross, before its rotting body beaches it in oblivion?"

"Maybe its dreams will outlive it," Zack said.

Through the darkness, steps approached. Zack turned to see Sephy beside him. She clasped his hand.

"Hope," the Captain nodded. "You mean Hope—"

"Yes," Zack said. "I mean Hope."

The Captain looked from Zack to Sephy. "Perhaps it's our death that Hope wants," he said. "Maybe she brought us here for that."

"Who made a home for Hope inside you?" Zack asked him.

"He makes a fine priest." The Captain smiled at Sephy.

"These dreams, these wishes—" Zack turned and looked into her eyes.

"We all wish for better," the Captain said. "Men and fish."

"I have to go." Zack touched Sephy's temple.

"The powder cache at Mind's Eye," she said.

Zack nodded. He kissed her, glanced at the Captain and stepped away.

Sephy watched him wind through the cots. She turned back with a troubled look.

"Have I done something to upset you?" the Captain asked.

"No," Sephy said. "It's a dream I've had."

"A bad one," the Captain said.

387

"Zack is found out," she replied.

The Captain frowned.

She closed her eyes. "I fear it's what Hope wants."

Twenty feet away, Genuine Jo rose from between two cots. Sephy had her back to her, and the Captain didn't see her. She gathered her skirts, stole through the infirmary and hurried across the stope, making a beeline for the madam's boudoir.

A minute later, Salt Lick barged through the doorway of the BMC enclosure. Her bodice was half-buttoned, her hair in disarray. Owen was there. She strode forward and grabbed him. "Where's Trill?" she asked, breathless.

"Somewhere below."

It was 1:20 a.m., forty minutes before curtain time. Zack met Inky at Meat Hook as they'd arranged. The drift where Zack first swung a hammer was dark and dead.

In the light from his lantern, Zack saw Inky raise a key between them. It hung on a small loop of thong and glittered as it turned. Zack took it.

"I've composed something," Inky said.

Zack watched him pull a scrap of paper from his coat.

Inky leaned closer, using Zack's light.

"For years he wanders," Inky read. "Then one day, his mind turns. He leaves the wide ocean with a strange purpose —to find a river, one river only. Through instinct and providence, he finds it and follows it. Farther and farther from the freedom of the sea, closer and closer to that moment he has spent everything to achieve, when he ascends the last freshet and twists his way into the pocket that fathered him."

Inky lowered the scrap. Zack looked into his eyes.

"We've traveled together," Zack said. "Hope is the river. She'll lead us home."

When Inky had gone, Zack took the bullets from the canvas pouch and loaded the mongrel.

At 1:30 a.m., Zack was looking for Trevillian. The miners on the 400 hadn't seen him. They spoke with pauses and sidelong glances—he felt distant and alone. On the 490, it was the same. The stiffs gave him plenty of space. As he boarded the winze, he thought, *Everything is about to change.* His life was a sketch done in chalk and it was starting to rain. The bucket clanged in the well—once, twice—then it began to sink. The cable's low hum mounted in the shaft.

When he reached the 770, a pair of miners on the platform nodded. The boss was at the end of the level—in the Seemly drift.

Zack stepped through the dimly lit corridor, boots crunching the gravel. Past Tempting and Lovesick, Promise and Giblets, walking between the rails. At the Seemly entrance, he paused beside a flickering candle and slid the mongrel out. He opened the chamber and checked his lead. Hammer back, trigger engaged, hammer forward. The crowd was expectant. He was alone, outside the arena, fighting his nerves and his mount. He slid the gun back in his waistband, straightened himself and headed into the drift.

He passed a candle. And another. Puddles where the corridor angled, and then the headwall came into view. Trevillian was stooped between a pair of muckers, picking through blast fragments.

As Zack approached, he looked up.

Zack stopped.

Trevillian rose slowly with suspicion in his eyes. "What are you doing here?" he said beneath his breath. "You're steering a mule cart next shift. Got your place from Owen?"

"Hope's disappeared," Zack said.

Trevillian studied him, as if expecting some gloating.

Zack met his gaze, serious, collected.

"Slights and stipulations," Trevillian burst out. "The backbiting tramp—"

"You made me the goat," Zack said.

The boss spread his hands and laughed.

"I was an easy target," Zack nodded. "I'd taken too much credit. There was too much pride in my love for Hope."

"Repentance," Trevillian said. "You know I like that."

"I was below just now," Zack told him.

Trevillian bristled.

"Doing some exploring on my own," Zack said.

The boss's right hand settled on the butt of the Reminder.

"You want her, don't you?" Zack said.

Trevillian's lips parted. He exhaled sharply, then he put his hand on Zack's shoulder.

"You didn't expect me to stay away from her," Zack said.

"No," Trevillian shook his head. "Where is she?"

"On the 930."

Zack turned on his heel. For two strides, he was on his own. Then he heard the boss's bootsteps following. As he exited the Seemly drift, Trevillian came up beside him. "We're blood," the boss said, as if to himself. "There's no pulling us apart."

They had just passed Promise when Salt Lick burst upon them.

"Trill—" She was gasping, eyes shifting from Trevillian to Zack.

"In the diggings?"

"I have to talk to you," she insisted.

Zack didn't stop and Trevillian kept on beside him. Salt Lick followed, grabbing the boss's elbow.

"Trill—"

The boss shook her off.

"Not now," Zack said without looking at her.

"You cannibal," she seethed.

Trevillian glanced at Zack.

"He's the enemy," Salt Lick raged. "The missing powder—"

Zack didn't halt. The lights of the 770 station appeared ahead.

"The waters are closing over us," Salt Lick shrieked.

The boss slapped her face.

"Trill, Trill—" She clung to him as if she were drowning.

The boss tugged her arms from around his neck. She sagged down his middle, hugging his thighs. Trevillian stepped free, leaving Salt Lick sprawled on the gravel. Zack didn't slow. The boss caught up to him.

They stepped onto the platform together. When they reached the winze, Zack pulled the bell wire. The iron bucket rose, thumping against the sides of the well.

Zack didn't look at the boss.

When the bucket arrived, they climbed into it. Zack signaled to descend. As the cable unspooled and the bucket dropped, his hand slid inside his open coat. His palm touched the mongrel's handgrip. The cable jerked as the windings slipped, and the bucket swung in the shaft. Zack kept his feet and so did Trevillian. Then the low drone of the cable returned.

The 930 landing rose to meet them.

As the bucket slowed, Zack eased the revolver from his waistband. When the bucket thumped against the platform, he cocked the hammer with his thumb. A metallic click sounded.

Zack pushed the muzzle out of his coat. The barrel gleamed in the lantern light, trembling like something alive. He pointed it at Trevillian.

"Get out," Zack ordered him.

Trevillian looked puzzled.

"I said get out." Zack's voice echoed down the well.

Trevillian touched his left pectoral. "The closest to my heart."

Zack shook his head.

"Brothers," the boss said.

Zack laughed.

The boss lifted his chin, daring him.

"You've got all of that you're going to get." Zack steeled himself, ready to fire point-blank at Trevillian's face.

The boss stared at him for a long moment, then he put his hands on the rim and climbed out.

Zack fished a cord from his pocket. It had a slipknot at one end. He bound the boss's wrists with his left hand and urged Trevillian down the 930 level, following behind, gun trained. The candles on the wall lit the gravel before them.

"Where are we going?"

Zack didn't respond.

They passed the mouth of Maidbraid. Their boots splashed through puddles.

"You need me," the boss said. "I'm your mirror."

"You're the fate I'm going to escape."

"Escape?" Trevillian said, as if amused.

The Guillotine scaffold appeared ahead.

"Step it up," Zack ordered. He kept his eye on the barrel and the boss's back.

Trevillian ducked beneath the blade and Zack followed. They began the descent toward Mind's Eye. Gas filled Zack's nostrils.

"Have you ever thought," Trevillian said, "that the blow that will kill you has already been delivered?"

The first wave of dizziness.

"A life without Hope," Trevillian said. "That's where we start, and it's where we must end." The boss stumbled and paused to steady himself.

"Hurry your hooves," Zack said.

Trevillian moved forward. Zack shifted his boots warily, feeling his legs rubber beneath him. They reached the bottom of the incline and the boss took the turn. Zack followed, mongrel trained.

"There's no cure for the wounds we carry," Trevillian went on. "Hope brings forgetfulness. Nothing more."

"Here," Zack said.

They had reached the entrance to Mind's Eye. Trevillian halted.

"Zack—"

The ring of hammers reached them from Rapture.

"Move," Zack said.

Trevillian stepped into the Mind's Eye drift.

"Do you feel nothing between us?" Trevillian was shaking his head. "You know what I've wanted."

The walls were scaly. The track had been removed. Over the sounds of their boots and breathing, Zack could hear the murmur of escaping gas.

"Hope is with me," Zack said.

Vapors enveloped them. Zack felt the tightness in his chest and then it grabbed. He reached his left arm out. In the light of a wall candle, his hand was rippling.

"She'll betray you," the boss said.

The mongrel's barrel glimmered. Zack's hand was shaking. "Another word and I'll shoot," he swore.

They rounded a bend in the passage. Beyond, the drift head came into view, thirty feet away. A lantern was hanging on the wall outside the powder cache. The gate was open, swung back on its hinges. Someone had unloaded explosives from the niche in the rock where they were stored. Boxes of dynamite were stacked to one side.

"That's deep enough," a voice spoke from the darkness.

A match was struck, crashing like a cymbal in the narrow space. Men emerged from the shadows inside the gate, firearms raised. Owen stepped forward, his shotgun aimed directly at Zack. DuVal shifted among the armed men, lighting the candles on their hats.

Zack hooked his arm around Trevillian's neck, holding him close.

"You're found out, high horse," DuVal said.

"Let the boss go." Owen moved closer.

Zack raised the mongrel to Trevillian's temple. "Another step and he's finished."

"Where's Hope?" the boss hissed.

"The Captain's taken," Owen said. "And Sephy. The powder's in our hands."

"Stay where you are," Zack warned.

"You're lost," Trevillian whispered.

"Repair yourself with the boss," Owen said. "You've been

his favorite. Perhaps he'll find the middle and go lightly with you."

Zack's pulse thundered in his ears. Hope was gone.

True Bluford stepped out of the shadows, rifle aimed.

A delusion, Zack thought.

Trevillian twisted to free himself. "Fire—"

Zack struggled to keep hold of him. DuVal advanced, barrel aimed at Zack's head. The boss's elbow drove at his ribs. Zack jerked him in front of DuVal's muzzle, swinging his revolver as Owen lunged, clubbing the foreman across the face. DuVal came around his left, muzzle probing, looking for an opening.

Owen was rising, his candle splashed light on the drift head. Something gleamed at Zack from within the niche—a blasting cap tin, rolled onto its side, watching him like a knowing eye. True Bluford stepped forward. Zack barged Trevillian into DuVal, jerking the goon's rifle aside as it fired. Owen leveled his shotgun.

Then Trevillian wrenched free.

Zack saw three barrels trained on him.

"Fire!" the boss raged.

Zack reached for Hope. *My heart*, he pledged, sending a stream of pure thought into the darkness, twitching his mongrel toward the knowing eye and fanging the trigger. An explosion like the end of the world burst Mind's Eye. A blinding darkness, a shattering deafness, a sucking expansion—the rock was a sudden void into which everything had been hurled.

18

wareness returned to Zack slowly, piecemeal.

A cool surface against his cheek. Pressure on his chest. Nothing to see, nothing but midnight. One leg was angled to the side. He was choking—the sound reached him through the droning in his head. When he summoned his right hand, it responded. He slid it closer. It touched his hip and crept around, reaching inside his coat pocket for a block of matches. Then his left hand—he felt along his flexed leg and pulled a candle from his boot.

He tried to stand, but his weight shifted oddly. When he straightened his back, his foot slipped. He hunched forward, feeling pressure on his chest again. His left thumb found the sulfur, he scratched it and a flame burst out. Without moving his body, he raised both arms and turned his face up, touching the flame to the candle wick. When it took hold, he peered around.

His eyes were flooded, but he could see he was on a steep wall, his chest against it, barely clinging. Around him, the surface lustered. He had crossed into a world of melting wax—everything was scalloped and puddled.

The surface was writhing and lobing. Things were shifting beneath the waxy covering. It was the end envisioned by Pollard, Zack thought. Entombed with the hopeless in Prowler's gut. He could see the sundered parts around him—fists and knees, shoulders and heads—dissolving in slime.

Zack wiped his eyes on his sleeve. His flame brushed water, guttering without quenching. When he looked again, the gleaming surface had congealed. He felt the lumps and pockets with the heel of his hand. Rock, not wax. He was alive, somewhere inside the mountain.

He drew a shallow breath and peered up. A dark eave resolved through the dimness—an overhanging cornice fringed with dripstone. He shifted the candle and gazed down. The wall below him was sheer. There was a balcony at the limit of his light, maybe forty feet below.

Zack put the candle between his teeth and tested a hold with his boot, sliding his hands, trying to keep his weight balanced on the slippery rock, descending slowly. His arms quivered, his legs jackknifed as the weight shifted over them. The droning in his ears was fading. Rising through it, he could hear a reverberant *plink*. His candle lit rows of tiny stalactites on the undersides of the gleaming lobes. Drops swelled at their tips and released into cisterns, raising a chorus of silver bells.

When he was a few feet from the balcony, he let go of the rock. He fell farther than he expected, spilling onto his side.

The surface beneath him was slick and wet. He rose, took the candle from between his teeth and turned to the left. The balcony was lined with sagging colonnettes. Where the shelf met the wall, drapes flowed over it, fluted and gleaming. The wall itself was dark and furred.

Zack dripped wax on a ledge and planted the candle in it. He removed his fuse belt and went down on one knee, searching for a shard with an edge. When he found one, he set his belt on the rock and sawed off a foot-long spitter. He stuffed what remained in his pocket and stood, scraping the spitter until the powder core showed.

Then he turned to the flame and held the spitter over it.

Light burst before him, hissing and white, flooding the balcony. At the corner of his eye, the dark fur came alive, shivering and expanding. It rose and swept over him—a panicked horde with frenzied wings, a wave of thick musk and mournful cries—and was lost in the darkness.

Zack turned, wondering. He bent and hurled the sparking spitter straight up. It rose like a star. "Where am I?" he shouted. And his words boomed back, as the heights of an enormous vault appeared—a hanging maze of seeps and teats and twisted vanes, with clouds of bats drifting beneath. The star descended, lighting silken walls, galleries and porticos, entrances to tunnels that glimmered in their depths. A void in the mountain, with gleaming sides and hollow arms. The star flashed before a cliff of flowstone and plunged into a fog at its base, igniting blue lightning, snapping like a flag in a storm.

All at once, Zack realized what he'd done.

Flames shot through the fog, the air shook with thunder and a ball of blue fire inflated, revealing the sanctum throughout, every inch glowing, extravagant as a pharaoh's tomb.

The Silk Cavern quaked, the cliff of flowstone parted. Zack teetered at the balcony's edge, watching huge torches flare from the cracks. A deep groan and the flowstone unpuzzled—and Hope appeared behind it.

Dazzling, behemoth—a white river rippling with crescent waves, hissing and crying, loosing batteries of flashes as the gold strobed through her. She lay with her white robe open. The lining was visible, crowded with rubies and garnets, the tribute of ages, still warm and pulsing.

Hope's home, he thought, or Hope whispered in his mind.

From here her veins flowed— Here she nested, dissolved in her own essence, communing with the dreams of those she'd blessed. Here their hearts flew to share her perfection, the chambered quartz mazing them in a golden trance, while the gas torches chanted and silver bells *plinked* down the walls.

As he watched, Hope shifted, emerging from the breakings like a figure cast from lost wax. The ancient body eeled out of its bed. Hope reared before him, effulgent, blinding—

I'm leaving, she spoke through the clashing crystals.

The nest exploded.

A hurricane of light blasted Zack against the wall, roaring

over him. The Silk Cavern shook, enameled cliffs cracking, clapping back and calving into the void. A crashing in the depths, the hiss of slides, waves of orange flame— Zack clung to the rock, scrabbling vainly for holds, torn loose and blown up the wall.

Was it gas combusting or the twisting of Hope? As the giant torches crossed her, Zack saw her turn in midair, half on her side. She banked and the edge of her robe was lit—a pink scroll woven with scarlet threads. A pink wave curling over on itself. Behind her, haloed grottos flashed and a heaven of stalactites glittered, their points like stars.

Leaving this mountain—

Her massive body vipered down. The leviathan neck disappeared into a tunnel, slick and gleaming, and her scaled trunk followed, essing and arrowing to pick up the slack. Clouds of bats swooped after her, entering the channel, and the chorus of squeals that echoed within merged with the hiss of Hope's crystals. The sound had inflection, meaning—

You know where to find me, Hope said.

A roar followed her words—the Cavern was collapsing. Deep in the tumult giant pipes were struck, carillons rhythmic and swelling as slope after slope joined in. Hope's purpose, Hope's plan, her long body stretching through a dark tunnel. Behind her lay memory, and before her—the future. Hope twisting, veering, the white tail disappearing—

She was gone. The Silk Cavern was still.

Zack struggled to his feet, choking, a chill wind biting his face. The depths below were screened by dust. A sporadic flicker lit the remains of Hope's bower—slides of rock with smoke coiling up.

In his boot, a fresh candle. In his pocket, the match block. He struck a sulfur and lit the wick.

He stood at the opening of a large tube, a horizontal tunnel gleaming with flowstone. It led into the rock. His candle washed the entrance with a spectral light. At its distant end, a sharper light shone. A ray from mankind.

Zack stumbled forward. Behind him, the ruined cavern went black. He shifted the candle, finding his footing. His face was hot, his center throbbed. There were shooting pains in his legs and something was wrong with his shoulder. *Hope's new home*, he thought. What tests, what struggles—

Pity the boss, Sephy said. *Pity yourself*, she meant. The golden dream, born from longing and despair—that was his slice. Sephy had sent him to the Throne. Somehow she knew.

Zack began to cry. Relief and dismay—for himself, for Sephy. For the people of the camp, and for Trevillian and the misfortunes that made them brothers. Did Hope hear him? Did she understand?

I will do everything I can to save you.

Was that Hope speaking?

The tunnel narrowed as Zack advanced, walls pleated around him like the inside of a bunched sleeve. He was moving up an accordion of ledges onto loose talus. The ceiling descended abruptly. As he mounted the talus, a box of light rose into view. He reached a ragged sill and clambered over it, tumbling down a broken slope on the far side.

Zack raised his head and looked around. A hanging lantern lit regular walls. He was in the Big Twist drift.

There was blood on his coat sleeves. Zack put his fingers to his cheek and they came away red. His brow felt gummy. He touched his crown. The hair on his head was burnt clean off.

Voices reached him from a distance. The danger of discovery was all at once real.

Boots sounded in the passage.

Zack lay still.

"Stop your clucking," Snell said.

"I'm leaning with Bluford—he was looking right at him," Carew insisted.

They were twenty feet away.

"Knox is atoms," Carew said.

"Well then, who would this be?" Snell raised his lantern.

Zack regarded the pair.

"I'll get the boss," Carew said.

"And Lloyd," Snell told him.

Carew passed Snell his rifle, then turned and hurried back down the drift.

Snell gave Zack a respectful nod. "Some story, I bet."

Zack got his feet beneath him.

Snell knelt to help him up, then thought better. "Wait for the doc. Somethin' might be broke."

"How do I look?"

"Like a tomato," Snell replied. "Missing skin in places." He pointed. "Your shoulder's crooked."

"Trevillian survived?"

403

"With hardly a scratch," Snell said. "The blast threw 'em all twenty feet down the drift. Owen got his belly flayed. Everyone thought you were smoke—but the boss."

"He'll be happy to see me."

Snell sucked his cheek. "Shouldn't have turned on 'im."

"The mountain shook," Zack said. "You must have felt that."

Snell looked at the hole in the Big Twist headwall, and when he turned back his eyes were wide. "It brought the guillotine down."

Lights appeared at the entrance to the drift and moved quickly toward them.

In Strongbox Stope, the miners were spooked. There was no one in the workings and the Wheel was dead. Men lay in their bedrolls or huddled together, awaiting news, sharing their fears. Their eyes went frequently to the walls, and conversations stopped while they felt the floor or listened for shaking deeper in the mountain.

Trevillian pushed past the anteroom blanket. Lloyd and Snell followed, carrying a body wrapped in canvas.

Faces turned, men stood. A hum of speculation rose. The body was set before the BMC enclosure, not far from where the Captain was curled with his arms bound behind him. Trevillian disappeared through the plank door. A moment later, he emerged with anchor bolts and a hammer.

"Arm yourselves," he ordered Lloyd and DuVal. The two men hurried into the enclosure for weapons.

Trevillian passed the bolts and hammer to Snell. "There," he said, nodding at the wall of crates.

Snell approached the wall and began hammering the bolts in.

Lloyd exited the enclosure with a rifle in his hands. Owen was right behind him. The foreman's middle was thickened by bandages and he walked with a limp. He was holding a shotgun and DuVal appeared at his elbow with another.

Trevillian faced the camp. A moment of silence and then he spoke.

"The Judas is mine." He nodded to Snell, who stooped and loosened the ropes around the body. "Hope didn't want him," the boss told the men. "She's thrown him back."

Snell helped the body to rise. When it turned, the stope was filled with startled sounds and shocked faces. A group of Blondes approached from the Wheel, Weasel among them. "What have you done to him?" she cried.

Zack's clothing was scorched from head to foot. He looked like he'd washed his face in fire. His hair was gone and his hands were bloody.

"All hail the fault finder," Trevillian proclaimed, unbuttoning the Reminder from the loop on his hip. "Strip him bare," he ordered Snell.

Zack scanned the stope. Dinesh was staring at him. Inky looked sick. Bob stood motionless beside Noel, eyeing the boss with cornered rage. Salt Lick emerged from the Big Wheel, leading Sephy out. Sephy's wrists were bound and her head was bowed. She lifted her face to Zack.

"Shoulder looks fine," Snell said. Lloyd had pulled his arm back into its socket as they were wrapping him up.

Snell reached for Zack's collar. He snagged it and tore the charred fabric away. Then he unbuttoned Zack's pants and drew them down.

The camp watched in silence as Snell grabbed the ropes from the floor and led Zack to the wall of crates.

"Face forward," the boss said.

Snell's brow furrowed. Then he turned Zack, backing him against the wall, tying the ropes around his wrists. "You'll be ugly as me," he muttered.

"Rise up," the Captain cried, trying to right himself.

"Let him go." Dinesh stepped forward.

Trevillian raised the Reminder, sighting Dinesh through its loops. "The smith," he barked at Lloyd. "Mark him down." He scanned the tense faces. "Hope needs every man. If you've fallen in with Zack, I'm willing to look past it. But whoever was with him—you'd better make your peace now." He unhooked his forefinger, letting the whip uncoil. Trevillian nodded to Owen and Lloyd and they turned their weapons on the crowd. Then he swung around, squaring with Zack.

Snell bent to roll up the canvas, but Trevillian waved him away. "Leave it for the pieces. DuVal—do the count." The Reminder larruped against his leg.

"You've angered her." Trevillian addressed Zack like a

judge passing sentence. "You've driven Hope away. And we want her back."

Zack stared his accuser in the face.

A long moment passed between the two men.

Trevillian snapped his wrist and the Reminder straightened behind him. His loins jerked, his fist leaped over his shoulder and the thong shot forward. A crack split Zack's ears and he felt a breeze on his front.

"One," DuVal said. "No blood."

Trevillian drew back and the Reminder shot forward.

"Two," DuVal said. "Still thirsty."

Trevillian came forward again. Lightning struck Zack's hip, shaking his frame.

"Three—"

"Humility," the boss assailed him. "That's what Hope wants. Shame and confession. And names— Those who are traitors to the faith."

"You're the pretender," Zack said.

Trevillian struck. Zack's left leg spasmed with pain.

"Your loathing sickens her," Zack gasped.

Crack. The Reminder went wide.

"You're not her priest." Zack's head jerked as the popper snapped at his cheek. A welt had risen on his thigh like a purple pipe.

"What's my count?" the boss said.

"Six," came the reply.

"I've been with her," Zack told the camp. "The Hope

you've seen is nothing. The real Hope is ten times larger."

"Ten times," Trevillian roared. "Ten times!" He struck with all his might. The whip bit Zack's middle.

"The boss doesn't know her," Zack raised his voice. There was fear in Trevillian's eyes. "He's an imposter, a fake—"

"Rise up, barnacles!" The Captain stood on his knees.

"Hope's left the mountain," Zack shouted. "There's a void below us that will swallow anyone who stays. Free me—I'll lead you to her. That's what Hope wants."

The boss wrenched around, thong shooting out.

The Reminder bit Zack's chest.

"Red," DuVal crowed.

"Blood," the boss cried.

Zack's chest was cut clean through. A scarlet thread raveled down his belly.

"Zack's your pilot," the Captain shouted.

"Silence him," Trevillian ordered Lloyd.

The doctor trained his rifle on the kneeling Captain. The miners were motionless. As Trevillian gathered the Reminder, Zack read their thoughts. Some felt for him, some hated the boss, but that wasn't enough.

Trevillian's whip struck his temple, dashing his head against the planks. A moment of darkness eclipsed one eye. *Help me*, Zack pleaded.

Speak my name, a voice said.

"Hope," Zack called out.

A quake jolted the stope. The piled crates behind him creaked and swayed.

Trevillian froze.

"A chasm, a void," Zack roared at the camp. "Show them!"

The floor sank. Zack hung suspended by the bolts and ropes, but the boss was flung down. He landed on his side, rolled toward the enclosure and crashed against the crates. Cries from the stiffs. Hollers, jabbering— Zack closed his eyes. Hope was swelling in his chest, winding through his mind, hissing and white.

"Dream Song," he said for all to hear. "The roof's cracking. Big Twist is choked with gas. In Mind's Eye, the floor is gone—it's caving beneath."

Men picked themselves up, looking around at the walls, too shaken to speak. Trevillian rose wild-eyed, doubling the Reminder.

"Free me or die with Trevillian," Zack threatened.

"Hope's with Zack," Inky shouted, stepping forward.

Noel slipped through the crowd, passed his pistol to Dinesh and bolted for the anteroom drape. Dinesh turned the weapon over in his hand.

Dog-Eared Bob drew the prospector's pick from his coat.

"Lies, lies—" Trevillian lunged at Zack, bludgeoning him.

Zack took the blows and the jolts returned. Men hunkered down, the boss stumbled back.

"This isn't Hope," True Bluford lurched to the front of the crowd, waving at the walls. "The diggings are weak."

"Knox is crazy," Carew shouted.

"This is her place," Arnie agreed.

"Die with Trevillian," Zack sentenced them. "Die, die—"

Jolts still fiercer—cracks appeared in the stope's western wall. Groans and yells, and then as they watched, the cracks opened like barn doors, blocks thudding from the gaps. The Big Wheel barricade tumbled to the floor.

A miner screamed and scrambled for the anteroom.

Zack could feel Hope racing through his veins, could taste her on his lips, the creamy essence coating his tongue.

"I'm her priest," he boomed. "I'm her priest!"

"Bar the way," Trevillian ordered.

Lloyd shuffled toward the cooks, between the crowd and escape.

Bob was advancing and so was Inky. A handful of rebels pulled knives and axes from their bedrolls. The boss had his back to them, but Owen saw them coming. He motioned to DuVal, who raised his firearm and stepped closer to the boss.

True drew his sheath knife from his hip. A dozen of Trevillian's faithful rallied to join him as the first rebels broke through the front of the crowd.

"Inky, Dinesh, Bob—" Owen shouted, singling them out.

Marcus Bunting slid his rifle from a clothes pile, and amid fresh quakes he pitched through the crowd. Snell saw the vise tightening and ducked into the enclosure.

"Lower the shooter," Bob threatened Owen, a few feet from him, pick raised.

Marcus burst through the crowd with his rifle pointed at Trevillian's face.

"Boss—" DuVal cried.

"Cut him down," Trevillian shouted.

DuVal fired and Bunting's arm flew apart. He fell to the floor screeching, clutching his stump. Bob whirled around. The rebels froze. True and his allies moved to circle them as Snell emerged from the enclosure with a shotgun leveled. At that moment, Weasel parted the gathering. She ran straight at DuVal and grabbed his arm. The goon struggled, jerking the barrel of his shotgun about her head.

"Shoot her," DuVal snarled at Lloyd.

The doctor turned his weapon on Weasel, then let it fall to the floor. Dinesh rushed him and three rebels followed, wielding knives and hand axes. They brought the doctor to his knees.

"Blast them," Trevillian raged at the foreman.

Owen fired his shotgun over their heads.

True and his men had Bob's group surrounded. Carew held his knife to Inky's throat. "Put that aside," he threatened Bob, whose pick was still raised. Arnie retrieved Bunting's rifle. Snell stepped forward, his shotgun on Weasel. "Sorry, Miss."

The jolts left off.

Zack watched, speechless, as the men who'd supported him lowered their arms.

Trevillian faced him. "It's the grave now."

"You're going with us," Noel said. He strode toward Trevillian, a half-dozen dynamite sticks strapped around one arm, a fuse sparking beneath. "There's forty more in the ceiling," he pointed at the ventilation shafts, "live as these."

Heads craned toward the roof.

411

"He's lost his mind," Owen said.

Dinesh pointed Noel's pistol at DuVal and fired. The shot opened DuVal's middle. A wad of gum spit from his pocked cheeks, and he folded on the floor like a suit of clothes.

Fresh jolts gripped the stope.

"We're doomed," Arnie bellowed. "Knox is right."

"She's turning the tide," the Captain croaked.

A man beside True broke rank and fled. Arnie dropped Bunting's rifle and headed for cover. Bob swung his pick, gashing Carew's arm, shouting to his fellows, urging them to fight.

Zack saw Sephy racing toward him.

Noel rushed Trevillian, trying to embrace him, but the boss swung the Reminder and dashed him to his knees. "Fire, damn you," the boss bellowed at his foreman.

Owen set his jaw and his shotgun roared at close range. Dinesh's chest exploded and four others were thrown back, grunting in agony. As Owen loaded fresh shells, he caught sight of Sephy rushing through the melee with a knife in her hand. He raised his shotgun. Out of nowhere, Lucky barged in front of it unarmed. "Enough," he scowled, grabbing the barrel. The blast destroyed both of his legs.

Sephy reached Zack and cut him free.

As he pulled away from the wall, Bob sent the prospector's pick arcing between them, end over end. Zack caught the handle in his palm and turned.

Trevillian saw him coming.

Inky stooped and took the pistol from Dinesh's dead hand. Len appeared at his elbow waving a straight razor, and with rebels on either side, they advanced on Snell. The gaunt man surrendered without a fight.

Miners were retreating from the impending blast. A group of men led by Bob had backed Owen against the BMC enclosure. Bob was weaponless, but the others waved hammers and axes. The foreman swung his shotgun from side to side to ward them off.

Zack hurled himself at the boss, pick raised. Trevillian heeled to the right, swinging the doubled whip. Zack tracked the boss, sending the pick's blunt end at his chest. The boss staggered, taking the blow on his collar. As Zack came again, the Reminder cut upward and caught his jaw. He swung blindly, wide of the boss's hip, and again, missing his chin.

Noel jumped Trevillian from behind, the sparking fuse dancing beneath his arm. The boss shook free. Zack swung as the boss brought his knee up, and the pick impaled his thigh. Zack jerked it loose, going for the shoulder. The blow glanced off. Again Noel rushed the boss. Trevillian jerked his lash to the ground, loops snaking around Noel's legs. The boss tugged, upending him, turning as Zack lunged at his middle. The pick struck ribs and something cracked.

The standoff with Owen ended abruptly. The rebels rushed him as one, and Bob grabbed him and threw him down. The fighter's fists found openings, cracking Owen's teeth, crushing his nose, battering his face again and again.

Trevillian was hunched over, gripping his middle. As Zack came forward, he looped Zack's neck with the Reminder and fell on it with all his weight. Zack's windpipe cinched, his legs flailed. He felt his neck bones grinding. He sickled his pick at Trevillian's back. It sank into the boss's loins. Trevillian wrenched the noose tighter, as if nothing had happened.

Zack struggled the pick free and drove it at the boss's face. The point pierced Trevillian's cheek, turning him aside for a moment. Then he was growling and bearing down, throwing all his weight onto the strangling thong. Zack tore at the noose with his free hand, vision swimming. He heard Trevillian rasp in triumph. The boss sank farther, down on one knee.

Zack's sight blackened at the edges. There was only a blurred image of Trevillian's head, bobbing like a puppet, steely eyes gleaming, face streaming with blood.

Hope shook them both—the stope tipped and slid, opening a space between them.

Zack raised the pick and drove its sharp end at Trevillian's chest. The cloth split. Zack felt the pectoral give, ribs parting around it, the point burying deep in the heart's cage.

The whip relaxed. The boss's eyes shifted, confused. His bloody jaw struggled, hatred and helplessness guttering together. Zack stood on one knee. Trevillian sank beneath him, lips quivering, nostrils flaring with defiance. He was staring at Zack's naked crown. A tremor passed through him and he let the whip go.

Zack held the pick firmly. He could feel Trevillian's pulse in the handle, what the spike was doing inside the man's chest.

"Mercy," Trevillian whimpered.

In his eyes, Zack saw the terror of a child.

Another jolt shook the stope. Trevillian's arms went limp, opening. Then he sagged off the pick, sprawling faceup on the canvas.

A gang of rebels with Inky and Len in front were advancing on True and his fellows. Inky was waving Dinesh's pistol at them, and Weasel came up beside him with DuVal's shotgun in her arms.

"Fire," Noel cried. "Fire in the hole!"

The two factions halted, stared at each other, and then all were scrambling to lift the wounded and bear them away. Lloyd helped the Captain hobble clear of the blast zone. Dog-Eared Bob sent his right one more time at Owen's head. The bloody pulp twitched and Owen blanked out. Noel yanked the dynamite bracelet from his arm, flung it through the entrance to the BMC enclosure and bolted for the anteroom.

Sephy grabbed Zack and together they ran toward the Wheel. People were crouched against the walls or diving into alcoves. There was a flash of daylight behind Zack, and thunder filled the stope. He turned to see tons of rock opening over the BMC enclosure and the figures stretched before it. Trevillian was peering up, searching that dark sky for the last time.

Zack shielded his face from the blast winds, and as the dust whirled, he felt Sephy close. A few moments later, she was removing her shirtwaist, pressing it to his chest to stanch the wound.

415

Weasel approached with a blanket and draped it over his shoulders.

"How did you get loose?" Zack asked.

"Francine cut my bonds," Sephy said, "and handed me the knife."

"Knox!"

Lloyd was twenty feet away, gesturing.

As Zack approached, he saw Lucky stretched on the floor beside the doctor. A blanket had been thrown over the remains of his legs.

"There you are," Lucky said as Zack stooped over him. "I'm ready for Hope."

"She's standing by," Zack said.

Lucky smiled. "Tell her to sit down and have a cigar." The smile froze, his head lifted, eyes flaring like a panicked horse. Then his eyes rolled up and his head fell back.

Lloyd felt for his pulse. "His luck's run out." His gaze shifted to Zack's chest. Sephy's shirtwaist was already soaked. "That needs stitches," Lloyd said.

"His hands," Sephy urged him, "and his face—"

Inky stepped forward. "We've got three men at death's door," he told Zack. He turned to Lloyd. "And there's others your guns have maimed."

"I'll mend who I can," Lloyd said sadly.

Len limped forward, escorting Snell. Bob was beside him.

"I didn't shoot no one," Snell was saying. He glanced at Zack.

"You stood by the boss."

"That's what ya do," Snell muttered, "beggin' your pardon."

Blondes emerged from one of the alcoves with Arnie and Carew in tow. Across the stope, through the thinning smoke, a tumulus was visible, covering the battleground completely. A man with orange hair and electricity in his step skirted the pile, headed for Zack with a lopsided grin.

"Ten times larger?" Noel said.

Thirty feet from them, a woman screamed.

"Someone— Please—"

It was the cashier. She stood outside Salt Lick's boudoir, waving her arms. Zack and Sephy hurried toward her, followed by others. The woman stepped back through the velvet.

When they entered, she was kneeling beside Genuine Jo. Before them, in the light of the lone candle burning on the dresser, Zack saw Salt Lick curled in a pool of blood. One sleeve of her shirtwaist was hitched above the elbow, and her wrist was torn open. A small wooden box was overturned by her knee, and the fragments of the Cupid lamp lay scattered around her. Her hand clutched a shard with a piece of Cupid's wing.

19

The camp applied all its energies to emptying the mine. In addition to ferrying essentials—food, stoves and the means of survival—Zack ordered the removal of animals, mining equipment, drills and explosives. Speculation was rampant—about Hope and the camp's future, about the things Zack had said under the lash.

Zack disclosed nothing, except to his closest.

At the end of three shifts, fresh tremors gripped the mountain. Zack called a halt to the transport relays and began evacuating people and their possessions. The wounded went first, along with the Blondes. Miners followed, bearing the slain.

He stood by the entrance to Strongbox Stope, watching the last of them leave. He wore a borrowed coat, and his brow and hands were bandaged.

Sephy and Lloyd approached with the Captain between them, splinted and tottering. On the far side of the dark tumulus, a crack was visible in the floor. The stope rocked, and as the threesome reached Zack, the crack shot toward the Big Wheel, dividing the ruined barricade and grounding on the disk. The axle slumped and a slow ticking rose through the rumble as the disk turned around.

As Lloyd passed, he saw Zack put his hand to his chest.

"Bad?" Lloyd asked.

"The stitches are pulling."

A shriek sounded in Zack's ear. The timbers at the entrance were twisting like barber poles. As he stepped through it, the cap beam splintered. Bob and two others were racing toward him. Zack led the group into the anteroom. Below them, the rumble was mounting—the sound of failure in the depths of the mine. The winged herald swayed on its chain like a trapped bird looking for an exit.

On the 310 landing, Inky was waiting beside the skip.

"The winze has caved," he said as Zack approached. "The 490's still in one piece, but the floor's sinking fast."

Another jolt shook the diggings and a stamping started up, loud and insistent, like a child throwing a tantrum. Rock was clattering down the main shaft. Lloyd climbed into the back of the skip, and together he and Zack maneuvered the Captain onto a seat while Inky and the miners boarded. Sephy sat on the second slat, Zack on the third. Bob stepped onto the first and pulled the bell wire.

The rails jumped, rattling the skip. Silence followed. Why wasn't the car climbing? Had something happened to the hoist? A low hum sounded. The cable squealed. The skip crept down the track, shuddered and began moving up it.

A picture came to Zack: the quartz that had filled the heart of the mountain had dissolved, turning back into fog. The Silk Cavern was caving, and the collapse of that great space was swallowing the mine, one level after another. First the 930, then the 770, then the 490—following the excavation of the vein.

Above, the collar of the main shaft appeared. Light streamed down. Zack looked at himself—scorched pantlegs, bandaged hands, the bulge of the battle dressing beneath his coat. Then he looked at Sephy. All he could see was her tangled hair and her shoulders. The back of her dress was streaked with grime and blood.

He tried to speak but could not. He reached and felt the back of her neck. When she turned, he touched her cheek and leaned forward.

"The barge," he said weakly.

"Was that us?" she said.

The mine grumbled in its throat, as if irked by their departure. The circle of blue was expanding. A comet-shaped cloud appeared with the sun in its head, throbbing with life. Zack put his hands on Sephy's shoulders and kissed her temple.

"I can feel Hope in my toes," the Captain said.

The well shrank to nothing, the sky spread on all sides. And then they were free, with the day full upon them. Noel was standing on the platform amid a clutter of knapsacks, mining tools and firearms. As the skip slowed, the gallows moaned. Noel looked up at the cables and turning wheels, and the passengers did likewise.

Zack rose and stepped out. Bob helped Lloyd lift the Captain from his seat. "A good wagon," Bob said, nodding at the skip.

True Bluford exited the hoist house with Snell.

As Sephy left the car, a low drumming filled the crater. Zack led the group across the trembling planks and up the path. Faults had opened beneath the hoist house. The plastered snow was fracturing, rustling with slides as they passed.

They crested the rim into a northbound breeze. Sephy shivered and Zack flipped his coat collar up. As they turned, the familiar contours of the Breakaway valley appeared. The high places still held their snow, but the warmth of spring was changing things. The lower slopes were netted with streams. The frozen river had buckled, and in the gaps between cakes, they could see water moving, glassen and sinuous, on its way to the sea. A thousand ducks rafted offshore.

The mountain faltered again, shifting beneath them. Zack imagined Strongbox Stope with its walls and ceiling collapsing.

"Hope was his curse," Lloyd said.

Zack gazed down the valley. "Patch up our boys," he told the doctor.

"You need something to cover that head." True took off his cap and handed it to Zack. "Men can sleep beside the coal bunkers."

Zack nodded. The way down the switchback trail was littered with what they'd salvaged. The people of the camp came and went, hauling sacks and bedding, crates and equipment. On a grassy bench lower down, mules were stumbling around, getting used to the light. "The girls can use the steam plant or one of the mill sheds. Sephy will manage it."

She eyed Zack uncertainly.

"You'll do fine at the helm," the Captain said, patting her shoulder.

"The camp adores you," Inky agreed.

Len rounded the last switchback and limped toward them.

"The Bang Boys have canvas up," he reported. "Hot chow tonight."

"We'll start felling timber," True said.

Zack turned to Lloyd and opened the doctor's coat, exposing his pocket ledger. "True will assign jobs," he said. "Start fresh."

"You're the boss," Lloyd nodded.

"What's the count?" Zack asked.

"Ninety-three," Len replied.

"How's Marcus?"

"He's still got one arm," Len laughed. "You've made a new man. Marcus believes."

"Keep the dead on ice," Zack said, wincing as he put the cap on. "When we get back, we'll give them the farewell they deserve." He motioned to Noel. "Let's go."

Noel slung one of the knapsacks onto his back and took a

rifle. Bob and Inky grabbed packboards and picks. Zack drew Sephy aside.

"Marry me," he said.

She bowed her head.

He kissed her ear. "You said yes once."

"And the child?"

"His line's lost," Zack reminded her.

"I know who he is," she replied. "I can feel his soul. I speak to him and I know he hears me."

A chill wind struck them. It seemed to Zack that it lifted them both.

"He'll be our firstborn," he said.

Sephy stared at him, then she began to cry.

Zack embraced her and drew her close. She flinched. "There's something sharp in your pocket," she said.

Zack drew out the key to the Mind's Eye powder cache. It turned between them, catching the light. He opened the loop of thong and slipped it over her wrist. "Hope will be with us."

Sephy laughed and wiped her cheek. "You're so sure."

He kissed her lips. "I'm sure."

Zack retrieved the remaining knapsack and rifle. He motioned to his companions and started forward, leading the way along the path that skirted the Glory Hole rim. Noel, the champion driller who walked away from his prize. Inky, ace reporter without a beat. And Dog-Eared Bob, who'd left the ring on all fours.

The victorious, Zack thought. You dig with the spades you have.

They followed the ridge with the ravages of winter around them. The ice was wind-scoured. Broken limbs lay twisted among the stunted spruce. The parchments of snow beneath their boots were dashed with black needles, as if the elements, in the midst of their fury, had tried to record something in the language of men.

Northward they went, finding their way over spurs and through valleys. It took them the rest of the day. The cold winds cut through their threadbare clothing, but the traveling was easy. The thickets were leafless and the soil was firm beneath their boots. Other than the first flushes of moss and the devil's club shoots, there was little green.

They reached the plateau at dusk and scouted for signs of Prowler. Satisfied they were safe, Bob and Noel raised a canvas in the lee of the Throne, while Zack and Inky trimmed boughs for bedding, and by then it was dark. There were clouds, but they were scattered, and the sky was full of stars. Through the groves of tall hemlocks, fingers of mist were gliding. High above, Zack could hear the cascades purring down the rock. And as he rolled beneath the canvas, he could see the Throne's snowy crest and the silhouette of its thorns.

When they awoke, the giant scallop was full of morning. They stood shivering, warming themselves in its light. Winter's mantle had changed it. The shelves were hung with cornices and the galleries were veiled with ice. With the rickracked amber and ocher showing through, the Throne looked like it had been lowered from the sky. Inky said a few words in memory of Winiarski and those fallen in combat, and they started to drill. It was late afternoon by the time they'd loaded the powder.

"Ready?" Noel shouted.

He stood at the base of the Throne. Zack was behind Prowler's sofa.

"Ready," Zack said, motioning to Inky and Bob. They sank behind a nearby mound. Noel struck a match and lit his spitter.

A scratching sounded in the thatch a few feet from Zack. A black-hooded junco was hopping and pecking, lost in its business. Behind it, the trail of ancestral prints stretched like bridges between islands of snow.

"Here we go," Noel cried.

Zack could see him parting the comb ferns, lighting the first fuse hanging down. Then Noel was scrambling along the Throne's base, following the scroll of pink rock, lifting the rattails one after the other, sparking and moving on. The lit fuses winked like stars among the scarlet threads. When he reached the hemlock snag, he spit the last.

"Fire," Noel shouted. And he raced down the slope, taking cover behind the shoulder of an abutment where they'd stowed their packs.

Zack leaned against Prowler's sofa. For a long moment, his own breathing was all he heard.

The charges hit like artillery fire in an unbroken sequence, jolting the earth and mounting to a roar. When the last *boom* sounded, Zack peered over the bolster. Smoke was billowing from the pediment of the Throne. A rain of rock fell on the thatched plateau, and slides were hissing down the skirting slopes.

He rose and started forward.

At first, there was nothing to see but the blast cloud. He quickened his pace, huffing and squinting, boots pounding the damp grass and laces of ice. He was on the slope now, inside the smoke, fighting fumes and talus, feeling the heat beneath his boots.

The obscurity wafered into drifting veils. Through a gap, Zack saw an ocher tongue twisting in cheddar. Then the tear extended, and a wedge of the Throne painted down. Gusts were stretching the blast cloud. He pushed through an eddy, breathing through the crook of his arm, the rock swimming before him. Amber and ocher, and below—the pink rock, the curled edge of Hope's robe with its scarlet arteries threaded through it. And below that—

A stiff wind struck the fresh surface, and a wave of particles broke over him. Through his tears, Zack saw the lining of Hope's robe—so crowded with rubies and garnets, the fabric was invisible. And where the dynamite had chopped deepest, there was quartz white as soap. Through the spume and froth her perfection flashed, golden flames crowded in crystal pockets.

Gusts swept the Throne, clearing the smoke. Zack scrambled closer, Inky beside him now, wide-eyed, gesturing at the quartz with a drill steel in his hand. It was so different here, beneath a blue sky with the sun full upon it. No dismal caverns, no poison gas—just splashes of milk from her furious river, and the fists of blood carried on her flexing trunk. Like the white cord that emerged from the wrangler's girl— For a moment, the yearning—that hollow he'd lived with—had a new meaning: it was the memory of his first home. There, Hope sustained him before his trials in the world began.

As Zack approached the quartz jags, one blazed like a torch. He pulled the pick from his belt, reached with his left hand, feeling for its points. Then he was swinging at the rock, chips flying. Bob and Noel appeared on his right. Zack pried a wedge of gold free and turned it before them. The four men stood mute, locked on the sight.

The reaches of Hope were hidden, but Zack could imagine her, winding through a fiery past, weaving her essence into a dazzling future. Hammered to foil for salmon fins, melted to tears on infants' cheeks, powdered into stars over distant skies—

Zack passed the wedge to Inky. "No one will doubt that."

"No one," Inky agreed.

"It'll be equal shares for the faithful." Zack slid the pick through his belt.

"We're back in business," Noel said.

He laughed and embraced Zack, and then the four of

them were hugging and beaming like fools.

"'Damned and Delivered,'" Inky spouted. "Exclusive, in *The Morning Sun*."

"There's powder enough," Bob said.

"Barracks will go there." Zack pointed at a sheltered spot that bordered the plateau.

Bob eyed the vein. "Maybe Fugazi will sell us his hoist."

"What are you talking about?" Inky said.

"You see where she's headed." Bob lined his rifle up with the pink scroll and the quartz beneath. It slanted into the earth. "I'll wager my piece of heaven on it."

"We'll cut a trail south," Zack said. "Find a harbor by those narrows. Give ourselves a supply line. Whatever men and equipment we need."

"We'll be mining Hope in a new century," Noel said.

A crash like lightning sounded behind them. From the Throne came a rumble. The four men wheeled.

"Slide," Inky cried. The next moment they were treadling, arms flailing, trying to stay upright as the slope carried them down. Bob spilled, then Inky. Zack outran the scree, tumbling in dry grass. As he turned to look, a ledge left hanging by the powder blast came away. The hemlock snag went with it.

Bob yelled and they scattered as the snag heeled back, booming onto the slope. The great tree skied toward them, its compass of roots foremost, turning and slewing, slowing and stopping forty feet from Zack.

A man was frozen to the footing of the tree. Like the rays

of a dark sun, the giant roots held him, his arms flexed at odd angles amid the twisted spokes. His face hung forward, white as quartz, eyes wild, lips parted as if about to speak. It was a face Zack knew. His coat was maroon and the arm was tatted where a chevron had been removed.

"The Private," Bob whispered.

The harrowing visage was surrounded by gold-studded quartz, and the shock and wonder in those piercing eyes brought back Zack's most tortured moments with Hope.

Inky pointed at the Private's arm. Light glinted on the brass buttons and the golden piping. On either side, the wooden sun was matted with fur.

"Prowler dragged him here," Inky said.

"And recommenced his snooze," Bob added, "using him as a cozy."

There was a fresh disturbance at the top of the slope, where the snag had stood. Something shook itself from beneath the boulders, heaving off rubble, swelling like a great boulder itself. Brown arms swatted one block and another, sending them tumbling to the side. Prowler was rising above the ruins, coughing and shaking his snout.

"My rifle," Inky murmured.

Only Bob had his weapon in hand. "Don't move," he said, lifting it.

Prowler humped his back and angled his head, squinting and blinking. His snout shifted, drawing scents from the breeze, then he bucked his shoulders and rose onto his hinds, clenching his claws as he peered down the slope. He spotted them. His mane bristled. He snarled and then he was vaulting over the debris.

Bob fired and missed. Prowler kept coming.

Zack had no time to react. The emerald eyes singled him out, charging straight for him. Zack doubled over. The next instant, giant claws raked his side. He was lost in a chaos of muscle and fur, trying to squirm clear, hellish nostrils blasting in his face. Quaking jowls, jaws spreading, the long fangs bared—

Zack tried to roll away, arms in, knees tucked— But when he looked up, Prowler was looming over him, heaving with grunts. Ice crystals were beaded on the brown belly, and they rattled as Prowler's arm came around. The great paw struck Zack's chest, driving the wind out of him, flattening him against the slope.

"Stay down," Bob shouted.

Bob was edging past Prowler's shoulder, aiming his rifle. With barely a glance, Prowler backhanded him. The rifle flew out of Bob's grasp and went clattering down the slope. Prowler roared in Bob's face, and then he turned those open jaws on Zack. Your body in ruins, your mind given over to terror and the void—

The great claws grabbed him and lifted him.

"Hey you—" Inky hurled his drill at Prowler's face. The bear turned and snapped, and Zack drew the pick from his belt. As Prowler turned back, Zack slid his fist down the haft. The black nostrils twitched and the lavender worm came to life, crawling on Prowler's brow as he opened his jaws to engulf Zack's head.

Zack swung his pick, the emerald eye flooded with fear and Prowler dashed him to the ground.

"Get out of here—" Inky hurled a rock. Bob and Noel joined him, pelting the bear.

Prowler wavered, claws clicking, squinting at Zack and the pick. He bucked his head and stood on his hinds, arms pedaling. Then his decision was made—he wheeled, dropped to all fours and bolted across the plateau.

"You okay?" Noel asked, kneeling.

Zack was too stunned to speak. Bob opened his coat and shirtfront, inspecting his bandaged chest. "No leaks."

Inky and Noel were on either side of him, helping him up. Zack drew a breath and got his feet beneath him. He rose slowly, worried his knees might give. The Private was staring at him. Prowler's roar echoed in his ears.

"We'll see him again," Bob said.

The great bear was moving quickly, bounding up the incline on the north side of the plateau, growing smaller each moment. On his back, a skin of winter ice flashed in the sun. As he approached the crest, he crossed from light to shadow, and then he was over the top and out of sight.